# Cat in a Midnight Choir

By Carole Nelson Douglas from Tom Doherty Associates

## MYSTERY

MIDNIGHT LOUIE MYSTERIES
*Catnap*
*Pussyfoot*
*Cat on a Blue Monday*
*Cat in a Crimson Haze*
*Cat in a Diamond Dazzle*
*Cat with an Emerald Eye*
*Cat in a Flamingo Fedora*
*Cat in a Golden Garland*
*Cat on a Hyacinth Hunt*
*Cat in an Indigo Mood*
*Cat in a Jeweled Jumpsuit*
*Cat in a Kiwi Con*
*Cat in a Leopard Spot*
*Cat in a Midnight Choir*

*Midnight Louie's Pet Detectives*
(anthology)

IRENE ADLER ADVENTURES
*Good Night, Mr. Holmes*
*Good Morning, Irene*
*Irene at Large*
*Irene's Last Waltz*
*Chapel Noir*

*Marilyn: Shades of Blonde*
(anthology)

## HISTORICAL ROMANCE

*Amberleigh\**
*Lady Rogue\**
*Fair Wind, Fiery Star*

## SCIENCE FICTION

*Probe\**
*Counterprobe\**

## FANTASY

TALISWOMAN
*Cup of Clay*
*Seed upon the Wind*

SWORD AND CIRCLET
*Keepers of Edanvant*
*Heir of Rengarth*
*Seven of Swords*

\*also mystery

# Cat in a Midnight Choir

## A MIDNIGHT LOUIE MYSTERY

# Carole Nelson Douglas

A Tom Doherty Associates Book

New York

CAT IN A MIDNIGHT CHOIR

Edited by Claire Eddy

A Forge Book
Published by Tom Doherty Associates, LLC
175 Fifth Avenue
New York, NY 10010

www.tor.com

Forge® is a registered trademark of Tom Doherty Associates, LLC.

Library of Congress Cataloging-in-Publication Data

Douglas, Carole Nelson.
    Cat in a midnight choir / Carole Nelson Douglas.—1st ed.
        p. cm.
    ISBN 0-312-85797-7 (alk. paper)
    1. Midnight Louie (Fictitious character)—Ficion. 2. Barr, Temple (Fictitious character)—Fiction. 3. Stripteasers—Crimes against—Fiction. 4. Public relations consultants—Fiction. 5. Women cat owners—Fiction. 6. Las Vegas (Nev.)—Fiction. 7. Cats—Fiction. I. Title.

PS3554.O8237 C2767 2002
813'.54—dc21

                                                                2001058281

First Edition: May 2002

Printed in the United States of America

0  9  8  7  6  5  4  3  2  1

For the original and real Midnight Louie,
stray cat extraordinaire,
nine lives were not enough

# Contents

Previously in Midnight Louie's Lives and Times . . .                     11

Chapter 1:    Serial Sunday                              15

Chapter 2:    Feral Foul                                 28

Chapter 3:    Midnight Consultation                      31

Chapter 4:    DOD: Domesticated or Dead                  33

Chapter 5:    Dead Air Time                              41

Chapter 6:    DAD: Desiccated and Dead                   54

Chapter 7:    Saturday Night Stayin' Alive               59

Chapter 8:    Asian Persuasion                           65

Chapter 9:    Sunset Boulevard                           72

Chapter 10:   Car Trouble                                78

Chapter 11:   The Sign of the Serpent                    96

Chapter 12:   Smoke Signals                             112

Chapter 13:   Signals Received                          117

Chapter 14:   Disappearance Inc.                        123

Chapter 15:   Vamp . . .                                128

Chapter 16:   . . . and Revamp                          142

Chapter 17:   Main Course                               153

Chapter 18:   The Laddy and the Vamp                    156

Chapter 19:   Magicians at Work                         163

Chapter 20:   . . . The Sting                           171

Chapter 21:   Tempted                                   177

Chapter 22:   Charming Fellow                            185

Chapter 23:   A Place of Concealment                     189

Chapter 24:   Men in Motion                              200

Chapter 25:   Missing Link                               206

Chapter 26:   Moonlighting                               208

Chapter 27:   The Lady of the House                      221

Chapter 28:   Stripped for Action                        226

Chapter 29:   The House of Midnight Louise               231

Chapter 30:   Irreconcilable Differences                 237

Chapter 31:   Shadows                                    248

Chapter 32:   Heads or Tails?                            253

Chapter 33:   Did You Ever See a Dream Walking?          255

Chapter 34:   Ritz Cracker                               258

Chapter 35:   Diamonds or Dust                           263

Chapter 36:   Cover Story                                265

Chapter 37:   Terra Incognito                            268

Chapter 38:   Baby Doll's Brand-new Bag                  272

Chapter 39:   Secret Showdown                            276

Chapter 40:   Midnight Choirboy                          278

Chapter 41:   No Dice                                    280

Chapter 42:   Final Jeopardy                             285

Chapter 43:   Max: Gloves Off                            297

Chapter 44:   The Third Man                              302

Chapter 45:   Molina: Face-off                           309

Chapter 46:   Hallelujah Chorus                          312

Chapter 47:   I Once Was Deaf but Now I See              314

Chapter 48:   Siren Song                                    317

Chapter 49:   Serial Chills                                 321

Chapter 50:   The Morning After                             335

Chapter 51:   Life's Little Addenda                         344

Tailpiece:    Midnight Louie Sings the Blues                347

              Carole Nelson Douglas Joins the Choir         349

**Previously in**

# Midnight Louie's Lives and Times . . .

As a serial killer-finder in a multivolume mystery series (not to mention a primo mouthpiece), I want to update my readers old and new on past crimes and present tensions.

None can deny that the Las Vegas crime scene is a pretty busy place, and I have been treading these mean neon streets for fourteen books now. When I call myself an "alphacat," some think I am merely asserting my natural feline male dominance. But no, I refer to the fact that since I debuted in *Catnap* and *Pussyfoot*, I then commenced to a title sequence that is as sweet and simple as B to Z.

That is when I begin *my* alphabet, with the *B* in *Cat on a Blue Monday*. From then on, the color word in the title is in alphabetical order up to the current volume, *Cat in a Midnight Choir*.

Since I associate with a multifarious and nefarious crew of human beings, and since Las Vegas is littered with guidebooks as well as bodies, I wish to provide a guide to the local landmarks on my particular map of the world. A cast of characters, so to speak:

To wit, my lovely redheaded roommate and high-heel devotee, freelance PR ace Miss Temple Barr, who has reunited with her only love . . .

the once missing-in-action magician Mr. Max Kinsella, who has good reason for invisibility: years of international counterterrorism work after his cousin Sean died in a bomb attack in Ireland during a post–high school jaunt to the Old Sod . . .

but Mr. Max is sought by another dame, homicide lieutenant C. R. Molina, who is the mother of preteen Mariah . . .

and the good friend of Miss Temple's recent good friend, Mr. Matt Devine, a radio talk-show shrink who not long ago was a Roman Catholic priest and who came to Las Vegas to track down his abusive stepfather, Mr. Cliff Effinger.

Speaking of inconvenient pasts, Lieutenant Carmen Molina is not thrilled that her former flame, Mr. Rafi Nadir, the unsuspecting father of Mariah, is in Las Vegas taking on shady muscle jobs after blowing his career on the LAPD . . .

or that Mr. Max Kinsella is hunting Rafi himself because the lieutenant blackmailed him into tailing her ex. While so engaged, Mr. Max's attempted rescue of a pathetic young stripper, Cher Smith, soon found her dead . . .

and Mr. Rafi Nadir looks like the prime suspect.

Meanwhile, Mr. Matt has drawn a stalker, the local lass that young Max and his cousin Sean boyishly competed for in that long-ago Ireland . . .

one Kathleen O'Connor, for years an IRA operative who seduced rich men for guns and roses for the cause, deservedly rechristened by Miss Temple as Kitty the Cutter.

Miss Kitty, finding the Mystifying Max impossible to trace, has settled for harassing with tooth and nail the nearest innocent bystander, Mr. Matt Devine . . .

while he tries to recover from the crush he developed on his Circle Ritz condominium neighbor, Miss Temple, by not very boldly seeking new women, all of whom are now in danger from said Kitty the Cutter.

This human stuff is all very complex, but luckily my life is much simpler, revolving around a quest for union with . . .

the Divine Yvette, a shaded silver Persian beauty I filmed some catfood commercials with before being wrongfully named in a paternity suit by her air-head film-star mistress Miss Savannah Ashleigh . . .

and a quest for peace from my unacknowledged daughter, Miss Midnight Louise, who has been insinuating herself into my cases, along with the professional drug- and bomb-sniffing Maltese dog, Mr. Nose E. . . .

and a running battle of wits with the evil Siamese Hyacinth, first met as the onstage assistant to the mysterious lady magician . . .

Shangri-La, who made off with Miss Temple's semiengagement ring from Mr. Max during an onstage trick and who has not been seen since except in sinister glimpses . . .

just like the Synth, an ancient cabal of magicians that may take contemporary credit for the ambiguous death of Mr. Max's mentor in magic, Gandolph the Great, and that of GG's former lady assistant as well as the Cloaked Conjuror's assistant's more recent demise at TitaniCon science fiction convention, not to mention a professor of the metaphysical found dead among strange symbols, Mr. Jefferson Mangel.

Well, there you have it. The usual human stew, all mixed up and at odds with each other and within themselves. Obviously, it is up to me to solve all their mysteries and nail a few crooks along the way. Like Las Vegas, the City That Never Sleeps, Midnight Louie, private eye, also has a sobriquet: the Kitty That Never Sleeps.

With this crew, who could?

# Chapter 1

# Serial Sunday

The drawing seemed like child's play.

Done by a preschool child.

A preschool child lacking any art talent.

Temple frowned at her own handiwork.

She had never had much drawing skill, but one would think a grown woman could do better than this.

One would think, for that matter, that a participant in an alleged ritual murder could do better than this.

The thought unleashed a montage of memory-pictures. Actual crime-scene photos flared in her mind's eye again like psychic flashcards wielded by a female homicide lieutenant who went by the name of C. R. Molina. All homicide lieutenants needed a sadistic streak, Temple mused. You didn't provoke betraying reactions by walking softly and carrying a sharp nail file. Not that Molina had fingernails long enough to file.

Temple shut her eyes against the vivid memories of a death scene and pictured the site when she had last seen Jeff Mangel alive in it: a bland classroom in a bland, boxy University of Nevada at Las Vegas building. Jeff had converted the uninspiring space into a small exhibition, mostly of posters framed in freestanding ranks like pages in a gigantic book.

With the painted paper eyes of Houdini, Blackstone, Copperfield, and Gandolph the Great looking on, the professor enchanted by magic had met a brutal death amid the paraphernalia of kinky sex. The weapon had been a custom-designed ritual blade.

Underneath it all lay the five crude lines drawn in blood on the floor, that had boxed in Jeff's body like a symbolic fence.

Those bloody lines had to mean something, perhaps both more and less than the crude attempts to invoke cults and sexual extremes had.

Temple had started this Sunday afternoon homework project because she'd promised Max that she'd try to find out what the strange shape represented, if anything. Thanks to her exposure to a cadre of mediums and psychics the previous Halloween, he now considered her an expert on the mantic arts.

Public relations people had to be quick studies, and since Temple had moved from TV journalism to fine arts public relations to the far less fine art of freelance PR in Las Vegas, she had become even better at being a jill of all trades. But an artist she was not.

She stared at the five rough lines linked into the askew shape of a house drawn by a three-year-old. Or . . . a rather clumsy bell.

Her sketch had been jotted down on the back of a flimsy restaurant receipt she'd found in her tote bag when Max had broken into the crime scene to show her the bizarre props littering it. The sketch would have fit on the palm of her hand.

In reality, in life, in death . . . it had been drawn on a vinyl tile floor in great sweeping strokes, large enough to encompass a dead body.

Had it been drawn before, or after, Jefferson Mangel had bled and breathed his last on the floor of his small exhibit room of magic show posters and paraphernalia?

Temple shivered a little, though it was a lovely spring afternoon. Las Vegas springs and falls could be numbered by days. This day was one where the bountiful sunlight poured through the French doors into her home office until the room seemed made of bottled radiance. Even shadows were lazy, innocent sketches on the warm, inadvertent canvas of her wood parquet floor. The room contained nothing sinister, except her thoughts . . .

. . . and the drawing from a killing ground . . .

. . . and something sinuous and black that brushed the sundrenched floor as if keeping slow-motion time.

"Louie?" She stood and leaned over the width of the desktop, an oak slab with a tight grain streaked like honey blond hair.

Only by leaning to the point of teetering could a woman as short as Temple see the owner of the serpentine tail, a huge black cat sunning himself in the hottest, purest pool of sunlight in the room.

"I'll thank you not to waggle that tail around. It looks too much like a desert snake that crawled in."

The cat's green eyes, slitted almost shut, angled open while its ears flattened. Midnight Louie did not take kindly to criticism. At twentyplus pounds of muscular alley cat, he didn't have to.

His balefully still image sank like a black sun behind the desk's horizon line as Temple sat down again. She could hear the grumpy metronome of an insulted tail thumping the parquet.

"This *is* a *work*room," she pointed out to no one in particular.

And maybe she was a little grumpy herself this morning, because her only roommate was a cat.

She pulled the gigantic mug that held hazelnut-flavored nonfat creamer diluted with gourmet coffee close enough to lift and sipped, slitting her eyes at the drawing again.

It had to mean something.

She needed to enlarge it, think in bigger terms.

Temple picked up the ruler and pencil and duplicated the figure at several times its original size on an eleven-by-seventeen sheet of blank paper.

The peaked "roof" was obviously the top, but why was the bottom foundation line slightly angled? An accident of freehand drawing, or intentional? And none of the four paired lines exactly matched, which was what gave the image its childishly askew look.

"It doesn't have to be a house," she muttered as she set down her implements and took up her coffee mug again. She would never admit that she was talking to Louie. "It could be a window. A Gothic window with a peaked arch. Like a church!"

Now that image was interesting. It brought to mind another murder of another person connected to the world of magic and magicians, as Professor Mangel had been: Gloria Fuentes, the late Great Gandolph's now late ex-magician's assistant.

"*Arghgghgh!*" Temple ran her red-enameled fingernails into her naturally wavy, coppery hair.

The source of her frustration wasn't just Professor Mangel's death, circumscribed by a crude outline, it was a lot of unsolved murders over the past year or more, all tangential to her life and the lives of those she knew.

She pulled a fresh sheet of large paper over the puzzling image and grabbed the ruler as if she intended to admonish someone with it: herself.

But her cri de coeur had disturbed the native.

Midnight Louie leaped with surprising grace atop the desk. He sniffed the contents of her mug until his dashing white whiskers twitched, then lay down on the edges of all her papers and began bathing his right forefoot.

"There have been too many unsolved deaths in this town for too long," she told him.

Louie took this declaration stoically, and switched to licking his other forefoot.

He may have been thinking, but Temple thought not. *She* did not tend to lick her toes when thinking, although she had been known to wet her lips.

At least she was drawing straight lines now. The ruler moved down the page inch by inch as she underlined it with pencil, dark and emphatic.

Louie stretched out a damp paw to follow her progress. Temple wasn't sure whether he was playing or putting his own stamp of approval on the form taking shape on the paper.

She might not be able to draw a decent stick figure in a game of Hangman, but she could trace straight lines to infinity.

Temple swooped the page around in a forty-five-degree turn and began drawing another series of lines crossways to the first.

"This is a table, Louie," she explained as the cat continued giving encouraging pats—or playful bats (with Louie it was so hard to tell when he was just being a cat, or was being just a cat)—as he supervised her progress down the page.

"There!" Temple spun the page around again. "I am going to list every mysterious death that I know of for the past year. Seeing it laid out in black and white ought to make something clear."

| WHO | WHEN | WHERE | METHOD | ODDITIES | SUSPECT |
|---|---|---|---|---|---|
| dead man at Goliath Hotel | April | casino ceiling | ? | | Max |
| dead man at Crystal Phoenix | Aug. | casino ceiling | ? | ? | ? |
| Max's mentor, Gandolph | Halloween | seance | ? | ? | assorted psychics |
| Cliff Effinger, Matt's stepfather | New Year's | Oasis barge | drowning | | 2 muscle men |
| Cher Smith, stripper | Feb. | strip club parking lot | strangled | | ? |
| Gloria Fuentes, Gandolph's assistant | Feb. | church parking lot | strangled | "she left" on body in morgue | ? |
| Prof. Jeff Mangel | March | UNLV hall | knifed | ritual marks | ? |
| Cloaked Conjuror's assistant | April | New Millennium ceiling | beating or fatal fall | masked like CC or a TV show SF alien | ? |

Temple leaned back to study her handiwork. It seemed that the last year had not showered pennies from heaven on Las Vegas casinos, but dead bodies. Parking lots came in second as a hot crime scene. Magic was a thread linking four of the victims, including the last three.

Louie lashed out a paw and, with what passed for retractable thumb tacks on his forefoot, drew the drawing closer to him. He actually appeared to study the layout for a moment with the usual feline solemnity, but immediately after rolled over on the paper and wiggled luxuriously, creasing wrinkles into Temple's crisp recto-linear design.

"Off, off, damn . . . *Spot!*"

Temple's expletives often displayed her years doing PR for the Tyrone Guthrie repertory theater in Minneapolis.

Louie did not heed Shakespearian admonitions. He didn't heed admonitions, period. He rolled onto his back, putting his curled limbs into what Temple called the Dead Bug position (well, Louie *was* jet black), the one that cats everywhere from Peekaboo the comic strip cat to Leo the Lion considered the safe-at-home, leave-me-alone position: Home Alone, for short. In other words, meddle with the cat sprawled helplessly on its back at your own peril.

Temple decided she was in no hurry to reclaim her paper and reached instead for the cell phone headset on her desk. The headset left her hands free to take notes while on the phone, which she had to do frequently, and also preserved her from possible cancer of the ear, eye, nose, throat, and, most creepily, brain.

She punched the autodial number for Max's cell phone.

Meanwhile, Louie twisted his torso in two different directions at once and took total possession of the papers on her desk.

"What's up?" Max's voice answered.

"Louie's legs. In the air. All four."

"That doesn't sound like a phenomenon worth reporting."

"It's the paper he's lying on that's interesting."

"The Sunday paper?"

"No. The list I just made of all the unsolved murders hanging over us . . . some of them quite literally. It's rather interesting when you spell it out in black and white. Thought you might want to see it. I also have an enlarged version of that crude symbol painted around poor Jeff's body."

Temple's glance fell on the small, crumpled, pale green receipt on which she had first drawn the palm-sized version of the symbol.

"Max," she went on suddenly, "isn't there some tradition relating to a five-sided figure, a pentagram, as a sign of evil?"

"If you're talking Universal Pictures from the forties, then yeah."

"I thought so! But I can't remember what. It isn't Dracula—"

"No way would he dirty his palms with pentagrams. Can't you remember?"

"No! That's why I'm asking you."

"A werewolf."

"Right!"

"So you think a werewolf is involved?"

"No, but somebody might want us to think so."

"So we'd look even more ridiculous to the Las Vegas Metropolitan Police Department?"

"A lot of the victims are people involved professionally in magic."

"That doesn't make them consorters with werewolves, Temple, m'dear. In fact, just the opposite. The magic professional despises any intimations of the weird or paranormal surrounding the art. We are illusionists. We create mysteries for others. We don't cherish any illusions ourselves."

"Hah! Shows what you know about your own self, Mr. Mystifying Max. Don't worry. I'd never suspect you of being a werewolf. No, you've got to be a vampire: shuttered windows, night person, wears black."

"Just to prove you wrong I'll pick up a pizza with garlic on the way over."

"Done!"

After she disconnected the phone, Temple wondered how to kill time. Max wouldn't take long to get there. Las Vegas boasted almost as many great pizza places as it did wedding chapels.

Midnight Louie had abandoned his tummy-up position and hit the hardwood floor with a thump. He stalked over to the French doors and gazed out on Temple's second-floor patio. Most people would assume the big black cat was watching for birds, but Temple understood that he was watching for Max.

Somehow Louie always knew when his predecessor in the role of roommate was coming over. Temple had never owned a cat before she had found Louie running loose in the exhibition hall of the convention center a year ago, and also had stumbled over, literally, her first murder victim. She hadn't realized yet that the verb "owning" was wishful thinking when it came to cats.

If anything, Louie owned her, and often acted like it.

Now that he was absorbed with guard duty, Temple pulled the papers back toward her, smoothing any wrinkles Louie had pressed into them.

She paused, realizing that Louie's maneuvers had left the strange figure upside down. And it looked weirdly familiar in that position. Not like something you saw every day, certainly, but like *something*. Some similar conjunction of crude lines she had seen. Somewhere.

Great! She would be the Queen of Vague when she trotted this sketch around desperately seeking a definition for it.

Movement in the sun-dappled room suddenly caught her eye: Louie trotting swiftly into the main room.

He seldom troubled to move faster than necessary, so Temple jumped up to follow the cat.

She hadn't heard a thing, but Max had materialized in the living room like the imposing magician he was, six-feet-four, lean and all in black from hair to toe except for the white-and-red cardboard pizza box he held before him like a tray.

"Not climbing the balcony today?" she asked, referring to his usual second-story-man approach.

"Didn't want the pepperoni to slide off the mozzarella. Vertical ascensions don't suit pizzas."

Temple was already rooting in the hip-pocket kitchen's cupboards and drawers for plates, knives, and napkins. Fingers would do for the rest.

"Are you still worried about being seen here?"

"Now more than ever," he answered fervently.

She saw that he was serious. "Why?"

"The forces of evil seem to be gathering."

"Of evil? Or crime?"

"I think it's just outright evil, but crime trails after evil like a kid brother trying to keep up."

"Evil. The Synth?"

Max pulled a triangular piece from the precut slab of crust, cholesterol, and tomato sauce as red as blood.

Eating it allowed him to mull his answer. "I started thinking about who would be in the Synth. I know or know of most of the professional magicians around. I can't see any of them being seriously irritated by the Cloaked Conjurer. At that level, they're institutions. Everybody knows they're trickmeisters, and their level of trick is not what CC is exposing. He blows the whistle on dated stuff; illusions we've all had to reinvent or forget. So the Synth—"

"Has to be 'nothing but a bunch of bloody amateurs!'" Temple declaimed in a thundering British accent.

" 'Bloody' may be eerily appropriate. Where'd you come up with that quote?"

"Spoken by the late great Tyrone Guthrie, the British director who founded a repertory company in the American Midwest, my alma mater in Minneapolis, after trying to coax a professional performance of *Oedipus Rex* out of some college-level theater students as a demonstration. He burst out with that sentence. It became a catch phrase around his namesake theater forever."

"I'm afraid *we're* 'a bunch of bloody amateurs' in the face of what's really going on here. Which is why I brought this."

Max reached into his pocket to pull out an object.

Temple was so stunned at the directness of the gesture—usually an ex-magician like Max couldn't resist producing physical objects out of thin air—that she stared at him instead of it for a moment.

The overhead kitchen fluorescent light cast an admittedly harsh shadow, but Max's lean face looked hollow instead of sleek. Temple saw strain in the taut tilt of his eyes, and he looked tired. No, dispirited.

"We never had time to go to the firing range," he was saying, regretfully.

"Ah, you did notice my extremely awkward relationship with firearms out at the Rancho Exotica? I'm better off unarmed."

"I don't like guns either. This is just pepper spray. You have to snap the cover open and move the spray head out of the guarded position. Then press away."

Temple curled her fingers around the molded edge of the leatherette carrying case, unsnapped the flap, and rotated the little white plastic nozzle into the armed position. It looked like a key chain giveaway, or something kids in a kinder, gentler time used to send for through the mail from ads at the back of comic books.

"You sure it doesn't double as a decoder ring?" she quipped.

"No, it just sprays very hot pepper. Be careful not to let any get in your eyes if you have to use it. Works against mad dogs, and Englishmen too."

She glanced at Midnight Louie, looking natty as a rug on the black-and-white-tiled floor. He was dispatching a pepperoni circle that Max had slipped to him.

"Who am I supposed to be using it against?" Temple asked. "Besides mad dogs and Englishmen?"

"Whoever chased you with the car at TitaniCon. Whoever was

getting pushy with your entire party at the convention. I don't know who, but you will if he/she/it/they ever have you cornered."

"Yeah." Temple kept silent to chew on pizza and a scene from the past: a parking garage, two strange men, blows, pain, humiliation, fear. She glanced at the petite pepper spray. Would that have helped her then? Only if she carried it where it was instantly accessible.

"And," Max said, not quite meeting her eyes, "it wouldn't hurt to put Matt Devine on your distant acquaintance list, since he seemed to be the main target at TitaniCon."

"Yeah, well . . ." Temple swallowed too much pizza too fast and almost choked. "The way he's been acting lately, that won't be a problem. Is something going on I should know about?"

"Nothing concrete." Max expelled a huff of frustrated breath. He got busy inhaling more pizza. "Never hurts to be cautious," he said finally.

That also held true for interpersonal relationships. Temple bit back a lot more questions. They sounded more like an interrogation in her mind.

Besides, it was time to put the leftover pizza in the refrigerator and show Max her handy-dandy list of murderous events.

She hopped off the stool, avoiding Louie who was still cleaning up undevoured pepperoni while a full, fresh bowl of Free-To-Be-Feline lay untouched not three feet away.

"You're spoiling him," she warned Max.

"Consider it a bribe." He glanced back with a grin, satisfied that the cat was remaining behind to finish dinner. "I always feel I have a Victorian father scowling at me whenever that cat's around the place."

"A Victorian father? Louie?" Temple laughed. "No, I picture him more as a Mob enforcer. You know, Louie the Shiv from Cicero."

"How about Louie the Lip from Jersey?"

They were laughing as they entered the office. The sun had moved to the other side of the building, so Temple switched on the student lamp on her desk. Its warm yellow light hit the enlarged drawing she'd made like a spotlight.

"All wrong." Max had stopped just inside the door to regard it from a distance.

"How?"

"Not your sketch. The original. It's too crude. Why go to the trouble of stabbing the professor with a custom knife with a hokey

Satanist handle, why import all the S and M paraphernalia, and then surround the man's body with such a plain-Jane arcane symbol? I've seen ritual markings. They're elaborate and based on something . . . alchemy or horoscope symbols, alien hieroglyphs. This giant 'house' is too bland for that kind of mind-set."

Temple took a deep breath. "Then *it* must really mean something, and all the other props are distraction." She waggled her left-hand fingers.

"And meanwhile the right hand is scrawling these five pathetic lines on the floor? It think it's all a distraction. Let's see your list."

Temple pulled it from under the drawing.

In the bright artificial light of early evening, with someone else looking on, her brave new approach looked as childish as the drawing.

"It's just a list," she said before he could point out the obvious.

Max had come close to read it, and stood with folded elbows staring down at the names, and especially the blank places.

"Why'd you include the dead men in the casino ceilings?"

"Nobody's really been charged with their murders, although Molina's pretty sure you had something to do with the Goliath one."

"Why is Effinger listed?"

"Molina turned those two thugs over to the DEA. Wasn't it assumed they'd killed Effinger, though proving it would be hard?"

"If Effinger was tied into anything, it was those two casino deaths, especially since the second guy looked like him. I happen to think that sequence has nothing to with the later murders."

"But . . . you call it a sequence."

Max just nodded. Then his long forefinger stabbed a blank slot under the "Suspect" heading. "You can put a name in here: Rafi Nadir."

"Rafi Nadir . . . what kind of name is that?"

"Lebanese, maybe Lebanese-American. I don't know."

"For Cher Smith's murder? Who is this Rafi guy?"

"You've met him."

"No way!"

"I wish you hadn't, but you did."

"How do you know—? Max, you were *there* when I met him!"

"Elementary, my dear Temple."

"Don't tell me," she ordered. She was already irritated that he knew something he hadn't told her. Now she would have to figure out on her own who this Rafi Nadir was and when she had "met" him.

Max wished she hadn't met him. It must have been recently, because they'd been hanging out together more. That creepy guy in the desert, the knife and chain-mail bikini maker. Mace was his name, though maybe it was a nickname.

She glanced at Max. He was smiling, watching her mental wheels turn, spin, and dig themselves deeper into a rut.

Somebody at the science fiction convention? But everybody there wore some stupid costume, and they certainly didn't use names unless they were Spock or Data.

*Max wished she hadn't met him.* A moment flashed into her mind. Looking over her shoulder at Max and seeing a deep flicker of fear beneath the surface anger. And looking forward from that moment, she was staring into the face of the Rancho Exotica guard who had made a point of lifting her down from the Jeep, an act she could have managed all by herself.

"The macho guy at the ranch. The guy you later told me had to get out of there at the end before the police came. I could tell you hated to see him leave the scene of the crime as much as you hated to leave it yourself. But Molina was coming. . . . so who is Rafi Nadir, Max?"

He nodded in tribute to her impeccable deductions. "Ex-L.A. cop. Went rogue. Does shady muscle jobs, like at the ranch. Which was why I was furious when he laid hands on you."

Furious, Temple remembered. And frightened. She had never seen Max frightened before.

"He also does bouncer work at the strip clubs," Max added grimly.

"*That's* how you decided he was a suspect?"

Max stared at her hand-drawn table as if an invisible rattlesnake lay coiled upon it. "Yeah. I saw him in the clubs. He liked to throw his weight around, particularly at a-hundred-and-ten-pound strippers. Someone . . . drew my attention to him."

Temple remained silent, studying her table, studying Max. He seemed to be talking and thinking on autopilot. Too little on his mind, or, more likely, too much.

Whichever it was, he was not about to share his deepest inner concerns with her.

Max mysterious was one thing: this was a given with a man who had made his living as a magician for so long. Max unable, or unwilling, to be forthcoming with her was something else. Someone else.

"Anything more I should know?" she asked suddenly.

He started slightly. That was also so unlike Max, showing surprise. "Know?" He was confused, playing for time while the cobwebs cleared.

"Any more suspects I haven't listed here, like this Nadir guy?"

"Oh. No. Except for the amorphous Synth."

"Rafi doesn't sound too sinister," she said, lettering it in.

"He goes by Raf."

"As in raffish?"

"As in you wouldn't want to win this bozo in a raffle. If you cross his path, stay away from him, Temple. He's major breaking news in the local disaster department, especially for women."

"Yet you let him get away from the scene of the last crime before the police got there."

Max's face froze as if she had said something astounding.

"Scene of the crime? How did you—?"

"I was there, remember? At Rancho Exotica."

"Oh, right, at Rancho Exotica."

That's when Temple realized that there had to have been another scene of the crime where both Max and Rafi were present, but she hadn't been.

"Apparently he's as eager to dodge Molina as you are," she said, probing now.

Again Max tensed, right on the name, which Temple had dropped the same way some people would toss a grenade into a garden party: casually, but with oh-so-lethal intent. The bombshell was the name Molina. Homicide Lieutenant C. R. Molina, lady cop, lady blood-hound when it came to Max and his vague past and all-too-often suspect present.

"Let's face it," Max said, deciding to hide behind humor, "what red-blooded man wouldn't want to dodge Molina? Except maybe Matt Devine."

Now Max was dropping his own grenades. Temple tried not to feel the spray of psychic shrapnel. When had their consultation become a chess game?

When the name Rafi Nadir had come up.

The one man Temple had ever seen who frightened Max. Excepting Matt, and that was a very different kind of fear.

Why? Who was Rafi Nadir, really?

And why wouldn't Max tell her a damn thing about him?

# Chapter 2

# *Feral Foul*

As everybody knows, the world-weary private eye must some-times tread on the dark side of danger.

Mean Streets R Us.

By us I mean the old-time guys: Sam Spade, Lew Archer, Travis McGee. We are a breed apart. We are not afraid to get our digits dirty, our eyes blackened, our whiskers wet, or our ears wiped.

You can knock us down, but not out.

Okay, sometimes you can knock us out.

But not off.

Anyway, having observed my Miss Temple struggling to make sense of the string of murderous events that have dogged her teeny-tiny high-heeled footsteps since we met, I decide to take action.

It was nice of her to share her deductive reasoning with me. I truly enjoyed our consultation over Sunday morning coffee. We make a good team. She is the cream in my coffee, and I am the caffeine in her cream. She is sugar. I am spice. But she can be feisty, and I can be nice when it suits me.

However, when it comes to ferreting out information from the lower elements, there is no way that I will allow my Miss Temple to dirty her tootsies with a walk on the wild side. I will go this part of the case alone.

I am not even taking my usual "muscle," the spitting-mad Miss Midnight Louise, who is my would-be daughter. I say that there are a lot of black cats in this hip old world (despite wholesale attempts to eliminate our kind since the Dark Ages, no doubt why they call it that), and we cannot all be related. Though even a macho dude like myself must admit that there are times when you cannot beat a seriously enraged dame for effective backup.

The successful operative will stick at nothing to get results.

Still, sometimes it is best not to show up in the company of a girl. She might be mistaken for your mother.

So it nears my namesake hour when I slink solo into a neighborhood where even the pit bulls and housing developers do not go.

This is the north side of town where the abandoned houses and cars are all older than the Nixon administration. "Run-down" would be a high compliment in this area, and run down is what careless intruders usually get.

I pass a few rats the size of Midnight Louise scurrying in the opposite direction.

One stops to hiss in amazement at my presence, and at the fact that I am heading in the direction that he and his cohorts are fleeing like the, er, plague.

I hiss back. His claws scrape the cracked asphalt like dry leaves as he skitters out of sight.

I shrug my coat collar up around my neck to keep the wind from picking all my pockets. It also looks as if I am making a fashion statement instead of just having the hair on the back of my neck at permanent attention.

The effective operative does not wish to look scared into a new hairdo.

Either somebody is fitfully beating on a hollow tin drum . . . or the trash cans are rocking in the wind. Or somebody is trying to stuff a body in 'em. Or, more likely, pull one out for supper.

I did mention that this was a rough crowd.

Of course now you cannot see a soul, not even a rat.

That is how I know I am just where I want to be.

I sit down to survey the place, casually clipping my toenails in the light of the only working streetlight within six blocks.

While sharpening my shivs, I regard a street in ill repair that cuts like a rusty knife through what amounts to one big empty lot.

Islands of trash thrust up from the flat desert landscape here and there. I recognize articles of furniture missing stuffing and upholstery, and large black-green garbage bags big enough and lumpy enough to hold sufficient dead bodies to populate a zombie movie, and maybe a sequel or two. Broken amber-colored empty bottles exhale the sour stench of beer so flat it is looking for a singing teacher.

However, my connoisseur's sniffer notices something else among the odors of decay: the whiff of fish. Oh, it is not the delicate, scaly scent of freshly caught fish, such as you find at the edge of a koi pond, but the odor of the canned stuff they sell in the stores. Being that my old man was once the mascot on a Pacific Northwest salmon boat, I prefer to catch my own, but it is clear that the pre-caught kind of fish is here to catch something else.

I rise and swagger over to the nearest hummock of trash.

It is not long before I am close enough to notice something familiar jammed in among what is left of somebody's Tia Evita floral reclining chair. I spot the familiar crosshatching of thin gray metal wires.

Normally such sights give me a chill of apprehension, but tonight I emit a soft purr of satisfaction instead. Everything is as bad as I had hoped it would be.

In not too long a time, I shall be at the mercy of the most fearsome street gang this old town has ever seen.

What I do to keep my Miss Temple out of danger and in arch supports.

# Chapter 3

# Midnight Consultation

Max stretched, pushed Temple's compilation of dead people aside, and consulted the watch on his right wrist as his long arms folded around her.

"Almost the witching hour. We could tune in Mr. Midnight for a bedtime treat."

"Listening to a bunch of strangers whine about the personal lives they don't have? Not me."

"You're not a fan?"

Temple yawned pointedly. "Who can stay up that late anymore?"

"You're right. I should let you get your beauty sleep."

"Since when have you ever done anything you 'should' do? Max, what's the matter?"

"What isn't the matter? Listen, Temple. You stood by me like, I don't know, like the brave little drummer girl, when everyone thought I was a cad and coward and a murderer."

"Everyone?"

"Well, mostly Molina, but she carries a lot of weight. It's not fair for me to ask this, but you might have to do it again."

"Stand up to Molina?"

"Always. I mean, stand by me."

"What's happening?"

"I can't quite tell. Can't quite say. I don't know what to think. I know." He laughed ruefully. "That's not like me. This is getting too much like Northern Ireland. Foes and friends mixed together in one bloody stew. You start to question friends, you start to sympathize with foes, and the upshot is almost always betrayal and death."

"Max! You've never talked this way before."

"I've never been here, in this precise position before." His hands touched her shoulders, then his thumbs reached up to caress her cheeks. "You're sharp. You're nobody's fool. You might hear some things about me. Don't believe them. No matter who they come from. I know. You've done it before, but it'll be worse now. What I've found is worse."

"The Synth?"

"No, nothing that exotic! Something down-home and downtown. Just remember, if I'm suspect, it might be because other people are more suspect."

"People? Or person? Is it this Nadir guy?"

Temple watched her stab in the dark ricochet off the wary expression in Max's blue eyes, like a stone skipping across one of her native state's vaunted ten thousand lakes, never quite connecting with anything, defying gravity, just defying. Everything.

She was close, but still too far away.

"Does it have something to do with Molina?"

"It always has something to do with Molina," he answered, laughing bitterly. "Try to keep it between us, Temple. Can you?"

"I always have," she said, no longer certain she could.

# Chapter 4

# DOD:
# Domesticated or Dead

No sooner I have applied myself to sniffing around the silver mesh than I sense a change in the air.

I do not hear a thing, mind you. Yet the empty space surrounding me has suddenly become not so empty. It cannot be rats. Rats cannot retract their shivs, so they always announce themselves, like Miss Temple in her high heels. Also, rats cannot refrain from chittering when excited, and the gang I expect knows how to keep its lips zipped tighter than a leather bustier on Pamela Anderson.

I flick a nail at the pungent glop of fish before me, then say right out loud, "Sucker bait. One bite and boom! You are in stir."

I turn to regard my audience. Gack. Imagine a ragtag road show of *CATS!* with the entire cast recruited from a feline *West Side Story*.

These dudes are lean, edgy, and ravenous. Their shivs nervously scrape the cracked asphalt. Their whiskers are broken and twitching. I spot one poor sod who was in a rumble with a car. His untended broken leg sticks out at such a bizarre angle he can only walk on his knee. I notice a duke's mixture of ragged ears—some neatly notched—and crooked tails, not to mention fresh and festering wounds. As for coats, this crowd looks like it has just come from the Ragpickers' Ball. Exiting through a shredder.

There must be a dozen of them. Three or four start circling me so somebody is always at my back no matter which way I turn.

This is when prior planning pays off. I retreat until I am pressing the nap of my coat flat against one wall of the wire grille. After this gig I will look like I am wearing monotone plaid from the back, but sartorial concerns are the last thing on my mind.

These are not just tough and desperate dudes; this is the original Wild Bunch.

A big tiger-stripe pushes forward until his fangs are in my face. "You got a lot of nerve coming onto our turf, a downtown dude like you."

This I already know, so I say nothing.

A marmalade tom with a broken front fang pushes so close I can inhale the Whiskas-lickings on his breath. "Fee, fie, foe, fum-bug! I smell human on your lapels. You are a housebroken cat."

"Not true," I hiss back. "I do happen to occupy a co-op off the Strip, but I come and go as I please and when and where I please."

"Where is your collar, dude?" taunts a once-white semi-long-hair I hesitate to describe as a lady. "No vet tags, Prince Chauncey?"

"Yeah," the tiger-stripe adds. "We need an address for where to send the body."

"At least I do not live in a road-kill academy." I glance at the street. "I bet they drag race their lowriders so regular along there that a lot of you end up as poster boys and girls: flat as a face card in a fixed deck."

I have hit a nerve, for several sets of green and gold eyes narrow to angry slivers.

"It is the rugrats like Gimpy," says Snow Off-white, with a shrug of her razor-sharp shoulder blades, "who get creamed."

I glance at the kit with the right-angle leg, and conceal a shudder. Poor sod would be better off with that seriously bum limb amputated.

"It is not so bad," the dingy yearling pipes up. "The winos and bums feel sorry for me because I cannot forage and see that I get McDonald's leavings."

Jeez, this lot is so low that the homeless *humans* show them charity. Chalk one up on the pearly gates for the homeless humans. I have always found that the have-nots are better at sharing than the have-it-alls who got plenty to share.

"What about this day-old fish market behind the grille here?" I say.

"We stay away," says Tiger, with a growl. "We think it is a trap. People come and take away the dumb ones that venture inside and cannot get out."

"And you never see them again?"

"We do," Snow Off-white says, eager to explain. I can always get through to the babes, which may be why Tiger and Tom are breathing down my epiglottis. "But . . . they are different."

"They are . . . drones," Tom snarls. "All the fight is out of them. They come back with their ears . . . and everythng notched and have zero interest in dames and just want to lay around and wait for free food and get fat like you."

"I am not fat. I am well built. If your lot was not half-starved, you would see that you are all way too skinny."

"That is better than the alternative," Gimpy bursts out in his high adolescent voice.

"And what is the alternative?" I ask.

"Death or domestication."

I digest this for a few seconds. It is no use to preach the joys of the domestic lifestyle to those to whom just living for the next day is a real achievement. They regard every human with fear and suspicion, and in almost all cases around here, rightly so.

Except, that is, for those beneficent bums and bumettes, and the feline birth control brigade responsible for the satellite clinics that litter this junkyard, one of them right at my back.

I realize, of course, that if this gang gets too rough I can always leap through the open door, grab the glop, and trigger the automatic closing mechanism. I will be caught like a rat in a trap, but I will also be safe from the Wild Bunch.

Ole Tiger seems to be reading my mind, because his yellow teeth show a Cheshire cheese grin. "Guess you would not mind a ride in a cage, being the domestic sort to start with. You would come back minus your *cojones*, though."

"You do not understand. I have already been rendered free of unpopular potential, such as progeny."

Gimpy has been slinking around the side. "He has still got them, boss. He is lying. He is still armed and dangerous to dames."

I sigh. "It is too difficult to explain to street types. I have had a fancy operation by a plastic surgeon called a vasectomy, and—"

"We are not interested in your medical history, you pampered sellout!" Tom spits. "Whatever you have had, what you will *not* have when you come back from the twenty-four-hour abduction is your hairballs."

I gulp. This mission is more dangerous than I thought. If I happen to fall into the hands of these do-gooders, they will have me sliced and diced for real in no time, because a vasectomy is invisible. I will be summarily cut off from my former self just as if I were a homeless, irresponsible, kitty-littering street dude.

"So," says Tom with an evil grin, digging his shivs into my shoulder like staples. "Why is a domestic dude like you risking life, limb, and liberty to come hassle us on our territory?"

"I am an investigator," I begin.

"Narc!" screams Snow Off-white, arching her bony back. "We hardly ever get any nip, just that awful weed that people are always selling on corners around here. We better take care of the narc personally."

They crowd closer, ugly mugs full of fangs and uglier expressions. I can handle myself in a brawl, but they have me pinned and my only escape is into the clutches of the North Las Vegas Neutering Society.

Shivs as edged as sharks' teeth are pricking my undercoat in warning. With this crew, one puncture wound, one whiff of blood, and they will go into a fighting frenzy.

I let them push me closer to the open door to eunuchhood. I'd rather take my chances hornswaggling a bunch of humanitarians than beating off a gang of wildcats any day. Where is that twerp Midnight Louise when you need her?

"Wait a minute," yowls a rough female voice.

A cat who is black like me shoulders through the mob to thrust her jaw in my face like a knuckle sandwich. Midnight Louise this is not.

This is a big-boned, rangy lady with a hacksaw voice. The white scar tracks crisscrossing her mug are not tokens of the plastic surgeon.

"I have been taken away by the aliens with the silver ships," she says, "and it is not so bad. I was tired of trying to eat for five or six every few months anyway. So if I were you, dude, I'd take the escape hatch. This gang is out for blood. Just being brave enough, and stupid enough, to come here will not save you."

I stare into her hard and weary green eyes. She stares into my hard and wary green eyes. Suddenly, I feel an embarrassing purr bubbling in my throat. I growl to conceal it, but it is too late.

She lunges at my throat, then twists her head and takes the nape of my neck in her teeth and shakes me until my fangs chatter. A big black mitt boxes my cheek.

"Is that you, Grasshopper?"

"Yeah," I admit sheepishly. I cannot stand being publicly mauled by overenthusiastic females who are not babes. "Ma. But they call me Louie now. Midnight Louie."

Well, there is only one thing that cuts it with a gang as down and out as this one: family. They are all so related to each other that if they were people they would be put in jail. In fact, I think a lot of them are a few whiskers shy of a full muzzle, but nobody cares about the family trees of our kind. Our mating tendencies go back to our godlike Egyptian origins. The Egyptians were not too nice to resort to marital alliances with brothers and sisters to keep the royal line going. I believe the term is inbred.

Anyway, by virtue of my long-lost mama being among them and being something of a top cat at that, my bacon is not chopped liver. In fact, they are all my kissing cousins now.

She has taken me aside for a family reunion.

"How did you remember me?" I ask as we settle down on a Naugahyde ottoman that has lost its stuffing until it is shaped like an inner tube. Actually, it is quite comfy. "It is not like you did not have dozens just like me."

"Oh, Grasshopper, there were none just like you. Naughty from the moment you lost your milk teeth. You were after those poor grasshoppers before your eyes were open. So. You are in business. Did I hear you bragging about a co-op apartment? Not smart with this gang." She boxes my ear again, as if dislodging mites.

"Actually, it is a 'cooperative' living arrangement I have with this babe who flacks for the Crystal Phoenix."

"It is a mixed marriage?"

I blink.

"She is human?"

"Um, pretty much so, but she has long red nails. I really love the way they sink into my . . . ah, we are just roommates, Ma. Purely platonic. My real ladylove is this shaded silver Persian—"

"A foreigner? And what is this 'shaded silver' stuff? You mean the chit is gray."

I roll my eyes. I am not about to explain the sublime and subtle mix of black, white, and gray hairs on the aristocratic form of the Divine Yvette.

"So tell me about your business."

"It is a one-dude operation. Private-eye stuff. That is why I am here. I am looking into a case involving some Big Cats."

"You know some Big Cats?" She actually sounds impressed. *I* am impressed.

"Some."

"Then why did you not bring one along for backup?"

"These big guys do not just meander out on the streets. There are laws."

"Well, boy, you are lucky I am part of this colony because your meatballs would have been chili powder in another couple of seconds, and I am getting too old to rumba without activating my rheumatism. So I suggest we go over and ask the boys what you want to know and then you skedaddle."

"Yes, Ma." There was never any point in arguing with her. She was the Sultana of Swat when it came to keeping her litters in line. "Uh," I add as we amble over to the others. "What is your name besides Ma?"

"That is it. Ma. Ma Barker."

"You are not a dog!"

"No, but I bite like one. Just remember that."

In a moment I am huddling with the Wild Bunch.

"I am looking for a man," I begin.

"Why come to us? We have nothing to do with that species if we can help it."

"I cannot argue with your good taste, but this man has a place where he keeps Big Cats. It is a hideout, see. No human knows where it is. I figure you guys"—Snow Off-white bristles and hisses—"and dolls might have an idea where it is. I know you get around and I figure you have your ears to the ground better than anybody."

"*Hmm*," says Tom. "We do not roam as much as we used to now that our numbers are being whisked away and returned all meek and meatball-less. But I wonder if you could be talking about the Dead Place?" He glances at the others.

Oh, great. Like I need to visit another Dead Place. "What is this joint?" I ask.

"I have smelled Big Cat there," Snow Off-white mews. She rolls her yellow eyes. "Very Big Cat."

"But nobody human goes there much," Tiger adds. "That is why we explore sometimes. It is not far from here and there are trees to climb."

"It is like a park," Ma puts in. A lot of these street types do not even know what a park is.

I nod. "It would be a rich man's estate, but no one would know."

Whiskers tremble sagely all around. "That is it, then. The Dead Place. People do not like Dead Places. They stay away and then we can come out and play. Not even the aliens with the silver ships who abduct us go there."

"I have been thinking of moving the colony there," Tom admits, "but we grow weak and fewer, and many like the free food too much. We have gone soft."

"Not very. Trust me," I reassure them.

So I get the general location of the Dead Place, which I am happy to learn is in Las Vegas proper, if there is any district in Las Vegas you could call "proper." I had enough treks into the desert during my last case to leave permanent sand calluses between my toes.

Then I bid the gang adieu. Ma escorts me to the edge of their territory.

"Imagine," she muses with a trace of fondness, but very little. "The Grasshopper hangs with Big Cats."

"You could come back with me. I am sure I can get you a cushy position at my pad, the Circle Ritz."

For a moment her eyes soften.

I press on. "Air-conditioning. Sunspots. Security. Down comforters."

She shakes her head. "They need me here. We are dying out, of course. That is the plan."

I try one last ploy. "Ah, Dad has retired on Lake Mead. Runs the goldfish concession at this eatery they named after him, Three O'Clock Louie's."

"Your father is a restaurateur?"

"Sort of."

She shakes her grizzled head. "I thought he had to follow the sea."

"He followed it to a salmon boat in the Pacific Northwest, but he came back here to retire." I look at her edgeways. "Maybe he wanted to find us."

"Three O'Clock! He always was a loner, that one. We had some good times, though. Nice to see you, boy." She cuffs me one more time. "But do not come around again. I may not be here to save your ashcan."

I gulp. I have not mentioned her maybe-granddaughter, Miss Midnight Louise. The maternal instinct is a hormonal thing with our breed: strong as steel when kits are coming and growing . . . gone with the wind once they have left the litter.

Still, her eyes are suspiciously shiny as I turn away and begin my long midnight stroll toward the Dead Place.

# Chapter 5

# Dead Air Time

Matt Devine pulled off the huge foam-padded earphones.

This heavy-duty headset always reminded him of the "earmuffs" people wore at target-shooting ranges.

Some nights, wearing them, *he* felt like the target.

"Rough shift?" a woman's voice asked.

For a moment he was disoriented. Without the strange, isolated intensity of a phone-line link to the whole, wide radio-listening world, the nearby unamplified sound of a normal human voice was surprising, even alarming. He'd thought he was alone.

Matt swiveled around on his stool. *Had she—?*

But it was only Letitia, the host who preceded him on WCOO's nightly schedule of moody music and listener requests followed by his Mr. Midnight call-in shrink gig.

"Letitia. I didn't know you'd stayed for my show."

She lowered herself to the empty stool. This was quite a production, because there was well over three hundred pounds of Letitia to lower.

"I'm your producer, after all." She folded her arms over her formidable chest and stared at him.

To the world of the airwaves she was her pseudonym, Ambrosia, the warm, maternal voice that teased mention of hurts and shy loves out of anonymous callers and then played the perfect song to celebrate or soothe. "You Light Up My Life," "The Rose," (Matt had to admit he liked the clean poetry of that one), that sort of thing. Most of the songs were soothers, and Ambrosia's hokey therapy worked wonders. Matt, formerly a priest in a fairly formal religion, tended to distrust easily accessed emotions, but he couldn't deny the magic Letitia/Ambrosia performed each night from seven to midnight.

Even her morbid obesity wasn't unusual for a radio personality. Radio was the ideal medium for the less-than-medium attractive. Garrison Keillor wasn't only a self-proclaimed "shy person," but one of the homeliest men in the public eye since Abraham Lincoln. It had made him a star. On radio, and then in books. Not on TV.

Hefty size aside, Letitia was gorgeous and dressed like an MTV queen. Tonight she wore a pleated tangerine polyester pantsuit draped with a chest plate of African beads. The seriously chubby fingers braced on her knees were choked with high-carat solitaires of semiprecious gemstones. Silky smooth brown skin set off her eyes the way black velvet showcases diamonds, and they were meticulously made up with metallic swaths of shadow. Looking at her was like regarding a bird of paradise.

"You look gorgeous tonight," Matt couldn't stop himself from remarking, though he seldom felt comfortable complimenting a woman on looks alone.

"Thanks." Her self-esteem preened visibly. "You look pretty good yourself."

"It's not anything I do," he said, instantly uncomfortable.

She just shook her head. "I told you when I hired you that you were too pretty to be on radio, but that's okay. They can hear it in your voice."

"People can hear how I look?"

"They get an image. If you have a nice voice, it's a nice image. Radio's the only place I can be taken for a size six, honey!"

A rich rhumba of laughter emerged from the bright drum of her huge body. She cocked her gorgeous head with its decorated dread-locks to hear herself. "Then again, maybe not. Too much reverb for an anorexic."

Matt couldn't help smiling.

"Now that's better, Mr. Moody Midnight. You keep smilin'. Remember, they hear it all in your voice. So what's the matter?"

"You hear something in my voice?"

"I hear everything in your voice, baby. It's nothing personal. It's my job. I read voices. Yours has changed."

"How?" He felt an irrational surge of defiance. If she could hear it, so could . . . anyone.

"Tighter, more cautious. Strained. If you were a singer I'd be worried. We got to get back that nice, easy open throat you were born with. So tell Ambrosia what's the matter. Don't think of me as your producer; think of me as that nice smooth-as-white chocolate voice on the radio."

She shook with laughter then, picturing herself as white choco-late. In a way she was, thanks to radio. Ultraslim, no-calorie white chocolate.

Matt sighed, relieved to have nothing to hide behind right now. Letitia was indeed his producer. If she detected something strained in his performance, then it was her business. And . . . half the world confided in Ambrosia and felt better for it. Maybe he could share a bit of that magic too. God knew he had a lot to confide.

"So tell Mama."

The admonition made Matt superimpose his mother's image over the gaudy mountain of Letitia. Mira Zabinski was small, pale, con-strained, lost like a pastel portrait by Degas against a lush Gauguin oil painting of the islands.

He felt a pang of disloyalty along with relief.

"When did you notice a change?" he asked.

She considered. "Around 'bout that time Elvis started calling you."

"Letitia, it wasn't Elvis—"

"Let me think it was Elvis. I'd feel better thinking it was Elvis. A lot of people would. He's kinda a patron saint for the dysfunctional, you know."

"I know! I heard that loud and clear from the callers back then. So I started going wrong then?"

"Wrong? Nothing wrong with you, then or now." She stood up. "Let's go get some fruity drink some place. I'm buying."

Matt knew then that it was serious. He was slower to rise. Half of him welcomed a chance to share the trouble he'd doled out piece-meal to the people he knew over the past few weeks, partly to protect them, mostly to protect himself.

Protecting yourself was constant, lonely, back-breaking work, and he was tired of it.

They paused at the door to turn off the lights. Their familiar studio landscape vanished like a stage set. After Matt's "Midnight Hour" program, the station went to satellite feed until regular programming resumed in the early morning. Only a lone technician kept the sound of music flowing over the air waves.

The hall was dimly lit and the tiny reception room seemed larger without people in it. Beyond the glass door, the almost empty parking lot looked like a staging ground for a UFO movie.

It was one-thirty in the morning, but in Las Vegas the bars were open twenty-four/seven.

Matt opened the door for Letitia, then followed her into the luke-warm night.

They'd dawdled inside long enough that the small gaggle of fans who usually waited for Matt after his show had given up and gone home.

"No groupies," Letitia commented.

"No groupies." Matt sounded relieved even to himself.

"You don't worry that your ratings might be slipping?"

"No, because if they were, I'd do what I did before I had ratings to slip."

"Which is?"

"I don't know. Whatever I have to do to pay the rent."

A form came barreling toward them from Matt's left side, from the shadow the building cast along its sides.

Matt barely had time to put his hands up before something as big as a German shepherd lunged at him. Hairy, too. Red hair.

While he was thinking Irish setter, the apparition's weight pushed him slightly backward and swiped his mouth off-center with a sloppy kiss.

It was five-feet-something of overenthusiastic girl and only the red hair kept him from pushing her away like an encroaching poodle.

"I love your show! I can't believe I did this! 'Bye."

And she dashed off around the building, giggling.

Letitia nodded. "Kiss-and-run groupie. Not bad."

Matt backhanded his mouth. "Where are their parents, anyway?"

"At home, wondering where their kids are, as usual." She chuckled, a sound as rich as water in a mountain stream plunking notes from a scale of river rocks. "Lighten, man. You've got fans and they're in the desired demographic. I don't know why you gotta see life in shades of gray when it can be a Technicolor paradise like the merry old land of Oz."

"You forget the wicked witch."

"Don't look at me. I'm not playing no ugly old thing with striped socks unless I get to keep the jazzy red shoes, bro. That's what it's all about. Life does not have to be a black-and-white film these days."

Letitia stopped to stare at a vehicle under the greenish glare of a security light. "There. See what I mean? Where's that kick-ass motorcycle of yours? Or that sweet shiny silver Volkswagen Bug that Elvis left for you? That just makes me want to laugh and cry at the same time, Elvis givin' people VW Bugs, even if they have been redesigned. Poor Elvis never got a chance for a redesign. I know what you're gonna say: 'it wasn't Elvis.' " She sing-songed along with Matt, nodding at his programed response. "But why you driving that white chocolate old Probe now? It isn't even white chocolate. It's just plain white, honey, and that ain't you. Trust me."

"Maybe I don't want to be me."

"Yeah, that's soooo tough. Easy job, good money. Raking it in on the traveling chitchat circuit. I don't get those gilt-edged national speaking invitations. Not yet. And I was here first. So what is it? Girl trouble?"

That question was so wildly off and so right on that Matt felt like Letitia did about Elvis's postmortem taste in giveaway cars: he didn't know whether to laugh or to cry.

"Boy trouble?" she asked when he remained silent.

He saw that he'd at least have to commit to declaring a sexual preference. Before he could, his feet felt a faint, almost spectral thrum. They knew that subliminal vibration but his mind couldn't name it.

"Damn it, Matt, my car's in the garage, so we're going to get in that Vanilla Ice car of yours and go someplace for a Bloody Mary and then you're gonna drop me home—"

He was frowning into the distance, black and empty. "Yeah. Let's get to the car." He took her elbow, or what he figured to be her elbow, and tried to hurry her across the black asphalt sea of the parking lot.

That was like a fishing boat trying to tug the Queen Elizabeth into port in double time.

"What burr got up your nose?"

Not only his feet felt it. Now his knees were humming with it, all his joints, and he could finally hear that distant waspish drone, sweet and scary.

"Come on, Letitia!"

They didn't make the car, of course.

Some things just overtake you, like hurricanes and tornados and very fast motorcycles.

It came spurting and bucking into the lot, as black and anonymous as the leather jumpsuited and helmeted figure that rode it. Zorro on wheels.

It came roaring toward them on a curving scythe like Death's particular sheep's crook, the dark side of the Good Shepherd. Matt cast a quick prayer at the nearest streetlight, a vigil light for the whole firmament and what might lie behind it.

He stopped moving and Letitia mirrored him.

"What's going on? Who's that speed demon?" she demanded. For the first time her deep, dark voice trembled like her flesh.

"That's my problem."

"Drugs? Somebody's after you?"

"No drugs. Just after me."

The black motorcycle, a Kawasaki model aptly called the Ninja, swung in a circle and tilted closer and closer until it ringed Matt and Letitia into an invisible circle of containment.

"It sure does stir up a lot of hot air," Letitia complained as her tangerine outfit expanded to blowfish proportions.

The Ninja revved and came whooshing by, forcing them to back step.

Matt circled Letitia, keeping between the motorcycle and her.

"Hey, man," she objected, "don't play the hero. I can take that thing. Who'd you think'd be left standing after a head-to-headlight?"

Matt laughed, his tension easing. "You're addicted to counseling, you know that?"

"It's cheaper than a lot of things. Oh, that machine is snortin' now. Here comes El Toro."

The dark motorcycle charged, cutting it even closer than before.

Matt tensed to pounce as it passed. Motorcycles were powerful, fast, and maneuverable, but they rode a very fine line of balance. If he could tip that balance he might be dragged over the asphalt, but the bike might skid, tip.

He lunged as the heat and sound roared at them like a dragon's breath. Grabbing at the handlebar jerked him off his feet, sent him rolling on the asphalt without the protection of biker leathers.

Khakis and a linen blazer kept the asphalt from breaking through and he was up as fast as he was down, but fifteen feet away from Letitia.

The Ninja cut a close, wobbly circle; its rider was forced to throttle down and drag a booted foot on the ground to stabilize the bike.

Then it revved again and drove straight ahead, between Matt and Letitia.

He tried to lunge and grab once more, but only ended up smacking the red taillight good-bye. Letitia huffed out a protest.

He glanced at her. Still upright. Still all right.

The vanishing bike's driver lifted a right hand off the handlebars and flourished something long and dangling like a trophy, or a scalp.

Matt ran toward Letitia.

"My beads!" she was bellowing. "That bastard ripped off my tribal beads."

"Are you all right? Your neck?"

"The world's worst Indian burn." Letitia removed her palm from her nape and examined it in the glare of the streetlight. No blood. "Now I really need that bleeding Bloody Mary. And you've got a lot of explaining to do."


The place was called Buff Daddy's and the clientele was all black.

Rap and hip-hop twitched off the sound system, the rapid-fire rhythms and lyrics as relentless as musical machine-gun fire.

Matt made his Polish-blond way in Letitia's wake to the corner table she commandeered like a petty dictator. The speakers were far enough away that you could hear someone talk if the language was English.

A tall, pipe-cleaner-skinny waitress with an awesome arrangement of interwoven dreadlocks took their orders. Matt joined Letitia in a Bloody Mary, suddenly reminded of another wise woman of color and size, this one from the musical *South Pacific*.

Her tangerine false fingernails curled around the tall thick glass of tomato juice and vodka as soon as it arrived.

"This is a three B.M. night," she announced. "Glad you're driving me home."

Matt noticed that her chocolate complexion had grayed to the color of cold cocoa. "Then one's my limit," he said.

"Didn't plan on getting you drunk and compliant anyway," she chuckled, drinking from a straw that rode alongside the usual celery stalk. She twiddled the celery like a swizzle stick and winked. "Good drink for dieters."

Matt just shook his head.

"No use playing innocent. What you got after you? The mob? Some crazed Elvis nut?"

"Elvis. That's what I thought the motorcyclist was at first. And a motorcycle did follow me one night . . . a motorcycle cop—maybe." He shook his head again, wanting to clear away the biker roar he still heard, still felt. "After tonight, I have no doubts. It's my stalker."

Letitia made a face, shook her celery playfully. "Not this kind of stalk, I guess. Stalk-er. What gender we talking about here, Matt?"

This time he laughed as he shook his head. "I didn't think anybody could get me to see the bright side of this. . . . Female."

"Ooh, well, then."

"If you say 'relax and enjoy it,' I'll steal your celery."

"Nobody steals one more thing off me tonight." Her mock defense softened into a radio cajole. "Tell me about this Leather Lady on wheels, Matt."

"First off, I didn't know she had wheels. I'd seen a motorcyclist following me, but like you I'd assumed it was male."

"You thought it was really Elvis! Admit it!"

"Well, it did occur to me. He *was* a speed freak. Things had been pretty weird, especially at the Elvis impersonator competition." Matt actually nibbled his celery stick.

He wanted to remain sober, after all. No, he didn't. For the first time in his life he didn't, and he couldn't get drunk. He had to drive. The story of his life.

"So how'd you pick this freako up? Through the show?"

"No. She came first."

"Now, no dirty talk. I might get outa control."

"Dirty talk?"

"How long were you a priest? Never mind. Where'd she come from?"

"Out of the blue. Looking for another man. She thought she'd use me to lead her to him. She seems to have gotten stuck on me."

"Like an old LP that gets in one groove and won't jump out of it." Letitia had drunk half her Bloody Mary and was working on the celery stick. "That pepper vodka really gives this bite!" She waved at the waitress for a follow up. "So. She's not the usual groupie."

"Definitely not. The second time I 'met' her, she cut me."

"You're not talking high school snub here?"

"Razor. Superficial, but a lot of blood loss."

"Jesus!"

He kept silent, listening to the piped-in rapper excoriate "ho's" and "hot mamas." Why'd anybody want this as aural wallpaper? It was like listening to Hitler. Except nobody here was really listening, which made it even worse. Cultural nihilism was easy to ignore until it got into the communal bloodstream and then it lashed out and bit.

"Jesus," Letitia whispered this time. "Where'd she cut you?"

Matt put a hand to his right side. Didn't mention it was where the spear had pierced the God-man she'd just invoked without much thinking about it.

Catholic kink might be a little out of Letitia's line, as much as she knew about human nature when it came softly over an anonymous radio line.

"Poor baby!" She was now halfway through the second Bloody Mary and growing a little unfocused.

That was all right with Matt. If he was finally going to confide the whole story to someone, he'd prefer a slightly tiddly confessor.

Her sympathy, her distance from the whole conundrum that was Kitty/Max/Temple made Letitia the perfect big sister. He could even picture her in a habit, with rosary beads instead of the African trade variety. Now, that would really horrify her.

"Say, Matt, you're doing okay here." She looked around the funky bar.

"What you do mean?"

"For a sheltered white boy."

He didn't bother to tell her that he'd haunted black Baptist churches for the music for years. If he hadn't become color-blind, he'd become color-immune.

"You're so strange. Way ahead of the rest in some ways, way retarded in others. Must be the priest thing. Anyway, what does this witch-woman want?"

"I think she really wants to destroy the man she was looking for and can't find. So she'll settle for me."

"She'll kill you?"

"No. Not physically. That would be too kind."

"Gee, Matt. You gotta remember you're dealing with Bloody Mary here. I am feeling no pain from my necklace rip-off, okay? But I am also feeling no pain, so 'splain it to me in teeny-tiny syllables of one word. Does that make sense?"

"Yeah. Okay. She wants my history. My past. Everything that was sacred in it. She wants my priesthood."

"I don't get it."

"What if somebody came to you and demanded that you do the one thing that most undid whatever you were, or everybody at the radio station would be killed? And that person could do it."

"Wait. I'm trying to think what would take that much away from me. Being made to do something would." Letitia's face suddenly sobered, grew ashen. "I wish you hadn't asked me that, Matt."

"I'm sorry. You wanted to know. I—"

Her extravagantly manicured hands cupped her exquisite face, which wore a mask of slack horror. "I hadn't thought of that for thirty years." Her eyes interrogated him. "How'd you know, Matt. How'd you know?"

"I don't. I don't know anything."

"Someone comes and stirs up the worst hurt, the worst hate in your whole life." Her hands entwined, twisted, the nails clawing into the dark backs until dead white moons appeared there. "The ones who call at night. Call us. They all have hurts like that. We make them feel better for a while, but we don't really cure anything for good. Only until tomorrow . . . when we talk to a whole new set who are all the same, really. God, if Someone came for me, she'd bring memories of Him back."

"God?"

"No! The devil. My own particular devil, whom I will now drown in a third Bloody Mary." She lifted a dagger-nailed forefinger, signaled the waitress. "Tell me about your devil."

For some reason, Matt felt obliged to distract Letitia from the monster in her past that his trouble had raised from the dead. He was a good counselor. He would sacrifice himself to prevent anyone around him from suffering. Just open a vein and he would bleed tomato juice and pepper vodka.

He understood how utterly Kitty O'Connor had trapped him.

"She wants my vows," he said. "My virtue, I guess. She wants me to sleep with her."

Letitia blinked. "I heard a hundred sob stories from girls up against it, but I never heard a guy complain."

"I'm not a guy. I'm an ex-priest. I made promises of chastity."

"Ex, baby. That's all history."

"No, it's my choice now. It's a sin outside of marriage."

Letitia snorted.

"In my religion it is. Especially for me, who was holier than holy."

"Listen, plenty of priests have made the news—"

"They are not me and I am not them. I was a faithful servant, okay? Think of me as a monogamous married man. I love my wife. I've been faithful to her. And some woman comes along and insists that betraying my wife is the only way for my wife, and me, to live."

"That's sorta like the reverse of that movie a few years back, where the rich dude offers a couple a million if the wife will sleep with him. People sleep with the wrong people every day. What's the big deal, really?"

"When it's wrong."

Letitia was suddenly silent. Her hands twisted. "Yeah. Sometimes it's wrong, no question." Sweat jeweled her forehead like a diadem.

"Letitia. You asked. If it's too . . ."

"Too what, Matt? Too big of a problem for Ambrosia? Too hard for a black Baptist to understand a white priest?"

"Letitia. I'm sorry. I shouldn't have tried to unload this on you. I was weak."

"You? Weak? You don't have a headlock on weak." She wiped a hand over her mouth, painted the color of a hot pink camellia. The lipstick washed off onto her palm, like a stigma. "It's abuse, that's what it is. Plain and simple. Doesn't matter how old you are, who's doing it, why. Forcing is abuse. You gotta resist. I didn't, but you gotta resist."

"Letitia."

"That's me. The lusty virgin. Pretending I'm gonna get you drunk? Who am I kidding. I couldn't ever get myself drunk enough for it. Not after . . . that. Oprah's not the only one, just the most, what, public, successful? Does she ever still get the night sweats, I wonder. Is that why her weight never stays off? Yeah, we're worldly. We know the score. We are too hip to hurt. Too old. Too successful. Huh!" She swiped the sweat on her face away with the back of her hand, streaking the exquisite glittering makeup, the mask.

Matt leaned his chin on his balled fists, watched her intently across the table. The music hummed like a buzz saw, a hive of venomous hornets. The music threatened, abused, and everybody ate it up like it was normal. No, just common. Not normal.

"That's why you can really help me," Matt said. "What can I do? You saw how she threatened you for just walking out of the radio station with me."

"Was that it? The bitch was jealous of me?" Letitia started laughing. "If she only knew—" Tears replaced the sweat beads on her cheeks. "Oh, Matt. You are my project, boy. I am not going to let anybody take away from you what they took from me when I was just a kid. Just a kid. I guess you're just a kid, too, in some ways."

"If I give in, everybody around me's safe. I know she'll keep her word, because she knows that their safety will sear me as much as their danger if the price is right. Or wrong."

"She's mean. She's bad. She might do anything, right?"

He nodded.

"Then you have to be ready to give in."

He drew away, sheer repugnance pushing him back like a fist.

"No. But on your terms. Your innocence is her price, right?"

He nodded.

"Then you have to lose your innocence. Even if she holds a gun to your mother's head, then you can give in and she hasn't won what she really wanted. She's not the first one! That's what they want, to get to you before you can say yes or no, to make you a fool forever, hopeless, weak, stupid!"

"But it would be a sin."

"So sin! That's better than being a victim. A martyr. Sin and get what—confessed, and it's all gone. Don't you believe that? Isn't that what Catholics believe?"

"Yes, but—"

"Yes, but. I didn't have any 'yes, but' when I was seven years old. I just did the best I could and it wasn't good enough. You're older.

You're smarter. You outsmart that wicked woman. You put yourself in a condition that whatever she gets from you, it isn't what she wants. And don't you dare get so damned nice that you fail to protect yourself. You owe it to every kid who never had a chance to do better than that. You take away what she wants before she has a chance to get it. Get it?"

Matt nodded numbly. Letitia was right. If someone holds a weapon at your head, disarm the weapon. Especially when the weapon is yourself, your better instincts, your conscience, your integrity.

"I get it, Letitia. Thanks."

"Okay." She sat back, gathered the externals that were Letitia and Ambrosia and his producer together. "You want my extra celery stick?"

"Thanks."

"I'd help you out myself, you understand, but it's better for our professional relationship—"

"You're absolutely right."

"You have any . . . candidates?"

"A few. Maybe."

"Honey, just look at the nightly groupies."

He frowned.

"I know the Elvis shtick isn't for you. But there must be a nice girl somewhere—"

"It'd have to be absolutely secret. To protect . . . her."

"That's done all the time, particularly in Las Vegas. This ho ain't God. She ain't everywhere all the time."

"No." But sometimes it felt like that. The obsessed could be pretty pervasive.

"You can lose her and lose your virginity at the same time. I know you can."

Matt eyed her soberly. One Bloody Mary-soaked celery stick wasn't going to undo the condition. "Am I some sort of surrogate for you here?"

"You bet your sweet ass you are. Just let me know when the deed is done. Ambrosia'll play something real special for you on the rah-di-o."

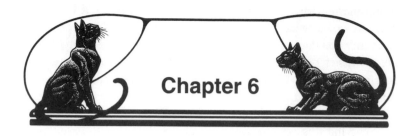

# Chapter 6

# DAD:
# Desiccated and Dead

I am happy to hotfoot it out of the feral territory. I am even happier to hop onto the back bumper of a bus downtown and get a ride almost all the way to my destination.

In another city, buses and traffic would be scarce as hens' hangnails in the middle of the night. Here in Vegas, things are always jumping, from dice to bailees.

I have to catch a cross-town bus and there it gets tough. Beyond the Strip schedules slow down appreciably.

Still, the moon has barely bar-crawled past the top of the sky when I trot the last few blocks. I had never noticed this before in my travels about the old town, but I find myself suddenly beyond the three-story apartment complexes and one-story strip shopping centers that fan out from the famous Strip in all directions.

Instead I confront a ten-foot-tall wall of shrubbery, like oleander but bigger, thicker, and taller. The sort of testosterone-overdosed vegetation you expect to find comatose princesses behind. When

I reach a cross street it is unmarked. It too is lined by an endless length of stone and iron fence, diminishing like train tracks in the distance.

Now this is definitely not the Las Vegas I know and love, and sometimes loathe. All the streets around here are the usual suburban sprawl, and Las Vegas has sprawled more than most urban areas, being that the landscape here is flatter than a tapped-out tortilla, so there is nowhere to go but up and out.

So I start ambling down the lane. The night is dark, but the moon is yellow and the leaves come tumbling down. Still, my built-in night vision is in fine shape. I notice that a lot of long green has gone into furnishing the grounds beyond the fence . . . not only the cash kind, as in long, green paper money, but long green grass. The upkeep on what the English call sward costs a bundle in this desert burg.

I know this is the right place because it is littered with small stone slabs, the upright kind that usually mark where a person is buried.

Strange that I have never before noticed an in-town plant-a-tarium, so to speak. That may be because my kind is so seldom interred. In fact, as I move down the road, I spot a pair of iron gates with the heavenly host on guard duty in the form of plaster statuary. On one of the big stone pillars is a brass plaque, and inscribed on the plaque in raised letters are the words "Los Muertos."

Now, when you live in a city called Las Vegas, and there is another burg of the same moniker in New Mexico, which also has a town called Las Cruces; when, in fact, Los Angeles is just three hundred miles west of where I now stand, you tend to get used to Hispanic place names and do not think twice about what the words mean, although there is often a religious connotation. Las Cruces means "the crossroads" and Los Angeles means "the angels." Even the early Spanish monks must have known Las Vegas was never going to live up to any Biblical ideal, except maybe Sodom and Gomorrah, because its name just means "the meadows" and there is nothing holy about that.

But *Los Muertos* . . . a few hours ago and in broad daylight I would have strolled by without a second thought. Now, though, I think. And it comes to me that *muertos* must have something to do with death, or the dead.

So I am in the right place, the Dead Place. Now all I have to do is figure out how to get into where nobody ever gets out.

I sit down under an overarching oleander bush and am rewarded by the hiss and sting of a venomous serpent on my rear end.

I bristle and leap around to face the attacker, which is a little too little too late, apparently. Ask not for whom Los Muertos is named: it is named for me. A sinking feeling in the pit of my pith tells me I may be done for. There is no antidote for snakebite way out here, alone, in the dark.

Unfortunately, I am not alone in the dark. I gaze into the chilling sight of a dark open maw with two world-class Dracula fangs bared for a second, totally unnecessary, lethal strike.

"You are sitting on my train, Pops," the snake hisses. "Move or I will staple you to the nearest prickly pear."

"Midnight Louise! What are you doing here?"

"None of your business," hisses my darling daughter-not, closing her maw to reveal her piquant little black face, which is purely feline.

"It is my business if you nearly give me a cardiac arrest. I thought I had been hit by a rattlesnake with a contract to kill."

"No one would sic a rattlesnake on you, Dads. You have not aggravated any feuding Mormons lately. Besides, you are a polygamist by nature. You would be kissing cousins with the early Mormon patriarchs."

"Leave the Mormons out of this. I want to know what you are doing out here alone at this late hour."

"Since when do you play the stern parent, Daddy Densest? The real question is what brought you here."

"Business, which is none of yours."

"So I guess we are even. This is what they call a Mexican stand-off. Unless you want a way in, which I can provide for a price."

"And the price?"

"We are partners."

The nauseous feeling in the pit of my pith lurches into a vomitous feeling. I sense the Mother of All Hairballs coming on.

"Throw up anything gross and you are on your own."

"I am merely . . . gagging. So show me the way to San Jose."

"Odd you should mention that. There is a handsome statue of St. Joseph just inside the gates, along with a raft of plaster-winged angels. And farther in, a quite nice grotto to Bastet."

"Bastet! She does not get any respect here in Vegas!"

"Perhaps you underestimate our esteemed Egyptian goddess. Like me, she gets around."

"The females of the species always do," I grumble. "That is what is wrong with the species."

"What? I did not hear you, Daddio Dearest."

She has turned her back on me and is wiggling through the oleander thicket and toward a stone wall.

There is nothing like a dame for pointing out that she is younger, sleeker, and more limber than you, particularly if she is claiming to be your offspring.

I belly down and crawl right after the minx. Midnight Louie can do night recon with the best of them. Black berets are built in with us.

The oleander stalks prick like barbed wire and my dress blacks will be sadly disheveled, but I manage to push myself through the tunnel of missing stones to the other side.

I allow my innards to expand, shake out my outer coat, and gaze upon the moonlight grazing among the short grasses and tall monuments.

"This is a cemetery," I complain. (I am too young to be in such a place.)

"*Hmmm,*" Miss Midnight Louise says thoughtfully, rubbing against my side.

Kissing up will not cut any crypts with this dude.

"So why are you here?" she asks.

That was my question, but it has been forgotten. "I am hunting Big Game."

"You are always doing that, to hear you talk. I suppose you want a tender reunion with Butch and Osiris."

"Tender I will leave to you. Reunion, yeah."

"Follow me."

This is not what I had in mind, but I have almost no choice. I am still trying to figure out what Miss Midnight Louise is doing on the premises when I find myself past all the monuments and tombstones and crypts and other gruesome but ornate set dressings.

I hear the tinkle of . . . a waterfall, I hope. Either that or the MGM Grand's giant Leo the Lion statue is taking another untimely, three-story leak.

There are walkways of flat stones, bowers of exotic plants,

patches of clipped thick Bermuda grass, sandy pits . . . this is either a really nice golf course, or it is—

A growl that sounds like marbles the size of basketballs being shaken together makes the ground vibrate.

I freeze.

"Do not worry," Miss Louise purrs in that superior tone that makes me want to slap her whiskers off. "It is a friend of ours. Of mine, I should say."

"You have earth tremors for friends?"

"Just *Lucky*, I guess," she answers with a grin that would make the Cheshire Cat frrrrrow up.

We round an outcropping of canna lily leaves and come face to face with this large black dude with a mug the size of a beach ball.

Black panther, no doubt about it. Lean, mean, and counterculture, if domestication is the name of your game.

A huge black paw lifts and hangs over Miss Midnight Louise.

I gulp, then leap forward to knock her to safety.

The looming paw does not descend, but Miss Louise swipes me again on the rear.

"Ow! What was that for!"

"Conduct becoming a male chauvinist porcine. I do not need protection from Mr. Lucky. Do you not recognize Butch from the Rancho Exotica? He is the one who shared his dinner with poor Osiris, thanks to me."

"Oh. Sorry, Mr. Butch. I mean, Mr. Lucky."

The paw lowers and tickles my ears, and my back and my everything.

"Is this your poor old dad?" the black panther's voice growls like thunder above me. "He was most valiant in your defense, although sadly ineffective."

"That is my dad. He wants to see you for some reason. I am sure he will update me shortly."

Well, what is a practical private eye to do? I am where I want to be, about to interview who I want to see. The only fly in the ointment is the odious Miss Louise, and telling her so would be highly self-destructive in present company.

So I do the right thing, ignore the chit, and get down to the chitchat with the Big Boys.

# Chapter 7

# Saturday Night Stayin' Alive

Women in strip clubs that catered to men either had business in being there, or no business at all in being there. Women with no business at all being there attracted attention, all of it either bigoted ("dyke!") or unflattering ("frigid freak").

Molina couldn't afford attention and she couldn't admit to her real business in being here at Saturday Night Fever—police business—so tonight she was a location scout for *C.S.I.: Crime Scene Investigation*.

It gave her a professional payback to name-drop the hit forensic science TV show that uses Las Vegas as a backdrop for its high-tech and personal look at maggots, body parts, and implausible police procedure.

Tonight, Molina was here on official business, and she was not alone.

Visibly alone, yes. Actually, no.

She glanced in the mirror behind the bar at Sergeant Barry Reichert, who usually did undercover drug detail. His dirt-biker ensemble and party-animal attitude fit right in at Saturday Night Fever.

At the moment he was stuffing ten-dollar bills in about six G-strings at a prodigious rate, all the time getting paid back in information that was worth hundreds.

Molina sipped her watered-down no-name whiskey and kicked back, despite the relentless overamped beat of music to strip by: loud, all bass, and brutally rhythmic.

She could relax and (almost) be herself because tonight she knew where Rafi Nadir was: being tailed by a plainclothes officer who had reported him across town at another strip club. Purely a customer now, not a bouncer.

She glimpsed her curdled expression in the mirror, as if she was drinking a whiskey sour.

Didn't want to think about why a man she had used to know hung out at strip clubs. Know? "A fellow officer" was the now-inoperative phrase. Another phrase followed, one even more painful to roll around in her head like ice in an empty lowball glass: an ex-significant other.

Barry unglued himself and his wad from the bevy of off-duty strippers and lurched to Molina's station at the bar.

"Hey, casting director lady!" he greeted her with feigned quasi-drunken camaraderie.

"Location scout," she corrected him for whatever public they played to during even the most private conversation.

"Whatever, babe." He grinned. Barry Reichert enjoyed getting into a persona where he could play fast and loose with a ranking female homicide officer. That was almost living as dangerously as risking his sanity and life among the crystal meth set.

Barry was an unstriking brown/brown: hazel-eyed, dishwater brown-haired, middle-American guy with scraggly coif, a five o'clock shadow aiming for midnight blue and missing by several shades, and scruffy casual clothes.

Like all undercover officers, he absorbed his role. He was "in character" night and day, even when a slice of reality stabbed through on the knife of a cutting remark.

Despite his apparent shaggy geniality, Barry reminded her of that walking immaculate deception, Max Kinsella.

Molina tried not to let her distaste show. She was playing at undercover work now herself, and it was entirely different from anything she had done in police work before except for a brief, early stint as john-bait in East L.A.

"Come on," Reichert was cajoling, maybe only half kidding in his womanizing role, "you could use a guy like me, admit it."

"Using is one thing; liking it is another."

"Ooooouch!" He shook a mock burned hand. "I'd be great on camera."

By now everyone at the bar had lost interest in their interchange.

Barry leaned so close she could smell his motor-oil cologne. "You getting any info?"

"A little. And you?"

He lifted her almost empty glass and sucked the remaining water and the ice filling it. "The girls are spooked." He spoke so softly that he might have been whistling Dixie through his teeth. "These parking lot attacks are getting to them."

Molina nodded. Strippers weren't dumb. They saw the axe from the first. "You see that man I mentioned?"

Reichert's shaggy yeti-like head shook. "No really tall guy like that here. You ever notice that guys who patronize strip clubs tend to be short? No? True. Must be compensation. For the height of what, I won't say." Grin. "As far as tall guys go, not even an Elvis in disguise either. Were you serious about that?"

"I'm always serious, Reichert."

He grinned as if she had issued him a challenge. "So I heard. The Iron Maiden Lady of Homicide."

She didn't react. Stoicism was the best defense. "Believe it. I don't care how much you're enjoying a break from the speed freaks, Reichert, I'm after a killer here, maybe a serial killer. He won't play the part, like you do, but he'll mean business. So you keep at it. I'm sure those bills are burning a hole in your . . . pocket. Enjoy."

She pushed off the bar and headed for the door. Halfway there a drunken topless stripper collided with her.

"Hey, who was that lady! Whatcha doin' here?"

"I'm a location scout."

"Location scout?"

"For a TV show."

"Oh, a TV show. C'mon, you gotta be in the picture."

"No." Molina pulled her arm away.

"We're all having our picture taken. It's Wendy's birthday. C'mon."

Molina didn't have to "c'mon." A bunch of strippers surrounded her, hanging off her shoulders and making her part of a topless chorus line.

"That's it, ladies," a guy shouted over the noise, "get closer now. Smile." The photographer backed up to include the whole impromptu row, the camera's long telephoto lens obscenely erect given the atmosphere.

Molina ducked her head, let the false hair fall forward over her face just as the camera flashed.

"Sorry, ladies, I'm outa here." She pulled away, the drunken one clinging.

"It's my birthday," she slurred, "you gotta say 'Happy Birthday'."

"Happy Birthday Suit," Molina muttered, making for the door.

She wasn't happy about being in a photo. These pro-am shutter-bugs always haunted strip clubs, selling prints to regulars and the girls themselves, cataloguing offstage life and likely illegal activities.

The whole scene had a stench that was almost smothering. She crashed through the door to the outside, suddenly understanding what prisoners must feel on release.

Air. Black night. Bright constellations falling to the ground, like angels, and becoming neon signs. Another night on Paradise. On Paradise Avenue in Las Vegas, a long, straight row of strip clubs magnified to infinity.

When you thought about the endless numbers of women who found a tawdry glamour and even self-esteem in flashing nudity at men, and the families they came from that made this strip-club life seem a far, far better thing than they had ever done. . . . Molina shook her head, though no one was there to see it.

In another moment she herself didn't see the gaudy neon tracks of signs narrowing into the distance like lonesome train rails. Her mind was back in the Valley Hospital room, watching a girl who called herself Gayla lying pale and lost in some monotone film nightmare produced by that low-budget pair of mind-numbers: pain and pain killers.

The injuries from the attack Molina had almost witnessed in the

Kitty City strip club parking lot were minor, but Gayla's voice rasped from a near-throttling. Her knees had been skinned, her wrist sprained. All minor injuries in a major-trauma world.

"Did you see or hear anything? Anyone?" Molina had asked.

Gayla's red-blond frizz of a hairdo had thrashed back and forth on the pillow.

"No, ma'am," she said, either reared in a household that taught children respect for their elders and authority figures . . . or that beat the hell out of them until everyone they met was a force to be reckoned with and kowtowed to.

"No, ma'am. If I'da seen something I'da screamed. You know? I just sort of slipped and my throat was all tight, and my elbows and knees burned and someone was leaning over me."

"Someone. Tall, dark?"

Gayla frowned. Every night she saw faces on the other side of the spotlights, all blurred and all Someones. "Dark. The hair. Maybe."

Maybe. Maybe Kinsella. Maybe . . . Nadir.

"Were the eyes dark, or light?"

"It was night." Gayla finally sounded indignant enough to speak up for herself, for everything she missed really seeing as it was because life was nicer that way. "I couldn't see eyes. I didn't see face. Just something . . . dark coming at me and knocking everything out from under me. And breath. It was hot on my cheek."

"Breath. Did you smell anything on it?"

"Wow. You know, when I was feeling sick there on the ground, it did seem my sense of smell kicked up. Like when you—"

"When you what?"

"You *know*."

"No, I don't. When?"

"During . . . it."

"Oh. That." Molina sighed. "So what was the smell in the parking lot?"

"What? I wasn't doing . . . it."

"The attacker's breath. What did it smell like?"

Gayla's faced screwed into such exaggerated concentration that she winced when her muscles hurt from it. "Gum, I guess."

"Gum?"

"Gum."

Molina chewed on that. Neither suspect was what she'd call a gum-chewing man. Unless he'd drunk something that often flavored gum.

"The scent. Was it cinnamon? Spearmint? Fruity?"

"I don't know. For just a second I thought . . . maybe spicy, I don't know."

Spicy. Did they put cinnamon sticks in anything besides hot Christmas punch? Or maybe it was breath mints! Any scents similar? Check it out. Check out every damn breath mint on the market.

"But you didn't see anything?" Molina pressed.

"I told you, no!"

"Did you sense how tall the man might be? He was behind you. He choked you, forced you down. Did he feel like a shadow of yourself? Not much taller, but stronger? Or did he come from above, like a tree, bearing down?"

"Gee. I don't know." Her vacant, pale eyes, no color to speak of, like her opinions, her testimony, blinked rapidly. "I can't say. It was like a . . . spike, driving me down. I just gave, without thinking about it. It was so sudden, I didn't know anything else to do."

Molina looked at this frail young woman. She was a willow, this girl. She would bend to any will stronger than hers, and every will was stronger than hers. That was why the attacker had picked her. He knew a beaten-down soul when he saw it. It was so unfair! Those whom life had already battered gave like reeds and took more battering.

Molina reached to cover Gayla's hand on the thin hospital blanket. "I'm sorry. We're going to find the man who did this. Stop him."

Gayla nodded, looked like she believed her. Smiled a little. Sadly.

"There's always another, though," she said. For the first time during the interview, she sounded very, very certain about something.


Molina's flashback faded, leaving her back in the Las Vegas night, standing alone on Paradise, not certain about anything except that she had to catch an elusive killer.

Too bad that arresting either of the two leading candidates for the honor would be disastrous for either her career or her personal life. Or both.

**Chapter 8**

# Asian Persuasion

It turns out that I need an interpreter with the Big Boys. By allowing Miss Louise to check out their circumstances at the canned
hunt club first, I have encouraged them to bond with her, not me.

You would think that male solidarity would overcome a little
exercise in charity like visiting the imprisoned, but no such luck.
Mr. Lucky, the black panther, and Osiris, the leopard, now think
that Miss Midnight Louie is the cat's meow, and I am merely a tol-
erated hanger-on.

At least I am allowed to eavesdrop.

"So how plush a pad is this?" she asks.

"Like the cemeteryscape up front," Mr. Lucky says, "this is a fine
and private place."

I do not think that he means to paraphrase a poet, especially a
Cavalier poet, but he does. I refrain from pointing it out. This is not
a poetry crowd.

"You will get used to the funereal facade," Osiris assures his new roommate. "It is a security dodge that protects all our hides, including that of our esteemed sponsor, the Cloaked Conjuror."

"An artful dodge," I put in with admiration. "Hiding behind a cemetery is what you might call ironic, as his life is always in danger because his act reveals the ploys behind some of the most famous magical illusions of all time. That is why the Cloaked Conjuror must disguise his face and voice even on stage. Of course he makes enough moolah at it to challenge that casino known as The Mint for the title."

"I do not know about him," Mr. Lucky replies with a hackle twitch. "That creepy leopard-spotted mask is insulting to the real thing, and his voice sounds like he is gargling rattlesnakes. I liked the Man in Black who stole us back from the ranch better."

"Mr. Max," Mr. Lucky purrs in basso agreement. "I have heard of him often on the Big Cat circuit. It is a shame that he has retired from the magician trade nowadays. He was the best. We guys in black are pretty hard to beat."

"Hear, hear!" I put in, but am ignored, except by Miss Louise, who corrects me. "Gals in black, too."

"Speaking of gals in black," I put in, hoping to be heeded for once, "I hear you two big guys are going to be working with a new female magician. How is that going?"

"How does a pipsqueak like you know about our secret sessions?" Osiris growls.

"I hear things others do not. It is my job. I am a private investigator."

"She does not wear black," Osiris says, "this new lady. At least not all the time, although I commend the truly long fingernails she wears. As long as some human females' high heels. Four inches, I would say."

"Awesome," purrs Mr. Lucky, cleaning between his own four-inch shivs.

I try not to shudder, knowing that the evil Shangri-La and her light-fingered mandarin stage-shivs stole my Miss Temple's ring as part of her so-called act three months ago. Besides, it is more important to know what Shangri-La is up to now.

"So Miss Shangri-La is indeed joining the Cloaked Conjuror's act?" I say idly.

"And that kitten of hers." Mr. Lucky lifts a paw the size of a catcher's mitt and licks it cleaner than home plate.

"You mean"—my breath catches in my lungs like a two-pound koi in the throat—"a piece of fluff about the size and weight of Miss Midnight Louise here, only pale of coat?"

"She is a funny-looking feline," Mr. Lucky says, "not a symphony in monotone like Miss Midnight Louise. Her eyes are an unnatural blue shade, her body is the pale liverish color of the pablum I am given when I am sick and off my feed—"

"Baby food," Osiris sneers. "They give you human baby food, buckets of it."

Mr. Lucky ignores the attempted ignominy, as I would do in his position. "And her extremities appear to have been dipped in some sort of mud. They are all dirty brown."

I chortle to hear the hated Hyacinth cut down to size by the Big Cats. My every encounter with her so far has ended with me caged or drugged, not a sterling record for a street-smart shamus. But even she would not dare to challenge these big dudes.

Midnight Louise is not amused. She never is.

"I have seen the cat in question. She is a lilac-point Siamese and is supposed to look like that, including the blue eyes, which are highly prized by humans. The only thing unnatural about her is the colored enamel on her claws, and that is perpetrated by her mistress, who presents a rather gaudy stage presence herself."

I cannot believe that Miss Louise has beaten me here to lay eyes on my bête not-noir in her new lair before I have! To lay eyes on both of them, in fact, Shangri-La and her hairy familiar.

"I need to check these babes out," I say.

"I bet you do," Mr. Lucky says with a wink. "I must say you get around for a little guy."

I fluff my ruff, but Midnight Louise is not impressed. "I have got the whole layout down cold. Come on along and I will show you. 'Bye, boys."

There is little left for me to do but to sashay after Louise like she is cheese and I am a rat. When I catch up with her, I decide to assert my age and experience.

And then I get a brilliant idea. These dames are big on family trees, and have I got a claw off the old cactus for her!

"Say, Louise."

"*Miss* Louise to you, since we are not related, as you keep reminding me."

"It is funny you should mention that. Before I came here I ran into a rather large piece of auld lang syne."

"Huh?" She stops and twitches her tail. "I am a Scottish fold, ye dinna hae ta speak Scots to me."

"I mean I encountered a figure from my past. My earliest years. It was quite a shock."

"I am surprised you remember anything that far back."

"Ungrateful kit! I am not about to forget my own mother."

"Mother?" She actually stops and sits, squashing that metronome tall of hers. "How can you be sure? You must not have seen her since you were six weeks old. I certainly did not see mine after that, though whether it was because she was dead or domesticated I cannot say."

"Well, my ma is neither dead nor domesticated. She runs a feral gang on Twenty-fourth Street, a pretty raw neighborhood. She has survived being kidnapped by the Fixers and is doing just fine. I would say she said hello if there was any chance that you two were related, but it does not look like there is."

"Liar!" she spits. "So my grandmother is alive."

I do not say anything to dissuade her. Dames love to imagine long lines of interelated individuals, whether they be human or feline. Perhaps that is why the human ones watch soap operas.

"Do you think she would know anything about my mother?" Louise asks.

"Could be."

"I suppose you did not ask, you irresponsible lug!"

"There was not time. I was about to be jumped by the Wild Bunch or whisked away for an unnecessary globe-otomy by the Fixers."

For some reason Miss Louise finds this amusing. Her shiny black lips curl like whiskers with a permanent wave. "Yeah. I suppose in your condition you could be mistaken for an unneutered male. Who would dream an alley cat like you had benefitted from a human-style vasectomy?"

"Not the Fixers," I admit with a shudder. "Now, where are these dames of Asian persuasion? I have reasons for tracking down Shangri-La and her evil sidekick Hyacinth."

Midnight Louise sits down in the middle of a flagstone walk between a luxurious growth of giant-leaved plants imported to give the Big Cats a touch of jungle clime.

I can tell right off that she is about to be obstinate.

"We need to make a deal," she says.

"About what?"

"Our relationship."

*Dames!* "We do not have one."

"I wonder if the delightful lady gangster you met on the north side would agree if she laid eyes on me."

"A mother may recognize a grown kit, especially when the kit in question was such a remarkably smart and personable little nipper, but no grandmother is going to recognize an offspring once removed. Let us face up to the common prejudice: we black cats all look alike."

"Actually, I was not interested in any personal relationship," she says silkily. "I was speaking purely of business."

"Oh. Right. You work for me. Sometimes."

"I have worked *with* you, sometimes, when it suited me. I believe it is time for a more formal arrangement."

"What? I should pay you?"

"We should be partners."

"Partners! I do not need a dame for a partner any more than I need a dustball dog for a sniffing substitute."

"Yet you have employed both on several of your latest cases."

"Aha! You admit that I do have 'cases.' "

"I will . . . if you admit that we are probably blood related."

"Hell, an average cat couple can create over four hundred thousand offspring in seven years, which I admit is a long run for your average street cat. All cats are probably related."

"Do not swear, Daddikins," she purrs in an odiously sweet manner. "It is a bad example for the boys."

I turn to find black and spotted muzzles parting the glossy leaves. "Ah . . . nothing to worry about. Just a little family discussion."

The leaves close like emerald curtains and we are alone once more.

"See," says Louise. "That was not so bad. We can consider this a family business. No one will think anything of it."

I think something of it, and it is not good! But I have not lasted in a cruel world so long without being a smidgeon adaptable, so I lick my lips and weigh how badly I want to track down the rotten

Hyacinth against how much I hate conceding anything to Midnight Louise.

"All right," I say. "You are in the firm: Midnight Louie and Son."

*"And son!"*

"That is what they usually name two-generation businesses."

"I am not a male!"

"Yeah, well, one could not tell by looking at you. You could be one of these poor souls the Fixers got. A business has to have a name the public will have confidence in: Midnight Louie and Son. What's not to love, like, and lap right up?"

"How about Midnight Louie and Daughter?"

I try not to snerk up my plush leather glove. The kit is so busy defending her gender she has neglected to note that I remain the first and foremost element in the billing.

"Who ever heard of a PI firm with 'and Daughter' in the name? Not that I concede that you are, of course. My daughter, that is."

"I do not care what you concede. I am not moving a foot on the way into that Fort Knox of a house until you come up with something reasonable."

When a dame uses the word "reasonable" she means her way, period.

I shift my weight from forefoot to forefoot. I must admit that Midnight Louise has certain talents she may have gotten from a brilliant second-story dude like myself. She does have potential, and I could use a schnook now and then. But I cannot stomach, in this life or any other of my remaining eight, "Midnight Louie and Daughter."

If ever I was called upon to be brilliant and devious, it is now.

I clear my throat. I hum a few bars of "Melancholy Baby." I rid myself of an irksome nail sheath.

"Quit stalling, Mein Papa. You are cornered and you know it."

I am at my most inventive when cornered, so . . . invent!

"All right," I say portentously. "We will be partners in a firm. We will have a sexy, Richard Diamond kind of aura."

"Richard who?"

"TV PI, had a secretary with a world-class pair of gams." (Which were provided by Miss Mary Tyler Moore, who went on to become even more famous for tossing a hat into the air at the opening of a TV show.)

Midnight Louise blinks. I do not think that she knows a "gam" from a "gat" or she would be all over me for that sexist remark. I swallow my smirk.

"We will have a name that says it all," I go on, caught up in my own scenario.

"We will be equal," she warns, flattening her ears and fluffing her fur.

I am not afraid of a family spat with Midnight Louise, but I am well aware that her lurking backup outweighs me twenty to one, and there are two of them.

I straighten, shake out my coat until it is in gleaming order, and pronounce: "Midnight Inc. What could be better?"

I catch her flat-footed and wimp-whiskered. "You mean like in India ink?" she asks, confused.

"No. As in *Murder* Inc. *Capisce*?"

"It does sound dangerous," she concedes.

"It is compact."

"It does include both our names."

"Indeed."

"It is gender neutral."

"Of course," I growl. I hate gender neutral.

"It will do."

With that she turns on her tail and struts forward, assuming that I will follow.

Having dodged "Midnight Louie and Daughter," I do. For now.

*I do.* The expression smacks indecently of wedding vows.

Well, there is always divorce and, in business unions, dissolution. And finally, in Midnight Inc.'s line of work, 'til death do us part.

# Chapter 9

# *Sunset Boulevard*

I stare at the pool behind the house.

It is big and old-fashioned, just a huge, deep rectangle of blue mosaic tiles seen through a glassy viewfinder of chlorinated water, darkly. Some jungle leaves the size of elephant ears float like lily pads, lending an air of disuse or of the macabre, I cannot decide which.

I almost expect to see William Holden floating facedown in the limpid water as I look beyond to the stucco mansion looming beyond the pool like the white cliffs of Dover.

"What a spread," I say.

"It belonged to Carissa Caine, a mistress of Jersey Joe Jackson before he lost his stash. That man had more mistresses than Howard Hughes had phobias."

Louise sits to tick off her research on her toes. Or perhaps she is licking off her research from her toes. Now that she is my partner, I will be darned if I will call her "Miss" anymore. Business is business. "That is why a spread of this size still exists inside Las Vegas," she goes on. "It was like Sleeping Beauty's castle. Jersey Joe went crazy and while the tabloids were busy reporting his slow self-destruct, Carissa faded away, as untouched as this mansion. She was a little touched in the mad sense of the word, because she didn't want to be alone after she died, so she turned the streetside acres into a cemetery. Everybody forgot about the house and grounds behind it."

"Only in Las Vegas can the façade become the reality," I note. "So the Cloaked Conjuror grabbed up this cold property when he started getting death threats for exposing the secrets behind magical illusions in his act."

"He wanted to be near the Strip, but needed to be discreet. Los Muertos was perfect."

" 'Lost' Muertos is more like it. And the Big Cats up front make dandy bodyguards."

"Oh, the Cloaked Conjuror has every security device in the firmament. Even the Mystifying Max would have trouble breaking into this joint."

"But you cracked it."

"I am small and subtle," she says demurely.

"Small, yes. So Hyacinth and her mistress now inhabit the house with the Cloaked Conjuror?"

"His friends call him CC. It saves one's breath."

"Yeah, one would worry about saving one's breath around this creepy place." My ears prick up, and then my nostrils flare. "Dogs?"

"Not just dogs. Rottweilers."

"Oh, *weinerschnitzel!* How do we get around them?"

For answer she leaps into one of Sleeping Beauty's thorny vines and starts climbing.

She may be small and subtle, but I am larger than life. I follow in her footsteps, but not without collecting as many snags as a cheap pair of nylons. All right, pantyhose. A guy must move with the times, although even my Miss Temple, the high-heel queen, hates pantyhose. I do not want to mention how many times she goes bare-footed and high-heeled, but I understand that this is all the fashion now among the starlet set.

I manage to muffle any cries of protest as I am raked right and left on the way up.

I suppose my reward is the sight of two Rottweilers, heads bowed and nostrils sucking sand, snuffling and whimpering at the foot of the vine that has been our high road to heaven.

Louise is already intently pawing a mullioned window.

I join her on the wide sill to lick down my worst wounds and cowlicks.

"Forget the grooming fetish," she advises. "No one will see us to care how smooth your coat is. I hope."

"So this Shangri-La is crashing with CC."

"Speak sense, Poppy."

"She is residing at the house. Do you suspect some hanky-panky?"

"Really! I choose not to dwell upon the disgusting mating habits of humans, which never cease. I suspect that since CC must remain in constant hiding, anyone who joins the act is forced to stay here so they can practice."

"Practice! Mr. Max Kinsella has never been seen to practice."

"No doubt he has his own hideaway for the purpose, unless you believe that magicians can really work magic?"

"Of course not. But what has brought you to trespassing on such sinister grounds?"

Midnight Louise shrugs the silver-tipped ruff that nestles around her shoulders like an open bear trap with a fun-fur cover. "I wanted to check up on the boys, make sure that they were being treated right here."

"Like you would be able to do something about it if they were not," I jeer.

She ignores me, which is very hard on a jeerer. "Everything was on the up-and-up on the outside, where the Big Cats are kept. It was what was going on in the inside that kept me sniffing around."

"How did you manage to breeze in through a window if the joint is so protected by security?" I ask, eyeing the cushy chamber beyond the mullioned window. A guy could film *Rebecca* here, the place looks so old-Hollywood-style lush, and creepy in that inimitable blend that only black-and-white movies can convey.

"I did not. Every aperture is wired for sound and fury, including the chimneys."

"Then how do we—?"

For an answer she flips her busy tail in my face and ankles off along the ledge.

I cast one last hungry look at the *Leave Her to Heaven* bedroom, all chiffon and brocade and oil portraits of to-die-for dames and tall glass perfume bottles that resemble a cityscape of midtown Manhattan.

Instead of busting into Manderlay I am taking the high road to agoraphobia.

At least Louise is doing point.

Way up here the oleander bush tops scratch on the brickwork and it is a hard twenty-foot fall to the foundation landscaping, which looks to be a variety of thorny hedge.

At last Louise pauses at a porthole the size of a salad plate and sits down with unpardonable pride.

"This is a peephole?" I suggest.

"This is the only unwired entry in the place."

I peer through the aluminum-lined opening. "I can see why. A snake would have trouble breaking and entering here."

"Luckily, the snakes stick to the ground cover."

I peer below, picturing serpents writhing among the thorns. No way do I want to go down.

"This is a perfect entrance," Louise goes on. And on.

It seems she has stumbled across a former clothes dryer vent pipe in a closet that everyone has forgotten was once an ultra-modern second-floor laundry room, only now it is filled with racks of costumes and stage props. The pipe, she says, exits into the back of a red-satin-lined cape, sort of like the escape chute on an airliner.

A moment later, the tip of her tail is vanishing into the pipe. She has not even paused to consider that I might be a rather tight fit. Young kits nowadays!

Normally the Rule of Entry and Exit is: if the head will fit, you must commit.

However, this helpful motto does not allow for individuals whose proportions tend more toward those of Nero Wolfe than the Thin Man.

I must admit to wolfing down my food more often than not of late, especially when I get out and have a chance at something other than that arid mound of Free-to-be-Feline Miss Temple keeps endlessly replenished at the Circle Ritz. Luckily, Las Vegas is as much a town to eat out in as to lose your lunch (and bargain buffet breakfast) in.

However, I cannot have Miss Louise saying I am the slowpoke of the outfit, so I nose my way into the pipe.

It is dark and cold as only bare metal can be in this climate. I can already feel my innards shrinking from the chilly contact, which will only do me good in slithering through this foul worm-hole.

Still, it is quite a job to wriggle through, requiring all my superior muscular strength. I recall an anaconda from a previous case and pretend that I can propel myself by rippling muscle tone alone, as Trojan did.

Finally my head pokes through into free space. I feel like I can breathe again, and grunt and huff as I pull my body through the eye of the needle that Miss Louise's wonderful, handy, forgotten entryway has proven to be.

I plop with a thump onto the advertised red satin lining of the cape, which is so slippery I can barely get the traction to push myself upright without flailing my battle-shivs through it until it is shredded wheat.

Altogether a most undignified illegal entrance. The only thing missing from this comedy of erroneous entry is the usual dead body I have a knack for stumbling over, especially in strange places, in the dark.

I attain my balance and swagger forward. Fortunately, this closet is so dark that the hypercritical Louise has not witnessed my struggles.

I step over the nearest supine human chest and sniff hopefully for Miss Louise's unmistakable scent.

I am sitting, sniffing, on a supine human chest and it is not moving: neither to sit up and unseat me, or to make like it is breathing in and out and going up and down. *Come on! Go up and down!*

No. Uh-oh. It is business as usual for Midnight Louie. Most of my horizontal humans are dead, not sleeping, unless I am safe in my bed at home, which is supposedly Miss Temple's bed, except that all beds are the immemorial and hereditary property in perpetuity of cats. Why else do they call them king- and queen-size models?

I am amazed that Miss Midnight Louise has held her tongue for so long when she has the opportunity to lord it over me and claim the body as her first find.

That is when I realize that I do not scent so much as a hair from Miss Louise's body.

She is not here.

It is most unlike Miss Midnight Louise to abandon a fresh kill.

Unless the departure was not voluntary.

# Chapter 10

# Car Trouble

Temple cast one fond farewell look over her shoulder at her aqua Storm. Although sun-faded, the car looked remarkably perky for its age. It had served her well but now it was sitting on a used car lot and she was moving on to a hot new property.

She felt like a traitor. A car took possession of its owner's history. It was a silent witness to life's big and small moments. She would be able to date certain occurrences from now on by whether it was before, during, or after she was driving the Storm . . . or not. Owning a car was almost like going steady.

The "or not" lay ahead of her in all its new-car glory.

So Temple let the Storm slip into the rearview mirror of her memory and advanced on the shining form of her new wheels, a Miata.

She knew every argument on the planet against convertibles: your hair will get scrambled, your eyes will get dried out, and you'll end up with skin cancer. But hey, the tiny trunk was *almost* big enough to hold a hat, and the glove compartment could certainly contain a small bottle of sunscreen, which she would apply, along with sunglasses and scarf, with the religious zeal of a redhead.

She opened the driver's door and got in.

The hat she hadn't bought yet, nor the sunscreen, but she could put on the sunglasses.

The sun warmed the top of her head. She looked around for someplace to stow her ownership papers so they wouldn't blow away. The tiny glove compartment.

She turned the key in the ignition, inhaled the sun-baked scent of new car and resisted looking back one last time at the Storm.

This was the first car she had bought all by herself. The Storm had been a Barr Family Production, at least all parts of the Barr family that were male, which most of it was, except for her mother and herself.

Her father and brothers had kicked the tires, negotiated with car dealers, done everything but drive it. This baby was hers alone! She had visited all the web sites, tracked down the MSRP, interrogated the local dealers, and finally decided who she would allow to sell her the car at her price.

Temple hoped that her price was the rock-bottom one it should have been.

She sighed deeply and then eased out the brake. Everyone always watched a new owner toodle away as if driving over shattered glass. Hah! She put the car in gear and spurted out onto the freeway access road like a crimson jackrabbit, safe but not sorry.

In a minute she was on 95, her short curls curried by the desert wind. The car fit her like glove leather, with which it was indeed lined.

The only negative was that her exit came up too quickly and she was soon trolling mundane city streets again (if city streets could ever be mundane in Las Vegas) at a sedate thirty-five miles an hour.

Taking a spin in her new car seemed like a good idea, but which direction could she spin it in? All dressed up and no place to go . . .

She knew: the Crystal Phoenix. The Grand Opening had been last week, so she wanted to sneak up on the crowds patronizing her various bright ideas there, the Jersey Joe Jackson Action Attraction, the petting zoo, the Domingo performance art garden. . . . Amid the opening crowds and hoopla, she hadn't been able to savor every little touch.

Temple spun the small steering wheel around the next corner, and the next, until she was on the car-crowded Strip, just another gawker in a mechanical bumper-car game of hot metal, lurching her way to Byzantium, or at least the Crystal Phoenix Hotel and Casino.

She drove up the long, curving drive, thinking everybody was staring at her, which they weren't. There were far more pricy and exotic cars in the queue.

She hopped out to let the valet take the precious car instead of parking it in the far back lot and hiking up to the hotel's rear entrance as usual.

Sticking the parking chit in her tote bag, where it was promptly lost, Temple strode into the main entrance on her high-rise heels.

Somebody whistled.

Obviously not at her.

She strode ahead as only a determined short woman can.

Someone whistled again.

She risked a glance over her shoulder: Armani suit at three o'clock high, bearing down on her in a cotton-candy cloud of unwrinkled wool-silk blend, no easy deed in Las Vegas.

So here she was: IDed, targeted, and shot down by a Fontana brother in full flight.

Whether Temple or the Fontana brother was in full flight was a good question.

She spun and stopped to wait for the inevitable to catch up with her.

"I am hurt," he said when within hearing distance. "Miss Temple Barr deigns to visit my brother Nicky's tacky little establishment and she intends to hit the front door without a suitable escort."

He paused to fold his hands in front of him and smile rebukingly down on her.

"Take off those extreme-price shades so I can see the whites of your fine Italian eyes," she said, "and can tell who you are. I don't accept anonymous escorts."

He shrugged and peeled off the wraparound Porsches.

Not Aldo, or Julio, or Rico, or Giuseppe, or Ernesto. Temple put her brain through boot camp. What were the other Fontana names? Not Vito. Or Fabrizio, thank Jove. Wasn't one named something unlikely? Panache? Pinocchio?

"Ralph, at your disposal," he said. "It appears that I am the only member of the family on hand to do the host's duty. How may I be of service?"

Temple eschewed the obvious, as was always wise with a Fontana brother. "Well, I could use a good guide."

"I am the best. To what?"

"To the best of the Crystal Phoenix. I'm here to give the new attractions a post-opening test drive, so to speak, as an unsuspecting member of the the public."

"Speaking of test drives, I see you have a snappy new car. I can get you a Maserati for a very good price."

"I don't doubt it, Ralph, but the car I drove up in is the best I can afford and I think of it as a Maserati in training."

"No doubt you are right." He offered an arm. "Am I right in assuming that the honor of being your escort on this occasion will mean an expedition on the Jersey Joe Jackson mine ride?"

"Why, yes. You have any reservations about the JJJ mine ride?"

"Many, all having to do with digesting a superb lunch of veal Venezia at the Rialto."

"Don't worry. I left special instructions that the mine ride personnel be equipped with, how shall I put it, barf bags?"

Ralph nodded with monkish resignation most unusual in a Fontana brother, and swept open a glass door by its gilded phoenix handle.

Temple moved into the chill air inside, onto the soft hush of thick carpeting, secretly hoping that she would soon see a suave and elegant Fontana brother screaming and shaking and losing his lunch.


Because she had dropped in without making previous arrangements like a proper PR person, Temple and Ralph had to queue up and pay up at the ticket kiosk like any tourists.

"I could—" Ralph suggested, easing a supple calfskin wallet from his inside jacket pocket as another, cruder sort of fellow might tease the butt of a Beretta forth from the same site.

"No tips, please." Temple frowned, employing her sternest tone. "I want to see how the system works without greasing."

"I hope they grease the tracks," Ralph muttered under his breath.

Temple noticed that his warm Italian skin now matched the pallor of his fine Italian tailoring.

The kiosk was manned by a Calamity Jane type. Temple had nixed the first suggestion of a dance hall girl with cleavage.

Calamity Jane came with side arms instead. "Howdy!" She paused in her spiel to aim her handy pistol at an animated bushwhacker in the faux desert terrain. "Don't mind him. Jest a claim-jumper. Guess he's jumped all the way back to St. Louis now. Jest follow the folks up front and keep to four lines and watch out for bushwhackers."

"This bushwhacker," Ralph asked. "Where did the expression come from?"

PR people are supposed to know everything, so Temple took an uneducated guess. "I suppose from all the missed shots miners fired at each other defending their claims. They probably hit more bushes than people."

Ralph nodded, impressed. All that had touched his land of origin in the last century or so had been world wars. "The Wild West."

"I hope so." Temple was buoyed to see that the line was long. They had to baby-step along behind a full complement of riders. Once they had moved into the Old West Saloon the lights grew dim, the piano music came up, and they were passing a laughing crowd of seated patrons watching a burlesque show on the stage.

Part of the scene were live actors, part animatronic figures, and the line moved just fast enough that you couldn't be sure which was which.

People around them laughed at the punchlines or buzzed about some subtle bit of business in one corner or the other. The scene was complex enough that repeated viewings would reveal new details.

*There!* Temple noted. In the corner. That byplay between the drunken snake-oil salesman, the temperance lady, and the visiting English duke was hers. She was a playwright!

She realized that people in line were turning around to eye her and Ralph. Did they know she was the creative genius behind this display?

Then Temple looked at the people looking at them. Tourists clad in saggy shorts and baggy T-shirts. She in high heels and Ralph in Armani looked out of place in the Wild West ambiance of the Jersey Joe Jackson Action Attraction. Jersey Joe Jackson had probably, and fortunately, never lived long enough to hear the word "ambiance" used.

Temple cleared her throat and looked down as their path led onto a crude wooden elevator. She catwalked onto the contrivance, set-ting each foot down so her spindly heels didn't wedge into the spaces between the rough board floor.

"Something of an impulsive outing?" Ralph asked.

There was little chance to answer as the influxing mob crowded them against the wooden struts that formed the elevator's sides. Otis Packing Crate Company, at your service.

"This is authentically rickety," Ralph commented as the mecha-nism creaked and lurched down a story or two.

Once they had been jolted to the ground level, they were in the sudden, cool darkness of a mine tunnel. Only the fluorescent lines on the cavern floor, between which they were ordered to queue up, indi-cated where they were to go next.

A rocky wall melted away like cheesecloth as lights penetrated it and an overhead voice urged them to move sideways. Temple grabbed Ralph's creamy sleeve and pulled him beside her.

"We want to sit together, we line up horizontally," she whispered up at him.

"Ah, you may not want to sit together." Ralph's suit was delicately yellow, but his face was tinted green. "I don't like violent amusement park rides."

"Nonsense. This ride is certified safe for an eight-year-old."

"I didn't like violent amusement park rides when I was eight years old."

Come to think of it, Temple hadn't at that age either.

Too late.

They were in the Disneyland-pioneered pattern: a controlled mob boxed into sequential spaces. Beyond the vanished wall sat a string of mine carts, miniboxcars. Convertible, of course. Open to the dank underground air. She who lives by the convertible will die by the con-vertible.

She and Ralph ended up shuffling into place on a seating bank of four, buckling safety belts across their laps. Ralph frowned to see the fluid drape of his suitcoat puckering like seersucker under the belt's firm clasp.

Temple's belt didn't seem to tighten enough. Maybe she would fly out on the first turn. Eight-year-olds, she told herself. Surely she wasn't smaller than the average eight-year-old.

The rich, whiskey-and-tobacco-salted voice rolling out from the concealed speakers described Jersey Joe's colorful Las Vegas history: paydirt-hitting prospector, early Las Vegas developer, founder of the Joshua Tree Hotel from whose ashes the Crystal Phoenix had risen in exquisite glory only years before, busted millionaire living on in a 1940s suite at the abandoned Joshua Tree until life abandoned him and only his ghost remained. . . .

The train of cars jerked into motion, then wrenched their passengers right and left as it careened through the serpentine tunnels under caged bare bulbs of light.

Light. And dark. Swinging, swaying light. And dark.

People shrieked, the uninhibited, pleasurable shrieks of kid-again wonderment, with an edge of adult unease that knew Something Could Go Wrong.

Ralph put an arm around Temple to hold her down. Her small frame was rattling around in her seat despite the belt. She screeched, exhilarated and a little nervous. Having primal fun, but part of the thrill was her reservations. What if she should slip out of her belt . . . if the ride should run off the rails, if—

Water dripped from jeweled stalactites onto the rising pinnacles of stalagmites as their ore carrier rattled through a wonderland of an underground kingdom seemingly decorated by Jack Frost Inc.

Kids were oohing and aahing between squeals, making Temple grin like a proud department store Christmas window decorator.

The passing stone walls flashed veins of silver and gold and other rich subterranean mineral finds, geodes as lavish as any showgirl's crystal-and-sequined costume, nature's naked glittering chorus line, all purveying actual mineral wonders. Genuine silicon silicone, so to speak.

The walls grew gauzy, revealing moving pictures from Jersey Joe's rise and fall of a life: the Joshua Tree growing out of the desert floor like a manmade geode, all angular stucco and early Southwest style ziggurats. Small planes descending on the spare desert landing strip like tribal thunderbirds, then cars coming, from L.A., many of them Thunderbirds. Then night fell and the lights in the Joshua Tree winked like stars, darkening one by one.

The riders grew hushed. The next scene showed the sun scorching the once-vibrant building, Las Vegas landmarks exploding around it like fireworks, the Joshua Tree a lifeless hulk amidst a neon jungle.

Then . . . a dark tunnel, like an umbilical passage. The cars sped into more darkness. The moving walls showed the Joshua Tree imploding, exploding, its stucco walls breaking open like the dull surface of a rock containing a geode . . . and the faceted, glassine elegance of the Crystal Phoenix was revealed at its center like the heart of a chocolate Easter egg's raspberry-ice nougat.

Faster the cars went, twining and soaring in the tunnel, passing scenes of glittering festivity, until finally there was only the intimate glimpse of a private suite, the decor harking back to the 1940s, a silver-haired ghost of a dirt-poor miner moving through the scene like a holographic host at a Halloween party.

Jersey Joe Jackson's faint image went to the prow of the train of cars, Tinker Bell as figurehead, leading them into the darkness and the future like a headlight.

Walls flashed by, dark and stony, lit by veins of unimagined richness. Subterranean minerals gleamed like phosphorescent fish schooling in some dry sea bed long deserted by a polar wave of warming.

Temple blinked. For an instant Jersey Joe's ghostly figure took on iconic form, white and gleaming . . . Elvis!

No, another illusion. Another dip into the collective unconscious. They were hurtling toward the light at the end of the tunnel, and it was solid, warm, and bright.

Daylight.

The cars rocked to a standstill. They had stopped in the Crystal Palace, a glass-domed tropical garden flooded with brightness. Fluorescent flamingos moved among the green leaves. Huge tropical flower faces sang in holographic harmony, inviting the admiration of an invisible Alice. A massive neon caterpillar rippled with rainbow segments.

Everyone struggled out of their seat belts and the cars, blinking, the scenes viewed in the darkened tunnels still imprinting their retinas.

Ralph smoothed out his suit coat, pleasantly surprised. "It was not as tumultuous as I had thought."

"But it was fun?" Temple was anxious to be reassured.

"An experience," he said, patting his inside coat pockets delicately until reassured as to the integrity of the contents of both pockets.

Temple tried to imagine hunting for a wayward Beretta in those dark tunnels and was glad this was just a fictional scenario.

People, buzzing as contentedly as honey-fed bees, fanned into the artificial garden the performance artist Domingo had wrought.

It was a garden of sound as well as sight, hushed songs from vintage radios, hushed soothing voices.

Temple ignored all the fascinating constructions, moving, blinking, changing color, changing voices, looking for one specific landmark.

"What are you hunting for?" Ralph asked.

"I don't know. A plaque, I suppose."

"Like on a public fountain?"

"Right," she said. "Some acknowledgment . . . He'd probably build it into the overall theme. Nothing obvious."

"Nothing obvious is ever worth hunting," Ralph noted with lofty Fontana-brother certainty.

Temple stopped dead. "That's rather profound."

"I'm sorry. The ride upset my stomach."

"Maybe I'm too short to see it. That's always a problem."

The problem was solved in an instant. Ralph bent and lifted Temple up, his hands fixed at her waist.

So. This is what it felt like to be tall. She gazed into the elephant-ear plants, read the hidden neon messages that flashed off and on like shy Rorschach blots. Domingo had said. He had promised to acknowledge Matt with this exhibit. How? Where?

It was a mystery.

A challenge.

Something necessary to solve.

"There!"

Ralph carried her where she pointed.

No one gawked. This was Las Vegas. One expected the unexpected.

He set her gently down by a lurid gaggle of overgrown neon kiwi birds.

"How did Domingo know?" Temple muttered.

When a world-famous conceptual artist decides to do something in Las Vegas, there are no holds barred. The entire project, a coup for the Crystal Phoenix, was courtesy of Domingo's high regard for Matt Devine. Temple might have cleared him of murder, but Matt in his role of hotline-counselor had cured him of a mid-life sexual addiction that was threatening to ruin his professional and personal future.

Behind the kiwis (so prominent in a more recent murder environment) stood the sinister figure of the Wicked Witch of the West holding a flamingo pink neon sign.

"Surrender Dorothy" it read in cursive script, with an added line beneath: "to Mr. Midnight."

Signed: "Domingo."

Really, Temple thought. Most . . . ambiguous.

And her without a pair of ruby red slippers to her name.


Temple pulled into the Circle Ritz parking lot, feeling in the mood for a brass band, but no such luck. It was deserted except for the landlady's inherited silver VW Bug, millennium model.

Temple pulled in right next to it. Take that, Elvismobile!

For a moment she wondered again why Matt Devine had traded this sleek if funky little car upholstered in blue-suede-shoe cloth for Electra's groady old pink Probe. Which he'd immediately painted an uninspiring shade of white. Of course, all shades of white were uninspiring on any car but a Stutz-Bearcat convertible to Temple.

She sat there in her snazzy red convertible, contemplating Matt's depressingly modest outlook on life. If it was quiet, unassuming, and dull, he was all for it. Perhaps that was why he'd never really fallen for her.

It had been a close call, though, interrupted by Max's sudden return from the missing-in-action lists just when she was beginning to accept that her live-in lover was gone for good. What if Max hadn't come back? Would she and Matt be sharing the whitewashed Probe now? Or a red Miata? At five-ten, Matt would probably fit in the Miata like Goldilocks in baby bear's bed: just right.

Temple glanced at the empty passenger seat beside her. Ghosts always rode with a single woman. Maybe some women wouldn't have taken Max back after he'd vanished for almost a year with no notice. But he was a magician. Vanishing was a professional hazard. And he had left to save her from drawing the attention of the bad guys on his trail. A noble act, really. Besides, they had been monogamous long enough and enough in love to flirt with a real commitment: marriage someday. You had to remain true to your school, and Temple's alma mater was monogamy in a bed-hopping age. Max had remained true the whole time he was gone, too. Mutual fidelity wasn't something you threw away.

Temple fluffed her road-whipped hair into a semblance of order in the rearview mirror, which reflected a lot empty of all the working tenants' cars, including her reliable old Storm.

Too bad you couldn't keep old cars like you did old pets: till death did you part, and a little box of rust at the end for your étagère. Then she thought of Max and his rotating stable of "cold" cars, courtesy of his international-operative friends. Temple didn't know what he'd be driving from one day to the next, and they were all perfectly service-able, perfectly forgettable vehicles. That was the point.

Temple patted the leather passenger seat beside her, hot in the sun. Maybe that's why she had made such an extravagant statement with this car. Maybe she wanted to shout that she didn't need to live the kind of self-denying life Matt seemed married to, or have to fol-low the kind of enforced low-profile pattern that Max's undercover work had made his lifestyle if he wanted to keep having a life.

Something tweedled, and Temple jumped. Every new car had its own literal bells and whistles that told you to take the key out of the ignition, or put your seat belt on, or to turn off your headlights.

But this signal was just from the cell phone in the tote bag on the passenger seat. She patted it down expertly, looking for concealed communications devices, and finally came up with her phone.

"Yes?" she asked after the fourth ring, basking in the open air, star-ing up at clear blue sky of spring.

"I hope I didn't catch you at a bad time," the voice said.

"Only on a most unusual day," Temple caroled back. She was in a good mood and would not be denied.

"This is Molina and all my days are unusual, so don't flatter your-self. I need to talk to you."

"You are."

"In person, where I can see you and you don't sound half-looped."

"I am not looped. I am happy. It is a natural human state in parts of Las Vegas you seldom see, Lieutenant."

"That's good to know. Can you come see my side of town?"

"Yeah. Now?"

"As good a time as any."

"For you, maybe." Then Temple pictured zipping up to the police department building in this jaunty set of wheels. What'd Molina drive, an ancient Volvo? "Okay, I'll be there in twenty minutes."

"Thanks," Molina's brusque voice said before the connection died.

Temple stared at her cell phone as if it had grown Dumbo ears. Molina gave thanks? To her?

Must be a trap.

Temple resolved to be on her guard despite a New Car High and welcomed piloting her new baby on a mission to Homicide Central. Might as well break it in early.


C. R. Molina's office was depressingly functional, but Temple had been here before. She sat on the molded plastic visitor's chair, her feet barely grazing the floor despite platform wedges that added four inches to her five-feet-zero.

Across from her, Molina was the same stark, brunette figure that sometimes stalked Temple's nightmares: Mother Superior incarnate, a female authority figure who wouldn't take no for an answer.

Instead of feeling chirpy about her flashy new car, Temple suddenly felt like a kid with a new red fire engine that all the adults were too busy with Real Life to look at.

This insight reminded Temple that she had often been too busy lately to look at Real Life, which was the only kind of life—and death—Molina dealt with daily.

Molina was shunting some paperwork aside. The statistics of death in Las Vegas. She reminded Temple of a school principal calling a student to her office. Except school principals were seldom nervous, and today the Rock of Gibraltar of the LVMPD was. Slightly.

She sat back, a nunlike figure in her dark navy blazer and denim shirt. "This is off the record."

"Which way? I'm not supposed to tell anyone, or you won't tell anyone?"

"You've never listened to me before, but I wish you'd prick up one tiny Toto ear and listen now."

Temple flushed at being compared to a dog. A small dog. A small cute film dog. "Which Wicked Witch are you warning me about now?"

"It's Wicked Wizard."

"Max? Don't you know by now that I don't listen to propaganda?"

"I do. Which is why I'm pretty stupid for even trying to open your eyes about him. You should know that he is suspected of some pretty serious stuff. That there's good reason to think he's committed a felony."

Temple's sun-warmed skin felt the sudden frost of an inner chill. "Felony."

"Grand theft, burglary, robbery, kidnapping," Molina noted tonelessly. "And murder."

"You're not back on that old sweet song again? Max is not a murderer. If he'd done anything even remotely wrong since he came back last fall, you'd have had him arrested by now."

"Easier said than done with the Mystifying Max. Magicians have a criminal edge second to none."

"Ex-magician."

"Too bad he's not an ex-boyfriend."

"Maybe he is. You don't know anything about us, really."

"I know more than you do about Max Kinsella."

"Now, really, that'd be going some."

"You're blinded by your relationship to the man. You so resented the implication when you were assaulted in the parking garage that the emergency room staff assumed you were a battered woman. But what does sleeping with the stripper strangler make you?"

"Max? Killed that poor girl? Cher Smith?"

"For starters."

"You think I wouldn't know if he were capable of that?"

Molina nodded. "Most of the worst serial rapists had nice little wives at home who were totally ignorant of their real natures. And some didn't. Some had willing partners in their crimes; women who preferred to see it done to other women than to suffer it themselves. Abused to the point of becoming accomplices."

"You have no idea of who Max is," Temple said, stunned at the darkness of the crimes under discussion, but unshaken. "I wish I could tell you, but you wouldn't believe me."

"Who's more liable to be deceived here: the girlfriend, or the police professional?"

Temple just shook her head.

"Remember that I warned you. He could go down for something seriously criminal, and then you really will be an accomplice, as well as a witness for the prosecution."

"Why do you need to prove Max guilty of something so badly?"

"Because it's my job to find and arrest the guilty. He may be guilty of more than you can imagine."

Temple had a Cecil B. DeMille imagination, so this was a real threat. If Molina was even more convinced now than a year ago that Max was guilty of something heinous, the situation was as serious as she said.

Temple answered seriously. "I know it looked suspicious when Max disappeared right after that dead man was found in the spy network cubbyhole over the Goliath Casino, but he *had* just finished his performance contract there. If—and I say *if*—he knew about the death, he might have gone underground because he was afraid of whoever did it, or of being arrested for it. Maybe he was set up—"

"You're telling me you lived with the man and he never explained his vanishing act to you?"

"Max keeps his own counsel. He said it was for my own protection."

"He's not doing a very good job of protecting you, or what's yours."

Molina finally lowered her laser blue eyes—so like that beautiful blue light of the glaucoma test machine at the eye doctor's that you're supposed to hold absolutely still for while staring right into it without blinking as it pushes closer and closer . . . and even though you can't feel it you know that gas-blue flame is drilling right into your cornea—ick! Temple blinked from just thinking about the eye test.

Maybe it had made her nervous (that epic imagination at work again), because she jumped when Molina tossed something across the desk that hit the papers with a thunk.

This was the usual police evidence baggie that you thought should be holding somebody's leftover tuna-fish sandwich, which usually turned to be something sad, like one earring, or grisly, like somebody's leftover bloodstained wallet. . . .

The object inside the bag was small and lumpy with a glint of gold.

Temple's ghoulish imagination conjured a flashy molar pulled out by the roots. . . .

"Oh."

She reflexively reached for the object. It was hers, after all.

It weighed heavily in her palm as her memory assayed it. She'd forgotten how utterly beautiful it was, the opals, the diamonds, the gold setting.

It had been hers for only a few days.

"Where? When?"

Molina was happy to dispatch the dispassionate facts. "In a park-

ing lot. A church parking lot. Several weeks ago. Near another parking lot body. It was identified, but the perp remains at large. A female
victim, of course."

"My ring was by the body?"

"By the edge of the parking lot, actually. A bright young uniform
found it. The body was thirty yards away."

"I don't understand." This time Temple could meet the laser eyes:
she stood on firm ground. "You know this ring was on my hand the
night we all attended the Opium Den to see that woman magician's
act. Shangri-La called me onstage as the willing audience schmoo,
took my ring, and then vanished with her whole retinue."

"You vanished too, and that black alley cat of yours, who gets
around like a case of the clap."

"But Max found me, and Louie too."

"I found you. Max was along for the ride."

"He found us. You were along for the ride. Maybe that's why you
hate him." Temple found a lump as big as the ring blocking her
throat. Holding the ring brought back her Manhattan "honeymoon"
with Max last Christmas, reminded her of his hopes, promises, that
he'd be able to duck out of the undercover life, live a normal existence someday with her.

"Max had nothing to do with this ring!" Temple said, her wits
gathering. "It was stolen from me by a woman no one has been able to
trace. She must have been involved with that drug-smuggling ring
you busted that night. Somebody must have pawned the ring and it
ended up in that parking lot. Why would this be evidence incrimi-
nating Max, except that he gave it to me? Is giving me rings a crime?"

"Not to my knowledge. Unless it was stolen."

Temple stared at the object in its sheath of cheap plastic, aghast.

"It wasn't," Molina admitted. "Purchased in New York, at
Tiffany's. For cash."

"Really? Tiffany's?"

"He didn't brag?"

"Quality doesn't brag. So how does this being on the scene of a
murder implicate Max? You admit the ring was his to give. You know
that it was taken from my possession in front of a theater full of witnesses, including you. You know that the entire magic act was a cover
for criminal activities. Why drag Max into it?"

"You haven't mentioned the murder victim. Of course you

wouldn't have noticed or known about her death. It got a three-inch mention in the local news section roundup column. Still, she was just as dead, brutally strangled. Not a young woman: sixty-two. Gloria Fuentes would not ring a bell with you or most people who read the paper that day."

Molina was wrong. The name Gloria Fuentes almost made Temple drop the evidence bag, but she clutched it tight instead.

"And the connection to Max Kinsella," Molina went on. "She was a former magician's assistant, long since retired. Still, magic is the link, isn't it? Between Shangri-La, the vanishing magician, between the late Gloria Fuentes, and between Max Kinsella, formerly the Mystifying Max and lately your non-live-in lover. I'll take that bauble back now. It's police evidence."

*No!* Temple wanted to shout. *It's mine! It's precious. Valuable. Mine.*

How cruel Molina was to flaunt her possession of Temple's only engagement ring. Temple felt a wash of anger, but it was rinsed away by fear. What if Molina knew what Temple knew: that Gloria Fuentes had been the longtime assistant to Max's mentor in magic, Gandolph the Great? She would really be able to add several rows of bricks to her wall of circumstantial evidence closing him off from the normal life he hoped for.

Temple held the baggie out to Molina. "Handle it carefully. Opal is delicate and the ring is valuable. You probably know just how valuable more than I do. If it's damaged in your custody, I'll sue."

While Temple met Molina's hard gaze with her own steel blue fury, the desk phone rang.

"Molina," she answered.

Then she was quiet. "I'm in the middle of something," she said finally, sounding much friendlier than she had to Temple. "I'll call you later. Yes. As soon as I can."

The call didn't sound totally professional, Temple diagnosed expertly. A public relations professional knows a lot about phone-voice language. So if this was a semipersonal call, who was it from? Not Molina's preteen daughter, Mariah. There had been none of that annoying Mother Superior-knows-better tone that Temple got by default.

A man. It was a man who Molina didn't need to intimidate, but liked. Since a female police supervisor needed to intimidate men all around her into giving her an even break, Temple deduced that the man on the line was not a colleague, but a . . . friend? When did Molina relax enough to have friends, of any gender?

"Where were we?" the lieutenant asked.

Temple raised an eyebrow. It wasn't like Molina to lose track of anything, especially something so potentially lethal. "I was requesting that you take good care of my ring, and you were talking about how I was married to the Mob."

"That would be better than the state you're in," Molina retorted. "This is a friendly warning. Kinsella is trouble and he'll take you down with him, no matter how many pretty rings he tosses your way. If you see him do anything that makes you think twice, let me know."

"If I do, I will, but I haven't yet." Temple itched to reveal Max's secret good-guy past, but secrets were supposed to stay that way and Molina would only call it defensiveness anyway. "Are you through with me?"

"For now." Molina eyed Temple as she stood up, barely looming over the seated police officer even when standing. "You see much of Matt Devine nowadays?"

"Around the Circle Ritz. But he's been . . . busy lately. Out of town on speaking engagements."

"I hear he has other engagements on his calendar, too."

"Oh?" Temple recognized a leading dig when she heard it. She braced herself again.

"Only that he's been working himself back into the social mainstream."

"Dating, you mean."

"I guess I do."

Temple gritted her teeth. She would not ask who. "That's good. Single guys should date." She narrowed her eyes like daggers at Molina. "Single gals, too."

Molina shrugged. "A lot of single gals Matt's age are single parents, though."

Temple resisted catching a gasping breath. *Molina* had that daughter, Mariah. Was this her way of announcing that she was dating Matt?

"I'm a single gal with a dependent myself," Temple said breezily, "only he's a cat."

"Doesn't count as a dependent, especially given Midnight Louie's untrammeled ways. I'm surprised you haven't figured out who Matt's new interest is. I thought you fancied yourself an amateur detective."

"In criminal matters. There's no crime in Matt's having a social life."

"There's a crime in that it took him so long to get around to getting one." Molina let her pencil rap back and forth on a manila folder, but kept silent.

Guess you could call this, Temple thought, a second "Manila Thrillah" only instead of Frazier and Ali going another brutal round, it was her and Molina. A Manila Molina, maybe? She be darned if she went down first.

Molina finally straightened, her mouth making a moué Temple couldn't interpret as approval or not. "Janice Flanders. He's been seeing Janice. I think they're well matched."

Temple had seen the sketch artist's portrait work, but never hide nor hair of her in the flesh. Curiosity was killing her.

"She's a wonderful artist," Temple said smoothly. "She must share Matt's insight into people and their problems."

Molina paused on the brink of saying something, then seemed to remember her own secret. "That midnight radio job keeps him off the streets during prime time. Not too conducive to a social life. Probably for the best. Funny, there was a time when I thought you'd go with him over Kinsella."

Temple was so flummoxed she couldn't say anything for a moment. "I don't think personal relationships are your long suit," she said finally. "Obviously, you were wrong."

"Oh, the show isn't over yet." Molina's Midnight Margarita-blue eyes narrowed speculatively at Temple, like she was an undercover operative Molina was unleashing on the world at large. An unwilling, ignorant undercover operative. "Just watch yourself. It's dangerous out there," she added, turning back to her papers, dismissive.

Temple tottered out of the office to the elevator, weak-kneed for a moment. The last admonition had sounded reluctantly sincere enough to be real. And it wasn't just Max that the woman was warning her about, Temple sensed.

Given how deeply Molina loathed and distrusted Max, it gave Temple chilling pause to wonder what *else* threatening Molina saw looming in Temple's own present and future.

# Chapter 11

# The Sign of the Serpent

If Lieutenant C. R. Molina had meant to destroy Temple's zip-a-dee-doo-dah mood, she couldn't have done better had she gone to graduate school in Killjoy 101.

Temple put the Miata's top down again, fussing aloud about the process and herself.

"There's no sense in taking anything that woman says seriously. She's prejudiced against Max and probably thinks Miatas are the Devil's workshop, too. What a puritan! She probably has the sex life of a cantaloupe. She certainly has the hide of one.

"I'd *hate* to be her daughter! Poor Mariah! It would take more than a Xena the Warrior Princess outfit to make that woman halfway human."

Still, Temple stopped and grinned to picture the towering, nononsense detective done up as a credible Xena in leather bustier, studded boots, and kilt. And she already had the Lucy Lawless Olympus-blue eyes down cold. The masquerade had been a ruse to catch a killer at a science fiction convention where Xena clones were about as unique as Bozos at a clown convention. Temple was surprised the buttoned-down Molina would go undercover in such an over-the-top feminine guise, but her daughter had been in danger and mother love is a desperate motive. Actually, Molina'd looked pretty hot for a homicide lieutenant in that get-up. Temple's grin faded.

Then she broke a fingernail on the convertible-top latch.

"Holy Aeolus! It's the curse of the Chakram Chick."

She got in the car and drove away, worrying more about what Molina might know about Max (that Temple didn't) than was good for her sanity.

She hardly noticed where she was driving, she was so upset. Seeing the ring Max had given her treated like a Cracker Jack token made her stomach churn. Contemplating how Molina might use it to tie Max into yet another murder made the churn start whipping out butterflies. She was hardly Max's keeper, she told herself. He'd been taking care of himself since high school and then some. Taking care of her, too. Loyalty and faith were hard emotions to defend; they were so totally in the mind and heart of the holder.

Had her supply of both run out on Max? He was mysterious, yes, but that had been a professional qualification for a magician, a charming quirk at first. Later . . .

She was driving east of town on Charleston. On her left the Blue Mermaid suddenly surfaced from a tangle of junky roofs and signs, her slowly turning serene plaster image a kind of Virgin Mary for the down-at-the-heels set.

And of course the Virgin Mary (which she was decidedly not) reminded her of Matt (which he decidedly was). Virgin, that is. Holy mackeral! What had she been thinking? How could she, a fallen away Universalist Unitarian, deal with an earnest ex-Catholic priest determined to re-enter the single lifestyle with eyes wide shut; to play by the religious rules even some Catholics had found unworkable? Talk about sexual responsibility. Before Max had reappeared, she might have and he couldn't. After Max had returned, he might have and she wouldn't. A tragicomedy of timing. Something to film for a joint HBO and Pax TV project: *Sex in the Psyche*.

The white-painted motel named in the mermaid's honor bore a huge new sign of its own, a temporary banner stretched over the portico:

PSYCHIC FAIR

Temple's foot hesitated over the brake for a heartbeat. She'd attended a psychic fair once. Even knew a few psychics. Maybe one of them would have a clue about the strange five-sided figure that had scribed professor Jefferson Mangel into a circle of death only a couple weeks before.

She was sure that the figure meant something arcane. Who better to ask than a psychic? It was doubly a pity that poor Jeff was dead. He was the one objective expert on the mantic arts she'd trust to have a scholar's dispassion on the subject. But she couldn't consult him anymore. . . .

Or could she? What had Max said? He'd borrowed some Ph.D. theses that mentioned the mysterious entity known in some magic circles as the Synth.

She twisted the small steering wheel right to shoot down a side street, rather dingy in this near-downtown neighborhood. Max would have wanted her convertible top up, pronto, if he were along. But he wasn't, and she quickly turned around in a deserted gas station lot and got back on Charleston heading west.

She hoped Max was at home and feeling like company. Maybe she could also find out what he had done lately to put Molina in her rabid-rottweiler mood.

The house was a picture of housing development serenity, like its neighbors. In the nearby houses, though, people were really away at work and school. Behind this house's hooded windows, Max probably spun plots like a spider in a suburban web.

Temple parked the Miata three houses down and hefted a businesslike folder from her tote bag. Maybe she'd be mistaken for an Avon lady if anyone was watching.

If anyone was watching. At the very least Max was. Like a spider, he was supersensitive to any stirrings on the fringes of his gossamer empire.

Why was she creating such unattractive metaphors for Max's perpetual state of siege today? Had Molina really gotten to her this time?

Temple paused in the sheltered entryway. Ringing the doorbell was a last resort. If Max was inside, he would materialize at the heavy wooden door and draw her within before anybody on the street noticed her.

When she came here Temple always felt like a magician's assistant being shuttled quickly into the next disappearing lady trick, as if the whole house were only an illusion, one big revolving door into a maze fashioned of hidden compartments and deceptive mirrors and sliding false walls.

Temple stood in the shade of the portico, designed as shelter against the daily Las Vegas Heat and Light Show. The door did not so much open as dissolve into deeper darkness.

A hand, pale as a formal glove, reached out to draw her inside.

Her eyes blinked, unable to adjust to the interior shadow.

Max's hand, conversely as warm as it looked pallid and cold, pulled her through the entry hall and into the well-lit rooms beyond.

Her eyes, still blinded, rebelled at the rapid-fire change in light.

"What brought you here without phoning first?" he asked.

"An interview with the vampire."

"Vampire? Before lunch? Let's go into the kitchen for a little healthy fluorescent light."

Temple laughed. Max always managed to banish his own most powerful illusions. It was just a darkened house, after all, kept shuttered against the heat, but mostly so he could see out without anyone seeing in. That's what a man on the run for eighteen years needed.

The kitchen was its usual gleaming, efficient self, the stainless steel appliance fronts reflecting and distorting their entering figures into gray alien forms.

"You didn't say why you dropped by." Max never forgot an unanswered question.

"I . . . I was happy."

"*Was?*" He never missed an implication either.

She studied him as he leaned against the walk-in refrigerator front like an extremely suave corpse propped against his coffin. Or a space vampire against a high-tech crypt door.

His trademark black clothing underlined the image, but Molina had carefully planted the sinister side of Max in Temple's brain. The policewoman had been working on that for a year, always questioning Max's whereabouts, his history, his sudden disappearance and reappearance in Temple's life. Maybe it was beginning to work.

Max turned away to pull open the stainless steel door, and spun back to face her, something in his hand. "Dreamsicle?" he asked

Molina's evil spell of doubt was broken.

"*Dreamsicle?*" Temple slung her tote bag and folder atop the huge kitchen island. "Where you'd get that? I haven't had one of those since I had scabby knees."

"You never had scabby knees."

"Yes, I did, and I sold lemonade at a stand, too."

"Shocking." Max handed her an orange-vanilla ice cream treat on a stick and unwrapped the thin white paper from his own. The label read Creamsicle now but they both knew these were Dreamsicles of old, of their youths. "And you worry about *my* past."

Uncanny how he could always target the unspoken issue.

"I don't worry about it as much as Molina does."

"She doesn't worry about, she just worries at it, like a demented Scottish terrier, only she would be an Iberian terrier."

"Not necessarily. She got those blue eyes from somewhere. Why not a Scot?"

"Bagpipes in the blood? I don't think so, Temple."

"I just saw her."

"Why am I not surprised."

"She warned me about you."

"I repeat: Why am I not surprised? That's nothing new."

"She warned me really, really hard about you. And she showed me something."

Max managed to tense without visibly moving a muscle. Temple only noticed it because she knew him so well. He had that perfect concentrated stillness that the stage required, the sense of something tensile ready to spring, like a big cat.

He didn't ask what.

"The ring," Temple finally said.

"The ring?" Max unfolded his arms. "How the *hell* did she get the ring?"

"Found it."

Max's face broadcast consternation. "Found it? Where?"

"Actually a street cop found it. And where is the problem. At the scene of another murder."

"A new murder? And the ring was by the body?"

"Not so old a murder, but not so new either. Gloria Fuentes. Remember? She was found strangled in the church parking lot."

"I remember," Max said grimly. "Another of your magic-linked murders."

"Not mine. I just noticed the connections."

"And the ring was there? But that was before—"

"Before what?"

Max relaxed enough to smile. "I'm trying too hard to anticipate you. Magician's bad habit. You tell your story at the right pace."

"It wasn't very near the body, at least. Maybe ninety feet away at the edge of the bushes. In the dirt. My ring! In the dirt."

"*Your* ring?"

"Well, it was originally your ring, until you gave it to me. I think that's how Molina thinks of it too. As *your* ring. As a nasty talisman associated with the demon Max. As more evidence to hang you with."

"That ring," he said faintly, blinking once. He leaned against the wall again. "That ring. So it's found. Has been for a few weeks."

"Isn't that just the meanest thing ever, Max? Molina had it, knew she had it, and never told me?"

Max smiled again. "It's mean, but that's police work. It was a wildly out-of-place piece of evidence. Of course she'd save it for a rainy day. Apparently she decided on today to rain on your parade."

"Well, it worked. It was horrible to see it in that tacky plastic bag, pulled out of a tacky desk drawer in a mean little office."

"I'm sorry, Temple." Max came to put his arms around her, creating a living ring. "I don't much like Molina having custody of that ring either. But it was lost weeks ago. We have to give it up."

"It's so beautiful, and it was from Tiffany's."

Max embrace hardened. "How did you know that?"

"Molina found out."

"She is starting to really irritate me."

"It's mutual, and don't you forget it. I reminded her that the ring was taken by that Shangri-La onstage at the Opium Den, in front of all of us, you, Matt, me, Molina. How can she suspect you of getting it back and then being stupid enough to drop it on a murder scene?"

"I got you and Louie back from the abductors, didn't I?" Max pulled away and retreated to the buttress of the refrigerator door, this time as if he needed the support. "Maybe Molina figured I found the ring during my search of the magical chambers, and palmed it. Then I decided it wasn't safe to give it back to you, so I took it along on one of my stalking expeditions and left it as a tip for a beat cop."

"Max, don't joke. She's dead serious. And it does look like somebody wants to implicate you in these murders. Maybe it's the Synth. Maybe that book you're writing on Gandolph is making them nervous. Whoever, it doesn't matter. Molina thinks she's got a hold of another coffin nail for you."

"Why'd she show it to you now?"

"Because she's convinced, she wants to convince me, that you're a monstrous criminal I should turn in to my nearest precinct house. She said you could be going down for something big, and that I could be a witness, or an accessory."

"What did you say?"

Temple had to work on finishing her Dreamsicle, which had melted like syrupy emotions while she'd been talking. It was hard to discuss serious issues with ice cream in your mouth. Disposing of the treat gave her time to notice that Max's insouciant attitude, both physical and mental, overlaid an uncharacteristic edginess.

He showed the strain, a magician's worst enemy.

"Is there something I should know?" she asked.

"There are a lot of things you should know, that I can't tell you." He pushed off from the refrigerator door's icy steel support, looking gaunt and haunted under the unforgiving overhead fluorescent light.

"Undercover work," he said, "which I did a lot of for a long time in a good cause, mostly requires keeping an ungodly amount of balls in the air. You deceive by telling the truth, or by telling slices of the truth to a lot of people, like doling out a piece of pie that's too rich for human consumption."

"I guess the food analogy fits a kitchen," she noted.

"Spy work is all oblique, all analogies. Yet there is a simple straightforward rule underlying the cut corners and endless angles. You must always respect your sources and their confidences, or the whole thing falls apart. That means you know pieces of everybody else's truth, but can never tell the whole truth. You tell lies—not to deceive, but to protect the truth that some people have the courage to tell. You must know more than any one of them. You must see the big picture, and prevent them from seeing it, or they will fall into it and die. And it will be your fault."

"You're saying you have to lie to protect people."

Max nodded. "From others. From themselves."

"But—"

Max leaned forward to collect the empty wooden stick from her and throw it in the trash can hidden behind an island cupboard. He waited for her to finish her thought.

"But . . . you're talking about professional espionage. Telling lies not to deceive but to protect people: isn't that where people go wrong in their personal lives?"

"Not so much committing untruth, but neglecting to mention truth, I think."

"You know what I think?"

He smiled. "No. That's what I like about you. I get to find out."

"I think you and Molina both know something that you don't dare tell anybody else, but that makes you mortal enemies."

Max folded his arms. "That's possible."

"Sure, play Mr. Stone Face. She does the same thing. Just glowers and intones warnings like a witch from *Macbeth*, but she won't come out and say diddly!"

Max was laughing. "A witch from *Macbeth*. I like that."

"Good, because you're Macbeth, trying to decide which way to jump."

"I'm not contemplating killing anyone."

"No, you want to stop the killing. That's always been your problem. Most people are happy to get a good job and retire with a gold watch, although yours probably would be a Patek Philippe. *You* want to end the Irish Troubles and put your dead cousin to rest."

"Sean will never rest."

"He will, but you won't. Max, being secretive about what you really do, your past, is hurting you with Molina. This could get serious. She could arrest you, or worse, shoot you. If you would only tell her a little—"

"She wouldn't believe it. She's made a hobby out of not believing me, and telling her a little could hurt a lot of people."

"She's in law enforcement, I can't believe she'd be so blind—"

"Believe it!"

Temple stiffened to encounter the stainless steel in Max's voice, an ungiving intensity she'd never heard before.

"Do you realize what you're doing, Temple? You're taking Molina at face value. Because she's a woman, a policewoman, because she has a career in law enforcement, you assume she's straight. You assume she doesn't have a personal agenda. You assume she's honest."

"Well, she acts annoyingly self-righteous. Are you saying Molina might be crooked?"

"She might have agendas that have nothing to do with the law or her job. I'm saying she might be human, and if she's human, she might go very wrong."

Temple leaned against the island's hard granite edge, feeling it dig into her back. It was straighter than a stone ruler, and could not lie.

People were another matter.

"You're right, Max. Ever since Molina came charging at me after you vanished, nagging, worrying, digging, like an annoying dog after a bone—you're right, I assumed that all she wanted was justice. She might be misinformed, or, in your case, *under*informed, but she really just wanted to catch criminals. You're saying she has a special interest in pinning these vague crimes on you. It isn't just dogged police work, it's . . . obsession? Self-protection?"

"I'm saying if someone is persistently wearing blinders, maybe he, or she, has something to hide from herself. And people with something to hide from themselves are very dangerous."

Temple tried to rearrange the chessboard in her mind. Molina, the Red Queen, say. Not just legal authority but a human being with human failings. Blind to any but one view of Max, because that supported an illusion she needed to maintain, no matter what.

"I wish I could, Temple," Max said softly, watching her think, watching her rearrange her assumptions. His voice was sad and tender.

"Could what?"

"Could tell you the whole truth. But I love you too much to risk it. I'll have to risk you finding out half-truths from everybody else and turning against me. It's just the way it is.

"I can tell you this. I spent more than ten years of my life worrying about danger that might befall strangers. Now, since I came to Vegas with you, it's become personal. I don't worry about strangers anymore. I'm cured of that delusion. Now I'm like everybody else who can't do anything at all about fate, and life, and death. Now I worry about the people I know."

"People?"

He inclined his head in tribute to her instincts. "People."

"Anybody I know?"

"Everybody you know."

Temple considered this unwelcome news. Max would always tell her the truth, as far as he could.

She nodded, and picked up her folder.

"Max, what happened to Professor Mangel's magical poster collection once the room was no longer a crime scene? Did anyone at the university care to keep the exhibition going?"

"No."

"No? What a shame! Even though the posters of you were missing after the murder, the rest of the material must have been invaluable."

"I'm glad you thought the collection diminished by my absence, but now it's enhanced by my presence."

"What on earth do you mean?"

"Come with me." He beckoned her toward the hallway.

"I haven't time for dalliance, Mr. Valentino. Or do we say Pitt nowadays?"

"I hope not. But dalliance is not on my mind." Max led her down the dark hallway to the large, unoccupied bedroom where he stored all of his and the late Gandolph's magical paraphernalia.

"I've seen this act before," Temple objected.

"I've got a new illusion." Max opened the door and switched on the light: no magic, just Thomas Edison and Hoover Dam in tandem.

Temple gasped anyway. Against one wall stood ranks of aluminum poster stands framing the mostly yellow, black, and red vintage placards announcing the great magic acts of the past century and a half.

"Now *this* is a magic trick. How, Max?"

"The magic of money. An anonymous donor offered the university a good price for the entire collection."

"How wonderful!" Temple flung her arms around Max's neck, dangling from his height. "What a wonderful thing to do. I'm so glad."

"Well, Mangel really and truly loved my act. He loved the acts of every magician whose posters he collected. Now they're in a private museum with the leftovers of Gandolph's magical career. In a way Gandolph and Jeff Mangel, and Gloria Fuentes, Gandolph's murdered former assistant, are all interred here, locked away from life."

Max's eyes grew distant as he gazed at the collection of magic acts in their most physical form. Temple had the oddest sensation of being in an Egyptian pharaoh's tomb, of seeing the things the ruler intended to surround himself with in the afterlife, even of witnessing the final enshrinement of the Mystifying Max and his career in magic.

The notion was so sad she let her arms fall slack and stepped away from him. She could say nothing. It was like being tongue-tied at a funeral because the corpse had sat up politely to listen.

"Okay," she said finally, trying to sound businesslike, and succeeding. "I'm here to do some research. I've got a murder to solve, or maybe six. Show me the books you took from Professor Mangel's office just before he was killed."

Max rubbed her shoulders, his fingers digging into the tense muscles ridging the nape of her neck. He put a fresh mug of coffee with Bailey's Irish Cream for flavoring next to her on the desk.

"Ye gods," Temple complained. "Haven't these aspiring Ph.D.s ever heard of a declarative sentence? This last one was two hundred and fifty words, all passive voice."

"I'm no writer. Sounds okay to me."

"I hope your book on Gandolph isn't written like this. What's happening with that anyway?"

"I've, ah, kind of dropped it. Got a little busy."

"You can't stop writing if you want to finish something."

"Yes, ma'am."

Temple frowned at the narrow pages bound in soft rag-paper covers. "What do they use for type size? Agate italic? Never mind what I'm referring to, it's a print-media phrase for very tiny type." She sighed and sipped.

"They're quoting medieval alchemists and Edgar Cayce and Gypsy tarot readers. Especially something called the *Tarot of the Bohemians*."

"These are probably academic cranks, Temple. Let's face it, magic is not the usual postgraduate discipline."

"No, but poor Jeff Mangel took it seriously as an art form, and apparently got killed for his pains. Listen to this: 'The key to ancient science of Egypt and India is *synthesis*, which condenses all acquired knowledge into a few simple laws. To save the laws of synthesis from oblivion, secret societies were established. In the West, they were the Gnostic sects, the Arabs, Alchemists, Templars, Rosicrucians, and lastly the Freemasons."

"The Synth. But tarot, alchemy, knights Templar, Freemasons . . . that's rank superstition, Temple."

"Superstition is one way of fooling yourself, and you just said a couple hours ago that self-deception was a dangerous state."

Temple turned a page and blinked.

"Another blasted star chart. These things make my head hurt. Sidereal time and minutes and planetary positions. I like to read my horoscope in the morning paper, but *please!*"

Max read over her shoulder. "This section seems to cover astrology. What that has to do with magic I shudder to imagine. Skip it."

Temple started to turn several pages at once, but two stuck together. She pried them apart. "Yuck, red sauce. Somebody was eating pizza over this tome."

"That's not red sauce, Temple. That's . . . blood."

"Double yuck!"

She stared at the pages sealed with a blot of blood as they parted under the pry bar of her fingernail.

"Max! That's it! Look. That's the symbol on the professor's floor!"

He leaned close to peer at the small drawing. Dots connected by lines. Stars linked in arbitrary patterns so that humans could put a name and shape to their geometry and call it a . . .

"A constellation," Temple said. "The figure is a constellation. What a weird word they call it: Ophiuchus. You ever heard of that before?"

"O-fee-*yuch*-uss? *Hmmmm.* Have you?"

"Or O-*fie*-a-cuss. Never."

They exchanged a glance.

"Web search." Temple hit the boot-up button on the dead computer sharing the desk with the books from Professor Mangel's shelf.

In moments a list of entries with the word Ophiuchus unrolled like a carpet containing a hidden Cleopatra announcing herself to Caesar.

Max and Temple studied the entries together, heads touching as they stared at on-line "pages" that showed the very drawing that had contained Jeff Mangel's dead body.

"Ophiuchus," Temple repeated almost reverently. "I've played around a little with horoscopes . . . when I was a kid, Max. I used to know the symbols for the planets even. But I never ran into a thirteenth sign of the zodiac. And this is it. Ophiuchus, the Serpent Beaver."

"Thirteen is not a lucky number."

"Don't give me the willies! I know that. Black cats and thirteen are unlucky."

"So far we're batting a thousand."

"Leave Louie out of this. He's just an innocent stray."

"And so am I?" Max raised a Mr. Spock eyebrow.

Temple elbowed him in the ribs, not hard enough to notice.

"Cut it out. Seriously," Max said, "this constellation has as long a history as any other recognized sign of the zodiac. No wonder some ancient zodiac systems included a thirteenth sign. It's probably as old as Eden. The serpent. Ophiuchus."

"Serpent. Sneaky, convoluted, quiet. Hidden. Poisonous. Enduring since the Fall."

"I take it you're describing the Synth."

"I take it that's how the Synth describes itself."

Max nodded. "Members of a secret cabal of magicians might flatter themselves that way. The snake has always been considered a symbol of guile, wisdom, and evil." He frowned for a moment. "I wonder if it's a parallel image of the Worm Ouroboros."

"The Worm Ouroboros?"

"You've seen the image: a snake devouring its own tail. A symbol of eternity and entropy: the way things fall apart and unite at one and the same time, over and over."

"How do you know about this stuff?"

Max smiled. "While you were dabbling in horoscopes, I was dabbling in mystical mumbo-jumbo. In some forms it's called philosophy. In others, superstition."

"We both must have had a very weird adolescence."

"Perfectly and normally abnormal, I'm afraid." Max touched the crude five-sided "house" that pinpointed the stars of the constellation Ophiuchus. "Like all secret occult societies, the Synth needs to leave a trail. That means it needs someone to follow and find it."

"Why?"

"Why does anything lethal leave a trail? To entrap. To destroy."

Temple looked at the book in which she'd found such a perfect clue.

She didn't feel like a mouse, but she could smell the strong, lilting odor of sharp cheddar.

\* \* \*

Max saw her to the door, his arm draped over her shoulder like a comforting shawl.

"Good detective work," he said. He squinted out the door. "And you did an excellent job of hiding your car."

"Ah, thanks . . . but actually I did a good job of changing my car."

He looked again.

"*That*'s yours?"

"What?" she asked innocently.

"Not the Odyssey next door. The little red thingamajig."

"It's a Miata."

Max's arm left her shoulders. "A Miata. Is that a good investment?"

"I don't know. It's a fun car."

"A convertible? For a redhead? In Las Vegas?"

"I'll get a big hat."

"Temple." Max turned her to look at him. "This is the first major purchase you've made since we've been together without asking me about it."

"Well, yeah. I suppose so."

"I really can't fit into a Miata."

"You can't? Oh. I didn't think of that."

"Oh."

"But . . . we always drive places in your car. Or cars. Or whatever They leave for you."

"It won't always be like that. Haven't you been listening to me?"

"Yes, but the Storm was worn out and I finally had some real income from my semipermanent floating PR work for the Crystal Phoenix and the Jersey Joe Jackson attraction is done and open and a big success and I thought I deserved something . . . and this seemed like fun at the moment."

"You used to think that what we did was fun at the moment. You used to consult me about big decisions."

"It's a . . . little car."

"It's a big issue. I don't fit in it. Are you sending me a message?"

"Max, no! Don't be paranoid. I wasn't even thinking about you."

The words hung there, an intended reassurance hoisted on its own petard.

"I didn't mean that the way it sounded," Temple said.

"No one ever does," Max said, and shut the door on any further discussion.


Temple felt awful. She wanted to blame Molina for it, but that was too simple.

The car looked like a toy as she approached it. Silly. Too small for anyone but a shrunken Alice in Wonderland. *Eat me.* Humble pie, that's what she should eat. She felt about two inches tall, and short stature was such an issue with her that feeling small meant she felt really, really guilty. Because she was.

She'd only been thinking of herself when she'd bought the Miata, and maybe not very maturely at that.

Despite the sun-warmed sidewalk, her feet in their Mootsie's Tootsies high-rise slides felt ice cold. This was a lot of money to spend on a whim. An impractical whim. A whim that hurt a significant other's feelings. Max always acted so strong she sometimes forgot that he had feelings to hurt.

She got in, arranged herself and her tote bag, glanced at Max's stoic house facade. Here she sat, in a brand-new car, with a brand-new clue in her tote bag, and she felt horrible.

The only thing to do when troubled was to get on with the routine of life. She started the car and headed back toward the Circle Ritz. She needed to stop at the Lucky's store first. Buy groceries. Her least favorite chore. She saw a lot more chocolate in her future than was healthy for her figure.


Forty-five minutes later Temple stood on a sun-baked asphalt parking lot, her arms cradling brown paper bags, bulging plastic bags dangling from both wrists, wondering where to put her groceries.

One brown bag could share the passenger seat with her tote bag if she squeezed them together and belted them in. The second brown bag and a couple plastic bags could crowd into the well behind the seats. The other two plastic bags full of bottled water could go in the trunk, such as it was.

Now. What would hold the groceries down while she whizzed along the street? Time to put up the top, roll up the windows, and turn on the AC. This would be one buttoned-down convertible for the trip home.

Misgivings nagged her the whole way. How could she have bought a car that Max didn't fit in, much less a few bags of groceries? She had bought in to a sales pitch without considering the practicalities. She had been suckered.

Her back straightened against the seat back as the AC wafted the curls off her face.

Maybe the car wasn't the bill of goods she'd been sold.

Maybe it was Molina who was the slippery saleswoman. Maybe her whole mood had shifted at the woman's dire predictions about Max, and her cruel revelation of the whereabouts of the ring. Come on, the Storm hadn't been just Max's size, either, although she had bought that car before she knew him.

No, the question was *why* Molina was bearing down so hard on Max right now. Why was she warning Temple? To get her to do something. What? Question Max. Break up with him. Throw him off balance. Distract him from Molina's moves against him.

Max had warned her. Had said Molina could have motives Temple might not even guess at.

That he wouldn't say more only meant that Temple had many more puzzles than Ophiuchus to solve.

# Chapter 12

# Smoke Signals

Hoping this was the about-to-be-perfect end of a perfectly dreadful day, Temple zoomed into the Circle Ritz lot. She parked the Miata as close to the door as she could while still sheltering it under the big old palm tree's erratic shade.

As she stood beside the car extracting her groceries from various nooks and crannies, she heard another engine pull into the lot: Electra's old pink Probe, now Matt's, and now painted the color of a white sepulcher.

Temple brightened as she balanced the two brown bags, her tote bag's considerable weight swinging from the crook of her right elbow. Her key ring was in her right fist.

Great. Matt was here just in time to help her with the bags.

He exited the Probe, locked it, and thrust his keys into the pocket of his khaki pants. Looking neither right nor left, but at the ground, he rapidly crossed the asphalt to the building's side door.

Temple opened her mouth to hail him, except that his haste, his almost deliberate avoidance of looking anywhere near her direction made her freeze in chill indecision.

In those moments of hesitancy, Matt was through the door and gone.

Talk about being the Invisible Woman! How could he have missed the sight of a strange red Miata in the almost-empty lot?

Fact was, he couldn't have. He must have spotted it as he turned in, and he could hardly miss her.

But he had.

Temple trudged toward the building's glass door, the darkness inside allowing the glass to reflect her overburdened figure.

She looked like Little Orphan Annie disguised as a bag lady. Or maybe Typhoid Mary. Matt had seemed distracted lately, and he did work late hours and travel out of state for speaking engagements. He was semifamous now. Guess Mr. Midnight no longer had time to hobnob with the locals.

She shifted the bags to one side as she prepared to grab the door handle and shoulder her way into the cool darkness beyond.

It opened of its own invisible accord, like the eerie door at Max's house. Temple dodged inside before her bags slipped and she found them lifting out of her arms.

"Sorry," Matt said, scanning the parking lot behind her as the door swung shut. "I was busy thinking about tonight's show and I didn't notice you out there. Is that a new car or something?"

"Ye-es! Thanks. You like the car?"

"Fine," he said, juggling grocery bags. Not the kind of tribute that the new owner of a racy red convertible expected. Matt still seemed in a hurry. "Can you press the elevator button? Thanks."

"Well," Temple commented, "everyone around here was switching cars—Electra with your Elvismobile and you with her Probe, so I thought I'd trade the Storm for a Miata."

He nodded, looking over her shoulder, then at the bronze pointer above the door that showed what floor the elevator was on.

Forget about Matt not paying proper attention to her new car, Temple thought. He wasn't paying *any* attention to *her*!

What was she today, a poor cousin of Typhoid Mary, Miss Poison Ivy?

Before she could say anything, the elevator door ground open and Matt leaped aboard. "Hit the floor button, would you?" he instructed.

No, she was Miss Elevator Operator.

They both seemed stunned into silence on the brief ride up one floor.

But once the elevator doors parted, Matt was again peering up and down the hall like a wary Doberman.

It was like he was afraid to be seen with her.

Surely he didn't think that her resumed relationship with Max meant she couldn't have male friends? That was the problem. She didn't have a clue as to what was going on with Matt these days. Something had come between them, and she didn't know what or why, only that she felt horribly left out on all fronts: with Lieutenant C. R. Molina, the Mystifying Max Kinsella, and now Mr. Midnight Matt Devine.

Temple was the youngest of a family of five brothers and the only girl. She ought to be used to feeling left out by now, but in fact the older she got the worse she felt about it. Would she never count? Was she always "too little" to tell, to take along, to trust, to treat like a mature adult?

"Temple?"

Matt was looking down at her, peering into her face as if reading some of her distress. Professional PR lady couldn't allow that!

"Yeah, what?"

"Uh, could you take your keys and open the door before I drop these jam-packed bags."

"Oh. I guess I overdid it at the store. I was . . . distracted."

"You? Buy groceries when you're distracted?"

"Well, you've been pretty distracted yourself lately."

"Busy," he said quickly.

"Right. Me too."

She still didn't move toward the door, but he started to brush past her as if expecting it to open on its own. *Open sesame*, wasn't that the formula? But Temple didn't think any magic phrases would work anymore, certainly not on her door, and maybe not on her, ever again.

The grocery bags ended up crushed between them so they actually had to look each other in the eye—eyes, which were so evasive and edgy and anxious that Matt took a giant step backward against the opposite wall and stood there like the boy with his finger in the dyke keeping out all the floodwaters of the North Sea, except he looked more like a carry out boy from Lucky's.

"Put . . . the . . . bags . . . down," she paraphrased Gene Wilder from *Young Frankenstein*.

Matt just looked bewildered. It was a vintage movie and Temple imagined one didn't see many movies in a Roman Catholic seminary unless they were about Lourdes or Joan of Arc.

But he put the bags down on the floor, propped up by the wall, and he put his hands in his pants pockets. And stood there, looking Brad Pitt-adorable if Brad Pitt had been really, really good-looking.

Temple leaned against her opposite wall and looked away. "It's been a bad day."

"I got that."

"First I had to listen to Molina tell me the sky was falling and then my new car decided it wouldn't even hold my groceries."

"Groceries? There won't be that many groceries if you return to your usual ways. You're not exactly Wolfgang Puck, you know."

"You mean Martha Stewart."

"If I was referring to your whole domestic mise-en-scène, yes, I would have meant that."

" 'Mise-en-scène'? That is giving my life way too high a profile. How about misery-en-scène?"

"Temple, what's wrong?"

"Wrong? Nothing. Max is in trouble so deep he won't talk to me about it, though Molina will, but nothing's wrong. You're running around with a sketch artist and won't talk to me, or even look at me, but nothing's wrong. Molina's gloating like a vampire at a blood bank and *she* won't tell me anything except that I'm moving in all the wrong directions, but nothing's wrong.

"There." Temple folded her arms and stared sullenly at her grocery bags slumping against the opposite wall next to Matt's khaki-clad legs. "Nothing's wrong."

He was silent for so long she was almost tempted to look up at him, but resisted. She felt very rebellious all of a sudden.

"I can see," he said finally, "why you'd think I was avoiding you, but it's just that late-night schedule of mine and the travel."

"That's a lie, Matt. You don't lie well. You want to avoid me."

"I don't *want* to—"

"Listen, you're free to do whatever you need to. I just thought that we were friends—"

"No."

She paused, startled into looking up.

"We might have been friends once, we might be friends once again. But now. Friends. We are not friends."

The wave of disbelief, of unallayed hurt that struck like the opposite wall moving and smashing her between it and the plaster at her back, was a tsunami.

Nothing, she saw, was what she had thought it was.

Lives were being lived apart from her, separate from her, and they were not what she assumed them to be.

Molina was right. She knew nothing.

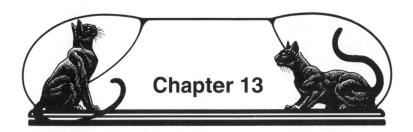

# Chapter 13

# Signals Received

Matt watched Temple's usual wall of blithe good cheer crumble into a shimmer of plaster dust around her.

He suddenly realized that of all of them, she knew nothing of the pervasive threats of Kitty the Cutter. He had confided in Molina. He had confided in Max Kinsella, of all penances the most painful. He had not breathed a word to Temple.

It was in the name of her own protection, but it had isolated her, infantalized her. His enemies and acquaintances he could tell. Temple, whom he most feared and most feared for, he had kept in the dark. And she knew it, sensed it, felt it.

"I'm sorry," she muttered. "I'll open the door. I can get the groceries in myself."

"We are not friends—"

She looked away again, in that heartbreakingly unfocused way too proud to show distress.

"—because we are too close to being something else. You know that. It's always been true."

Now she didn't dare look at him, and he found his hopeful, craven brain thinking, thinking . . . here, this tiny hallway. Not even *she* would, *could* have it bugged. Here. Now. Up against the wall. It would solve every dilemma but sin, and sin seemed such a small fault when hearts and souls were at stake.

"Not friends," she was saying faintly. "Oh, that's part of it, you know."

"I do know. Know more than I ever did before. And now I know that friends is not enough."

She stared at him, against her better judgment.

He understood he had the power. Just had to use it. He stepped forward, brought himself close to her. She didn't blink, didn't flinch, couldn't.

She'd always known, but had hoped he wouldn't, because then there'd be no one to say stop. No. The known norm is better than the imagined nirvana.

She knew more than he about what could be. He felt it, though, as he never had before, and his own self-interest was so strong, both subjugated to her and dominant over her, it was like sensing a hurricane in his heart.

His fingertips touched her shoulders.

Just that.

It seemed they stood in some still center while an electric dervish whirled around them.

Impulse mattered, not thought. Feeling, not fear.

He bent his head to hers.

She turned away.

He turned away.

They were closer than ever.

He turned.

She turned.

They couldn't avoid each other.

Always, always, turning, turning until they came round right.

Temple closed her eyes.

Anything, anything could happen. He could make it happen.

Suddenly the magnetism reversed itself. Or he did. He could make anything happen now, and he chose reversal.

They drew apart, leaned against their separate walls, said nothing.

"I don't understand," Temple said, her always dusky voice hoarse now. "But I will someday, won't I?"

"I hope so."

"Will I—" She hesitated, almost braced herself for something. "Will I ever understand why you knew that Molina had found my lost ring at a crime scene, and she told you and not me? And why you never told me that she had it?"

If she had wanted to throttle a moment and its aftermath, she had committed bloody murder right now.

"Ring?" he repeated, suddenly remembering the loathed object on his key ring: his own crime-scene memento. Only that crime scene had been his apartment.

"My ring. You know, the gorgeous opal-and-diamond-studded band Max got me in New York, that you both saw me wearing when you went together to the Opium Den to see Shangri-La perform."

"That ring."

"You make it sound so . . . common."

"I don't mean to. It was police business. Molina told me in confidence. She wanted me to distrust Kinsella more than I did already, maybe use it against him. I wouldn't be manipulated to hurt you. And then, the circumstances . . . it was a professional confidence. I didn't feel I could pass it on."

"The privilege of the confessional! Great. You were already with Molina that evening. Hand in glove. Why should I ever think you owed anything to me, even honesty?"

"She browbeat me into going with her that night. You know how she's always dogged both of us about Kinsella, trying to get us to crack, betray him. It was all part of her game plan."

"That Dragon Lady magician calling me up on stage and then making my ring disappear wasn't part of Molina's game plan."

"No, neither was your complete disappearance from the onstage chamber right after that."

"The one time I get to be part of audience participation at something," Temple went on bitterly, "and it turns out to be a kidnap attempt."

"Maybe worse," Matt said, his voice darkening. "Nothing we're talking about is anything to underestimate. You were abducted and that magician and her whole crew vanished. Then your ring was found later near where a woman had been strangled, an ex-magician's assistant, no less. Molina's games are not for the heck of it. She's trying to close down a lot of unsolved cases, and, like it or not, Max Kinsella seems to be at the heart of most of them."

"So. You're so busy now, with your own life and times, you should care about any of this, about me?"

"I care more than I can—"

"Wait. Let me finish. Or you do care, hallelujah, you care so much you'd like to see Max slapped in irons and taken away to death row, because then he'd be out of your way."

"No, Temple. What I care about or don't care about doesn't matter. It's what I'd do. I'd never hurt anyone for my own gain. But I can't betray a confidence either. Molina told me a piece of police business. I didn't want to know it. I understood that she was using me, that she was hoping I'd tell you and undermine your confidence in Max, don't you see? But I didn't do that. I honored her confidence and by doing that, I avoided being manipulated by her."

"You didn't avoid betraying *me*!" Temple's eyes burned with anger. "If we really were *friends*, you wouldn't try to protect me by concealing things from me. Maybe Molina was trying to drive you and me apart. Telling one person a secret that leaves another person out is a pretty time-tested way to do that."

"Molina has no personal interest in all this."

"Are you sure?"

"Molina? She's the Great Stone Mountain of the Metropolitan Police Department."

"Are you sure?"

Matt let his mind pull back, start wondering.

"Why is she so down on Max? Why does she never let up? Does she need a fall guy? Why does she try to use you to split Max and me apart? Does she really want Max? You? You've been thinking of her as a job, a function, a career, not as a human being. As a woman. Maybe she has agendas you haven't even imagined."

"And if she does, what was her agenda in showing you the ring? Now?"

They both paused, breathless, to consider their own charges.

" 'Oh, what a tangled web we weave,' " Temple quoted Sir Walter Scott.

" 'When first we practice to deceive'? That's not what we have

here. I don't think anyone wants to deceive," Matt said. "But to protect."

"Protecting means you put yourself above the protected. You know
better."

"It's a parental role, yes."

"Or a priest's?"

"Or an undercover operative's?"

"Or a policewoman's ?" Temple, laughed, not happily. "I guess
lowly PR flacks are stuck being the protectees. Nothing noble and
elevating about my job."

"Temple."

"I am tired of being protected by people meddling in my life for my
own good. It's my life. I'm allowed to mess it up all by myself."

"But not to lose it."

"That's what you're really worried about?"

He nodded, unable to speak, to voice the anxiety.

She relaxed a little.

"There's something you're not telling me, too. Just like Max and
the lieutenant. Join the club. I hate what people do to you for your
own good. I hated it when I was five years old and I hate it worse
now."

"It's worse when they think about doing something to you for their
own good, and not yours."

Her eyes grew suddenly shrewd. "That's what almost happened a
little while ago with you, didn't it?"

He nodded miserably.

That seemed to cheer her up considerably. "You were being selfish,
really?"

"Irresponsible," he admitted. Almost lethally irresponsible.

"So it wasn't my own good you were thinking of?"

"For a few, unforgivable seconds, no."

Temple let out a huge breath. "Well. At last! Somebody who's acting like a human being around me. What a relief!" Her voice grew
mischievous, if not quite flirtatious. "We'll have to try it again sometime."

Matt bent to pick up her groceries.

"I'll take the stuff in. Just go while you're ahead. That's what they
say at the craps tables."

He did.

He had never been so close to the perfect end of the fairy tale, but he realized that the witch would have been waiting to extract her price anyway. Temple wasn't his way out, no matter that she was the most tempting way out. He'd have to find another one.

That's when he knew that there were no perfect endings, just endless wishes that there were.

# Chapter 14

# *Disappearance Inc.*

I have spent the night not panicking.

This is hard to do when you are locked in a closet in a strange house that is hidden behind a forgotten cemetery. Especially when sharing said closet with you is a bunch of spooky magician's gear and a stiff stretched out on the floor like a rug du jour.

I mean this guy—and I have pussyfooted enough over the *corpus delicti* in the dark to know that it is a guy—is harder than the concrete they wrapped around Ugly Hugo Manicotti's tootsies before taking him to diving school in Lake Mead back in '59.

Eventually I settle down to the head's-up detecting I am noted for and realize that my closet corpse is so wooden for a reason: he is a giant-size Pinocchio, a mere dummy probably used in some body-switching illusion or another.

This is what comes of taking a supposed relative for a partner: the usually canny operative loses all sense of proportion when the partner in question goes missing.

I revise my previous conclusions. If Miss Louise had figured out the dead guy is really just deadwood, she would have had no compunction about moving on from our point of entry to other, more interesting, and thus more perilous, places. We two need to have a serious talk about not pressing forward on our own, leaving the senior partner in the dark quite literally.

I tromp over Dead Fred's nose, which is not prevaricatingly long (although the dummy maker must have had a sick sense of humor as something else on this anatomically correct stiff is), and nose the door open a smidge with my own admirably proportioned schnoz.

That it obliges my nudge tells me Miss Louise has gone this way. I slip out into the semidark and pull the door almost shut again.

Of course I am at a loss, while Miss Louise has obviously scouted this terrain previously.

I am really going to bawl her out for numerous acts unbecoming to a partner when I find her. I eye the room. It is vast, shadowy, and smells of mothballs and dustballs. I am guessing it is a mostly unused storeroom. The Cloaked Conjuror had hit Las Vegas like a leopard-spotted tornado only months ago. I imagine clandestinely finding and purchasing this hideout was a difficult job, and did not leave much time for dusting every nook and cranny.

Housekeeping is such a bore anyway, which is why it is better done by the female of the species. I note with disgust that my particular female of the species has carefully used her fluffy rear member to blur her distinctive footprints across the wood-plank flooring.

I must follow in her footsteps, but more slowly, lacking the built-in feather duster, as my aft member is long, strong, and buzz-cut. See what I mean about females being suited for domestic tasks?

After backing to the door and doctoring my trail with dust-busting swipes from my front mitts, I am able to nose another door open and survey a long hallway with the kind of railing that nasty Damien kid from the *Omen* films would love to push an unwary relative over.

I am nobody's unwary relative, not even Miss Louise's, so I look sharp both ways before pulling the door almost shut behind me— I believe in rapid retreats—and tiptoeing down the long, threadbare carpet that looks like something Queen Elizabeth tossed out at Windsor Castle. After the fire.

Wherever my wandering waif has gone, it is somewhere in a decaying mansion filled with the ancient traces of—I sniff the air—rats, bats, and . . . cats!

Somehow I do not believe that Miss Midnight Louise all by her lovely self in a few hours has accounted for the distinct attar of cats I sense in the air. Nor is that a lingering scent of days gone by, as is the essence of rat and bat.

These are contemporary cats. Alarmingly current cats, and of a strange, potent, malodorous breed I have not encountered before, not even in my wide and long travels.

That darn brat! She has rushed in where her elders would hesitate to tread, and now I have to get her out of trouble before anything drastic happens. I sniff again, though I am sadly lacking the specialized skills of even the smallest breed of dog. Ah! A waft of willfulness. An odor of the nunnery. A scent of superiority. Midnight Louie has his quarry and he will hunt her down.


Easier vowed than done.

I soon discover that the house is vast and rambling, a shadowed stucco labyrinth accessorized with enough black wrought-iron railings and lighting fixtures and hardware to supply the Spanish Inquisition for a couple hundred years.

Corners that aren't occupied by vintage magical artifacts are the property of empty suits of armor or such wall ornaments as fully loaded medieval cross-bows.

While human occupation seems distinctly sparse, I scent enough passing cat tracks to make me think the place is haunted by unseen felines. Maybe Los Muertos are really Los Gatos Muertos.

The hair rises on my hackles at that encouraging thought.

Worse, with all the Big Cat spoor, I cannot detect the delicate trail of Midnight Louise. It had been a black day (excuse the expression from the senior partner of Midnight Inc.) when she had undergone the politically correct procedure: it had neutered her scent trail as well as her feminine nature. Not that Miss Midnight Louise had ever displayed much of a feminine sensibility, before or after her operation.

I rest in the shadow of another of the empty-headed knightly guards and ponder what to do next. This joint must have as many rooms as a yuppie has flavors of exotic coffee to brew in the granite-kitchen-countertop Krups.

I think like a crook.

What would be the creepiest, most inaccessible, unsuspected part of this mausoleum where I could get up to nefarious doings uninterrupted?

There is only one answer. Well, two. Either the attic or the basement.

Now, basements are a rarity in Las Vegas. Hot climates don't lend themselves to cramped, damp, clay-walled holes in the ground. Most homes here are built on concrete slabs. Residents know that there is nothing creepier under their toes than some flattened scorpions crushed during construction.

Myself, I will take a dusty, dry old attic over a dank, dark basement any day,

Which is why I suspect this joint is old enough, and was lavish enough in its heyday, to have supported such a nice, built-in set decoration as a basement. I mean, the place already is a perfect setting for a slasher movie.

The only nice part about hunting for a basement is that the entrance is usually near my favorite part of any domicile: the kitchen.

So I pad over cool tile, keeping near the walls where I can always slink under a piece of furniture at a moment's notice. I finally find the stairs, snaking up the wall like a boa constrictor up a banana tree trunk.

And there I finally hear something: sound and motion in what has seemed until now a dark and deserted house.

It looks like I will be visiting the attic, after all.

And then I freeze, so still my whiskers would snap like whips if I were to move again.

I am not alone.

Not only that but the presence I now sense is not one of the many domestic cat trails I have crossed during my wanderings. It is not feline at all, which is odd in this house so marked by the presence of my kind, small or gigantic.

It is man. One man. As black as the night we share. I watch him move like a tide of shadow up the staircase, always rising, never seeming to move much, yet eating up steps like the ocean swallows sand.

I allow one whisker to twitch in recognition. Or tribute. It is the only human I would consider for a partnership in Midnight Inc. It is the incomparable cat burglar in the midnight cat suit. It is Mr. Max Kinsella himself out for an undercover stroll, right where I have decided all the action is. Or where it would be did either of us know what most of this action was about.

I wonder if Miss Temple knows that he goes wandering around at night without her.

I suppose she does. She is a very modern lady. She certainly knows that I do, and what is good for the Tomcat is good for the Maxman.

Frankly, I am pretty impressed by Mr. Max's savvy and nerve. He is a lot bigger and thus easier to spot than I am.

I decide to follow his lead and pour myself up the stairs like a sinuous Slinky toy defying gravity and going up, not down.

No one notices Mr. Max, and Mr. Max does not notice me.

That is the way it should be.

If only Miss Midnight Louise was not a loose cannon somewhere in the vicinity, I would not have a thing to worry about.

Not that I ever worry.

## Chapter 15

# *Vamp . . .*

Shaken by the imagined lethal consequences of his own scenario, Matt dialed Molina's office as soon as he got back to his apartment.

She had said "later." Now was later. Maybe too late.

"I've really got to talk to you privately right away," he said as soon as she answered, skipping the usual greetings, not even saying who he was. He sounded more like her than himself, but none of the usual social chatter seemed necessary anymore. "Right away."

"That's obvious," she said. "Where? You're apparently too freaked to tolerate a police station meeting."

"Freaked." The word made his mind speed down emotional dead ends like a rat navigating a maze of brain tissue. "I guess you could call it that. Some place where no one could draw the wrong conclusions. Some place . . . happenstance."

The other end of the line went silent. Finally: "One of the hotels?"

"No, a lot of bad stuff has happened in the hotels around here."

"You're not kidding."

"How about—?" He knew she wouldn't like it, but he did. "The Blue Dahlia."

"No."

"Why not?"

"I haven't shown up there in ages."

"Why not?"

"Because . . . none of your business."

"Because a woman's body was dumped in the parking lot, and it became your business, that's why. You really need to get back on that particular horse, Carmen."

"You're telling me what *I* need? You're the one with a stalker who won't let you breathe without looking in your rearview mirror."

"They must miss you at the club."

"I always came and went when it suited me. That was part of the deal."

"Part of the charm. You don't want to lose that outlet."

"Singing?"

"That, and being unpredictable."

"You think I've been predictable?"

"Lately? Yes."

A long silence on the phone. It wasn't just that being predictable was insulting. In her line of work it was dangerous.

"You oughta be a psychologist, Matt, anybody ever tell you that?"

"My guidance counselor in high school, and look where it got me."

"Okay, Mr. Midnight. Carmen rides the high C's again. The Blue Dahlia. Tonight. After nine. Watch your back."

Matt was smiling as he hung up. He felt the same satisfaction as when sweet reason had encouraged a radio caller to take a baby step past some personal stumbling block.

He understood why Lieutenant C. R. Molina needed to moonlight as the semianonymous jazz singer Carmen. No last name. Molina always said she sang because she could, and she was right: her voice was a terrible thing to waste, a smoky contralto born to carry '40s torch songs to the Casbah and back. But there was much more to her clandestine singing career than that.

Somewhere, far in the past, young Carmen had died a necessary death, resurfacing as the gender-neutral C. R. The only time her birth name came out to play was on the tiny stage of the Blue Dahlia and only when Lieutenant Molina decided to loosen the leash. Carmen showed up when she showed up. The trio that backed her knew that, and most often played sans vocals. The Blue Dahlia management knew that. The customers knew that.

And they all liked it that way. In her fashion, Molina was a magician, appearing when and where least expected, then vanishing again. It was odd she so detested Max Kinsella, since they had that arbitrary magical showmanship in common. But sometimes Like loathes Like just because it recognizes itself through a fun-house mirror darkly.

Matt found his thoughts jerked back toward the woman he really had to worry about: Kathleen O'Connor. Did he detest her because somehow, in some way, they had *too* much in common?

It made his skin crawl to consider such a hateful soul akin to his in any way, but the years as a priest had shown him that evil was almost always a distortion of good. Evildoers always had a self-justification. And so did inveterate do-gooders. Which made them closer relatives than either would care to admit. Killing and kissing cousins.

Matt decided it was time, a little late in fact, to search his rooms again for listening devices. Every time he left home, Kitty the Cutter could pay him a surreptitious visit. Would she have bugged Temple's hallway? The notion seemed ludicrous, but what would she do if she had heard, or seen, that surreptitious scene? Matt studied his sparely furnished three rooms, hunting hidden cameras. Having a stalker was like having a ghost for a roommate, a malign, murderous ghost with a license to kill in physical form.

THE BLUE DAHLIA.

The words were etched like acid on the black-velvet Las Vegas night: on the classic, cursive, lurid neon sign that made every bar in every podunk town across the country a little Las Vegas for the evening.

If Matt loved anything about Las Vegas, it was its neon. And the Blue Dahlia owned the epitome of the art form: a lush magenta blossom arching over the cool blue words like an orchid corsage from a long-ago prom, a 1940s prom, when girls wore shoulder pads and their hair rolled high at the sides to match, and guys wore fedoras and boutonnieres.

The parking lot asphalt should have been rained into patent-leather slickness to complete the film noir setting, but this was Las

Vegas, the desert Disneyland. The best it could do for any atmosphere was ersatz everything.

Matt parked the Hesketh Vampire near but not under one of the glaring security lights. He hadn't ridden the motorcycle in weeks, but he wanted any pursuer to dismiss this as a solitary outing. A man on a motorcycle traveled solo. Miss Kitty had shown a disconcerting interest in anyone he might pair up with.

Inside, the hostess, a wispy nineteen-year-old, mounted on those clunky Minnie Mouse platform shoes they all wore nowadays, showed him to a small round table for one. His chair faced the token parquet dance floor in front of the tiny stage. A trio as classic as a loaf of bread, a jug of wine, and thou occupied the tiny stage: a bassist, a saxophonist, and an electric keyboarder.

The music broadcast the relaxed yet jazzy insistence of updated Bach by Louis Armstrong. Be-Bach. You could let it be background Muzak, or get lost in the fascinating rhythms.

Matt used the oversize menu as a cover to study who was already there. He ordered a scotch on the rocks while he apparently dithered over the menu. His watch read 8:45 P.M.

No one had come in after him and only a scattering of customers littered the tables on a weeknight.

The quiet made him edgy. Expecting someone dangerous was more nerve-wracking than seeing him—her. It wasn't Molina's entrance that was the question mark but whether Miss Kitty would show up. And she might not look exactly as she had the last time he had seen her. He'd hope not! She'd worn motorcycle leathers then, like a punk London messenger boy. Before that . . . he'd always remember the day he'd first seen her at the Circle Ritz poolside, immaculate in a green silk pantsuit that matched her eyes, her Snow White coloring as startling as a billboard of a chorus girl in its high-colored photogenic perfection.

A new instrument was harmonizing with the trio, meaningless syllables riffing up and down the scale in inspired improvisation.

Matt shot a look at the stage. She was there now. Appeared from nowhere like a musical magician. Carmen. In the soft single spotlight, a portable mike in hand, she wore her draping long black velvet gown like a '30s socialite in a Marx Brothers movie, a flash of bare arm through the shoulder slits the only pale spot on her figure besides her face in its dark helmet of hair.

Oddly enough, Matt found the feminine side of Molina more intimidating than the plain-Jane facade she wore on the job. She was a big woman, just shy of six feet, and there was nothing delicate about her bones or her blandly practical manner and manner of dress. But here she donned some of that '40s dame toughness, even as her voice toyed with and tortured the rainy day lyrics and throaty sounds of Gershwin.

Matt could guess why she kept her songtress side under wraps. A singer sells raw emotion and that can make a performer seem vulnerable, especially throbbing out the torch songs Carmen was born to croon.

Matt didn't see vulnerability as a weakness, but as a strength. Being human made it possible to rise above human fears. Molina was one of the few people in the world he felt was competent to handle anything, whatever she called herself, or whatever she wore. And despite the words of woe she sang so eloquently.

So he relaxed more deeply at the Blue Dahlia than he had allowed himself to do for days. When the waiter returned he ordered the sirloin tips in béarnaise sauce, a baked potato, as if he was actually going to enjoy this excuse for a secret meeting.

And he did. Everything had arrived and been savored by the time Carmen's set ended at ten o'clock.

Matt studied the tables. Ebbing diners had been replaced by ranks of drinkers, who chattered now that the music was instrumental again.

No one who could have been Kathleen O'Connor in disguise or out of it remained in the room.

Matt left cash in the padded leather bill holder, got up, and followed Carmen's exit through a narrow green velvet curtain spotted with fingerprints.

The short hall beyond led past a cigarette machine and the restrooms to a couple of closed doors. It smelled of cooking oil and spilled Coca-Cola.

Matt knocked softly at each door. The second produced a muffled "Come in."

The room beyond wasn't large but the huge circular mirror on a vintage dressing table reflected almost his full figure in the doorway.

He looked out of place in his khakis and lightweight navy nylon jacket. No fedora. No striped suit. No red carnation in his button hole.

Molina wasn't sitting at the table but leaned against one of the pillars of drawers on either side.

"I'm going to kill you," she announced.

"Not you, too."

"My threat is serious. Do you know what you've done? My voice is creaky, the range is shaky. I can't believe that a few weeks off could work such ruin."

"You sounded great. Very Barbara Stanwick."

"Yeah, thanks. She didn't sing." Molina shook her head. Her no-fuss bob wasn't quite in period but somehow seemed to match the shabby nightclub ambiance. She pulled the blue silk dahlia from the side of her hair. It contrasted dramatically with the only visible makeup she wore, a dark-lipsticked '40s mouth, but a moment later it lay on the pedestal like a crumpled blue tissue, frail and expendable looking, like a dead stripper.

Matt knew that the recent unsolved death of just such a blossom in the dust was gnawing at Molina's professional and personal life.

"Odd," he said.

"What?"

"We've both got similar problems."

She arched her dark eyebrows that Temple always fussed could use a plucking. Matt saw them as a strong frame for the remarkable blue-dahlia eyes that were her most memorable feature, as coolly hot as neon.

"You've got a killer who just barely eludes you," Matt explained, "and I've got a killer I can't quite manage to elude."

"So what's your nemesis up to now?"

"A nemesis is an avenger seeking justice. Kitty O'Connor isn't that. She doesn't even know me. She's a . . . persecutor."

"What's she done now?" Molina looked like she should be lighting an unfiltered cigarette, but she wasn't.

"She showed up where I work."

"The radio station."

"Yeah. I was leaving for the night, the morning, actually. About one-thirty, with my producer. And this figure came racing in on a Kawasaki Ninja, leather-wrapped from neck to toe. She charged us like a bull on that cycle, tore a necklace right off Letitia's neck, then went roaring off flourishing it as a trophy."

"Intimidation."

"I know what it was. I want to know how to stop it."

"What did you do then?"

"Tried to keep between her and Letitia. Tried to grab a handlebar and tip the cycle over. Not much that worked."

"She's just harassing you at this point, not doing any real damage."

"She did real damage her first time out."

Molina glanced at his side. Matt could feel the scar, the tightness, if he thought about it. He felt it when he made any major move. A razor slash, now a faint long, thin, white line, like a wound just before the blood wells to the surface and overflows.

"She seemed to be taking something out on your producer," Molina said finally. "Showing off to you and hassling the lady."

"Right. She doesn't like me to associate with any females. That's pretty clear."

"What sort of female is your producer?"

Matt hesitated at the impossibility of summarizing Letitia. "Gorgeous black woman, maybe thirty, maybe three hundred pounds."

"Three hundred pounds. And this psycho chick was jealous?"

"I don't know if it's jealousy exactly. It's more like . . . possession. Yeah, I know that's a form of jealousy, but Kitty O'Connor is more like a demon than a woman."

"Whoa! You *are* spooked. She's a sick chick with issues, that's all. I am not in the demon-exorcizing business and I think you'd know better than that by now."

Matt stuffed his hands in his pockets to keep the fists his frustration made from showing. "This O'Connor woman is a wasteland of spiritual desolation. You can't reach her by any human means. So don't call her a demon, although that works for me. Call her a psychopath."

"She hasn't done anything you could even get a restraining order for. You can't prove the slash."

"It's not me I'm worried about. It's what she might do to someone around me."

"Listen, this town is teeming with dangerous types. You have no idea what you're brushing up against as you amble down the Strip on a Friday night. If the police are doing their job, and we mostly are, you and the tourists will never know."

Matt held his tongue for a while. It ached to pour out the strange history of Kitty O'Connor. If he could only tell Molina about her connection to Max Kinsella. . . . But Molina bared her teeth like a Rottweiler when any scent of Kinsella tainted the air. And those confidences weren't Matt's to share. Though he wasn't still a priest, he was used to keeping the seal of the confessional, to keeping everybody's secrets in their individual, sacrosanct boxes, like little coffins containing rotting lilies left over from the thousand natural wakes a human being holds for all past sins and uncertainties.

All he could say was, "I know she was fanatically involved in the IRA. She would seduce wealthy men for money to buy weapons. I imagine she was downsized from her job during the recent seesaw of peace accords. I'd guess she's an unemployed terrorist looking for a victim."

Molina nodded seriously, but her eyes narrowed. "We're all taking that pretty seriously nowadays. How do you know about her international terrorism history?"

Matt wasn't about to blurt out, "Max Kinsella." He flailed for a logical dodge that would still salve his Catholic conscience for truth at all costs. "Ah, Bucek. Frank Bucek at the FBI. He was in seminary with me. We've talked on the phone a little. He looked her up."

"Bucek looked her up for you when he couldn't give me diddly?"

"Fellow ex-priests . . ."

"Fellow guys, you mean."

Before Molina could wind up some feminist rant, someone knocked on the door. "Bar call," a man's jovial voice caroled.

Molina looked inquiringly at Matt.

"Scotch on the rocks," he finally thought to say. She yodeled a double order of same through the door.

"Sit down." She pointed to one of those round-seated wooden chairs with the bentwood backs that was stained so dark it looked like it had been sitting here awaiting him for decades. Probably had.

Matt took the seat, though it was uncomfortable, and Molina finally sat in a matching chair placed before the dressing table.

She shook her head at herself, her face as sharp-boned as Lauren Bacall's in the time-spotted mirror. "Sometimes I expect Bogey to stroll in here asking about Maltese falcons. Those were the days: treacherous greedy crooks, psychopaths disguised as cheap hoods, and manipulative dames. Okay." She scraped the chair legs on the concrete floor to turn her back to the mirror.

As she braced her elbows on the matching pillars, Matt was startled to see in the mirror the black velvet curtain of her dress part in back from neck to waist. She couldn't have been wearing, well, anything under it. This was not something he wanted to think about here and now, or anywhere at any time, really.

A knock at the door.

"Enter!" Molina called out grandly.

The barman came in carrying one of those small, round, scuffed brown trays that have held drinks since Methuselah was a wine steward.

"Thanks, Steve." Molina watched him set the tray on the opposite drawer pillar like an offering. "I love to impress company with my lavish backstage perks."

Steve, a toothy guy with receding gray hair, grinned. "Courtesy of the management. We're glad to have you back."

He winked at them both in the mirror as he left.

"They pay you for this?" Matt asked suddenly.

"Yeah, they pay me for this." Molina sounded indignant. "I wouldn't do an amateur gig. Lots of cops moonlight. This is less conflict of interest than most."

"I didn't mean . . . what I meant is they're happy to pay to have you back."

She leaned forward to hand him a lowball glass richly amber with about three ounces of scotch. He sipped. Johnnie Walker Black. Very happy to have her back.

He sipped again, feeling tension drain down his arms like a bloodletting. "This is the first time I've felt out of that woman's reach for two weeks."

Molina lifted her own glass in a distant toast. "Happy to hear that. What's the reason?"

"A bodyguard?" he said, laughing.

"You aren't kidding." She crossed her legs.

The motion would have been coy in another woman clothed in floor-length vintage black velvet, but now it simply revealed the small, lethal-looking gun attached to her ankle by some industrial-strength black holster of nylon webbing.

Matt almost choked on a quarter ounce of scotch too good to spray on the concrete floor. "Do you always do that?"

"Always," she said. "Nobody's going to die because I was in a Luby's Cafeteria with my gun in the car."

He nodded, remembering the case, another massacre in a public place by a single psycho gone ballistic. And that brought them back to Miss Kitty. "I can't carry a gun. I can't shoot her. So that makes me a perpetual victim?"

Molina nodded while she savored her drink. "This ought to oil the old pipes for the next set. You are keeping me up late tonight, Mr. Midnight." She twisted to check a small clock on the dressing table.

"No problem. I'm not due at work for a couple of hours."

She glanced at his glass. "Can you drive—?"

"I had a heavy meal."

"Then enjoy. I imagine you haven't enjoyed much lately. Back to your . . . bête noir? Is that better than 'nemesis'? Here's the deal. Here's what every woman with an abusive ex on her tail finds out. Nothing and nobody can help you. If you were a woman, I'd advise you to get a gun and shoot the guy the next time he showed up. No, I wouldn't. I can't. But that's the only defense they've honestly got, a lot of them. I am so damn sick of picking up the phone and hearing some woman was blown away in the parking lot of her office, or a grocery store, or a fast-food joint, or a day-care facility, or a school by some maniac man who can't let go because he can't live without a victim.

"And it's always just when the woman finally gets a little starch and tries to get away, when she's defending her kids where she couldn't defend herself, when she's being a heroine instead of a whipping girl, and then they kill her.

"Enough about my job frustrations. Now, about yours. Your job is to *foil this woman.* You can't give her what she wants."

"That's what Letitia said."

"Letitia."

"My producer."

"Oh, right. The Lane Bryant black Venus. You know, this Kitty woman is nuts. She really wants you."

"Thanks."

"No." Molina leaned forward, elbows on her knees, a hoydenish posture for the elegant gown. She sipped premium scotch. "She's dead serious about that. She wants you untouched by any woman. Weird. It's not an uncommon attitude among abusive men, but women aren't usually so . . . macho."

"That biker outfit was plenty macho."

"Why you?"

Matt wanted to shout, *Because she can't torment Max Kinsella. She can't even find Max Kinsella.*

But he couldn't. He did have a few clues as to why he was the designated Kinsella stand-in, though.

"She likes to corrupt priests."

"You know the answer then."

He nodded. "Letitia laid it out for me, too."

Molina sipped. Her electric blue eyes were softening to the color of natural blue topaz, Virgin Mary Blue, mild and misty. "You need an understanding woman who will remove that which Miss Kitty covets."

"Who won't get killed for the honor," Matt added drily. "Hell hath no fury like a woman scorned."

"I don't think so. She's nervous. That's why she's darting around, threatening these women. Once the deed is done, you're worth nothing to her. The whole house of cards falls down. Anticipate her, disarm her. Hell, sleep with her then, if you want to. It would kill her."

"Carmen. I'm not like that. I don't do these things lightly."

"That's where she's got you! You want to be got, cling to your odor of sanctity. You want to live, do what you must."

" 'And do it well.' "

"Huh?"

"A quote from a songwriter you'd never sing. Well, maybe you would." Matt took a deep, burning swallow of scotch.

"Any candidates to predate Miss Kitty?" Molina probed, perhaps a bit too curious.

"Nobody I'm willing to endanger," he said shortly, swallowing without the benefit of scotch, the afternoon's interlude in the Circle Ritz hallway returning on aching waves of might-have-been.

"No volunteers?" she pressed. Matt noticed that her lipstick had left a red half-moon on the edge of her glass, decided through a veil of pleasant haze that they were both relaxing too much, discussing things too dangerous to act on. Guns and sex and psychosis. "A good-looking guy like you?

"Janice? Letitia?" She left one name hanging until he thought he'd strangle on it. Why had he ever thought Molina might become an ally? She was a policewoman. She always needed to know the full story.

"No woman strong enough to risk."

"Ah." She leaned back, elbows braced on the twin pillars of the dressing table, the drink glowing topaz against the black of her gown. Molina?

God, he must be drunk.

But the idea started caroming through his brain. She was armed and dangerous. She just said she thought he was good-looking. Lots of people did, but Molina *saying* it . . . thinking it.

If he was caught in some sexless limbo because of his religious past, she was a single mother in a man's world. What kind of personal life did she have? Did she dream, as Janice did, of an Invisible Man who would come through her window, a puppet with no strings attached, like Errol Flynn on a rope, and go away leaving no traces, no obligations, no guilt, like a dream?

But there were always hordes of swordsmen after Errol Flynn as Don Juan or as Robin Hood, and a dalliance with a wanted man always backfired on the woman, even if her ankle was armed. Molina was not invulnerable, just professional.

She was not strong enough to risk, but he didn't dare tell her that.

"I can't. I can't involve any woman in this who might be the object of Kitty's murderous attention."

"Hmm," said Molina. Carmen. Looking lazy and contemplative, looking pretty luscious, as a matter of fact, maybe because of what she was thinking. He was thinking it too. Where had his friendly neighborhood earth mother gone? Luscious? He must be deranged.

Matt set the half-full glass of scotch on the small table near the wall. He had to be on live radio in under two hours.

"I just came here for some professional advice."

Her eyes suddenly focused in points like acetylene torch flames.

"Professional. From the mouths of babes. That's it, Matt!"

"What?"

"You need a professional. Someone Kitty wouldn't even notice. A pro."

"With a gun?"

"No! Listen. This is Las Vegas. *Las Vegas*. You get yourself a six-hundred-dollar-a-night room at the Oasis. The Goliath. Whatever. You tip everyone in sight, and you ask the bellman to send up some private entertainment. Tip him a hundred."

"Carmen!"

"Listen. I know this town. A hundred. You can afford it to save your virtue for the right wrong girl, right? Okay. For that you'll get a thousand-dollar call girl. She'll be beautiful, intelligent, gorgeously dressed, consider herself a sex industry professional, not some cheap, downtrodden hooker. She'll argue her right to sell her services with such sophistication that you won't have an answer. You'll tell her your problem, not about Kitty the Cutter but your personal history. She will *love* helping you out. She considers herself a mental-health field worker and, besides, you're not hard to help out. You will walk out of there much poorer, but not what Kathleen O'Connor wants: an innocent man. You will have endangered no one. The call girl will vanish from the hotel as she always does, with a great story to entertain another john. You will be absolutely . . . adequate, right? You will have taken advantage of no one, as talking to one of these awesome sexual entrepreneurs will convince you. They are nobody's victims, believe me, and consider themselves worth every c-note. It'll be *Pretty Woman* all over again, only with this strange role reversal all the way through. Make sense?"

"Carmen. No."

"Why not? It's brilliant. It's a scam. You out-sting the stinger. Why not?"

"Because . . . it's a sin."

"So is caving in to a sexual blackmailer. So . . . confess it afterward. You believe in absolution, don't you? Don't you have to?"

"Yes. But—"

" 'Yes, but' are the two most dangerous words in the language. Do it or pay for not doing it. Wait to see which innocent woman will pay. Maybe Temple Barr. This Kitty doesn't sound blind, just demented."

Matt fingered the key ring in his pocket, feeling the hard cold, gold circle of the snake ring spinning against his skin. He remembered how it had appeared in his apartment, with the equivalent of an Alice in Wonderland note: *Wear me.* The controlling Miss Kitty clandestinely invading his space again, claiming his attention.

It reminded him of Molina's cold-blooded investigative strategy in keeping the whereabouts of Temple's ring secret. In then sharing its whereabouts with him so he became complicit in her cruelty. He wanted to protest their conspiracy of silence he had only broken when Temple had figured it out. To accuse her, excuse himself.

But the damage had been done. To Temple, not to Kinsella, whom

Molina really ached to hurt, nor to him, who had been the stooge, the patsy.

Temple's ring was recorded history now. The ring Kitty O'Connor had forced him to install on his keyring was still a secret, still an issue, still lethal.

Still the eternal threat, the Worm Ouroboros, wanting to slip onto a finger like greased lightning and burn him, and never, ever come off.

# Chapter 16

# . . . and Revamp

"I'll think about it," Matt said. He already had, far too long. "I suppose it'd be easy to lose Kathleen if I dodged into a megahotel."

"Use a phony name. Pay cash at the front desk like a big winner. Take one room there and then call down and change it. Find something wrong. Somebody smoked in a nonsmoking suite, that kind of thing."

"You've got some tricky ideas."

"Not me. Everybody I've ever arrested. So." Molina's wild-blue-yonder gaze softened with scotch and satisfaction. "You gonna take my professional advice?"

"I don't know. I'll think about it."

He stood, took one last sip of the very fine scotch and left.

In the hall he could hear the trio killing time until Carmen's next set with jazzy crescendoes. He kind of liked this place, right here. Alone in the hall, between the dressing room and the stage, the public. Ignored, invisible.

He moved along, wove through the clotted round tables, arranged to be intimate and now in the way.

It was a weeknight. He had dragged Carmen in for a half-empty house, but she probably appreciated warming up with only chairs to hear her rusty voice. Most of the chairs were empty now.

So was the parking lot when he pushed open the big door with the round porthole window. Round windows seemed so decadent, as if blocking out a sinister subaquatic world.

He homed on the familiar tilted shape of the Hesketh Vampire, appreciating its sleek lines from a distance, savoring a fondness you'd feel more for a horse than a vehicle.

A nondescript black car sat between the faded white lines a few spots away. That was all. Matt knew the staff parking lot was on the other side of the building. This lot was for customers and, a few weeks ago, the dumped body of a dead woman.

He winced a bit to recall her. Killed for not being quite Catholic enough in someone else's warped view, when he might be killed for being too Catholic.

Why dumped here? Because the killer had associated The Blue Dahlia with nightlife and corruption.

He reached in his pants pockets for the cycle keys, eyed the waiting helmet, almost craving its anonymity, its implied safety.

A small click in the night.

Maybe the touch of a high heel on the asphalt.

Maybe the snick of a switchblade.

Maybe the mechanism of an opening car door.

Maybe all three.

Matt whirled to face the dark car with its windows black-tinted like a limousine's. It was a boxy, anonymous vehicle. He couldn't even name the model and maker.

It looked like a cut-rate hearse to him.

Someone was stepping out of it.

*Stepping out with my baby . . .*

A woman.

*. . . a face in the misty light . . .*

No, not Laura from forties film noir . . . just Kathleen. Kitty. Any haunting songs written for such a common name or nickname? Only raucous Irish ditties and a soulful Celtic ballad or two.

*I'll take you home again, Kathleen . . .*

She wore something long, dark, and glittering. It hung from rhinestone straps on her shoulders. She was done up like a disco prom queen. Her high heels clicked on the pavement as she approached. Scarlet rhinestones dripped like blood from her earlobes. Not rhinestones maybe, rubies . . .

She clutched not a gun but a small, bejeweled purse shaped like a kumquat. The innocuous bag was more suggestive, more chilling. What was in it? A folded razor? A tiny automatic pistol? A lipstick case? A vial of poison? Or of holy water?

"Don't be in such a hurry," she said. "The Midnight Hour is still a lifetime away."

He was alone this time. He didn't have to worry about her hurting anybody else. He moved toward the motorcycle again. It could outrun any car.

"You've come here before," she called after him, softly as a song. Her voice still held the faintest musical lilt of Ireland, a siren's lure. "I was wondering why."

He didn't pause.

"Actually, I was wondering *who*."

He turned, stopped, spoke. "What a small world you occupy, Kathleen O'Connor. There is not always a why, or a who. Sometimes there's a what. Not for you, though. You're hooked on whys and whos. That's what makes you so ignorant."

"*Me!* Ignorant? I've lived all over the world, visited casinos that make Las Vegas look like Disneyland for the double-wide set. I've drunk the finest wines, worn designer jeans that cost more than that whole damn motorcycle—"

"Impressive," Matt said without stopping or turning.

"If you really want to be impressed, maybe you should peek in the backseat of my car."

Her voice wasn't musical anymore, but raw, as metallic as a zipper slowly opening, grating. Kitty was sure that what she was about to reveal was raunchy but irresistible.

Matt knew it was a mistake not to resist, but her voice had become so smugly threatening . . .

He turned. Kitty O'Connor cut a sophisticated figure in the blue-green parking lot glow. The car behind her was a shiny black box. He remembered sensing it as a hearse. Whose hearse?

He started toward it, she spinning and clicking on those high heels to reach it first, as if now they were in a race. Her staccato steps reminded him of Temple, but he didn't want even her name crossing his mind in the presence of Kitty O'Connor.

The woman had paused by the back door on the driver's side of the four-door sedan to unlatch the hard little jeweled bag. She brought out something black and oblong. A remote control. The car's rear window opened with a can-opener whirr.

It sliced open on a band of red hair. Matt's heart stopped, but the window kept descending until a third of the way down. He saw frightened eyes and a duct-taped mouth, like a robot's featureless silver orifice pasted onto a human face.

Matt's heart throbbed like a jungle drum as he recognized not the fractured face but the mane of red hair: the teenaged fan from last night at the radio station parking lot.

The window was rising again like a dry dark tide, obscuring the terrified eyes and obscenely cheerful red hair. Had Kitty chosen the girl because she had been there, or because her hair was red?

"She's just an—" he began.

"Innocent bystander?" Kitty tucked the remote control back into her purse as casually as if it was a cigarette case. "My favorite kind. Besides, I don't buy your assumption that anyone is innocent. Even you."

"I never claimed I was."

"You claimed you were a good priest."

"A good priest isn't innocent. A priest needs knowledge of evil."

"You must be an even better priest now," she said, slithering forward like vamp on a nighttime soap opera.

"A priest needs knowledge of evil," he repeated, "like a seductress needs a touch of innocence to be believable. Seducing me won't work."

"Just remember the girl in the backseat. Next time she might be somebody you really know."

He choked back his anger at her constant threats, her theatricality. Did she need to be the star of her own show this much? Apparently. And what did that tell him about her?

"Relax," she was saying. "I've planned a quiet evening for just the two of us. And"—her dark head jerked over her shoulder toward the closed window—"she can't see us. No one inside the car can see out except the driver. Aren't you wondering who the driver is?"

He hadn't considered that. If Kitty was not alone tonight, if she had a hostage, she might also have an accomplice. An accomplice was needed for what? Chauffeuring? Ferrying captives . . . carrying bodies?

"A quiet evening—?" he repeated to gain time.

"Sure." She walked around to the car's front passenger side.

He heard the heavy metal door open, then Kitty began unloading objects onto the car's long black hood. Two champagne flutes. A silver ice bucket. A green bulbous bottle of Perrier-Jouët twined by painted art nouveau flowers.

"Come here," she said.

He didn't, of course.

"Come here or I'll have to get my petite straight razor from my purse and attempt to cut that poor child's duct tape off."

She poured one tall flute too full of champagne, and waited.

He moved in her direction, around the front of the car, wondering if her anonymous driver had orders to run him down.

But the engine stayed dormant and only the bubbles in the long tall glass moved.

They spun frantically for the lip of the glass, pearly strings and ropes twirling up like deep sea divers trying to outrun the bends. Bubbles, tiny bubbles of frantic, tiny final breaths.

A tearful bound girl trapped in a stranger's car with her mouth taped, breathing anxiously through her nose, fighting for each breath as congestion clogged her sinuses and nostrils.

"Let her go."

"No."

"Let her go, or I go."

"You wouldn't. You couldn't."

He shrugged, walked away, turned his back on the bubbles.

"You don't dare risk it," her hoarse whisper called after him.

He heard furious heel clicks, rapid, angry.

The whirr of a car window opening. The driver showing himself? Pointing a gun?

He kept walking.

Heard a muffled cry.

Turned.

Kitty stood beside the rear car door, now gaping open, the young woman tumbled to the asphalt in a fetal position, still bound, still gagged. Eyes still wide open.

"There. She's out. On her own. I'll leave her here. Now, come back."

Kitty strode around to the car's long front hood gleaming like a black steel coffin and lifted the heavy champagne bottle, a hostess as impervious as patent leather.

"It's rude to walk away when you're the guest of honor."

At least now the car couldn't take off with the girl captive.

Matt obeyed, or, rather, did what he thought was best at the moment, which was to seem to obey.

She poured another shaft of champagne trembling with manic bubbles as he approached and handed him the glass, her hand rock steady.

She sipped. He followed suit, wondering what playing her game would get him or cost him.

Her payoff was instantly obvious. Satisfaction. She fairly purred with it, arched her dark eyebrows, licked the smoothly rolled glass rim of the flute as if it were jagged and she had a taste for blood, even, perhaps, her own. Or perhaps mostly her own.

Matt rolled that idea around on his tongue as he swallowed the madly fizzing wine. He'd never thought of champagne as a hyperactive beverage before, manic, bipolar, as ready to go flat as erupt.

Like Miss Kitty?

Could he drag her down to the dark side of her nature? Depress her? Paralyze her?

"This is a joke," he said. "A scene out of a B movie."

"My movie, not yours."

So control was everything. She unholstered the remote again and aimed it at The Blue Dahlia, at the roofline along the building's side.

Instantly, a few blue notes of sound came rolling over the parking lot.

" '*Someone to watch over me*'," crooned a homicide lieutenant, spreading her vocal wings after too long in a cramped cage.

Matt couldn't help turning his head to puzzle out the illusion; the band sounded as if it had moved outdoors.

"How'd you do that? Never mind. Not telling me is half the fun. But why the sound effects?"

"You come here to hear the music, right? Can't be the food?"

"It's not too bad."

Her shiny dark head shook. "Must be the music. Tell me the truth."

"The music," he agreed. "The name of the place. Getting away from anyone who knows me. I don't know."

"Liar!"

He kept quiet, wondering if she'd already figured out the connection between him and Molina.

"You're trying to get away from someone you *know*," she accused instead. "*Someone who watches over you.*"

Her smile emphasized a mouth painted rambling rose red, a pretty mouth, small and pointed, not particularly sensual, almost pleasant peeling back over those small pearly teeth.

*Oh, the shark, dear . . .*

"Is that what you think you're doing? Protecting me?"

"Protecting my investment." She came nearer, set her champagne flute down on the hood. "Let's dance."

"I don't."

"You will."

"When someone's lying helpless and terrified only feet away?"

"Of course. The whole world dances when someone's lying helpless and terrified only feet away. Haven't you watched the evening news? But don't ruin our outing with politics. Aren't you glad I didn't come in and upset the help? We can have our evening out here, under the stars."

She took the glass from his fingers and set it on the hood. The surface curved, so everything on it tilted, faced imminent falling, destruction. The whole world tilted, facing the same fate, particularly his tiny corner of it.

Had Kitty somehow learned of his long-ago "prom" expedition into the desert with Temple? But how? Impossible. Yet she was duplicating it in some devilish way. Maybe that was how; she was the demon Molina would never believe in.

Molina.

She might be closing down her set and coming out soon, but to a different parking lot.

Did he want Molina to come to the rescue? Could she end up a captive?

While he worried, Kitty had insinuated herself against him, broadcasting an elusive, probably expensive perfume. Her curled hand rested on his shoulder like a fallen blossom. Her other hand was slipping into his palm where the champagne flute had been.

*. . . a face on a passing train*

This was so bizarre, and to hear Molina's voice wafting over the empty parking lot . . .

Kitty started swaying against him, seductive no doubt. Besides his deep disinclination to respond to anything she offered, despite the haunting image of that innocent girl as a mute witness to this insane scene, the real turn-off was her choice of music to seduce by, her Mantovani and Iglesias and Rod Stewart all rolled into one was a moonlighting homicide lieutenant's dusky contralto.

"You *don't* dance," she was saying. "I'd shuffle a few steps, if I were you. Your faithful fan is out of the car but not out of reach." She prodded a long fingernail into his chin.

Matt shuffled, resenting the infringement of her body, relieved that he felt absolutely no interest in mere proximity.

"Let's do talk politics," he said.

"As long as you dance."

"You must sincerely believe in the Irish cause."

"Must I? I mustn't do anything, haven't you figured that out by now? I could have a folded razor in the hand that's on your shoulder. It would take a millisecond to cut your face to shreds."

Her sensed her hand, a loose fist at the corner of his eye. It could indeed hold a weapon.

He suddenly took control of her other hand, so lightly laid in his, and spun her out, away from him. "Maybe we should swing dance."

The sudden move surprised her, maybe even pleased her. She caught her breath like a teenager, laughing a little.

He suppose it had felt like being on a thrill ride, and Kitty the Cutter liked thrills. Maybe needed them.

She tried to close in again, but he took her other hand off his shoulder and kept moving away, remembering patterns he'd seen on PBS shows about jazz and swing music. That kind of dancing was a constant tension: pull close, push away. Not so different from the choreographed discipline of the martial arts. With Kitty the Cutter, dancing was a martial art and Matt had just figured out the steps.

Luckily, Molina had swung into an up-tempo song.

*Jeepers, creepers.*

She wasn't kidding, and that *kid'll eat ivy, too.*

"Apparently," Kitty said, not unhappily, "you like fast dancing."

"I like anything that keeps you at arm's length."

"You can't keep me there forever."

"No, but this'll do for now, while we talk."

"What's to talk about?"

"That girl. You'll leave her here, unharmed?"

"This time."

"So what do you want tonight?"

"Where's your ring? I should say *my* ring? The deal is you have to wear it."

"It's here. In my pocket."

"That's not 'wearing'."

"I'm wearing it on my key ring. You didn't say where I had to wear it. I suppose I could wear it around my neck."

"Splitting meanings, just like a damn politician. Or a priest. How many angels dance on the head of a red-haired girl?"

Matt's heart stopped, hoping that Kitty meant only the unknown girl she'd kidnapped from the radio station. Had she held her captive since then? Or only taken her tonight? How many angels danced on the head of Temple Barr? An entire chorus.

"Just one," Matt answered Kitty, more blithely than he felt. "One guardian angel."

"Who?" The jeer twisted her beautiful features—Snow White, the fairest of them all, suddenly the Wicked Stepmother. "You? You can't even protect yourself from me."

"Guardian angels are invisible, Kathleen. Don't you remember that from catechism? No one can see them, not even the soul they guard. You have one, you know."

"Fairy tales! Like Santa Claus."

She was getting breathless from spinning in close and out far. Matt kept it up, relentlessly. She wanted contact, she would get it. He was in control, her hands in his, unable to wound. She had only her voice.

"I don't believe in Santa Claus," he said as they seesawed in and out, moving in small, furious circles on the asphalt. What would make her let him go, so he could help the young woman?

"The music's stopped, so can we," she said.

"Has it? I hear music."

He moved to an unheard rhythm, like telling the beads on an endless rosary, rote motion. The car sat as if abandoned with the battery dead. He doubted there was a driver. Only Kathleen O'Connor, a one-woman terrorism squad. And now she was breathless putty in his hands.

She craved control. To use it and perhaps to feel the object of it, as well.

"They'll be coming out. The band," she said. "Now that they've stopped."

"What do you care?"

"You . . . you're crazy."

"That's projection."

She tried to wrench her hands out of his. "Psychoshit! You're all full of it."

"All who? I'm only one guy."

"No, you're not. Your name is legion."

He laughed. "Now I'm the demon." He spun her quickly 360 degrees, lifting his arm so she twirled, a human top. Her long, snaky earrings flashed like comets.

She reeled a little as he resumed the relentless step in, step out, pull her close, push her away motions.

"You mean my ex-profession," he said, a little breathless himself. "We priests are all alike."

"Yes! Liars and hypocrites."

"Some, I suppose. There are some of those everywhere. Are you so perfect then?"

"No, but I admit I'm bad. I know I'm bad. I don't pretend to try to be good."

"Sometimes pretending to be something is the only way to become it."

"A liar's way. Is that what you are, someone who pretended to be a priest?"

She glared as he pulled her in, her eyes pure hatred now, the seductive veneer rubbed away like a cloud of silver polish on a mirrored tray.

"And are you pretending to be a temptress, an assassin? I don't think so. I think you've done all that. I think you're exactly what you want the world to think of you as: a very bad girl."

She finally was able to pull one hand free, although it must have hurt.

He let the other go. She was dizzy now, not only from the dance but from something inside of her he had released. It wasn't pretty, but at least her actions were hurting her for a change, instead of some-body else.

"Then don't mess with me. Don't make me do something you'll regret."

"Either way, I'll regret it."

She smiled, tilted her small, dainty head. "Now you understand. It's a lose-lose situation. You might as well get it over with."

"Maybe you're right. Where? When?"

She backed up, went around to the passenger side of the car. She downed the rest of her champagne in a long-throated gesture. Then finished his mostly full glass. She started stashing the equipment in the car's rear seat.

"No. You don't get to plan. To prepare. The next time you see me. I choose. If you want to enjoy it, you're allowed, you know. But I think you'll hate it. All I can say is just think of England. Or your landlady or that island mama you work for, or this little carrot-top wetting her Gap capris." She gestured at the other side of the car, where Matt didn't dare look because he didn't want to remind her she was leaving him with another woman.

"What if I surprised you?"

"You can't. That's what's so delicious about it. You couldn't sur-prise me in a hundred years. So keep that ring warm for me."

She darted into the front passenger seat and slammed the car door shut.

The engine started with a quick, quiet hum. The car pulled away, the tires peeling like black Band-Aids from the loose gravel on the surface.

Matt rushed to pull the girl away from the departing tires. Her ankles and wrists were circled in duct tape.

She mewed behind the silver gag.

"It's all right. It'll take a while to get this tape off without hurting you." He looked around the deserted lot, then pushed his arms under her knees and back, picked her up, and headed toward the Blue Dahlia.

# Chapter 17

# Main Course

"It's a good thing they trust me to lock up," Molina said, pouring lighter fluid onto a cleaning rag she had found behind the hall door, the one that didn't lead to her dressing room but to a maintenance closet.

"If they couldn't trust you to lock up, who could they trust?"

She gave Matt a look—a long, hard Molina look—then soaked the tape over the girl's chin. "There you go. I know you want to sing out right now like Britney Spears, but ripping this tape off would give you a rug burn for a week. In the movies, they just tear away duct tape, but that's make-believe. There. It's coming. Just a bit more, and don't lick your lips unless you like the taste of kerosene."

While Molina calmed the captive and eased the gag off, Matt dowsed the girl's wrists with fluid.

The reek was stomach-turning. He watched her pale face turn delicately green.

"Off!" Molina announced the obvious.

She squatted beside the girl they had propped on a restaurant chair, looking like a den mother in her jeans and vaguely Native American suede jacket with odd bits of beads and fringe.

"What's your name?"

No "dear," no "honey," Matt noticed. Nothing infantalizing. She wanted this victim to feel like an adult. In charge again. Able to answer. Able to point fingers.

Matt started untwining gummy duct tape that had adhered to him as it released her.

The girl noticed the phenomenon. Her lips trembled into a small smile. "Guess I got Mr. Midnight into a bit of a jam."

"*You* were in a bit of a jam," Molina said, sympathetic but not enabling. "Your name? It's okay. You've lucked into an off-duty cop."

"You?"

"Yeah, me. Lieutenant Molina. Now . . . you."

"Vicki. Vicki Jansen." She glanced at Matt, almost apologetically. "I never expected to see you again so soon."

"Same here," he said.

"Who was that witch?"

Molina eyed Matt, curious to see what he'd tell an innocent bystander.

"A . . . rabid fan, I guess."

"Kinda like me."

"You weren't rabid."

"A little." She flushed. Redheads had that tendency. "It made her mad. That I kissed you."

Molina's frowning eyebrows told Matt what she thought of that.

"You were just impulsive," he said. She shouldn't blame herself.

To him guilt was an untallied cardinal sin. He didn't want to lay it on anybody else. But he wished Vicki hadn't confessed her indiscretion outside the radio station. Still, Molina had to know. A gushing nine-teen-year-old throws herself at him at 1:00 A.M. one night. The next night she's a captive audience for Kitty the Cutter's elaborate revenge.

"Are you all right, other than sticky?" Molina was asking, working on the ankle tape. "Anybody you need to call? You'll have go to the police station to make a statement. Don't worry. I'll take you. It'll be very discreet."

"I just have a couple roommates at UNLV. I dropped my purse in the dorm parking lot there when she . . . held that gun on me."

"What's the address?" Molina picked up her cell phone. "I'll have a patrolman drive by, try to get the purse. What time did this happen?"

"Gosh, eight P.M. or so. What time is it now?"

Matt jumped up. "It's after eleven. I've—"

"I know." Vicki smiled up at him despite the reddened skin the gesture aggravated. "You've got to get to the station. Thanks so much. It was really wonderful the way you distracted her and made her let me out of the car."

He could tell Molina was itching to hear his version of the encounter and shuddered to think what Vicki might tell her while he was off doing his job.

"Sorry." He pulled out his key ring, immediately spotting the ugly reminder of Kitty's ring. "I guess I'm making everybody have a late night."

"That's your job." Vicki smiled again, this time with tremulous, fannish adoration. "Keeping us all up late."

"She'll be fine." Molina sounded brisk and possibly annoyed. "I guess we all just *love* being kept up late." Definitely annoyed.

Matt rushed out to the parking lot, mounting the Vampire and donning his gloves and helmet, looking for lurkers and finding none. He peeled out of the lot. He had a lot of anonymous listeners to think about. And one no-longer-anonymous tormenter.

# Chapter 18

# *The Laddy and the Vamp*

In no time flat, or round, or oblong, we are up on the third floor.

Only if this upper chamber is an attic, then my refound mama is Mae West in drag.

This is a ballroom.

Or was.

It is a wide room, but six times longer than it is wide. Arched windows with a mosaic of glass set into wooden struts fracture the night into a faceted jet-black mirror that will reflect even our dark presence if we do not watch ourselves.

It is easy for me to whisk under a settee by the wall. Mr. Max does not whisk, but he can melt, and he ducks into a pool of shadow thrown by a pedestal surmounted by a fern as big as a weeping willow tree.

Everything up here is big, like a movie set that predates the Edsel.

Speaking of big, so is the other cat dude that unknowingly

shares this space: a leopard. While I was taking the scenic route, Leopard Boy was imported here by the actual residents.

There are two humans in the room, but they are less interesting, at least to my sniffer. I see that they have the Mystifying Max's undivided, though covert, attention, however.

Osiris, for it is he, the only leopard I have a nodding personal acquaintance with, lets his huge nostrils fan like bat wings. He knows Mr. Max's scent and my own, but since we were both involved in his recent rescue, I trust he has the smarts to keep his animal edge to himself and let the scent-blind humans with him do business as usual. Which is to say, remain in the dark.

I have, of course, seen the Cloaked Conjuror before, from a distance. He is garbed like a hero or a villain in one of these science fiction/martial arts/Arnold/Jean-Claude films. Big, but enhanced even more by built-up boots and body building and impressively padded armor, wearing a leopardlike face mask that disguises his voice as well as his features.

Him I have seen and heard before, and he does not scare me. I happen to know that some of the magicians in this town, and beyond, have taken issue with his best-selling act: debunking the tricks that magicians have used to hoodwink audiences for decades. The brotherhood of the cape and the cane do not take kindly to being outed. Whew. The brotherhood of the cape and the cane sounds like they are tap-dancing vampires, but that is too amusing a characterization to convey the menace that a cadre of lethally annoyed magicians could evoke.

So let us look at the lady present.

I have seen her up close once before, and when I realize who, and what, she is, it is all I can do to swallow a betraying hiss.

This witch took my Miss Temple's fancy new opal ring Mr. Max had given her, took it right from her finger onstage at the Opium Den and then saw to it that Miss Temple, and I, who was rushing to the rescue, and the ring, all disappeared from that stage, perhaps never to be seen or heard of again.

Happily, we resurfaced, thanks to a little help from our friends and a couple of enemies. All except Miss Temple's ring.

I must admit I am not surprised to see Miss Shangri-La in attendance on the Cloaked Conjuror. He had admitted to Mr. Max in a private conversation earlier, which I made certain to overhear, that he was hooking up with this female magician-thief. Seems he thought his act could use some sex appeal.

I cannot for the life of me see how a Dragon Lady in the mandarin-nailed, oddly berobed getup of a ghost from a Chinese opera adds sex appeal to anything. She is wearing a mask, but it is all makeup: chalk-white paint that blushes blood-red high on the cheekbones and makes a mask over the slanted black-drawn lines of her eyes and eyebrows. The painted lines draw her features tauter than a plastic surgeon's scalpel. She looks mean, and wind blown, as if a demon held her captive by the end of her long, black hair and was fighting to pull her back into hell.

If this is sexy, I am Father Christmas.

However, I long ago gave up trying to understand what humans find enthralling, other than my own breed, which is quite understandable.

I can see that they are hard at work here: the masked man and woman and the barefaced, hair-faced leopard.

It is a trick as old as illusion: the lady becomes a leopard and the leopard becomes a lady.

Shangri-La's elegantly tattered robes (they look like my pal Osiris has used her for a scratching post recently) part as she moves to reveal a glittering leopard catsuit beneath the frills.

This sight gives me a chill, I admit. I am always chary of humans in catsuits. To me, it bespeaks a primitive need to hunt us for our hides. Although I call Mr. Max's second-story outfit a catsuit, it is merely black slacks and turtleneck sweater. But Miss Shangri-La wears the real thing, like a second skin, except for me the mottled pattern is more reminiscent of a large, suffocating snake than of an elegant jungle cat.

I wonder if she is wearing Miss Temple's ring, and then I do not wonder much more, because a sharp nail taps me on the shoulder, and it is not one of Miss Shangri-La's four-inch nail-fangs, as she is still across the room.

You cannot call what I have just then so much a premonition as a sick headache all over.

I glance over my shoulder to see the baby-Bluebeard blue eyes in their own lavender-brown mask of velvet fur. (Okay, Bluebeard was a guy monster, but just pretend he had a sex change operation and you would have Hyacinth.) I glance to check the color painted on those lethal toenails so close to my jugular vein: not tinted blood red or poison green today, but gangrene teal.

Once again the evil Hyacinth has found me before I found her.

I just hope Miss Midnight Louise is still lost, because I would never want a maybe-relation of mine to be found in company such as this. Especially me.

The only good thing about this revolting situation is that Hyacinth only has eyes for me.

She has missed Mr. Max Kinsella entirely.

I guess that is the price of living in a cat-centric world. I have long accustomed myself to dwelling among humans, and while some street dudes would consider me a traitor to the Code of the Road, I have always found it more of an advantage than a disadvantage.

So my path is clear here: I must keep Miss Hyacinth distracted and allow Mr. Max to do his strange, solo, human nosing around.

"You just cannot seem to keep away from me, Louie," Hyacinth purrs in the odious way of a female sure of her lures.

Vanity, thy name is feline fatale!

"Who could?" I reply.

Now I must confess, privately, that I have never been much attracted to these lean, mean ladies of an Eastern persuasion. They make like they are so demure and all the while they are practicing kamasutra violin or sushi tiramisù, a lethal variety of either marital or martial arts (sometimes they are the same, in my humble observation) nobody else in the world has ever heard of or knows any more about than they do Mr. Sherlock Holmes's bar-itsu, an Oriental art so obscure it has never been heard of again. If only I could say the same for Hyacinth.

But I make the chitchat with the cat-lady while watching her petite mistress curl herself into a box until she seems to disappear. Osiris obediently crouches in a matching box, ready for the cloth to be flourished away and reveal him in her "place."

"You enjoy watching these laborious delusions?" Hyacinth asks.

"This house does not seem to be equipped with cable," I say with a shrug. "Do you have something more provocative in mind worth watching?"

"Besides me?"

"There is no one besides you," I flatter outrageously. "I see that you have forsaken the film world for the live stage."

"Not permanently. I'm up for the lead in a cat food commercial."

"Really?"

"They are searching for the perfect partner for me. A Bombay is the leading candidate."

I shake my head. "Too rangy, too shorthaired. Your unique appeal would be better enhanced by contrast, not a competitor."

"What did you have in mind?"

I polish my nails on my exquisitely groomed vest. "Sophisticated dude about town, formal black coat, luxurious satin lapels. The Cary Grant type."

"Hmmm. You must come up and see me sometime."

"Ah . . . I think I have done so already. I mean, an attic is 'up,' right?"

"This is no attic." Hyacinth shows me her scrawny tail as she turns and slinks along the wall toward the stairs.

I follow, as I wish to give Mr. Max free rein.

"This," Hyacinth goes on, "was a ballroom, screening room, and assignation room for the late great film star Carissa Caine."

"Now it is rehearsal hall," I note.

"All things decay with time."

We are retracing my steps down the stairs. I wonder if we are headed for the basement. Oh, joy. No doubt that is not a basement but a wine cellar, film vault, and temporary dungeon.

Above us, behind us, I hear man, woman, and cat debating their various roles in an illusion.

So where is Midnight Louise?

"As I was saying," Hyacinth goes on, her lisping purr reminiscent of Peter Lorre in his more pussyfooted impersonations, "I might be able to put in a good word for you on the TV commercial circuit."

"I have other fish to fry, or chow down at least. I could not care less about being an Á La Cat spokescat."

"Other fish! You refer to your dubious appearance on the TV court show, no doubt, where you made a spectacle of yourself with that pallid little tart of a Persian."

I bite my tongue. Literally. Such a description of the Divine Yvette is blasphemy to Bastet herself. But let the Goddess take her revenge in her own time. I am working undercover and must not betray my true purpose, which should be easy because I am not quite sure what it is yet.

"Yvette is a good match to her mistress, I suppose, although I do not think Savannah Ashleigh is of the Persian persuasion. And your own lovely mistress, what breed is she?"

"Shangri-La?" Hyacinth sits to add lip gloss to her already gleaming and unnaturally painted nails. "I have never seen her without her mask of makeup. We are both members of masked breeds, perhaps that is why we understand each other. She is small and lithe, like myself, and I flatter myself that she is of a similar kind, an ancient race from the East, wise and inscrutable."

"*Hmmm,*" say I, who loathe the word inscrutable. To me it is a synonym for "stuck-up."

"*Ommmm,* Louie?" Hyacinth mistakenly quotes me. "Are you meditating? That is a very enlightened thing to do, perhaps more Indian than Asian."

I am not about to remind her of the glorious Persian's roots in Afghanistan, just above India. She does not seem capable of appreciating the many attributes of the Divine Yvette.

"*Ommm, hmmm,*" I reply diplomatically, managing to straddle both East and West. I am not convinced that Hyacinth even knows the origins of her deceptive mistress. I suppose I will have to leave solving that mystery up to Mr. Max.

I chafe, sorry to be no longer eavesdropping on the humans and the leopard upstairs.

Miss Hyacinth mistakes my unease for other urges.

"I am working," she says shortly. "I do not have time for dalliances."

*Hallelujah!*

"Now that we have met again, without prison bars between us," I gabble like the lovesick swain.

"The bars between us were always of my doing, Louie. I am devoted to my role in life. My mistress has plans for us that are so much more ennobling than making fools of ourselves on stage or on sets. I realize that you have developed a hopeless passion for me, but you must realize that it is midlife crisis on your part. I am too far above you to encourage your pathetic attentions. I cannot allow myself to be distracted from my mission by personal concerns. You may kiss my hand before you go."

Right. Like smack her in the kisser with my mitt. But she has handed me an advantage, however odious. So. I am an obsessed admirer, am I? Gives me an excuse to turn up where I need to. We obsessive types do not give up, do we? I get the impression this dame likes it that way. I let my eartips dip.

"I am desolate, chèr Hyacinth, but I understand, my dear Ilsa. I will remain here in Las Vegas, hunted and haunted, while you fly away to more elevated planes."

She bats her demon blue eyes. (They look a lot like Lieutenant Molina's peepers, come to think of it.) They wink like the three rows of faux blue topazes in her collar. (She wears a dog collar, of course, like any self-respecting subversive dominatrix rock diva.)

My eyes fasten on something below the collar . . . not her chest hairs! A gold charm dangles below the crystals and the shape is oddly familiar. Fortunately, or unfortunately, my avid interest is taken as personal rather than professional.

Hyacinth's true-blue eyes cross with self-satisfaction. "Console yourself with that low-bred Persian, if you must, Louie. That would be for the best, rather than aspiring beyond your means. There is a certain tragic nobility in your dedication to such shop-worn goods."

My shivs are itching to show Hyacinth some dedication she has never encountered before, but such is the role of the undercover operator. You must sometimes play Caspar Milquetoast. So I bat playfully at her neck instead, a clumsy gesture that she blocks with a right cross.

"I must truly leave?" I mew piteously.

"Alas, yes. And now!"

Yes, sir! She has shown me to an open window onto the dark, wide lawn leading back to the deceptive barrier of the cemetery.

I leap to the ledge. In like smoke, out like Flynn.

"Adieu, my lady fair."

I pound down to the ground and hotfoot it across the sward before somebody unleashes the hounds of Hell that guard this weird outfit.

I sense Miss Hyacinth's eyes upon my exit all the way to the exterior wall.

Good. More time bought for my partner-in-crime, Mr. Max Kinsella.

I just wish I knew where Miss Louise was.

Somewhere cushy, no doubt.

She can't possibly have gotten into bigger trouble than I have.

# Chapter 19

# Magicians at Work

Max found an upright curtained box to slip into like a man donning a cape.

Some people found upright, coffin-narrow boxes claustrophobic. To Max, they were home. Children were supposed to be seen but not heard.

He needed to be *unseen, and* unheard.

*Gimme shelter. Put me on a stage, the invisible man incarnate.*

Max eavesdropped, nostalgic, on the intermittent murmurs performance professionals make when they are rehearsing, as they consult one another.

*The cage closer? You stand here? No, there. What about the cat? He's fine where he is for now. And this turns when . . . ? On a count of eight. And you are—? Here.*

Max had worked solo, so his constant Q and A had been with a technical crew, not costars. Still, the ritual, the mind-numbing, boring repetitiveness of it, offered a stability and comfort he had found in nothing else. He wondered if that was what Matt Devine missed in say-ing the mass. He knew Matt Devine missed saying the mass. He had to.

You don't give up a leading role in the theater, or the Church, without losing a primal connection to something bigger than yourself, something more than tradition, something intimate and sacred. . . .

Max cut off his thoughts.

His role of magician had been only a cover. The real role was hid-den beneath the illusion. He was here to play his real role: spy, pro-tector, thief of other people's secrets.

Booted footsteps finally announced the arrival of groundsmen ready to collect the leopard. They sounded like storm troopers among a ballet troupe.

Osiris snarled, grumpy. Max smiled unseen in his upright coffin. The leopard reveled in his role, in work. Max had sensed that when he had "liberated" him from the Animal Oasis. This particular caged beast was not exploited, but occupied that rare boundary between wild animal and animal that had learned to enjoy a degree of domes-tication. The only problem was that so few people were fit to interact properly with such an animal. Better that this truce between the species had never been negotiated.

Still, Max knew the Cloaked Conjuror, trapped as he was behind the mask of his own stage persona, himself caged, loved the leopard and would protect him as he would a human colleague.

Shangri-La he could not speak for.

She was quick, a talented illusionist, and a conundrum. Why would she bother playing second banana in a major Las Vegas act? How deeply involved was she in the drug transportation scheme that had been used to kidnap Temple? And Midnight Louie, although he was obviously an afterthought.

When Max heard the light retreat of footsteps now that the leop-ard was gone, he tensed, his hand on the curtain. Exit Shangri-La. Enter the Mystifying Max. It would be best to surprise and confuse the Cloaked Conjuror, to convince the magician that the magician-turned-spy's illusions were superior.

Max waited, listened, timed himself.

When CC had turned away to deal with the equipment, Max slipped out of the box, climbed atop it and jumped to catch onto one of the huge wrought-iron chandeliers marching down the center of the ballroom.

He swung for a minute, silent as a pendulum, then used his remarkable upper body strength to pull himself up among the swaying branches.

In seconds he was arranged like a deus ex machina in a Greek drama, the god descending from the heavens at the play's end, thanks to a creaking stage mechanism that playgoers chose to consider part of the Olympian miracle.

"Osiris is ready to work again," Max commented casually.

CC spun away from his props, stared at the blank-eyed rows of windows, looked toward the stairs leading to the ballroom.

"Heavens, no," Max said sardonically.

Of course CC looked up at that. Even his expressionless mask seemed to frown when he spotted Max.

"You! How—? I'm the debunker, not you! But you keep turning up where you're not supposed to be."

"I saved your rear, and your leopard, the last time I 'turned up,' didn't I?"

Max swung to the floor, lithe as a chimpanzee, despite out-of-condition muscles that protested. The illusionist landed as lightly as thistledown, or Tinker Bell.

*Clap if you believe in fair play.*

"What are you doing here?" CC said.

"Curious." Max dusted off his palms and prowled among the equipment. "Curious about your new partner, for instance. I had considered getting a female partner, before I . . . retired."

"You? You always worked alone. It was your hallmark."

"Times change. Why did you hire Shangri-La?"

"To spice up the act, I guess. She's masked herself, in her way. You don't think we make a good team?"

"You make a provocative onstage statement together."

"Thanks. That's why, I suppose. Just any other female magician wouldn't have been worth recasting the act for. But she's, ah, well, you've seen her. Highly feminine but not blatant about it, small enough to manage the usual acrobatic illusions, and she brings multicultural dimension to the act, not to mention that incredible performing Siamese of hers. It's uncanny! You'd almost think that scrawny little devil could think. Rather sinister in its way—"

"Almost like a witch's familiar? If you believed in witches."

"Why do I think you just might?"

Max laughed. "I'm a fifteenth-century kind of guy? Seriously, I agree Shangri-La's a great match for your act. Her and her cat. How'd you find her?"

"She found me. Pulled a surprise visit at the theater, like you did the first time. Came swinging down from the flies like Peter Pan in that Jackie Chan-in-Chinese-drag getup of hers."

"So you've never seen her face, without makeup."

"No, and I like it that way. She's probably as ordinary as I am underneath the costume."

"Just Clark Kent and Lois Lane?"

"Not even that interesting. Listen, there's nothing . . . whatever between us. It's a working partnership, like with the big cats."

"And you like her little cat?"

"Hell, no. That thing gives me the creeps. Have you seen the painted claws on it? Reminds me more of a monkey than a cat sometimes. Besides, I'm partial to the big boys. Those are the real cats. These domestic versions are like toy dogs, a perversion of the original."

"*Hmmm.*"

"You can't say you've seen a street cat that could compare to Osiris or Mr. Lucky."

"As a matter of fact, I have. But then I know a better breed of street cat than you." Max smiled, stretched. Like a cat. "Speaking of Osiris, how is he doing now that he's out of captivity again?"

"He's one happy cat."

"I see that. Quite an operation you have here."

"And how the hell did you find it? I've spent millions keeping my residence secret."

"And I've spent a lot of time learning how to find out what I need to know. How do you suppose I got Osiris back for you?"

"I paid you well."

"True. But we both know that the story isn't over. Osiris was taken to damage you. Your enemies are still out there."

"Everybody successful has enemies."

"Not enemies like these. Rogue magicians. You think I can surprise you? I *know* they can surprise you more."

"And you?"

"They can surprise me, too."

"Why do you think I'm the key to whatever will-o-the-wisp you're chasing?"

"Because my prey are your enemies. They flutter around you like fireflies. Taking Osiris was just an opening shot. Besides—" Max grinned. "You're about the only person in Las Vegas who can afford to fight them. And you'll need to."

"And I'll need you to do it, I suppose."

Max nodded. "If I found you here, don't you suppose that they already have?"

The mask he wore hid the Cloaked Conjuror's every expression, but his body language spoke for him. His massive form was still, mute. Max's point had stabbed home.

Nowhere was safe.

In the distance outside, one of the big cats roared, a deep, ragged, sharp sound like nothing on earth.

"Do you hire out as a bodyguard?" CC asked at last.

"No. I'm just a guardian angel. I'm not allowed to be on anyone's payroll, but I'd be interested in who's on yours. Let me guess. I bet you just hired a new guy, a new bodyguard, am I right?"

Could a mask pale?

No.

But it could nod, very faintly, "Yes."

"I'm feeling lucky." Max paused to pick up a large painted globe. With a twist of the wrist, he separated it into halves filled with colored scarves. "Is the new bodyguard's name Nadir? Rafi Nadir?"

"I'll get rid of him," vowed the Cloaked Conjuror's growling mechanical voice, flat and lethal.

"A mistake. I'd rather know than not where that particular gentleman is."

"I'd rather not be surrounded by treachery."

"You already are. Better to not let anyone know that you realize that. How many people do you employ?"

"Here?"

"Here and at the hotel."

CC strode impressively toward the dainty ballroom chairs that lined the room and had come with the house, lemon yellow Louis XV fripperies, and sat on one. It was as if Darth Vader had perched on an egg crate.

"Here," he said, sighing. His sigh sounded like a lizard's hiss through the voice-altering mask. "About sixteen, indoors and out. But they are all investigated."

"Who does your investigations?"

Had he a lip visible to bite, CC would have bit it then. "I see what you mean. Any system is corruptible. And another twenty at the theater."

"They are less likely to be corruptible."

"Because they're attached to a bigger institution, like the hotel?"

"No." Max folded his arms and leaned against the wall between two lavish swags of drapery. "Because they're union."

When CC was silent, he went on. "Union stagehands are paid well enough to have something to protect. They don't like anybody messing with their jobs. They feel they have enough muscle on their side to resent outside muscle telling them what to do, which is simply their job. That's probably why your stagehand was killed up in the flies during TitaniCon. Have you figured out who it was?"

"Of course. With days off and such it took us a few days to realize."

"You tell the police?"

The massive feline head shook. "I couldn't maintain my own security if I let the police in on it. Robbie Weisel was a divorced guy, no kids, kind of a loner. He was a pretty loyal guy, like you guessed. Straight-shooter. If he got killed because somebody was trying to move in on me and he stood in their way, I'm not going to undo his sacrifice."

"Sacrifice is right. He probably was mistaken for you. You had him wear a backup costume, right? When he was up in the flies getting ready to unleash a leopard illusion on the people below? Part of your scheme to embarrass the science fiction TV show that had ripped off your look for its alien race of baddies."

"So it was a juvenile stunt! I resented the hell out them making my individual stage look part of a damned hive. Suing 'em would have taken years. One big splash of embarrassment would have gotten me ink all over the world."

"Only it got your man killed."

The Cloaked Conjuror's mask hid all human expression, but his gloved hands clenched and unclenched in the rhythm of a big cat pumping its claws in and out. With the cats, it was a sign of pleasure and security. With the Cloaked Conjuror, it signified guilt and impotence.

Max knew he was being fairly merciless, but he had to convince the man to go along with his master plan for unmasking the people behind a whole slew of Las Vegas mayhem and murder.

And besides, he wasn't entirely sure that the murder of Ron Weisel didn't cut the other way too: some resentful science fiction convention attendee could have mistaken the magician's disguise for the TV show alien.

CC was talking again. "You say this magician's coven who hates my work is behind this stuff. Okay, I don't want to blow unmasking them. I want to turn these Synth bastards over to the police, all wrapped up."

"You also want enough evidence on them from other sources so your personal security and privacy aren't compromised."

"Is that so despicable?"

Max shrugged. "I can see that in your case it's necessary. And I see that you need me to do it."

CC nodded. "I have a lot of money. I can pay you when it's done, when the Synth's teeth are pulled."

"Can you give me what I need now?"

"What is that?"

"Whatever I ask for."

"To . . . a degree."

"You mean to the degree that you can see sense in it. Here's what I want now. It doesn't cost a thing, except self-control and discretion." Max came close, braced his bare, bony hands on the lemon-silk-upholstered arms of the dainty chairs, confined the Cloaked Conjuror to a temporary witness box in an empty court of law.

"I want you to tell no one. Not a long-lost relative, not a trusted associate of decades, not a woman in your bed. No one. Your life depends on it. And mine. And if you're ever tempted, or ever that thoughtless, just remember Robbie's lifeless body hanging like a puppet from the flywalk. He saw too much, he could have talked. He paid the price."

"My God, my life is already circumscribed. I have no face to most people I deal with, no true voice, no body. You're saying I should be a prisoner within this costume, not relax my guard for a moment."

Max straightened. "Not every moment. You can work and play with the big cats. But don't share your troubles with them. Someone might be listening. Someone might have bugged their collars, the environment. Trust no one. No place. No time. Nothing."

"A man can't live like that."

"Yes, he can. If he must."

"You?"

"Sometimes. For a long time. Again."

"You think this is a . . . conspiracy."

Max nodded. "Conspiracies are big, clumsy, well-aged anachronisms, but don't underestimate the elephant. It's the largest surviving land animal, and it has a long reach and an even longer memory.

"And it can crush a Big Cat with its front toenail."

# Chapter 20

# . . . The Sting

"This music could drive a person crazy," Molina shouted to Morris Alch.

She was hoping he had attained an age group where he'd agree with her right off.

Instead, he just smiled.

"Sorry, can't hear you over this racket, Lieutenant." His forefinger patted his earlobe. "Hard of hearing. What a blessing sometimes."

He gazed around like a kid who'd run away to see a traveling carnival.

This was a side show, all right, with the hoochie-coochie girls front and center. Morrie gazed up at their undulating everythings with innocent amazement. He was working, after all, even though it was past midnight when he met her here.

Molina wasn't sure she was ready to watch another man fall for the obvious.

"I should have brought Su," she shouted. "She'd keep her eye on the prize."

Alch screwed a finger in one ear as if to twirl out wax. "Can't hear," he shouted happily.

Maybe, Molina thought, the awful, knee-knockingly loud music was part of the attraction. Some men seemed to crave not having to talk, or think.

The music made her teeth grind. It was what she thought of as jackhammer rock: screeched lyrics you couldn't understand, screaming guitar, a dominant, body-vibrating bass deep enough to stop pacemakers for three blocks around.

She glanced at the small, glassed-in booth where the teenage troll responsible for this hellish hullabaloo was nodding his scraggly head to the beat like a palsied muppet.

They were here on official business, waiting for a brief break in the festivities.

Morrie stared up at the stage, where the only view was of Frederick's of Hollywood thongs being put to very skimpy use.

You'd think Alch had never been to a strip club before, she thought, and then Molina considered the likely fact that he probably hadn't, not often. He didn't strike her as the type to rowdy out with the boys. Maybe that was why she'd always liked him, as much as an impartial superior officer could like an underling. Not playing favorites was the key to effective management, but she realized that she trusted Morrie more than most.

Which meant that she was relying on him to trust her enough to be useful and not ask too many questions. In other words, enough to use.

She let a few dead strippers romp through her memory to remind herself why this case had her covering up for her enemies and keeping her colleagues in the dark.

If progress was made tonight, if they could get closer to a chargeable suspect on the Cher Smith murder, the pressure would ease. The charade could stop, and she could go after the quarry she really wanted with brass knuckles: Max Kinsella, signed, sealed, and delivered for assorted felonies. Or Murder One would do. Maybe solving this case would take care of that matter for her at one and the same time.

The idea was so satisfying that she smiled.

The music stopped. Silence was more shocking than sound.

"Quick," Molina said under her breath to Alch.

He heard her. The barefoot boy with mouth agape was gone, replaced by a canny investigator. Their quarry was momentarily accessible.

Together they burst like gangbusters through the small wooden door with its upper half all window.

"Police," Molina said before the kid in the hot seat could do more than squirm.

He half stood, gulping like a guppy, trapped in his fishbowl of a booth, a place so transparent that almost nobody ever noticed it. She had.

"Police," she repeated, aware of their plainclothes.

"Take it easy, son. This is just a routine inquiry."

This was why she'd brought Morrie along. There was hardly a savage soul to be found in Las Vegas that his easygoing manner couldn't soothe: antsy, acne-ridden, teenage DJs among them.

"This is Lieutenant Molina," Morrie was saying. "My name is Alch. I know, it sounds like I'm burping. Just think of mulch or gultch. But you don't have to think of anything but what you might have seen. Answer a couple questions and you'll never see me—us—again."

"Questions? I only get a five-minute break."

"That might be against labor laws," Molina said.

"So what?" the boy demanded. "You think I'd give up this cool job just for a longer break?"

"What's so cool about it?" Morrie asked. "Besides the scenery?" His suited shoulder shrugged toward the empty stages.

"The music, man. I get to do it all. Next step is my own radio show."

Molina nodded, leaning against the closed door. "Who picks the music?"

"The girls mostly. They have their routines worked out. Sometimes I get to suggest numbers, though. Depends on the girl."

"Okay, son . . . say, what's your name?"

A silence held that matched the unnatural sound of silence in the larger room beyond.

"First name," Alch settled for.

"Tyler."

"So, Tyler, what's the attraction with this here job, other than cutting a career path to the top ten radio stations. Hours sort of stink. Nobody notices you much."

"Are you kidding, man? The girls notice me plenty. They'd be lost without me. I miss a cue, they look stupid. Like I say, I help a lot of them with their routines. All the guys in my class would kill to have this job."

"Just what class are you in?" Molina's tone implied "underage."

"Senior," he said. Sneered. Didn't like teacher types asking him to account for himself, big man like him. "I'm okay to work here, nights or whenever."

"I wish I'd had a job like this at your age," Alch put in, pulling the kid's attention away from Molina. Teenage boys didn't like female authority figures. It takes a few decades to get used to it. Did for Morrie anyway. Maybe kids today were faster studies. He doubted it.

He glanced at Molina, broadcasting his thinking.

She subsided, amused.

He didn't often get a chance to take the lead with her. He was surprised that she didn't care, but she didn't. He realized that this was why she'd ordered him along. Male bonding. Sort of.

"I gotta admit," Morrie went on, doing his Columbo imitation, "it's pretty hard to hear the music out there. It's all boom box, you know?"

"Yeah. It's a generation thing. The point is the beat, the bass. That's all there is. You're not supposed to notice the lyrics or anything. We're selling beat, bump, oomph."

"Well," Molina said, "we're not selling anything, but we'd sure buy an ID if you can make one. We figure from your booth here you get a good view of the whole place, including the regular customers."

"Yeah." The kid nodded, glancing at the stage where a purple spotlight glared on empty wood flooring. He twisted a dial up, then down, but the sound system remained mute.

"See, Tyler," Morrie said, "we're counting on you having sharp eyes, even if you're half-deaf from this music."

"I hear fine."

"I don't. My little middle-aged joke. Don't get like me."

"Deaf?"

"Middle-aged."

Tyler looked truly appalled at the thought. From zits to zip, not a happy notion.

"So," said Morrie, "we brought some pictures. Could you eyeball them and tell me if you recognize anyone?"

"It's about that stripper that was killed a while back, isn't it?"

"Maybe. We're not allowed to say exactly." Morrie glanced at Molina like she was the one who had made the rules.

"Yeah. I'll look. But make it quick. I gotta rev up these girls pretty quick for the next set."

"Sure." Alch produced the first of the papers Molina had given him: a full frontal photo of a powerfully handsome guy with that soft rot of something wrong in the character working its way out, the way Qaddafi had looked once, or the self-declared Reverend Jim Jones before he had served deadly Kool-Aid to the whole damn cult at Jonestown back before this kid was born.

This kid was nodding, as if in time to some music only he heard. "This guy's Rafi, sure."

"Rafi?"

"Not much weirder than 'Alch'."

"Got me there, Tyler. Kind of a bouncer, isn't he, around the strip clubs?"

"Yeah. He got around. Worked 'em all: Kitty City, Baby Doll's, Les Girls. Haven't seen him lately, though."

"Not lately," Molina stressed, wanting to be sure.

"No." Tyler shrugged. "Used to be around all the time."

"When did he drop out?" Morrie asked.

"Don't know. Haven't thought about it. A couple weeks ago? Hey."

"Hey what, Tyler."

"After Cher Smith was killed, I guess. That's all."

"That's all," Alch repeated, pulling away the photo.

He traded it for a piece of heavy, nubbly paper.

"This a police sketch?" Tyler asked, impressed.

"Naw. The person who drew it did police sketches in the old days, but we use computers now."

"Yeah. I use computerized equipment too. It's all digital, man."

"We're not digital yet. Funny, that used to mean doing it by hand. Anyway, this guy's face ring a bell?"

Tyler frowned, squinted, visibly thought.

Molina said not a word.

"He could have been wearing something different, could have looked different," Morrie put in so smoothly no one would ever know he'd been coached. Maybe not even Morris Alch. "Tall guy, I hear, way over six feet."

"Now that's something that'd stand out around here." Tyler's sneer was back. "Most guys who come in are on the short side."

"Really? I've never heard that observation before."

"Like you said, I get to eyeball the whole place. I'm here mostly for the music, but I notice things. Tall guy would stand out."

"You look like you're not missing any inches, so you mean most of the customers are like me."

"Yeah." Tyler stood up to stretch, showing off. Five nine maybe. "Not shrimps exactly, but no, uh, Schwarzeneggers."

"You think Arnold's that tall, really? Or just overbuilt?"

"I don't know. Maybe not as tall as he looks in his movies. This guy, though? I haven't seen him. He must be a bad dude, he gets his own police sketch. Computer too good for him?"

"We like to try different methods." Molina pulled the image off the small table crowded with buttons and dials where Tyler had dropped it when he couldn't make the subject. "People react to different things."

"Yeah, and I gotta make sure this crowd reacts right to that little honey about to strut her stuff onstage. Sorry."

Tyler sat down and started playing the tabletop dials and buttons like the Phantom of the Opera pulling out all the stops on the organ.

Molina eased the door open, admitting a blast of earsplitting sound.

She and Alch slipped outside, sealing Tyler into his cocoon of equipment and the sound of silence.

"Get me chapter and verse on the kid," she told Alch. "School, parents, age, everything." Molina shouted into Morrie's better ear as they wove their way through the cheesy tables to the door and the parking lot.

"You get what you wanted, Lieutenant?" he asked when they stood at last on the pulsing asphalt, the building behind them thumping like a herd of buffalo but thankfully muffled.

"No, Morrie. You did."

# Chapter 21

# Tempted

If the nights were no longer his own, belonging to WCOO and, more recently, Kitty the Cutter, the days were Matt's to do with what he would.

The Circle Ritz parking lot, he was relieved to see the next mid-morning, was bare of a red Miata.

He got into the sun-warmed, whitewashed Probe that had been his landlady Electra's once-pink signature car and drove onto streets thronged with white vans, pickups, and sedans designed to repel the relentless sunlight.

He didn't know where he was going, just somewhere else. To think. Ethel M's cactus garden crossed his mind. So did the shore of Lake Mead.

Instead, he found himself heading into Molina territory—not on her account, but because the stucco spire of Our Lady of Guadalupe beckoned him like a parental finger.

The church was in its midday lull, between services, empty.

Matt dipped his fingers in the stainless-steel-lined holy water font—no longer bracketing bowls at either side of the entrance arch, but now a footed and carved stone structure upheld by angels.

That's what he loved about Our Lady of Guadalupe. It was always in retrograde, like a planet frozen in its eternal orbit. The more modernity shouldered into Catholic churches, the more Our Lady of Guadalupe became a quaint, intractable anachronism. In an ecumenical world, OLG remained staunchly Catholic with a capital C. Matt genuflected before entering an empty pew, noticing that his knees were beginning to begrudge going through the familiar motion.

The vigil light signifying the presence of the Eucharist burned true-blue blood red above the elaborate altarpiece. The altar itself had long ago been turned to face the pews, one glaring concession to change. Matt remembered masses said with the priest's back to the congregation, so he faced only the crucifix and the presence of God. That made the ritual more solemn somehow, when the congregation eavesdropped over the priest's shoulder. Secrecy always conferred solemnity, or else why whisper during confession in those dark, private booths in the old days?

Matt's eyes inventoried the familiar artifacts: the embroidered altar cloth, the flowers provided by the Ladies' Altar Society, the simple pulpit awaiting a preacher the way a clay pot does its plant. The Stations of the Cross marched down the side aisle walls, the bas-relief wood carvings resembling petrified flesh. Everything was as soothing and familiar as it had been when he had come to church as a child, sitting silent beside his mother (nobody in the congregation spoke responses then, but were seen and not heard like good children of God). He realized the peace he had felt in church was literal. It was the only place he and his mother had escaped the bitter harangues of Clifford Effinger.

No wonder he had hoped to make the church his permanent home.

A door cracked open behind the altar.

Matt smiled at the familiar, secret sound, betraying the rich liturgical life that was always being led behind the scenes in a church. Every day had its meaning, its patron saint or significance in Church history. The Church calendar was a phantom image of the secular calendar, with its major "feast days" only reflected in a few secular holidays. The word "holiday" was itself an evolution of "Holy Day."

And the secular calendar was Gregorian, after all, determined by a Pope hundreds of years ago.

Father Raphael Hernandez crossed from the sacristy door to genuflect painfully on the red carpeting in front of the altar.

He wore the long cassock abandoned by most modern priests but its solid black dignity suited his angular Iberian features. He was the model of the reserved, dedicated priests Matt had known as a child. The father figure he had aspired to become.

The vigil light glinted off the small round black buttons closing Father Rafe's cassock from neck to hem. Matt found himself remembering Temple wearing a soft black knit dress that buttoned up the front, and him undoing some of them.

The vigil light's red heat seemed to flood his face. He wanted to censor the thought, then resisted. Too much had been censored. Self-censored and confessed. What he had felt and done had been natural, honest. That part of himself was as worthy of embracing as the urge for commitment and service that had brought him to the priesthood.

Father Rafe spotted him, started a bit theatrically, and then came striding forward.

"Matt. Nice to see you here. I've missed you at a few masses."

Matt rose, shook the thin hand. "I like to visit other parishes. Different decor, different music."

"I wasn't implying you had missed a Sunday—"

"I know. I wasn't implying that your sermons were anything but inspirational. I did that even when I was . . . a priest. Visited other congregations."

Father Rafe sighed. "I'm so involved with my little world here. That's what got me into trouble." He frowned and looked hard at Matt. "Are you troubled?"

Matt nodded, relieved.

"You need the sacrament of reconciliation?"

"Not . . . yet, Father. Just to talk. To discuss ethics. Right and wrong."

"If it's something involving the female sex, I admit I'm not your man."

"Nothing like that. At least not directly. It's about the nature of evil."

"Evil?" Father Rafe frowned again. "You mean that literally."

"Yes."

"Sit down." He gestured to the polished oak pew as if it were an easy chair.

Matt knew that there were no easy chairs in church. He sat, though, jamming his feet under the descended kneeler.

"I know a homicide lieutenant," Matt began.

Father Rafe nodded, understanding that this was prologue.

"She deals with the results of evil, day in, day out. I honestly don't know how she does it, faces so many dead souls, knowing they were killed by malice. I admire her."

"It is a debilitating job. I have such a one in my congregation."

Matt didn't acknowledge the relationship. OLG was Carmen Molina's parish, this was a story. No names would be given, to protect the innocent as well as the guilty.

"Like you, Father," Matt went on, "I've heard confessions . . . administered the sacrament of reconciliation as we say now. I like the old, plain title better. Confession. I liked absolving people of their sins, which they themselves had named. You and I know that as we priests became aware of the true wrongs in society we had to read between the formulas to find the violent spouses, the child abusers, and persuade them to seek help beyond mere forgiveness."

"Forgiveness is never 'mere.' It is the greatest of the divine gifts."

"Yes, I know that. Especially since I've been led to forgive beyond reason, beyond right myself."

"Forgiveness heals the wronged as much as the one who wrongs."

"I know that too. I've seen evil in human form, and have seen that the origin of that evil is all too human. But."

The priest's dark, peaked eyebrows lifted and held the position.

"What if, Father, you encountered truly irredeemable evil? Someone who would slaughter innocents, persecute children, spit in the face of God only because it was there?"

He thought about it, the implications. "You are discussing demonic evil."

Matt nodded.

"Inhuman evil."

"It would seem so."

Father Rafe considered it. He had a face that could have sat judge for Torquemada. Of all the priests in Las Vegas, he was the only one that Matt could imagine conducting an exorcism.

"I believe in pure evil," the older man said, speaking slowly. "I believe in the Devil. I believe the Devil can make use of humans who let him." He tented his fingers, considering every implication of Matt's question. "I believe in you, Matthias, named after the disciple who replaced Judas. But I do not believe that any human being is so unremittingly evil that he would be on an equal footing with the Unholy One."

Matt absorbed this. "Then anything once human keeps some lost core of humanity, no matter how debased?"

"I believe so." Father Rafe grimaced. "It is an act of faith, my belief in ultimate good. It is an act of reason to admit the existence of pure evil."

"Is it a sin to do what is necessary to save someone else from pure evil?"

Again the eyebrows raised. "I'm just a parish priest, not a theologian."

"That's why I'm asking you. You see people at their best and worst every day. Theologians do so only on Sunday."

Father Rafe chuckled. "Theologians are theorists. Very necessary, but sometimes annoying. So are parish priests. We don't say what you want to hear."

Matt shrugged. "As long as you tell us what we *say* we want to hear."

"I'm sorry you've encountered such evil. Your stepfather—?"

"Was a piker. I've learned to . . . forget him."

"Forgive him?"

"I suppose so."

"And this other evil?"

"I've truly never encountered anyone so devoted to destruction for its own sake. My conundrum is how to stop it."

"No."

"No? Innocent lives may be lost, ruined."

"No. Your conundrum is how to heal it."

"Heal evil? This evil demands my soul."

Father Hernandez was silent, then crossed himself, his lips moving in prayer. "I don't doubt that you are tried. Remember Our Lord, taken by the Devil to the top of the Temple and offered every worldly thing."

"Mere materialism. He was not offered the chance to save the lives of his disciples, to do good by doing wrong."

"One can never do good by doing wrong."

"If a kidnapper holds a child with a gun to its head and won't surrender, isn't it right that a police sniper shoot him?"

"That's between the police sniper and his conscience. But suppose the kidnapper's gun is defective and can't fire?"

"The only way to find out is to risk the child. Sacrifice the child."

"Or to negotiate."

"And while you negotiate, the kidnapper panics and shoots."

"You are not a hostage negotiator, Matt."

"Yes, I am. If you only knew how much I am."

"And the item under negotiation? It can't be a child."

"It's my soul."

"Your soul. You and I know what that means. Your soul is immortal, as you are not. You must not sacrifice it."

"But what is sacrifice, and what is self-defense?"

"I don't know enough about the specific situation to say. Surely the Devil has not appeared before you to tempt you."

"He has," Matt said gravely.

Father crossed himself again.

Seeing the ancient gesture invoked was strangely comforting.

"I'll pray for you," Father Raphael said. "Every day at mass."

Some would have said that was no solution. Matt respected the power of prayer, even if prayer might not solve his problem.

"Thank you, Father."

The man's hand leaned on his wrist as he pushed himself to his feet. It was a gesture acknowledging Matt's comparative youth and strength. "I can't tell you how to defeat this devil of yours. I was not very good at defeating my own devil."

"But you did."

The older man smiled, an expression that turned his stark, ascetic face handsome. "Yes, I did. With your help. I am sure that you will find a way to outsmart your own devil, which is not of your making, is it?"

Matt shook his head.

"You are fortunate to share with Our Lord the role of an innocent tried. I hope you find an easier path to redemption."

Matt did too. Perhaps the answer was to renounce all hope of his own salvation.

He let his knees sink into the padded kneeler, remembering the oak-hard kneelers of his childhood. Even here things had become easier, less deliberately harsh. It made for less agonizing decisions.

Kitty the Cutter had placed him back on the cutting edge of ethics. That's what she really wanted—not his body, but his divisive soul. Should he be the Lamb of God and go peacefully to the Cross to save the world? Or should he be the Soldier of the Lord, ready to smite Satan in all His forms?

He remembered the sadistic charade of the Blue Dahlia parking lot.

With Temple he had glimpsed his passionate, loving, sensual self.

With Kathleen O'Connor, and with Cliff Effinger before her, he had glimpsed his passionate, hating, homicidal self.

Which was the best/worst way to save his soul? A sin of the flesh, or the sin of murder? Cain had been the Judeo-Christian culture's first murderer but before that his parents, Adam and Eve, had lost paradise through a sin of intellectual superiority, though succeeding generations had chosen to convert hubris into a sin of the flesh.

Europeans, for centuries less puritanical than their American brethren, had long ago learned to rank sexual sins low on the totem pole. Americans called them cynical; they called themselves realists. Americans still flourished the scarlet letter: better death than disgrace. That presumed the death of the innocent. What about the death of the guilty at the hands of the innocent?

American society still had, today, a legitimate role for the executioner as well as the executed.

Matt let his mind and his emotions dance an interlacing pavane of imagined action and reaction.

He recognized that he could kill Kitty O'Connor. He knew the martial arts moves that would do it. Everything would stop there. Certainly his brave new secular life. He'd be lucky to get life imprisonment but what was he facing now?

He knew a hatred of what she was doing that shook him, made him think the once unthinkable.

She had revived his rage against Cliff Effinger, that childish fury of knowing the whole world was turning a blind eye to a terrible wrong, and the urge to right it by the most violent means, by yourself.

Weighed against the dark balance of his thoughts now, murder, a spiritual and social violation, a sexual act seemed trivial. He began to see the European point of view, and it wasn't cynical, it was practical.

So. He would sleep with someone not of his choice, of his free will.

Would letting it be Kitty spend her poison and save others at the sacrifice of his self-respect? Or would cheating her of her prey make her deadlier than ever?

There was only one way to find out. He must act and find out before her game became lethal to some innocent bystander. When she'd found out what he'd done, maybe she'd kill him.

He stood, still not sure what he'd do, directing a prayer to the altar: that God would give him the wisdom to sin in the manner least hurtful to the most people.

He genuflected on the way out, and touched the water from the font to his forehead, chest, and shoulders. Head, heart, and arms to act with.

# Chapter 22

# *Charming Fellow*

I am pretty excited when I hit the home place again.

I know I am hot on the trail.

My Miss Temple has been playing with a sketch of the very charm I have seen dangling on Miss Hyacinth's neck.

Only this interesting item is no longer dangling from that stringy and fuzzy throat. It has been nicked. It is caught close in the second shiv on my right mitt. And let me tell you hiking home the whole long way with one foot cramped to hang on to my prize has not been easy.

Several Good Samaritans have spotted my limping form and given chase, trying to save me by condemning me to the city pound.

The dedicated operative lets no discomfort dissuade him from the necessary heroics. My Miss Temple is interested in this bauble, so like any swain I have snagged it for her. Too bad it was at the sacrifice of playing the cringing toady with Miss Hyacinth. I could retch at my masquerade, except I am picturing my Miss Temple putting two and two together, and not having any notion of how to make it four.

Perhaps if she discusses it with Mr. Max they will finally make some progress.

Not that I wish to encourage her discussing anything with Mr. Max. He is much too big to share our bed.

So I claw my way, three-handed, so to speak, up the slick black marble face of the Circle Ritz to our patio and cast myself panting on the cool slate stones shadowed by the sole palm tree honoring our exterior.

It is not unusual for me to arrive at Chez Ritz by the dawn's early light, so I pop the easiest French door and finally stagger onto the parquet tiles of home. My mitt is numb from holding onto my prize. I can barely loosen my grip to release the item onto the floor.

I collapse, knowing nothing but Free-to-be-Feline lies in my bowl as goad and reward. I might as well have headed straight for the Crystal Phoenix koi pond, where there is some real eating adventure.

After recovering from my night of long treks, I amble into the bedroom, relieved to spy a familiar lump under the comforter. Like many a tea drinker, I like only one lump, not two, of sugar . . . so I am even more relieved to see that this is the case, although how Mr. Max Kinsella could have beaten me back here even with the assistance of wheels I cannot imagine.

I leap upon the bed, ignoring my sore pads, and excavate the edge of the comforter most likely to cover the end where intelligence resides in my Miss Temple.

"Luffffuhhh," she finally murmurs affectionately. Well, she murmurs. It might be more of an annoyed murmur.

I spot a stray red curl escaping the zebra stripes that cover her and snag it affectionately. Well, it might be with more of an intention to annoy.

With roommates of such long duration as Miss Temple and I, the line between affection and annoyance is always whisker-thin.

"Owww, lufffuhhh!" she complains, her endearing murmur having escalated into a less endearing mewl.

Aha, I am making progress.

I pat at her nose, just visible now.

"Owww!" She sits up, fully aroused. "Louie! Did you just knife my nose with your claws?"

It is so hard to be misunderstood.

I reach out a mitt again, and massage her nose.

"*Louie*! That hurts. What is the matter with you? You do not often put your claws out, not at home, at least."

Could I sigh, I would. But that is another rare thing that dogs are better at than my breed. I lift the paw again and dangle my prize from it, hoping that her eyes are open enough to see that my shivs remain in a gentlemanly closed position. It is the trinket I have snatched from Hyacinth that has scratched her.

"What is that? Have you got some tinsel caught in your paw? Did you walk on a open can while you were out!" She is sitting up now, all attention, torn between concern and annoyance, like a fond parent. "Let me see, you poor baby. Hold still!"

I sigh metaphorically and let my grasp relax, so that the item drops to the comforter.

"Where are my glasses?"

As if I would know. In fact, I do, and I paw them off the night-stand, also onto the comforter.

She claws at the black-and-white pattern until her one of her pathetic fingernails clicks against the red metallic glasses frames and she installs them on the same nose I was forced to abuse.

"I swear I saw your paw pierced by a piece of tin can. . . . Is there blood on the coverlet?"

Please. If I were bleeding, I would be licking it.

She feels the comforter surface again and finally, finally pulls up a plum: my offering, fresh from the sinister collar of the treacherous Hyacinth, who after a stint on cable TV has been reunited with the same evil mistress who stole Miss Temple's semiengagement ring only weeks ago.

Of course I cannot tell Miss Temple all this. I have to leave something for her to figure out on her own.

"Louie . . ." She leans over to snap on the bedside light. We both blink in the flood of artificial sunlight. "This isn't a piece of tin. It's gold. Real . . . eighteen-karat-marked gold. And I've seen it before. At the Rancho Exotica. And now I know what it is. Ophiuchus!"

Miss Temple practically stands up in bed, she is so excited.

"This is it! The charm I spotted on that woman at the Ranch. The larger-than-life symbol that was used to contain the dead body of poor Professor Mangel! The thirteenth sign of the zodiac! The sign of the Serpent. The calling card of the Synth. Louie!"

She comes back down to terra cognita again and hunkers down beside me, kisser to kisser.

"Where on earth did you get it?"

And she waits.

Like I could tell her.

Like I would.

## Chapter 23

# A Place of Concealment

"Aren't you afraid," Molina asked when Matt called, "that your girlfriend might be tapping your line?" She sounded weary and annoyed.
Annoyed with him.

"That's why I got a cell phone. I'm calling from the Circle Ritz
parking lot."

"Don't mention parking lots. Too many bad things have happened
in them lately."

"How is Vicki?"

"Fine. Except for being scared to death. The scariest part is that I
can't do anything to protect her. You've got to get me some solid information on this madwoman of yours, or she'll really do some damage."

"She's not *my* madwoman!"

"Anger is a deadly sin. You sound tired too."

"Yeah, well, I imagine we're both pretty much at the ends of our
ropes. I'm sorry, Carmen. It's my fault that the Blue Dahlia parking
lot has another bad memory for you."

"Bad memory? Not this time. This time I'm just . . . aggravated. Who the heck does that woman think she is, playing mind games on my territory? Was she alone?"

"She always has been when she's encountered me . . . or when she sees fit to confront me. You mean did she have an accomplice last night, with Vicki?"

"Yeah. It took planning. That outdoor sound setup was installed around ten yesterday morning. A couple of BD employees saw someone in white coveralls and a painter's cap on a ladder messing with the roofline but it was near the neon sign and they thought it was maintenance."

"Man or woman?"

"Couldn't exactly tell, even when pressed. Workmen and mail carriers are the world's most invisible occupations."

"So what happened to Vicki?"

"Took her statement, gave her a card for a good trauma counselor, suggested she stay off the call-in lines of The Midnight Hour and away from you and WCOO. She didn't see who nabbed her. The car had a dark-tinted glass privacy panel between the back and the driver's compartment like a limo. Some of the car services around town do that. She saw and heard mostly you when she was on the pavement. She thinks you're God's gift to damsels in distress, though, despite not knowing what was going on, and is grateful you 'saved' her. I am not hopeful that she'll have the smarts to avoid calling your radio show. Girls today are way too boy crazy way too young. It's a shame that Mariah can't skip adolescence like you did and go directly into the convent instead of junior high, but I guess nunneries are a dying institution."

"I can see why parents get into that kind of repressive thinking."

"This Kitty scenario doesn't make sense. Sure, women can become obsessed, they can stalk, but, as usual, they tend to hurt themselves, not others. They get arrested, ridiculed, mentioned on the nightly news, put into mental hospitals. They don't turn dangerous like this."

"I don't think Kathleen O'Connor 'turned' dangerous. I think she always was."

"Then you *do* know something of her history."

He did, and he teetered on the brink of telling Molina on a need-to-know basis. Something stopped him. Keeping other people's secrets was too ingrained from his life as a priest. Maybe he could persuade Kinsella to come clean about this himself. Yes. This latest incident would persuade him if nothing would. Kinsella couldn't stand innocent bystanders getting caught in the crossfire. It was the one trait he shared with Matt, that old Catholic guilt syndrome. No one must pay for my actions, my sins, but me.

"Well?" Molina was demanding.

"I'm thinking." True. So true. "I guess if we haven't lived in a politically and religiously segregated society like northern Ireland it's hard to understand how deep the hatred goes. That's what she's acting out: that bred-in-the-bone hatred where rage becomes your life's blood, your air."

"Unemployed terrorist is your explanation? Downsized into Stateside harassment of ex-priests? There's some more primal motivation, some ritual, just like there is with serial killers, that I know."

"You think she's really a killer?"

"I think she likes to put chaos in motion and sit back and watch the carnage. As you said, and Mr. Oscar Wilde before you: 'Each man kills the thing he loves. The coward with a kiss, the brave man with a sword.' "

Matt nodded to himself. The most virulent hatred is rooted in love betrayed. His own hatred of his abusive stepfather was his reaction to a father figure who was anything but. *You are supposed to love and protect me,* the abused child cries. And no anger, no fury is stronger than the final, unavoidable realization that the protector has betrayed his role and is really the destroyer. But it takes a while to find out that the unthinkable is not the status quo, and that your daily "normal" is very abnormal to a larger world.

"So." Molina was interrupting his silence again. "What can you give me? Something solid, other than this crackpot IRA theory. I don't know where you got that anyway. I called Frank Bucek and he didn't remember finding anything like that about Kathleen O'Connor, although he did remember you asking him to do a search and retrieve on her."

"I don't know. She may have mentioned something herself. She's said a lot of wild things to me."

"I still don't get how she found you, why she targeted you."

"It was when I was trying to track down my stepfather. She noticed I was on his trail. She mistook me for a hit man, I think. When she found out I wasn't one, she got angry, as if I had disappointed her."

"You're just too good to be true, that's your problem. It's very annoying, take my word for it."

"I guess women like the bad boys. Russell Crowe. Puff Daddy."

"Some who need their heads examined do." There was an odd silence on the line. "The bad boys have a way of introducing themselves as Mr. Right. But Miss Kitty seems to have a thing for good boys. I suppose she's no different from overcontrolling men who pick on naive girls."

"I may be innocent, but I'm not naive."

"So there's nothing you can give me, nothing concrete on tracking Miss Kitty?"

He thought, remembered, decided to lie. One small sin down the slippery slope.

"No."

As soon as he had hung up on Molina, Matt punched in another number.

Kinsella answered. They were now both plugged into cell phones. Matt pictured the whole world with a hand and phone clamped to one ear, mouths moving like cud-chewing cows, eyes gazing vacantly into the sky or the ceiling.

"Devine here," Matt said, brusquely.

"Gad, you sound like you've taken lessons in phone etiquette from Molina."

"Maybe I have. I've just gotten off the line with her."

"My condolences."

"Your Irish friend has crossed the line. I need to give Molina a real lead on her. All I can think of is that sketch."

"What's stopping you?"

"It's been our little secret, we three."

"Secrets are made to be shared."

"That's not the way you act."

"I'm a mass of walking contradictions."

"I know, and that makes you not as unique as you think."

"What do you want?"

"Your permission to bring Molina in on the Kitty O'Connor loop."

"My permission?"

"She *is* your demon."

"It *is* your sketch. You commissioned it. Why an ex-priest would want a pinup picture of a demon, I don't know."

"This is not just an amusing game of harass-the-clergy anymore. A girl was involved in the latest incident. And Molina was there."

For once something Matt said stopped Kinsella the Kool cold.

"Okay. Where can we meet?" he said. "When?"

"I don't know if we can. That woman is watching my every move. It's not just my apartment or my job anymore. It's me, twenty-four/seven."

"Go to the Oasis Hotel back parking lot. Park in the exact middle, as far as you can tell. What are you using for wheels now?"

"A white '93 Probe."

"Gack."

"So I hoped."

Kinsella laughed. "Your boring taste is impeccable. I congratulate you. Good work. Park the Ignoro-car and walk on a zigzag course toward the lamppost with the Sphinx on it. Drop to the ground and get under the car parked nearest to the lamppost. Did I mention you should wear Rough Gear clothes? I'll come by in a black Maxima."

"A black Maxima? Isn't that a little iconic?"

"Only you would ask if something was iconic. Yes. Just get into the backseat when I pause, and stay down until I say. It may be a while."

"Have you always lived like this, like James Bond or Howard Hughes or somebody?"

"Longer than you'd care to think about."

"I still don't trust you."

"Funny. I've always known I could trust you. It's what I've disliked about you most. Later."

Matt lay on the shaded asphalt, road grit prickling through his clothes.

He felt like a fool. Then he remembered how Vicki Jansen must have felt lying on the Blue Dahlia parking lot, bound and gagged.

He was here of his own free will, if against his better judgment.

He was doing what Max Kinsella had told him to do, and it was darn undignified.

He supposed Kinsella got a kick out of that.

But he was the undercover expert, and their enemy was now mutual.

Funny, a woman had made them rivals and another woman was making them allies.

Matt guessed that was life in the noncelibate world. He began to understand the deep fears of the Church fathers who had called woman the Devil's tool.

It wasn't demons they had feared, but their own impulses, both noble and base.

Groveling in the gravel did lend itself to philosophical and theological contemplation. It recalled his ordination, the long minutes of lying prone before the altar.

*For I am a worm and no man.*

Was that truly the thought of Jesus as he made the Way of the Cross? Was self-abnegation the only gateway to Godhood, or to any kind of religious transcendence?

Waiting obediently for Max Kinsella to show up was giving Matt all kinds of second thoughts.

He heard and saw some tires seize to a stop in front of him.

What he could see of the vehicle's rocker panels was black.

He scrabbled out from his ignominious shelter, scraping his palms on sand and glass, and hurtled through the open rear door, crouching to pull it closed.

Maybe he'd hitched a ride with a lady blackjack player with a broken rear door latch. Maybe Kitty the Cutter was at the wheel, having eavesdropped on him with some demonic high-tech device.

Whoever was driving turned up the CD in the player as they lurched away.

*Oh, my sweet Lord . . .*

Only Max Kinsella, always the impresario for his own one-man show.

Matt pulled the black blanket on the backseat over himself and tuned out.

Many, many gratuitous bumps later—Matt suspected that Kinsella enjoyed every pothole—the car came to a gravelly stop. He heard the tires slow as if stuck to adhesive.

More likely desert sand. The CD player stopped.

"All right if I do a gopher and peek out?" Matt asked.

"You can jump on the hood and tap-dance if you want."

Matt, blinking in the flat, bright light, glanced at endless scrub through car windows. "Where are we?"

"Where only the nuts and the G-men will find us."

Matt dusted off his khakis, staring into distant nothingness.

"We're on the fringes of Area fifty-one," Kinsella added. "We go any farther in, we attract unwanted federal attention. I figure even Kathleen O'Connor doesn't want federal attention."

"Really. This zone is that touchy?"

"Area fifty-one is the Holy Grail of conspiracy nuts. It's also real."

"Can I get out, get in the passenger seat?"

"Why? Don't fancy feeling like a mob abductee? It's better than being an alien abductee."

"I don't 'fancy' being anybody's abductee, including hers."

"Sorry. Sometimes I slip into a European expression. It's habit, not pretension."

Matt got out of the car without comment, paused to be ironed by the searing desert heat, then slammed the back door shut. He opened the front door and entered the idling car. A blast of air conditioning ruffled his hair and soothed his indignation.

"Is all this drama necessary?"

"You said she was on you twenty-four/seven."

"Seems like it."

"Tell me."

The trouble was that Kinsella looked and acted so bloody competent compared to the rest of the world. Matt knew most of it was stage presence. A magician is the ultimate controller, next to God Himself. A magician's biggest and best illusion is the myth of his own omniscience.

Matt had been trained to honor omniscient figures, but now he resented it. So he laid out the details of Kitty the Cutter's terrifying omniscience. Maybe it took one to outwit one.

Kinsella listened, his hands still clamping the steering wheel, unwilling to relinquish control.

Matt described the attack on him and his producer as they left the radio station. The ghastly setup in the Blue Dahlia parking lot, with the enthusiastic fan as an abducted witness.

"Why were you at the Blue Dahlia?" Kinsella asked.

"I wanted Molina's advice on this. I figured it was a safe place to meet her."

"Apparently safe places are no longer on your route now."

Matt glanced through the car's rear window.

196 • Carole Nelson Douglas

"This is safe, for a while. Now you understand how terrorists work. They never rest. They're always scheming. It's not that they're everywhere. They can't be. But their victims are everywhere, and when they strike, it looks as if no one is safe. They have generated terror."

"She's one woman."

"Is she?"

"That's what Molina asked me, if she worked alone. Yes, until last night. Last night I couldn't be sure. She could have had a driver. Witnesses saw a workman, or woman, putting up the sound equipment earlier in the day."

"That's the terrible beauty of being a terrorist. You put all your time into plotting, and it looks superhuman. Invincible. Not unlike a magical illusion."

"It feels invincible too."

"I know." Max Kinsella lifted something off the seat between them, thrust it at Matt.

The morning paper. He read the second headline, not the one across the top, but three thick lines above the fold on the right.

IRA OFFERS TO DESTROY ITS ARMS

"So? They've been dancing the peace shuffle in Northern Ireland for three years. It's been one step forward and two steps back every bit of the way."

"So. This is how Kathleen discharged her anger for almost two decades: selling herself to buy arms. She's not going to take this well. Peace is a threat to someone like her. It undoes all her life's work. She's more liable than ever to lash out at innocent bystanders."

"She already has." Matt gave him the short and sweet version of Kitty's treatment of the girl.

"And this girl she kidnapped was just a groupie at WCOO?"

"I don't like the term 'groupie'."

"Swell rock star you'd make. How'd Kathleen pick her out of the crowd?"

"Judas kiss."

"Ah, Kathleen's obsession has gotten seriously possessive. So this poor girl assaulted you with a postshow smooch and within twenty-four hours she's the main course at Kathleen's not-so-impromptu picnic at the Blue Dahlia parking lot?"

"How could Kitty know I was going there?"

"Had you ever been there before?"

"A couple, three times."

"Molina does trill a good torch song."

"So how, on the basis of my going there a few times, does Kitty know?"

"How many other spots around town do you patronize?"

"Uh, none. Not since I stopped hitting the joints looking for my stepfather."

"She's just covering all the bases, like a good terrorist. But you're right. She's tailing you twenty-four/seven. Or someone is."

"That's why I'm sneaking around to see Molina."

"Strictly business, huh?"

Matt remembered the subject of his last discussion with her and felt a reddening surge of guilty fluster.

"Sorry. None of my business." Kinsella's smooth smile annoyed the heck out of Matt.

"Just business," Matt managed to say, "sordid as it is when that O'Connor woman's involved. You know she's only tormenting me because she can't find you."

"I don't know that. Why would she think you had anything to do with me?"

"We're not complete strangers. She devotes all her time to it. She's superhumanly omniscient, remember?"

"So she is."

Matt couldn't resist an urge to flash some omniscience himself after contemplating the varieties displayed by these two mortal enemies.

"Temple knows where her ring is now. Your ring."

"Ring?"

It was Matt's turn to look smug. How could Kinsella have forgotten Temple's almost-engagement ring? "How many have you given Temple? The one the magician swiped. Sha-nah-nah or whatever."

Max reclaimed the newspaper section and folded it into crisp thirds as if trying to bury something inside it. "The ring? Where is it? Who found it? When?"

"I don't know when. I guess we could figure it out if we tried."

"Why should we?"

"Because Molina has it. In a plastic evidence baggie. She's had it for some time but just showed it to Temple a couple of days ago, along with a warning that it tied you to yet another murder and that Temple had better ditch you fast."

"Another murder? How?"

"I'm not too sure, but Temple sure didn't like the connection."

"Where did Molina find it?"

"It's evidence from the case of that woman killed in a church parking lot about the same time as Molina found the other poor woman's body in the Blue Dahlia parking lot. I'm not sure why Molina's so convinced the ring's being found there links you to the murder. We all saw the ring taken by a third party."

"Seeing things with her own eyes wouldn't change Molina's mind about me," Kinsella said absently. "She's like Kathleen, absolutely blinded by her wacked sense of political correctness. That dead woman in the church parking lot had been a magician's assistant years ago. That's the connection Molina sees. And she probably believes I got that ring back the night it disappeared because I got Temple and Midnight Louie back. She probably figures I palmed it and then dropped it while strangling Gloria Fuentes. That was the dead woman's name. She used to be quite well known in magical circles in this town."

"I'm sorry." Matt Kinsella's bleakness when speaking of the dead woman made it seem as if he had known her. Not good if he had. It only bolstered Molina's theory.

"Magic is dead," Kinsella pronounced with finality, the way Matt had heard some people chant "God is dead" twenty years ago. "There's more profit in debunking it."

"You could say the same thing about religion."

"So you could. We invested in the wrong careers for the times, didn't we? But you're still trying to save souls on the radio and I'm still trying to save lives with magic tricks."

"At least we're trying."

"Very trying." Kinsella grinned, unfolding the newspaper into a tattered patchwork that Matt took dazed custody of when Max put the car into gear. "Especially you. You must drive Kathleen nuts, as if she needed any help in that direction. Want to hop in the back again?"

"Not really." Max opened the passenger door to admit a wave of pure dry heat. It felt clean. "What are you going to do?"

"What I've always done: my Invisible Man act, try to control everything and be seen nowhere. As for your question, sure, give Molina the portrait of Kathleen. I'd appreciate it if she'd get off on persecuting someone else for a while."

"Can anyone actually persecute a psychopath, even if they're the police?"

"I could. If I could find her."

"Looks like you and Kathleen are at an impasse."

"I think we have been for almost twenty years. So don't sweat Miss Kitty. I outrank you."

Matt dropped the magically savaged newspaper on the passenger seat as he moved to his place of concealment in the back.

# Chapter 24

# Men in Motion

Matt rang the Circle Ritz penthouse doorbell, feeling oddly nervous.

He hadn't seen his landlady, Electra Lark, in so long that he felt like a fraud to be calling on her for a favor. A menial favor at that.

And he still hadn't thought up a good excuse for asking her to do it. Kitty O'Connor had driven him to the point that the truth was only a method of last resort.

The door swung open.

"Matt! I was just thinking about you."

"Why?"

"I get these sort of premonitions." She dimpled like a teenager. Not bad for a sixty-something. Electra and her apparel, the usual blooming Hawaiian muumuu that more often seemed to wear her, stepped back to admit him into the tiny octagonal entry hall that was covered in vertical Mylar-faced blinds.

It was like walking inside one of those spinning mirrored balls that hover like UFOs over scenes of mass ballroom dancing.

"Gracious, you haven't taken up wallpaper sales on the side, have you, dear?"

Matt lofted the cardboard tube he held like a clumsy sword. "No, this is why I came up. I was wondering if you could mail it for me. It's awkward for me to do it myself, I can't quite explain why—"

"If you were going to be late with your rent I'd need an explanation. If you need a favor, I'm not about to demand one."

Being a good guilt-ridden Catholic, Matt gave her one anyway. "It's a poster." A Wanted poster, in its fashion. "I taped an envelope to the top; what's inside should cover the postage."

Electra waggled plump fingers of dismissal at his scrupulous accounting. "Listen, Matt, I'm so pleased to have a media celebrity residing at my modest little residence I'd probably send a hundred-pound box of Ethel M for you gratis."

"A hundred pounds of Ethel M candy? That would be overkill."

She took the cardboard tube and leaned it against the doorjamb. "This is a featherweight. I'll mail it this afternoon. Can you come in for a minute?"

"Sure." Matt didn't like to beg and run. Besides, he was curious to see the penthouse.

"I keep things rather dim up here," Electra warned, preceding him through a split in the mirroring blinds.

The large room beyond was indeed bathed in eternal dusk, thanks to more vertical blinds, although these were a lot less flashy.

"I grew up with furniture like this." Matt eyed the sprawling, overupholstered forms that grazed on the dark wood floor like baby elephants.

"It that a complaint or a compliment?"

"I don't complain. It becomes chronic."

"That's for sure. Especially in my age group. If it isn't 'my aching angina' or 'my inflamed tendon' or my 'inverted intestine' or whatever, it's a marathon discussion of doctors and HMOs and prepaid burial plans. No thanks!"

Electra plopped down on a long, dark sofa shaped like a '40s Ford. Matt tried a '50s sling chair.

"So why did you paint my Probe white?" she asked. "It looks like a bathtub on wheels. I know the pink was a little sun-faded, but you could have gone for something zippier."

"White is the most practical color in this climate; reflects sunlight, keeps the interior cooler. And its high visibility makes it the safest color to drive. You're less likely to blend into anything and get hit."

"Oh, don't sound like a spokesman for the automotive council. I know all that, but a car isn't just a safety cradle. It should be fun."

"I have the Hesketh Vampire for that," Matt said.

"Which you hardly use. If it weren't for my Elvismobile and that new red Miata I've spotted in the parking lot just recently, the Circle Ritz would have to be renamed the Circle Ho-hum."

"The Miata is Temple's," Matt said, happy to divert Electra's wide-ranging curiosity from his choice of vehicle color, which was a defensive move, not an option.

"Well, at least you know what she's up to these days. Where on earth is Max?"

Matt was tempted to answer, "Out at Area fifty-one," but refrained from paraphrasing Bob Dylan's early landmark line "out on Highway 61." Temple had assured him Highway 61 actually had been a major Minnesota highway to Dylan's Iron Range hometown of Hibbing back in the '60s. Like a lot of major fabled highways, including the iconic Highway 66, 61 was mostly history now.

And now was Matt's turn to pump Electra. "You mean you haven't seen Max around here? I've been so busy working nights and giving out-of-town talks that I didn't realize he was doing another disappearing act."

"I worry about Temple. She waited around months for him to show up once, and now she's waiting around again."

"Oh, Temple's pretty resilient. I wouldn't worry about her."

Electra patted her short white hair, which was au naturelle today instead of being sprayed to match her floral-print muumuu. "Maybe you wouldn't, but I would. It's no fun waiting to see when a significant other is going to bow back into your life. That's why I had to lose number three."

"Husband number three?"

"Well, I'm not talking about gerbils."

Matt blinked, because just then he had seen paired pinpoints of red flashing between Electra's well-planted ankles. Did she have . . . rodents in the place?

"Do you keep gerbils?" he asked.

"No! And I didn't keep husband number three either. Those kids were such a happy couple when they moved in here. I just hate to see that go the way of all relationships."

"If all relationships deteriorate, Electra, it was just a matter of time."

"Maybe, but I marry 'em in the Love Knot chapel downstairs and I like to think some of them do better than I did. You aren't going to be in the market for a JP anytime soon, are you?"

"Me? No. I don't exactly have a social life with my work hours."

"Then get a different job."

"I don't see myself doing this radio shrink work forever, but—"

Electra leaned forward, hands fisted on her flowered knees, pewter eyes sharper than honed steel. "You never know, Matt. You never know when something will take life away just like *that*. Like a bolt of lightning. You don't want to be so absorbed in making a living that you don't live."

Between her slightly swollen ankles, the baleful red eyes regarded him as intently as she did.

"What makes you think I'm in danger of losing anything?"

"We always do, as life goes on. And I hate to see you young people so absorbed in running to this obligation here and galloping to that event there. You're just rushing your lives away."

Matt relaxed into the canvas sling. Electra was only bemoaning the up-tempo pace of modern cell-phone, belt-beeper, jet-speed, overbooked life. She didn't have any special insight into any of their lives, only that they seemed more isolated than her generation had.

And of course she had no idea of the secret waltz they were all doing to survive the fixed attention of one elusive psychopath.

He was glad that Electra was safe, then wondered if she was.

"I've still got time to worry about dating later," he said, hoping that Kitty had bugged the penthouse too, and her jealous spleen had heard his landlady bemoaning his lack of social life.

Maybe it was Kitty's eyes glowing ember-red beneath the sofa. Like a rat, she could probably gnaw her way in anywhere.

He excused himself, fought his way out of the chair, and left with one last glance at the innocuous cardboard tube in Electra's entry hall.

He hoped Molina could get further with that sketch than they had.

\* \* \*

Max called Temple at four in the afternoon, when her shoes were off, her bare feet were tucked under her on the office chair, and her computer screen was blank because she had run out of words. Or thoughts. Or energy.

"What's up?" she asked, trying to sound upbeat.

"Short notice."

"Is that some kind of sneaky personal slur?"

"Never. I was hoping you could dine with me tonight at the Crystal Phoenix."

"The Phoenix, why?"

"Because all your grand remodeling plans are now open to the public."

"How nice of you to remember."

"It wasn't hard. They made all the papers."

"Well, six."

"Including *USA Today* and the *Washington Post*."

"They both happened to be planning a Vegas update travel story. The timing was right. How did you know about the *Post?*"

"Web search. '*Crystal Phoenix. Fabulous show. Brilliant PR woman.*' Just type in the right key words and the Web will take you anywhere."

"Just murmur the right words and I'll go anywhere. How dressy?"

"Very."

"Hmmm. We must be going to Nicky's place at the top."

"It's a surprise."

"It always is when you feel you can afford to appear in public."

"Apparently my star has faded. I'm not in the world-wide demand I used to be."

"That would be wonderful!"

"Wouldn't it? Seven P.M. I'll meet you in the lobby. Please don't mistake a Fontana brother for me."

"Max, I never thought of the resemblance before, but darned if you don't make a natural—what would it be, thirteenth?"

"Unlucky number for dinner, so forget that."

Temple did as she got ready for her evening out, trying to forget the depression that had dogged her since a certain lieutenant had slapped a certain plastic evidence bag onto her desktop.

She took a long, neck-high bubble bath.

She did her nails.

She threw shoes around on her closet floor, finally sitting down and trying them on one by one.

The new Crystal Phoenix attractions were a rousing success. She thought, *What next?* She had a kicky new car. She thought, *Why care?* Matt Devine had gotten both too close and too far in the last forty-eight hours. She thought, *Who cares?* A ring that had once been lost, now was found. She thought, *What next? Why care?*

"This girl has a depression," she told a pair of purple leather high heels she had rejected and tossed back into the closet. Her whole life was like dressing for dinner: she didn't know what she wanted, what would make her happy, or if anything would.

Once just knowing that Max dared to take her someplace public was a triumph. Once glimpsing that Matt wanted her was a thrill. Once worrying about where she lived, what she could afford to drive, who would pay her for freelance work was a concern, a worry, a set of circumstances to overcome.

Now she thought, *Is that all there is?* And could hear Peggy Lee's world-weary voice sighing the same question to music.

# Chapter 25

# Missing Link

After a nice long nap preceded by a concerted pedicure, I wake up with all my ruffled edges soothed, particularly my journey-roughened cuticles.

The place reeks with that absolute quiet that means you are the only living thing on the premises (except for assorted illegal aliens of the vermin variety).

Last I remember my Miss Temple was a tad out of sorts because I had presented her with an object that was both a prize and a conundrum.

Sorry, that is the way I operate. Look, I could be one of those uncouth dudes who think bringing home a limp lizard is enough to thrill the lady of the house. At least I brought her something with some high-carat value, not to mention tantalizing links to crimes past and future.

What more could a high-heeled gumshoe of a little doll want?

A grasshopper?

That reminds me of my mama's long-forgotten nickname for me. How embarrassing!

I am glad there were no witnesses who knew me to this humiliating incident. This thought leads me to Miss Midnight Louise. I shudder to think the variations of demeaning nomenclature she could work on the nickname "Grasshopper."

I have naturally been absorbed by the females at opposite ends of the spectrum in my life: Miss Temple, my sponsor and ward, and her utter antithesis, the evil Hyacinth. Now I decide I should look up Miss Louise, admonish her for leaving the scene of the crime solo, and flaunt my trophy from the expedition.

I immediately trot into the office and hop up on the desk to collect the prize.

It is gone!

I check the French doors. Night has already drawn its shades on the day. I see my own green peepers reflected back at me, thanks to the desktop lamp Miss Temple has left on in her haste to gather up drawings and Exhibit A and go.

I have no idea where she has gone, except that it requires the wearing of A-list shoes. But I know where I must go. To the Crystal Phoenix to roust my defecting (I could say defective, but that would be too catty) partner and give her a piece of my mind.

Partners indeed! She has not the first notion of the word.

# Chapter 26

# *Moonlighting*

"What's the opposite of a harvest moon?" Temple wondered aloud.

"A sowing moon?" Max asked.

Their window table allowed a panoramic view of the glittering icons of rival hotels and casinos, an entire constellation of mythical beasts like the Sphinx and a giant gilded lion, and flocks of neon flamingos.

"I've never heard of a sowing moon. I can actually see the real thing over your shoulder."

Max swiveled in his captain's chair to look. The moon was low yet, just above the bristling skyline of the Strip establishments. It paled in comparison to the acres of manmade illumination. Still, it was big and solid and warm, like a sun fashioned from a wheel of cheddar cheese.

"Is the moon over my shoulder a lucky sign?" Max asked, swiveling back.

"You never used to mention luck."

"I never used to need it."

Temple sipped from her exotic martini, the latest fad in cocktails. Every fad came to Las Vegas first, and left it last.

"What is the occasion?" she asked.

Max reached into his side coat pocket like an ordinary man and pulled out a small, perfectly square box.

He placed it by her knife tip.

Temple hesitated. She was beginning to regard certain items of jewelry as akin to striking snakes.

"It's not what you think," he said.

"How do you know what I think?"

"It's fun to pretend. You might be thinking I've had a duplicate ring made up of the one that was lost."

"You could, and you would."

"And you wouldn't like that. Some things are irreplaceable."

Temple nodded.

"You could assume that this is the bauble from Fred Leighton you wore as a 'disguise,' shall we say, at Rancho Exotica."

"That would be incredibly extravagant."

"I agree. So. Open the box. It won't bite."

Temple did, gazing at the ring inside by the flickering light of their table candles.

The stone was small, green, solitaire.

She looked at him, questioning but mute.

"I thought at this point you'd trust modest more than anything else. That's all I can offer. Modest guarantees."

Temple nodded again. Max making the modest gesture was somehow heartbreaking.

"It was mean, what she did," he added.

"Molina?"

"I won't forgive her for it."

"How did you know—? Not Matt?"

"He was furious with himself for keeping Molina's confidence. We agree completely. She never should have ambushed you like this. It goes beyond police work. I warned you. She's desperate."

"To accuse you?"

"No. I'm just a means. To clear herself."

"Clear herself?" Temple absorbed the implication. It wasn't the first Max had made.

She took the ring out of the box, held the slender band between her fingers. Such an innocuous ring, neither engagement ring nor wedding band. Something simple you might give to a child on her confirmation.

"It's an emerald," he said. "Not a bad one, but small. Sincere."

"A piece of the Emerald Isle." A piece of his heart and soul.

He shrugged. "I don't know what I can promise you any more, Temple. I've always been a master of the impossible. Now even the possible seems out of reach." He moved his silverware, inward, outward, both futile gestures, one negating the other, marking time, wasting energy.

"You and Matt, conferring? About me. And Molina?"

"Strange times make for strange alliances." Max straightened in the chair, spun to look at the gibbous moon, spun back. "I'd even say he was your best bet, better than I, except he's even more dangerous for you now than I am. And that's going some."

"Max, I am not contemplating a change of allegiance."

He didn't seem to believe her, or, if he did, it didn't seem to make much difference.

"I've got to go underground again."

"Canada?"

"I can't say. I won't be around to protect myself."

"And me?"

"I hope I'll be protecting you. That's my priority."

"You've always tried to protect people. I hope you include yourself in that."

"I have to, don't I? First piece of business."

"Speaking of business . . ." Temple pulled a small box of her own from her slightly larger evening purse.

"For me? I hope it's not cuff links," Max said. Max the chronic wearer of turtleneck sweaters.

While he opened her box, Temple slipped on the slim ring. It fit best on her third finger, left hand. Max knew her ring finger size. He had left her no choice but an ambiguous one.

"This was the charm that Courtney the secretary wore at the canned-hunt ranch." Max turned the slender charm in his fingers so it caught the candlelight. "She vanished after the arrest. Where on earth did you get it?"

"Master Midnight Louie. He came limping in this morning and

threw this down on the bed. Do you think he knew what he was doing?"

"Impossible. He was out at the ranch. He must have found this in the area where everyone was milling around—man, woman, and beast. He's an alley cat. They're used to biting their way into garbage bags, through plastic and tin foil and into tin cans. He must have snagged it then."

"And kept it and waited until I had a drawing of this very image on my desk and then plopped it down on my bed, just by . . . alley cat-ness?"

"Yes. Because if you're trying to make me believe that Midnight Louie pulled a Lieutenant Molina and tried to ambush you with a lost piece of evidence . . . then he should be climbing the career ladder at the Las Vegas Metropolitan Police Department. Although I would enjoy seeing Molina outmaneuvered by a cat."

"Max, what's really going on?"

Their dinner orders had been taken so not a soul was hovering around to interrupt them. Max rested his elbows on the table anyway, to better to lean forward, lower his voice, and still be heard.

"I just finished giving you a speech a few days ago about how someone in my profession has to keep confidences. Somehow, I feel no obligation to keep this one now."

His caustic glance ricocheted off the ring on her finger. His anger had nothing to do with her or the ring, Temple realized, but everything to do with the Tiffany ring kept in a sandwich baggie at the LVMPD, as everybody now knew.

"You know how I encountered that sad young stripper, Cher Smith, the night before she was murdered. Strangled in a parking lot at another strip club, Baby Doll's, the 'new' venue I'd advised her to find?"

Temple nodded. "Another Sean to avenge."

Max ignored her parallel. He would neither deny nor defend his obsessions. Being a magician from an early age had sealed that fate.

"Molina put me there. In that strip club, on a collision course with Cher Smith. That one move also made me the last person known to have seen Cher Smith alive."

"Molina? How?"

"I was working for her."

"No way!"

"Yes. She had a personal problem. Wanted me to check out a certain guy. Can you guess who?"

It didn't take Temple long to remember the uncharacteristic fear in Max's eyes at the Rancho Exotica, his strange insistence that the ranch guard leave the scene of attempted murder before Molina and the police arrived.

"Rafi Nadir," she guessed. "That creep who just had to lift me out of the Jeep as if I were a southern belle. I thought you'd strangle him. And then, later, you protected him, I never did understand why."

"Understand now." Max's voice grew so deep and intense Temple had to lean inward to hear it. "I wasn't protecting Nadir. I was protecting Molina. And I hated every second of it."

"You? Protecting Molina?"

"She wanted me to keep an eye on this Nadir guy. That's what got me into the strip clubs, where he worked as a bouncer. That's how I met Cher Smith. He was hassling her in the parking lot and I stopped him.

"You know the rest. I took her home. Tried to tell her how to get away from Nadir at least, from stripping too. The next night she died in Baby Doll's parking lot. Strangled."

"Nadir, you think?"

He shrugged. "He's a bully, likes to throw his weight around on women. He's always on the strip club scene like an arsonist at a five-alarm fire. Trouble is, strip clubs were his scene."

"Apparently hunt clubs are too."

Max reached out to touch the small thin gold charm, a mere outline really. "Not so much hunt clubs, I think, as the Synth."

"The Synth? He's connected to the Synth?"

"He's working as a bodyguard at a site I think the Synth is targeting."

"What has all this to do with Molina, other than her asking you to keep tabs on a creepy guy?"

"The 'creepy guy' is the father of her child, and doesn't know it."

Temple opened her mouth. Closed it. Closed her eyes. Tried to picture this. Failed. Opened her eyes.

Max was regarding her with the ironic gaze he was famous for.

"And I thought *my* life is complicated," she said, taking a swan dive into her martini.

\* \* \*

An hour later the moon had vanished, but the carnival panorama of Las Vegas after dark more than made up for it.

Max had suggested they top off their excellent dinners with Bailey's Irish Cream liqueur instead of dessert.

Temple never disagreed with Max when his impulses matched her own.

During dinner they had discussed nothing more innocuous than the old days before chaos and crime has disrupted their Las Vegas unwed honeymoon. The change of subject had given Temple time to digest the new information on Molina and Nadir along with her sea bass.

"So why'd Molina ask you to track Nadir?" she said after savoring the first sip of Bailey's, now braced to return to ugly realities.

"Two reasons: One, no one in the police department knows about him and she wants to keep it that way. Number two: he doesn't know about Mariah, and she wants to keep it that way."

"Why she'd have to do anything about him in the first place?"

"His description had been noted on routine police reports, I guess. It, uh, rang a a very big bell. Remember that time I took off for Los Angeles without much explanation?"

"Yes! You did."

"I was checking out Nadir for Molina. To see if he was still in California. He was a former LAPD officer gone bad. And he wasn't still in LA."

"I don't get it. She called on you for help. She's your worst enemy. Well, maybe not your worst enemy, but your closest and most official. Why'd you do it?"

"Any opportunity to learn more about an enemy's secrets and vulnerabilities is rarer than rubies. Her theory was that I was sneaky and crooked enough to scent out her sneaky, crooked ex–significant other. She was right."

"Molina and Nadir? That's like . . . Queen Victoria and Yasser Arafat."

Max chuckled. "Thanks for painting another indelible picture. I thought so, too, but not nearly as imaginatively. I really don't get it, but I'm convinced Molina is telling the truth this far: Nadir is Mariah's father and she'd move all the neon in Las Vegas to keep either one of them from finding out."

"So you helped her out. Why wouldn't she ease up on you, then? Has the woman no gratitude?"

"None. And that's a key element of human nature, Temple. If you learn somebody's deepest, darkest secret, even at her own invitation, she eventually comes to fear and loathe you for having that edge, for having had to give it to you. Especially a hardnose like Molina, who thinks she can do it all alone."

"Max, how did a veteran like you get caught in the middle like this?"

"I know. I should have rocketed like the Roadrunner away from all this. But after Cher Smith was killed, I couldn't."

"Shades of Sean," Temple said soberly.

"Every senseless death is a shade of Sean." Max swiveled to scan the night sky. Nothing outshone the constellations of Las Vegas. The sky was black and blank. Not even Ophiuchus could be seen, could anybody but they recognize it.

Temple didn't know what to say. Scratch the surface on any part of Max and you always opened the scab of his cousin's death.

So instead she tried to picture Molina and Nadir as a couple and mentally choked on the image. Like the fabled O. J. Simpson glove, it did not fit.

"I did say," she mused, "when you asked me what I thought of Nadir, that he would appeal to a certain kind of woman."

"Molina's kind?" Max had whirled back.

"No. Not at all. But Mariah is what . . . twelve years old? Add almost a year for gestation. We're talking a much younger Molina. Maybe dumber."

"Nadir's a bad enough guy that she doesn't want him to come anywhere near Mariah. I wonder what the kid will make of this if she finds out later. But you see Molina's problem. If she used official police avenues to check out Nadir she'd have a lot of explaining to do. Whys and wherefores. At that point, no strippers had been killed, at least not in the current sequence."

"Hence you. She must have been desperate!"

"Thanks." Max's wry smile faded quickly. "When Cher Smith was killed, it brought everything to a head. I had witnessed Nadir threatening her, but I was the last man known to have any substantial contact with her. It doesn't help that a few days ago I was undercover at a strip club when another girl was accosted in the parking lot. I came on Nadir kneeling beside her, and then Molina came on both of us. I recognized her despite the undercover drag but Nadir didn't."

"What did you do?"

"What she told me. She had a nine-millimeter semiautomatic

pointed at my head. Nadir ran and she let him. I wanted to go after him, stop him, but she wouldn't let me. You tell me what she was thinking. She made it pretty clear that she could forget she saw Nadir and 'remember' just me. She had me dial for assistance on her cell phone and then told me to get out of there."

"What about the girl?"

"She was basically all right, just knocked down. But somebody had her by the throat first, and it wasn't me."

"Then Nadir is the killer!"

Max hesitated. "He could have arrived on the scene just moments before I did. We all could have heard the girl scream. I can only say that he was there first, but Molina has a lot of reasons for not believing that. If she nailed me for these crimes, she could close the casebook and be pretty sure that Nadir would discreetly fade away."

"She'd rather see an innocent man convicted than deal with an old boyfriend?"

Max grinned. "I'm not an 'innocent man' to her. Never have been."

"If only you could reveal your counterterrorism past. Don't you have someone who could testify that you're a good guy?"

"No. We don't operate like that. We can't. You're taking it on my word that I'm a good guy. As far as any official trail shows, I'm an iffy guy. It served me well when I wanted to infiltrate a rogue operation, but it's left me without a safety net. About the only respectability I could claim is my magician career and that ended on a suspicious note, to say the least."

"You're trapped in this . . . circumstantial straitjacket, and every time you try to wiggle out of it, you just draw the buckles tighter."

"Thanks for another vivid but depressing image, appropriate but discouraging."

"What can you do?"

"Find the real killer. Make sure that Molina doesn't overlook, or bury, that person in her zeal to cover her past with Nadir. I suppose you could regard her as an enraged rhino protecting her young."

"Stop! You're going to make me snort with laughter. That's so undignified. So . . . rhinolike! Talk about a vivid image."

"The trouble is, she's out there herself, undercover, in the clubs, covering her tracks and Nadir's. I run the risk of falling into a trap I can't get out of. And then it's her word against mine."

"And mine."

"You're not a witness. Well, maybe a character witness. And even there you can hardly defend me. I've had to keep too many aspects of my life hidden, even from you. No, this charade is between me and her and whoever killed Cher Smith."

"If it's Nadir and he's working somewhere for the Synth, which you're being really canny about not telling me where, he's out of the strip club scene, from what you said."

Max shook his head. "He gets time off. Can't stay away. I've seen him."

"Yuck. How could Molina ever have shacked up with a man like that?"

"You still have some professional respect for her?"

"Well, I like to see women making it in a man's world. I like to think they can bring more sense and integrity to the bull pen, less posturing and selfishness."

Max blinked.

"All right. I know women can be as corrupted by power as the next guy, but I like to think that I would have integrity and compassion even if I got a lot of power."

"There you go. You're imagining what you would do in her place, but you didn't have to go through what she did to get to her place. It changes you, Temple, grappling with a corrupt system, and all systems are corrupt. You have to compromise somewhere."

"I have to admit that Molina always struck me as fairly uncompromising. That's why she irritated me so much. A closed mind is a terrible waste. On the other hand, I never saw her taking the easy way out, or giving it to anyone."

"I warned you that you'd inadvertently overestimated her. She may not sell out for money or power, but she's a mother. She'll do anything to protect her kid."

Temple nodded. She could see that. Couple Mariah in danger with Molina's inbred distrust of someone with a revolving-door past like Max, an elusive sort by profession, and you had ice and water in conflict. Enough ice could chill water to a lethal degree, but mobile, shape-shifting water could wear down ice and even stone all the way to the bottom of the Grand Canyon. It just took a lot of time.

Temple decided she'd put her money on always-flexible water, but that ice had taken over a good part of North America in its day, and had trapped a lot of lost species in its path.

"Don't be glum," Max prodded her, the performer in him incapable of letting anyone wilt in his presence. "I've handled much worse than Molina before. With Nadir somewhat removed from the arena, his presence will be easier to track."

"You almost had him at the last attack scene."

Max nodded. "I need to catch him doing something dirty somewhere that Molina isn't policing."

"It blows my mind, Molina hooked up with a scumbag. Hey . . . maybe that's why she's never had any respect for my faith in you. She assumes all women hook up with scumbags."

"Thanks for the spirited defense. I think. I assume you mean that I am not a scumbag."

"Absolutely. Way too responsible to be a scumbag. 'Course, Molina doesn't see you as responsible, but as irresponsible. You'd think a cop would be a better detective."

"I think you've been up too late, eating and drinking too lavishly. Time to head home."

"And where is that? Don't say second star to the left and straight on to Ophiuchus." Temple leaned her chin on the heel of her hand. She was feeling a little punchy.

"Circle Ritz for you, where Midnight Louie will no doubt be waiting with a perfectly logical explanation of his eighteen-carat deposit."

"Not in his box!"

"Not in his box, but on your bed. Then back to my lair for me."

"Or out joint-crawling?"

"Whatever it takes, Temple. I have to find the one who's been attacking strippers, or Molina will build a case around me. A non-metaphorical straitjacket."

"But going out there hunting makes you look more suspicious."

"She's doing the same."

"She's a cop. She's not going to be suspected of anything except overwork."

"All I can say is, the next time we go head-to-head over a crime in progress, Molina won't be crooning 'The Man That Got Away'."

Matt checked his watch. Almost midnight. Almost time for him to take over from Ambrosia.

He liked to come in early and watch Letitia work. Her voice was melted milk chocolate, and the words caught in the tide were pure caramel.

"So you're feeling bad, honey, that you didn't trust the dude and let the relationship wither. Can't go back. All you can do is admit what you lost and go on. We all do it. Every day. In every way."

Her Valium voice trailed off in a tone of regret that felt personal as she cued the song she'd selected, "The Man That Got Away."

Funny, Matt thought, that title could almost be a cops-and-robbers anthem.

The content, though, was all bluesy self-torment. Matt saluted Letitia's therapeutic instincts in letting the caller wallow in her regrets in such gorgeous style. Showed the feeling was classic, constant, human. Showed you could make art from misery, and warned that you could make misery into an art.

The singer was one of the oldies, Jo Stafford or somebody, but Matt could hear Molina doing this song, if she'd ever subscribe to a song so hopeless, where the woman was so low-down and blue.

It was a great ending to the show, but the clock was a few minutes shy of quitting time. Ambrosia whispered into the mike over the song's closing notes.

"Time for one more request. Once more with feeling. You out there, lonely and blue? Need a little soul music to go on? Come talk to Ambrosia tonight. The moon is full, and so is my song chart."

"I need a special song, Ambrosia," a female voice whispered back.

Matt stiffened to sense the barest lilt of a brogue in it.

"I can't remember the name of it. Can't remember who did it. But I hear it in my head night and day, day and night."

"Maybe it's Cole Porter, honey." The smile in Ambrosia's voice was its own kind of lilt, clean, honest.

"No, something a lot more modern."

"Who's it for, someone you lost?"

"Maybe. Maybe more for someone I haven't completely found yet."

"He's special."

"Oh, yes. Rare, even. But rather elusive."

"The rare ones always are. So have you thought of the song yet?"

"I can't quite remember. It says something like 'I know everywhere you go, I know everything you do'."

The soft, seductive voice on the phone had become a mean-business monotone. "What is the group that does that?"

"The Police." Ambrosia's liquid voice curdled into hard candy. "I don't play that one. It's a stalking song. I don't like to see anyone stalked, even a guy."

"I guess you don't mind hanging onto someone else's guy when you strut out into your own parking lot," the voice taunted.

That's all it said, and the ominous words never made the air.

In the control room, through the glass picture window, Letitia made a horizontal chopping motion, her model's face a mask of fury.

Matt nodded at her through the window. He had recognized Kitty's cold, even tones. The trace of an Irish accent had only enhanced the sinister message. She whispered as if in a confessional, and her voice echoed in his ears though it had never reached the public, his audience.

Letitia, no trace of gentle Ambrosia in her face or figure, stood and motioned him into her seat. They had only two minutes before he would take over.

"That b-woman," Letitia said. "She is beginning to get on my nerves."

He sat down, the leather chair was still toasty, and set up the earphones, the mike, his big glass of water. "My nerves have been gotten to for a long time."

"Well, we've got her vocal tone down. She won't be able to call in here again."

"It'll only make her meaner."

"You ain't seen mean until you've seen me in action. Now forget her and do the show. Don't let her rattle you. She's just a spoilsport."

Letitia left the room but took up a post on the other side of the glass. Guard duty. Nobody was going to mess with the mind, heart and soul of her prize find, Mr. Midnight, late-night advice guru extraordinaire.

"I'm so worried, Mr. Midnight," came the shaky vibrato of a new female voice, a normal if neurotic female voice, through his headphones.

Funny how uncertainty made a female voice supposedly seem "normal." Kitty O'Connor had ditched the presumed normal female role. But she had messed with the wrong woman in Letitia.

Letitia sat like an island idol on the other side of the glass. She no longer left after her stint as Ambrosia, the feel-good soothing music shrink, had ended. Instead, she sat guard over Matt and his callers, a grim powerful presence, more household god than producer, determined that Kitty should not mess up her concept, *The Midnight Hour*, or her on-air personality, Mr. Midnight.

Matt was beginning to feel like an airwave Frankenstein, the misunderstood creation of both his inventor and his worst enemies. A puppet whose strings were tangled between opposing forces. Even those who meant him well somehow became caught in a sick power struggle.

# Chapter 27

# The Lady of the House

A quick scan of Miss Temple's bedroom and her bedroom closet, both left in shocking disarray, tells me that she has decamped in full battle gear: high heels and Opium perfume. So I need not expect her back until near my midnight hour.

I would love to knead my nails in the piles of delicate feminine fripperies, but my timetable does not permit a self-indulgent lingerie fest.

So I rush to run a nail under the French door with the wiggly-waggly latch. In a jiffy it is sprung and I spring through the slit, pausing to pull the door shut behind me.

I am balanced on the patio railing and about to leap onto my escalator to the ground below, the trunk of the canted palm tree, when I hear a hissing from above.

I look around for snakes. Then I look up to see a familiar pair of red eyes gleaming down at me.

Some see signs and portents in the heavens. Ophiuchus, say. I see Karma.

Not mine. Miss Electra Lark's. Karma is the name of her excessively self-confident Birman roommate.

"Louie," she cries from her distant perch. "Come up and see me."

*Sometime!* I want to spit back at her, but I have found it bad luck to ignore Karma.

So I shinny up instead of down the rough palm trunk, and in a Las Vegas minute (which is about three, since people in Las Vegas lose track of time) I am hurling my fighting weight over her railing to land with an impressive thump.

"Oooh! You should join Flab Ferrets, Louie. Methinks that you have been spurning the Free-to-be-Feline of late."

"It does not take a psychic or a Sacred Cat of Burma to figure that one out, Karma. I am not the health food type."

"Obviously."

She is a substantial lady herself, rather Victorian in her way, wearing a flounced ecru dressing gown and a set of snow white mittens and gaiters on her extremities. Her eyes are Prussian blue, but she is no Persian, despite her longish coat. The Birman is a very particular, I might almost say peculiar breed. A distant ancestor supposedly died to protect the life of a dalai lama, and they have never gotten over the honor. So the living ones like to lord it over inferior souls. Like me, for example. I am always handy as an example of an inferior soul.

"I am on my way somewhere," I say. "What do you want?"

"I want to warn you."

"Not that again! I do not need visions of lurking danger. I could use a good lookout at times, but you are a dedicated homebody, so that is out."

I do not like to say it, but Karma, for all her superior spiritual gifts, is something of an agoraphobic, which does not mean that she is allergic to cats of the angora kind but that open spaces terrify her. That is why she never leaves the shadowed environs of Miss Electra Lark's penthouse. I am sure Miss Electra likes light—why else would she be living and working in Las Vegas?—but assumes the shuttered existence in deference to her companion's nervous tics.

"Louie, I must warn you. Forces assemble against you."

"So what else is new?" I sit down and smooth an unruly eye-brow hair. "As long as you are interrupting my exit, I might as well ask if you have heard of a certain Ophiuchus dude."

See, this is what the trained operator does. I do not just ask a simple question, I ask it in such a way that she could make all sorts of wrong assumptions, and from her answer I will learn what she is hiding, if anything. Or if she knows anything. Or if I should care.

"Ophiuchus," she hisses, all the hairs on her housecoat stand-ing straight up. "How do you know of such a sacred and secret sign? You are an unwashed unbeliever."

An unbeliever I may be, but unwashed? Never!

"Listen, nobody runs the tongue concession as frequently and effectively as Midnight Louie. I do not get this black satin coat for nothing."

"I mean that you have not been dipped in the font of eternal knowledge and wisdom."

"I have been dipped in the koi pond at the Crystal Phoenix repeatedly, and can tell you that my wisdom quotient has gone up with each dip, also my nutrient level. Can this 'font' stuff and tell me what you know about Ophiuchus."

"Ophiuchus is a Forgotten One."

I nod. I have not heard of him before, so this must be true.

Her blue eyes narrow. "He was beloved of the Ancients."

"So are a lot of things that are kaput nowadays, like examining entrails."

"As a matter of fact, several of our kind still seek signs in the entrails of birds. I speak of the hidden priestesses of the Raven Cult, for instance."

Yuck! I say, eat 'em or leave 'em, but do not play with your food. These so-called "spiritual types" are the most bloodthirsty on the planet, if you ask me.

"So this Ophiuchus—?"

"Is the Sign of the Serpent Beaver."

"Why is the constellation shaped like a house?"

"Louie, Louie. You have been corrupted by too much human contact. The constellation is not in the shape of a house but of a trap. The Serpent wraps around its victims, ensnares them in its coils. There is no escape."

"This is just a bunch of hot gas jets in the sky, right? Not even the newspaper astrologists remember its name. That is fifteen minutes of fame minus fifteen in my book. Face it. Ophiuchus is the last millennium's teen sensation. History. Forgotten history."

"You are asking about it."

"That is because I have weird friends."

"The stars are eternal."

"Not according to the latest wrinkle in the Big Bang theory. I watch the Discovery Channel."

"I channel discovery."

"My mama is bigger than your mama."

"I do not think so. My mama is a snow leopard."

"Mine is a . . . gangland leader."

"A gangland leader? Surely you are not proud of that, Louie?"

"As a matter of fact, yes. This is the twenty-first century, Karma. Our kind need street smarts these days. Now, if you do not have any practical advice, I will be on my way."

The news of my mama's occupation appears to have tumbled Karma off her high horse. Or perhaps for her kind it is an elephant.

"I just wanted to warn you, Louie. The unseen planet of the hermaphrodite has entered the house of Ophiuchus, the Sign of the Serpent Beaver and thirteenth sign of the Invisible Zodiac. This is not a beneficent sign for you and yours."

"Sure, sure," I say, taking my leave.

In a minute I am down the palm tree trunk and into the foundation plantings.

I am in such haste to leave Karma and her dour rantings behind that I knock my noggin on the leg of an aluminum ladder some careless handy man has left standing.

A love tap on the brain-box does not slow Midnight Louie.

I dash through the parking lot, where my forefoot sends some round gold metal object spinning away like a Frisbee and crashing into a post.

Naturally, I cannot leave without investigating.

The object has split into two halves. My nose fills with a sickly sweet perfume as I accidentally inhale a cloud of fine dust.

Is this some druggie's party kit? Have I taken a fatal dose of some disorienting, illegal, aphrodisiac hallucinogen?

Alas, no. It is merely a compact of ladies' flea powder.

The rough journey, however, has shattered the mirror in the lid.

I see my face reflected as in a microwave oven window, darkly, looking like a living jigsaw puzzle in the web of broken glass.

Who needs to linger in front of an unflattering reflection, other than a masochist?

I am quickly on my way again, leaving Karma's silly predictions and bad omens behind like the insubstantial fairy dust they are.

# Chapter 28

# Stripped for Action

"You!" Lindy Lukas snorted, inhaling cigarette smoke and coughing it out again with her foggy-throated words. "Nobody'd believe you as a stripper, honey. You're too damn short."

"If you only knew how much I hate to hear that," Temple said.

"That nobody'd believe you as a stripper?"

"That I'm too short. That is blatant heightism. Aren't four-inch heels part of the uniform? I'm an expert on spikes."

"So are volleyball players, and they're not stripper material. You can't grab just any old girl and turn her into a stripper. It takes talent."

Temple gazed at the ladies doing their thing onstage at Les Girls. It was the only stripper-run place in Las Vegas, but that didn't mean the classic bump and grind was dead here.

"I suppose I could do you up as a twelve-year-old," Lindy said through her smoke-slitted eyes. "That appeals to some customers."

"I am not doing Alice in Wonderland in a G-string. That is really sick."

"If you have to play a role," Lindy went on, "I'll get you a metal ring of thongs and you can be a costume hustler. You've seen how that's done, I guess."

Temple nodded. Her one backstage experience with strip shows had included a G-string of murders. Strippers were perennial targets for the demented. In a way, she was glad that Lindy had ruled out the role of victim for her. With what was happening to girls in strip clubs in the last few weeks, Temple might be mistaken for a real candidate. And that's not what she wanted, to play decoy. She wanted to play detective.

"Do you have any idea," Temple asked, "who might have killed that one stripper and attacked another one in the club parking lots?"

"Lots of ideas. Too many. It's my job to watch these guys, but it's a hard call. These places attract hustlers. Some of them are customers, but not usually, or self-appointed 'freelance' photographers or serious loose cannons. See that guy over there, who looks like he just left the orgy set of *Gladiator*?"

Temple nodded at the apt description. The man was a kind of Hugh Hefner clone, old and stringy but surrounded by busty Barbie dolls wearing attire stringier than he was. His white hair was combed forward into a Roman fringe designed to camouflage a hairline that had receded like the Tiber in a drought.

"The perfect suspect," Lindy went on. "Wants those girls young enough to be his granddaughters hanging off of him by the dozen. Spends mucho dollars keeping that harem around him every time he comes in.

"After all the money he spends on the pleasure of their public company, you can picture him waiting in the parking lot and assuming one of them could be persuaded in giving him the pleasure of her private company."

"And would she?"

"We're strippers, not hookers. If an individual girl feels sorry for the old coot, that's up to her. But most of 'em can't wait to get out of here. They have lives like everybody else, kids, and boyfriends, husbands."

"So Caesar in his would-be salad days over there really isn't a good suspect?"

"Could be, but I doubt it. He's here to bask in the public attention."

"You ever run into a guy called Rafi Nadir?"

"Raf, yeah sure."

"You *know* him?"

"Well, he never worked for me as a bouncer, if that's what you mean. But he used to come in as a customer."

"Why didn't he work for you? He seems to have been associated with several clubs."

"That's the advantage of us running our own place. I've been retired from stripping probably almost as long as you've been alive, but I've seen it all. Raf was okay as a customer, but give him a smidge of authority and he'd get carried away. It just went to his head. He'd get overaggressive with customers who were basically pussycats, boss the girls around like he was the manager or something. I never gave him the chance to go into overdrive here, and he was fine."

"You're saying he was a petty tyrant, all bluster."

"Unless things went really wrong. That's the trouble with a guy like Raf, you can mostly count on him to be sound and fury, but then that one time . . . all bets are off."

"If somebody he'd been pushing around, a woman, got away and then he ran into her alone again, would he be dangerous then?"

"Like in an empty parking lot? You're asking could he have killed that Smith girl. If the right 'wrong' chain of events came up, yeah. But ordinarily, no. That's my take. I could be wrong." Lindy lit another cigarette off the glowing butt of the last one.

The smoke was making Temple's eyes and throat clog, but she could hardly ask an expert witness to give up an addiction. So she blinked hard to clear her contact lenses and eyed the room again.

She wasn't sure what she would turn up if she visited the strip clubs, but something would be better than nothing. She already had a new angle on Nadir: all bark and less bite. This from a woman who had made it her career to size up men in a New York minute.

Nadir was Molina's bête noir, but there were always two sides to a story. Despite his trashy background, he might not be a killer.

Did Molina think so also? Is that why she let him escape the compromising circumstances, and therefore had to let Max go too? Or was she simply too desperate to risk bringing Nadir in? If he knew she was in town, he could find out about her. He probably would. A man of bluster would not want to leave the past alone. And then he would eventually hear about Mariah. Temple pictured Nadir demanding parental rights, and shuddered.

"You okay?" Lindy said after a hacking cough subsided. "I said I thought Rafi could be less dangerous than he looked, not more."

"I was thinking about something else. Who do you think killed Cher Smith?"

"Oh, hard to tell. Someone who just ran across her, I think. Stinking luck. If she hadn't been in that parking lot at that exact time, if he hadn't happened to have been there. That's the kind of crime it usually is. He probably propositioned her and didn't think she ought to go turning him down. She probably panicked instead of kneeing him and running. Sniffled or tried to scream. That's how these things happen. He panics and is afraid she'll tell."

"So if he's afraid, the killer, there must be somebody he's afraid of."

"Besides the cops?"

"Yeah. If it's all one thing leading to another, escalating. Maybe he's a pillar of the church, or just married. But he's got somebody to answer to."

"Don't we all?"

"Do you?"

"No. But I worked at getting this way a long time, honey. This is all we old broads have to show for the struggle. No one much bothers with us anymore.

"Now. When do you want to become the little G-string girl? I have to get one my suppliers to fork over some of her wares."

"I could sell them for her. I mean, I'd need to look legitimate."

"That's already your problem, Temple. You look way too legitimate to be in here."

"You're right. I don't want to attract undue attention in the clubs."

"Coming in with quick-change stuff will help that. But you need to lose that red hair. Can you get a wig with a kind of hippie bandeau around the forehead, like retro flower child? If you look slightly street-person you can come and go as you please."

The idea of a wig hunt perked Temple right up. Not only was it an instant disguise, she always liked to see herself as other than she was. It was her version of the human potential moment, or her long-buried theatrical urges coming out.

The right wig and not even Max would spot her! Maybe.

"When do I get the costumes?"

"I'll get 'em if you can give me a hundred down. Then, whatever you sell you get to keep."

"Down and done," Temple said, slapping palms with Lindy before digging in her tote bag.

"You didn't say why you want to do this."

"Oh, research for an upcoming job."

"PR work certainly gets into weird areas."

"Certainly does."

Temple spun off the bar stool and passed through the dim and mostly empty club into the dazzling daylight of the Strip. Strip was sort of the key word in Las Vegas: a town that would strip you of your money and your clothes as soon as look at you, and it often did if you were stripped.

Why did she want to do this?

Because she needed to do something to hold off the tightening noose Molina had thrown around Max. Now she could see how quickly his conscience had led him into a quagmire, how much it would suit Molina's hidden and public agenda to arrest Max for Cher Smith's death. They were engaged in a secret duel to the death. A referee was desperately needed.

Max had said the homicide lieutenant was driven by the desire to protect her daughter at all costs. Temple didn't share that maternal fierceness, but she'd seen it before. It was considered a noble urge, but it also could be blinding and dangerous.

Temple had her own to protect, though not a kid, decidedly not a kid. Max had always done everything he could to protect her. It was time she returned the favor. Her conviction about that was very . . . fierce.

*So, c'mon, mama. Let's see who can nail whom first.*

# Chapter 29

# The House of Midnight Louise

It is a long hike over to the Crystal Phoenix and along the way I have plenty of time to brood about Karma's usual mystic mutterings.

I must admit that I have had an itchy-twitchy feeling that has nothing to do with psychic channeling and everything to do with plain old instinct.

I am worried about my little dolls.

You will observe the startling new use of the plural.

Miss Temple, in my opinion, has been lower than a polecat at a limbo contest of late.

I know that she is worried about Mr. Max. And Mr. Matt. And Miss Lieutenant Ma'am C. R. Molina. In some cases she is worried about the sanity and safety of the persons in question. In others—well, one—she is worried what the person in question might do to threaten the safety and sanity of the others.

And I know Miss Louise. She is not one to miss an opportunity to tweak my tail. Yet here I have proceeded, completely tweakless, for almost half a day. Is it possible for a hardnosed dude to miss abuse? I do not think so. But it is possible to deduce that Miss Louise may not be absent of her own free will, because she would never choose to loiter around a spooky old mansion when she could be persecuting me with her presence.

I must proceed logically. Miss Temple is relatively safe with Mr. Max for the night. That is to say, she is safe from anyone other than Mr. Max, and she apparently thinks that is an all right place to be.

So I must first make sure that Louise is missing in action, and then return to the scene of the crime and decide how to find and spring her from Los Muertos. If I did not cross her trail in the house during my previous visit, she might be held prisoner someplace secret and inaccessible, of which that joint has as many such places as a slab of Swiss cheese has mouse holes. What? You thought they were air bubbles?

The Crystal Phoenix's showgirl Big Bird is fanning its neon tail feathers three stories high as I approach. I avoid the sweeping entrance drive and veer around to the side, where the lights are low and the tourists are utterly absent.

I do not expect to be seen, but still dart from palm trunk to palm trunk.

Imagine when I find one of my refuges already occupied.

He growls and I hiss. We face off. It is too dark here to tell exactly what our opponents are, other than natural enemies.

I swipe the air and snag a shiv on a hairy bit of coat.

The growl deepens.

"Listen," I say. "I am just minding my business. I suggest that you mind your own business and we go our separate ways."

I head forward and bump brows with something knee-high to a dump truck.

"I will go right, and you will go left," I suggest.

"No dice. I go right."

"Fine."

We move again. Right into each other.

"Uh, do I go to my right, or your right?"

Oh, great. A Ph.D. candidate. A Doctor of Phoology. "You go to your right and I will go to my right."

We move, dancing in the dark. We stub our toes on each other's hangnalls.

Apparently the tree trunk is no longer between us.

"I demand satisfaction," my invisible partner grumbles.

"Fine. There is a floodlight out behind the service entrance. There is also a pretty big Dumpster near it that should offer plenty of satisfaction."

"I mean a duel. Face to face."

"You have not sized me up yet."

"It does not matter. You have stepped on my toes."

I realize that the doofus means that literally. I have stepped on his toes—and he on mine—and he wants me to fight him over it.

I shrug in the dark. A gumshiv expects frequent challenges to defend his . . . masculinity.

I head forward again and this time do not run into anything, although I do hear the click of large nails alongside me all the way to the back of the building.

As the broad fan of light thrown by the security bulb grows nearer, I glance sideways to check out my companion. For all I know, I could be accompanied by a stork in tap shoes.

No such good luck. My sparring partner, I finally see, is a Great Dane. Must weigh about one-twenty.

"What is a purebred like you doing loose in Las Vegas?" I ask.

"I have run away from home."

"There is not much in the way of single-family housing on the Las Vegas Strip."

"I live at a hotel."

"I did not know that the hostelries around here encouraged dogs on the premises, unless they were greyhounds and running at the track that day."

"This is not a people hotel. That is why I ran away. It is a nasty segregationist institution. I am making a political statement."

The way he says "segregationist institution" I know he has gotten that phrase from someone else. From their brain to his lips.

"What is the name of this joint?"

"They call it the Animal Crackers Inn. You can see that even the name is denigrating. It implies that all animals are crackers."

"Never assume ill will when idiocy could be a cause. You know that people have a disgusting weakness for cute names when it comes to animal-related businesses. It is nothing we of the superior species should take personally, unless we wish to waste our time on human foibles."

"Foibles?"

"Ah, quirks."

"Quirks?"

Why do I think this guy's brain cells have also run away from home, without him?

"It is their problem!" I say. "My problem is why a big bozo like you has a hair-trigger temper. My shivs need sharpening but I prefer a less lofty target. Not that I could not slice the nose hairs off King Kong if I had a mind to."

"Oooh." The Great Dane sits down and still manages to be as tall as Miss Temple barefoot. "I do not feel so well. I have an upset stomach."

"That is what you get for accosting everybody who crosses your path in the dark."

"No. It is all the rich food that the chef leaves out for me."

"You ran away from home—okay, a hotel—and you have a chef feeding you? Some political statement."

"Chef Song means well, but his style of food is alien to my diet."

For a moment my mind boggles at a Dane subsisting on bok choy and egg foo yung, although I do think that they would have sushi in common, or pickled herring at least.

"So you are another pet of Chef Song," I say, my mind always on my investigation.

"I am no one's pet," he growls, leaping to his nine-inch-nailed feet, which scrape the concrete as chalk does a blackboard.

This gets my back up of course, and it looks like our little back-alley do-si-do is on again.

"Wow," he says, his artificially perked ears backing off a little. "You look just like those Halloween dudes. Pretty spooky."

"Now that is an out-and-out stereotype," I say as I de-arch my back and let my electric hairdo settle down into the usual sleek pompadour. I have learned to speak his language. When that happens, fisticuffs can be avoided. "You should be ashamed of yourself, a denigrated species in your own right, passing on the prejudice."

He lies right down, snugs his huge black nose between his fawn-colored paws and whimpers. "You are right. I am a bad dog."

Great Bastet! These self-accusing sessions try my patience. It is too easy these days to chew your own mitts instead of looking around for the mitts that pull the strings.

"Look," I say. "I do not care if you are a pit bull on speed or Charo on chew sticks, I just want some information. I am looking for a dame. A little doll. Looks a lot like me except she is smaller, fluffier, and, er, meaner. She is one of Chef Song's favorites."

"Oh, Louise! Why did you not say you were a friend of Louise's? She is the cat's, uh . . ." He thinks, visibly. ". . . peignoir. Such a sweet little gal. She is the one who hooked me up with Chef Song after I had fled my life of enforced luxury."

"Happy to hear it," I grit between my teeth.

My supposed partner has never lifted a whisker to negotiate a truce between my and my worst enemy on two legs, Chef Song, who is sentimentally attached to a food source, his koi and mine, our mutual gold mine, the fascinating fins in our lives. You would think a chef who serves sushi would understand my wee addiction to koi fresh from the pond. I cannot help it that he has made the odd decision to watch these fish instead of serving or eating them.

"When did you last see the little . . . dear?"

"Hmmm. Yesterday. It was egg drop soup and szechuan shrimp. Made me sneeze and rub my nose."

When I look blank he adds, "Lunch."

"Lunch yesterday. You say that Louise ate this disgusting slop?"

"She is quite the . . . connoisseur."

"Why do you pause so long between words?"

"I must remember my mistress's expressions. She speaks to me only in . . . French."

No wonder the poor fellow is so confused and an easy target for extremist political activists. Why cannot his mistress speak his language, Danish? People are so self-centered.

"And what nationality is your mistress?"

"Ah . . . Californian. Or is it Vegan?"

No wonder! I did time at an upscale Palo Alto motel in my youth, and the sympathetic ladies used to leave out chocolate cake for my starving pals. Maybe to them chocolate *is* protein. At least it is not fatal to cats, as it is to dogs, though it is hardly the nutrition needed by the starving.

"Well, I will leave you by the Dumpster here. Perhaps you will find something succulent, besides me, inside. You need to get off that foreign food."

I have what I needed to know, so I skedaddle. I leave the Great Dane torn between two cuisines: Chinese and Chinese, fresh or well-aged junk food.

It is obvious that a rescue mission is called for at Los Muertos.

I recall the trail left indoors by unseen hordes of cats. If Midnight Louise has run afoul of a gang, she could be minced mouse by now.

My pace quickens, though I am not much paying attention to where I am going. It disturbs me that I found no trace of her on my previous visit.

The idea is strangely upsetting. I am almost run over by a skateboarder.

Of course if I can recruit Osiris and Mr. Lucky to my side, I might stand a chance.

But how to get them into the house? It will not be through Miss Louise's discovered dryer vent pipe, of that I am sure. Unless Mr. Max Kinsella can shrink two Big Cats to the size of Pomeranians.

And of course there is the matter of where he might be even if I were able to find a way to persuade him to come to Louise's aid. We do not talk the same language, the Mystifying Max and I.

# Chapter 30

# *Irreconcilable Differences*

"Tess," Temple said, figuring that she'd react most naturally to the same first initial as her real name.

She glimpsed her shoulder-length ash blond hair in the facing walls of mirror, fascinated by how different she looked. Besides, it was less stressful than eyeing her conversation partner.

"So, Tess," said the tall, virtually naked woman standing in the middle of the room. She did wear very high heels, however. "How long have you been selling this stuff?"

"This stuff" was the gaudy array of nylon spandex concoctions that hung from a giant version of a steel key ring hoop around Temple's right wrist.

"Not long. This is my sister's stock, but, well, she's a little freaked by the parking-lot attacks."

"So are we." The woman's long artificial fingernails paged through the bountiful patterns of skimpy stretch fabrics and cut a silver lamé number from the herd. "Let me try that one."

Temple spun the hoop until that item was near the latching mechanism. She sprung the hoop open and lifted off what looked like tangled suspenders . . . or, to her mother's generation of women, a sanitary napkin belt . . . or to eleven-year-old boys, maybe even a slingshot. Or maybe not, considering how sexually sophisticated eleven-year-old boys were getting nowadays.

"Cute." The woman twisted to face one set of mirrors, crushing the fabric strips against her naked torso.

*I have been here before, I have seen this before, I am not uncool about it.*

Temple repeated this mantra once more, still searching for someplace neutral to look. She had never gotten into the girls-in-the-buff health club scene, but always ducked into shower stalls or toilet cubicles to change clothes in decorous privacy. Perhaps that was because she was small . . . and, ahem, small . . . and would seem even smaller in all departments by direct comparison.

"Great!" The happy customer delicately stabbed her four-inch spikes through certain openings in the fabric like someone doing a Highland fling. The stretchy fabric was pulled up into snug place, becoming a teeny tiny thong on the bottom half and a random arrangement of straps on the top that could take a passing swipe at covering her nipples. Sort of.

"How do you know where all that's supposed to go?" Temple asked. "And doesn't it . . . chafe?"

"Oh, it's not on long enough to do much of anything. And it goes where I say it goes. How much did you want?"

Temple had been coached, but the ridiculous price stuck in her craw. "Forty-five dollars."

"Fine." The woman's nails rifled a lime-green sequined bag big enough for a cell phone and some paper money to pull out a fifty-dollar bill. "Keep the change. I really just love this."

She writhed into various poses in the mirror, working the straps off her shoulders, down her stomach. Every move was judged through narrow, dispassionate eyes.

"You've got some sexy fabrics there," she told Temple.

"Thanks. You've got some sexy moves."

"You ever stripped?"

"Ah . . . I'm too short for it. I'm told." This was the only time in her life Temple had been pleased to be found wanting in height.

"Oh, don't listen to anyone else. You could build a real exotic act around being so little. You know, china doll, or Catholic school girl. That's always a popular one. The guys go wild over those little plaid uniform skirts."

"Oh, really. Why do you think that is?"

"Grade school repression, silly! When you work up an act, you gotta think: what would a horny twelve-year-old find sexy?"

"That young?"

"Oh, they can be sixty or seventy and still think like that. Generally, they like the illusion of really, really innocent or really, really naughty. So what's your sister's name?"

"Ah . . . oh, my sister." Desperate. "C-Carmen."

"Carmen? That doesn't exactly go with Tess."

"Theresa," Temple said.

"My real name's Monica Mary, and now I get it. Theresa and Carmen. You girls could do a sister act, you know, a real nun thing. Go over big."

"Not with the Vatican, I think."

"I got news for you. They don't come here."

"Anyway, if you like our stuff, I'll be around for a while."

"How come you're not afraid of the Stripper Killer?"

"Ick, is that what they're calling him?"

"That's what we're calling him. So you're not afraid."

"I am, but I need the money more than . . . Carmen. What do you think? Are any of the clubs a bigger target? Am I safer here? What about when I should leave? I hear that poor Cher Smith was attacked at two A.M. Maybe if I made sure I was out of the clubs by one A.M.—"

"Hey, two A.M.'s a good time. It's when we kind of shift off, although here in Vegas you can go all night."

"You mean that a lot of you leave around two A.M. Wouldn't the parking lot be crowded then?"

"It's not like we run in packs. We're all pretty much loners. It gets intense in the dressing room, but what we like about the life is we can come and go when we please. A lot of us get picked up, you know? We don't have to worry about parking lot prowlers when a Hell's Angel on a Harley shows up to carry us home."

*Swing low, sweet chariot.* Temple nodded, thinking she'd rather take her chances in public with the Stripper Killer than have a Hell's Angel in her private life.

The door to the dressing room banged against the wall. Two women came caroming in with the speed and impact of bowling balls, toting tiny purses and huge gym bags.

"Monique! That's absolutely adorable, girl!" screeched the black woman with blond hair.

Monica Mary, aka Monique, stretched and preened in her silver lamé slingshot.

"Where did you get it?" demanded the white woman with the long, jet-black Afro.

Obviously, exotic was in. Guess they didn't call it exotic dancing for nothing, since that was a sound-alike for erotic.

Monique's daggerlike nail pointed at Temple's hoop of overpriced Spandex.

By the time Temple departed, her hoop was lighter and her wallet was fatter.

She had glimpsed the girly backstage atmosphere at strip clubs before. It always made her feel sad, the sooo high school element of girls having a good time experimenting with makeup and clothes. Only these girls were here to take off the clothes. Once they'd been cheerleaders and prom queens, or maybe not either. That was another route to the black lights that cast an ultraviolet purple haze that made whites look lurid on cheesy stages in every major city and minor hamlet across this land.

This backstage interaction was the oddly innocent side of the industry, and it struck Temple as more real than all the calculated moves and pouty faces under the spotlight. It was a female support group, only most of their support seemed to come from ultra-narrow spandex. *A band of spandex is comin' after me . . . comin' for to carry me home.* Only it wasn't a band of angels that had carried Cher Smith home.

Girls just want to have a good time, but some of them never learned a liberated way to have it.

Temple checked her watch before diving through the door that led to the major sound-system assault in the club area. Just past midnight. Matt Devine would be taking his first call of the night at WCOO's Midnight Hour. To watch the two P.M. "shift change," Temple would have to kill some time and she didn't want to spend it backstage slinging spandex suspender sets. *She sells spandex suspenders at the strip show.* No thanks. Let sister Carmen handle that part. Carmen. Why had her subconscious been unable to dredge up any name but that one? Weird.

In the performance area, Temple managed to climb onto a bar stool and sat facing the club, her ring of costumes covering her lap like a folded coat.

"Drink?" the bartender hinted behind her.

Nothing was free in a strip club, especially not a barstool.

Temple dug out a ten-dollar bill and asked for a margarita. That ought to buy her about half an hour.

"Sell any?" he asked when he plunked the pale, snot-colored drink in front of her. She would bet that there was about as much tequila and lime in the glass as there was Carmen in her Northern European soul. *Nada.*

*Sell any?* Temple was fleetingly tempted to take umbrage, but then she remembered the rainbow of glitzy fabrics on her lap.

"Yeah, several. I thought I'd watch some of the girls' acts. Get more ideas for outfits."

"You do whatever you like," he said, "as long as you feed the kitty or you feed the bartender."

Temple glanced stageward. A lone girl was striding across it to a drumbeat, squatting every now and then to wrap her fingers around some moonstruck guy's neck and let his fingers jam paper money down the skimpy pocket of her Tess-sold thong. Temple presumed that was "feeding the kitty."

She sipped the pallid margarita. It tasted more of lemon water than anything else.

*The stripping profession is a lifestyle choice,* she reminded herself. Who was she to judge? According to Molina, Temple was in an intimate relationship with a suspected murderer, and Molina ought to know, having been in an exploitive relationship with another murder suspect.

Speak of the devil.

Temple gazed across the huge room with anxious recognition. *Wasn't that him?* Rafi Nadir? Standing in the first row of tables, watching the woman onstage. He nodded as she passed. She winked back.

So he was indeed a genuine habitué of these places. A bouncer, Max had said. A man who liked to hang around naked ladies, who wallowed in the loud, sleazy atmosphere.

Her disguise was great, like wearing sunglasses on the street, Temple decided as she checked herself out in the mirror. Her actress aunt, Kit Carlson, would be proud of her. Amazing what one heavy-haired wig could do. She could watch everyone, just some idling costume pusher waiting for the next shift of dancers to come in and grab her wares.

Associated pros often came and went at strip clubs: photographers, costume hawkers, maybe even undercover cops.

*O holy nightgown!* Nadir was heading her way.

Temple turned back to the bar to swig from the smudgy margarita glass. She did *not* want to be caught making eye contact with a murder suspect. Also, he had seen her before, sans the Dyan Cannon locks. What had Max said? An ex-cop? He'd be good at penetrating disguises.

"Hey, Jay," his deep voice addressed the bartender behind her. "Anything shakin' tonight besides booty?"

"The usual usual," Jay answered, filling his order for scotch on the rocks.

Temple noticed that Nadir's drink had more color and needed less color of money to pay for it than her watered-down drink had required. Apparently he was known here.

"No suspicious characters?" Nadir asked.

"Just you." Jay snickered. "You're not hired heat anymore, why worry?"

"This used to be my beat." Nadir's eyes, so dark the black pupils melted into the surrounding iris, scanned the entire club.

Temple wondered if his pupils were dilated from being high on something, or if he just came with creepy jet black eyes, like a larger-than-life cartoon villain.

She remembered Thomas Harris's one chilling fantasy touch in his description of Hannibal the Cannibal Lecter. He had "maroon" eyes.

How could Molina suspect Max's true-blue eyes (sometimes disguised by contact lenses as alley-cat green) when here stood a suspect with eyes as black as his presumed heart?

Supposedly Molina had at one time fallen for this man, this hired muscle, this jaded strip club junkie.

Just as her description of Nadir was yearning toward truly extreme heights of distaste the man himself turned to her. "You're new."

"Not according to my mother."

He was speechless for a second, then laughed. "So you sell overpriced elastic bands. How's business?"

"Good. And they're not overpriced. It takes tremendous skill to make the 'gather' setting on a sewing machine pay off. These costumes have to survive a lot of . . . stress."

This time he exploded with laughter, his dark eyes almost disappearing inside the fleshy eyelids.

"You got that right, kid. So, is your sister a stripper? How'd you get into this scene?"

"You got the sister part right. She does this." Temple shook her hoop like a Salvation Army girl her tambourine. There was no noise, though, which wouldn't have been heard over the sound system anyway. She and Nadir were shouting at each other, although only two feet apart.

Yikes. She was sitting *only two feet away* from Molina's ex–sleaze-a-squeeze and the only man in Las Vegas, or anywhere, that Max Kinsella had shown any fear of. Wow.

"Say, you're kind of cute," he said, as if just noticing that. Having a strip club epiphany of sorts.

Anyone else called her cute, she'd raise a ruckus.

This was the fearsome Rafi Nadir, so she'd accept it. "Thanks. I won't say you're kind of cute yourself."

Again he laughed. She got the impression he didn't do a lot of that and he enjoyed the novelty. He was . . . gasp . . . enjoying her.

"What's your name?"

"Tess."

"That all there is?"

"That's all there is around here."

"Smart. You never know who you're talking to."

"Well?"

He shrugged, let a smile touch his lips, smugly. "My name's Raf."

"Smart."

He aimed his forefinger like a pistol. "Bang. You're faster on the uptake than most of the broads around here."

"Maybe it's because I'm not a broad."

He digested that along with some sodium-rich snack sticks salted with about three peanuts from a bowl on the bar that Temple had rejected forever after one try. Salty snacks encouraged drink orders, and bloating in the female of the species. Better dead than bloated.

"You want to go someplace where we can talk?"

Temple couldn't believe her luck: Rafi Nadir, feeling talkative, all to herself.

Too bad she didn't dare risk going as far as the jukebox with him, not that there was one here.

He read her hesitation so fast she thought he was Max. Predators were like that. Funny, she'd never thought of Max as a predator before.

"How about a quiet table?" he suggested.

"There is one in this place?"

He jerked his head toward a far corner. "There is one in every place. You just gotta know the terrain."

She shrugged her acquiescence and slid off the barstool.

"Leave that," he said, stopping her hand from reaching for the drink. "Send over a real one for the lady," he growled at Jay.

Temple was glad she had ditched the high heels, the better to disguise her daily habits, the better to run for her life.

His hands were always on her: between her shoulder blades to guide her toward the right table, at her elbow to thread between the tables, on her shoulder to follow her down onto the chair he pulled out for her.

With a man you were attracted to, it was a barrier-breaking, seductive exercise.

With a shady character, it was stomach-knotting. Temple wanted to use her fabric ring like a barrier to fend off his attentions, but undercover junior G-girls didn't get any good leads that way.

"Amazing," she said after Jay had come and gone, leaving a margarita with a high lime color behind. "It really is quieter here."

Nadir pointed to the ceiling. "In Vegas you always gotta check the ceilings. They're not only where the spy cameras lurk, but the loudspeakers. This is a loudspeaker-free zone."

"How'd you know all that?" Temple asked, sipping her margarita through its short, obligatory straw like a teenager at a soda fountain. She figured the more naive and impressionable she acted, the more information she'd get.

"It's my business."

She waited, sucking on her straw. Whew. This margarita had a tequila kick.

"I'm in security. Right now I'm working for a major Strip celebrity, but before that some of the strip clubs asked me to check out their systems."

"Wow. How do you get into that kind of work?"

He hesitated. The urge to impress won out over discretion. "I've got a history in law enforcement."

She bet he did! What was the expression Max had used? Rogue cop.

"So you went from the LVPD to private eye work."

"Private security," he corrected her. "Private eyes are rip-offs. Their rep is all from books and the movies."

Temple was still congratulating herself on leaving out the M in LVMPD. Unlike many cities, Las Vegas's police force was called the Las Vegas *Metropolitan* Police Department, because there was also a North Las Vegas Police Department. If she had used the official set of alphabet soup to refer to the force, Nadir would realize she knew a bit more than she should. Which wasn't much, but at least it was a fine point or two, thanks to her brushes with Molina.

Molina! Was married to this guy! Or shacked up with him! *Imagine that. No, don't imagine that,* she told herself on redirect. She didn't want to gag on the only real drink she had ever gotten in a strip club.

She had to admit that Rafi Nadir knew how to operate around here. That meant he would also know how to operate unseen and unsuspected around here. And certain murderers, especially sex murderers, loved to revisit the scenes of the crimes.

"Are you cold?"

"Huh? Oh, goose bumps. Just nervous."

"This is all new to you, right?"

"Yeah. My sister does this stuff. Does all right with it too. But she's—"

"She's what?"

"Scared. There was a stripper killed not too long ago at one of the clubs. Outside one of the clubs. And another girl was just attacked. She had all these, ah, suits made up and decided she didn't have the nerve to hang around and sell them, so I said I would."

"What makes you such a brave little girl?"

*Grrrrr.* Temple hated condescension, even coming from potential serial sex killers. "I lost my job, so I guess I was just desperate. Anyway, I'm glad to see that the clubs have security experts like you working to keep us all safe."

She apparently had hit the litany of buttons that made Rafi Nadir resonate like a choir boy singing soprano, or ring like a slot machine that had just coughed up three cherries in a row.

246 • Carole Nelson Douglas

"Don't you worry. This creep'll get caught."

"You sound pretty certain. Any reason?"

He leaned close. Even with this "quiet" table, the grinding rock music was always pounding the edges of your attention, flattening them like tin.

"I was there."

"There?"

"In the parking lot of this one club. Secrets. Some guy was with Cher Smith. I stopped them to make sure it was on the up-and-up."

"And—?"

"He cold-cocked me. Moved faster than a whipsnake. I don't often take a hit. Cher drove off. I think he followed her."

Temple frowned. She'd heard this story the other way around. Oddly, Nadir's version jibed with Max's, except. . . .

"That was the killer. She was dead in another strip joint parking lot the next night. I saw the killer. That's why I come back and hang around, even though I've got a better job elsewhere. I saw the guy. I'll see him again. Guys like that don't stop."

Temple was speechless, probably the best thing she could have done.

Nadir was setting up Max to be the killer. If Molina could ever overcome her extreme prejudice against crossing paths with Nadir, that's the story she would get out of him and it would give her every-thing she'd ever wanted.

How ironic.

"Now don't be afraid." Nadir reached out to pat her hand. He didn't. His own closed over it, trapping it against the slick tabletop. "That's why I'm here. I saw the guy. He wears disguises, but I'll know him again."

"How do you know you will?"

"Because I did see him again. That girl who was attacked outside Kitty City? I was there too. He got away. Some dumb-ass undercover narc bitch was there and blew my one chance to nail the guy. I had him in my reach, but she held a gun on us both. She arrived just after I came on him with the girl down. She couldn't tell which one of us was the real killer so the stupid . . . broad let him get away, and forced me to go after him."

"Did you get him?"

"No. He had too big a start on me. He can disappear like Lance

Burton, this guy. But don't worry, unless you see some guy over six feet tall. That he can't quite hide. Tall guy. You look out then."

Temple nodded, sober despite the kick-lime margarita. She could swear that Nadir believed his own story. But then, pathological killers always had some self-justifying notion.

She pulled her hand from under his to pick up the big glass bubble of the margarita glass in both palms and drink from the rock salt-slathered rim.

Her lips curled at the caustic taste, even as her skin crawled.

She had either just heard the twisted spiel of a stone-cold killer, or there was more to these murders than Max, Lieutenant Molina, and even Rafi Nadir knew or was telling her.

"So where'll I find you tomorrow night?" he was asking, as if she'd want to be found by him.

Maybe she did.

She leaned in to whisper one word to him.

# Chapter 31

# *Shadows*

Matt couldn't help thinking about computer hackers as he stepped out of the small WCOO office into the empty parking lot.

You never saw them, hackers, but they came knocking on your cyber-door, and huffed and puffed until they blew your house down. Their only motive was spite, pure and simple. They didn't have to know you to hate you. They struck and ran, leaving your entire system slowly eating itself. They were thugs, vandals, cyber-stalkers.

Kitty was like that. Maybe, like hackers, she took pride in mindless destruction. It was more fun to ruin a stranger than an acquaintance. Some poor Job who stood there naked and bleeding, asking the universe, "Why me?" Evil without motive, logic, gain, was more unsettling than all the seven deadly sins combined.

Letitia had left a few moments before him, at his insistence. He said he had to be a "big boy." Basically, he had to make sure she wasn't with him in case Kitty showed up.

He'd ridden the Hesketh Vampire tonight and every night since she had accosted him and Letitia in this very lot.

The Vampire was one sleek, shining, silver gauntlet thrown down on the empty black asphalt. She wanted to play motorcycle nightmare on her Kawasaki, he was ready to play back.

He figured they were pretty well matched. He had the anger and she had the nerve. Anger could betray you, of course, but it also was a fearless motivator.

He unlocked the cycle, took the helmet off the handlebar, put it on, donned the leather gloves, mounted, kicked the stand up, balanced all the bike's awesome weight on his boot-toes for a moment before throttling up and cruising down the smooth asphalt.

He was alone except for the shadow he cast in the pink-grapefruit-color parking lot lights high on their standards, like artificial moons stuck on fence posts. Pumpkin heads on scarecrow stalks.

His shadow was a low-rider, a sidecar running alongside the Vampire's high-profile bulk. The motor throbbed like hard-rock music, guttural and insistent, announcing itself to the night.

There was no way to be subtle on a motorcycle. It was an instrument of the self-advertised, married to a machine. *I am inhuman. Hear me roar.*

Overweight people, outcast people, overcontrolled people all found freedom on a motorcycle.

Matt wondered if that was why he had hated the Hesketh Vampire at first: too flashy, too noisy, too look-at-me.

Now he thought that he had been the too-too one. Too modest, too quiet, too self-effacing. Was that what had drawn Kitty O'Connor to him? Bullies always needed a victim, and a bully was what she was. Motorpsycho nightmare.

He watched his side mirrors. The helmet muted sound; it was like cruising inside a noisy silent movie, the familiar cityscape sliding by, sometimes at a pinball-machine tilt.

And then it was there: the black ball of a gadfly in his right mirror, moving up fast.

He tilted, swept left down an unknown street. Then right, swerving. Skating the dry warm streets, bike and man moving to a Strauss waltz, like the space station in *2001: A Space Odyssey.*

It was past 2001 now. It was past odyssey and into obsession.

He rode for the sake of it, for the oneness of it, only visiting the mirror now and then, finding the black spot clinging to him like a burr, but still a block or two behind.

What did she really want? What could she really do? Try to crowd him off the street into an accident? She didn't want any accidents to happen to him. *She* wanted to happen to him. So . . . if he wouldn't rattle, would she rock and roll? Quit? Give up? Just enjoy the chase and drop out?

He had nowhere to go. Nowhere to lead her. She knew where he worked and lived. She didn't know a thing about his internal landscape, except what she guessed or hoped to produce.

There was a strange freedom in deciding she could do him no harm, that she was trapped by wanting to harm him in certain limited ways.

She was gaining on him. He didn't particularly care. Maybe he'd spin around in a 180-degree stop. Wait for her. See what she'd do.

At least it was just him and her. No innocents in the way. Did she understand that trapping him alone with her was not the threat; it was trapping him with someone else?

Yes, or she'd never have brought that poor girl along to the Blue Dahlia.

He had to make her think that the game was more interesting when she came solo.

So he did it, swept the Vampire in a tight, tilted circle and dragged his toe along the ground to balance it to a swaggering stop.

And waited for her.

Like a fly you're about to swat, she played coy. Throttled down to a dull grumble, hovered three hundred feet away, the Kawasaki snorting and smoking like a stalled dragon.

It reminded him of a bull, so he revved up and raced at her, a toreador on ice.

His aggression caught her off guard. She swept away left down a dark, unlit street.

He followed, on the attack for once, liking it far too much. The worst thing an enemy can do is to make you like him. Like Cliff Effinger, mean, violent, hair-trigger. Still . . . he had seen, learned from a master. Maybe he needed a little of Cliff Effinger to deal with Kitty O'Connor.

He was an amateur.

She had roared out of sight, then silenced.

When he moved past an intersection, she shot out across it like a cannonball.

He almost spun out sideways in order not to hit her.

And the point was made.

He still wanted to avoid conflict. Crashing. Charging.

He turned the Vampire in a large circle and roared away, the chased rather than the pursuer now.

And now she retaliated. Buzzed up close like a wasp, agitated his jet stream, wobbled close to his wheels. It was like the chariot race in *Ben Hur*, nerve and dirty tricks and only the power of one Christian God to pull his fat from the fire.

He recognized his earlier hubris, the misplaced faith in the machine, in his new devil-may-care attitude. All the devil cared about was pride going before a fall, and Matt was pushing, was being pushed into taking the Vampire into a hasty, bruising scrape along asphalt and concrete.

He felt a pain, as if the machine's metal skin were flesh and blood and he would be responsible for its grazing.

He jumped a curb without thinking about it, the jolt bone-jarring. He was barreling along sidewalk on a thankfully deserted street, ducking unclipped shrubbery.

Innocent greenery snapped away from his helmet, his handlebars.

His side mirrors reflected slashes of the rare streetlight. He sensed his pursuer rather than saw or heard her.

All he heard was his own breakneck progress and the thought that this had to end with a mistake, badly, in a crash.

Ahead loomed the deserted industrial park he had used to dodge a pursuing motorcycle before, long before he knew that Kitty O'Connor was after him.

It was odd, the motif of the pursuing motorcycle, like a nightmare, like a cop, like the Hound of Hell or Heaven, like fate.

Matt twisted the hand throttle, poured on the power, turned a 45-degree angle around a building whose glass eyes had all been shot out.

The buzz was right behind him. He was going to cut the next corner too close or too far and he and the Vampire would go sliding horizontal into the dark night and hard ground for a long, long screech of yards.

Something came slicing behind him, crossways, like a buzz saw.

Another cycle. Big. Gaudy. Older than the Vampire. Bigger than the Vampire. All bristling chrome and wire wheels, a red vintage Harley-Davidson.

It swept a huge circle and came up behind him.

The motor throbbed like Wagner's Pilgrims' Chorus, like the Valkyrie on the warpath.

The rider wore no helmet, just a pair of wraparound sunglasses as pitch-black as tar.

His hair was windswept tar. His knuckles on the handles were white in the night, ungloved.

He wove behind Matt, left and then right, and every swerve put itself between the Vampire and the Kawasaki that followed.

Then the huge machine moved up on Matt, slowly but certainly.

He rode in Matt's left blind spot, like a cowboy herding a steer.

Matt couldn't engage with the other motorcycle. This interloper had interposed itself between them. He found himself resenting the intrusion.

It had been him and Kitty O'Connor and now they were three.

He was being herded out of the empty shopping center back toward the freeway and civilization and speed limits and population.

It occurred to him that he ought to be grateful, but he wasn't.

Maybe this would have ended it, once and for all.

He was being herded too damn fast.

His speedometer in the lurid dashboard lights read ninety miles per hour and he'd hardly noticed it.

His escort pulled abreast without revving up a decibel.

He glanced over, saw the lacquered hair, the thick sideburns.

Elvis saluted and pushed inward to force Matt onto the entrance lane of Highway 95.

In his right mirror Matt saw the overbuilt motorcycle turn like Leviathan to face the oncoming black blot of the Kawasaki.

Damn, but he wanted to see the outcome of that collision!

The night swallowed the images of the two motorcycles. He was awash in headlights and taillights and seventy-mile-an-hour lane changers and overhead lights as bright as the morning star.

This was Las Vegas, and his money was on Elvis. There was no percentage in messing with a living legend, especially after he was dead.

Matt felt a new swell of appreciation for the time-honored religious tradition of patron saints.

Elvis made a troubling spiritual figure, despite his clumsy aspirations to the role while living, but as a ghost he was pretty damn impressive.

# Chapter 32

# *Heads or Tails?*

At least I am able to return at a decent hour.

I manage to beat Miss Temple back to the Circle Ritz and am lounging on the comforter with my rear leg hiked over my shoulder like an Enfield rifle on parade, grooming an intimate part of my anatomy, when she comes waltzing in.

"Still up, Louie?" she asks the obvious . . . unless it is a question of a personal nature and therefore not so obvious.

Either way, I do not deign to answer, as usual.

I am too miffed by her bizarre appearance to deign to notice her.

When she leans over the bed to give me a midnight smooch, I turn my head away. Has she not looked in a mirror lately? Not that I go for dames who would place looking in a mirror over looking at me, but an occasional peek could spare another individual much distress.

"What is the matter, Louie?" She backs off, puzzled, her adorable little muzzle all wrinkled like a shar pei's, who are not so adorable. Then she runs into herself in the dressing table mirror.

"I bet it is the wig! You did not want all this blond Dynel rubbing on your whiskers. Well, this is history. For now."

She strips off the Lauren Bacall "do" to reveal her own sassy curls all crushed beneath. This girl could use a good grooming, but my tongue is not for hire. I have enough square footage of my own to tend to.

"These are wild," she says vaguely in my direction.

I hear a click and then the large silver ring on her forearm snicks open.

All is forgiven! An armload of cat toys!

I bound from the bed and leap into action, batting, snagging, toothing.

"Louie! These are borrowed goods. Let go. No! Bad boy! Please!"

That is Miss Temple's idea of domestic discipline, all right. She wields the Carrot of Cajolery and the Big Stick of Superior Force in such rapid turns that a guy could commit sixteen felonies or hara kiri while she was making up her mind whether to slap or tickle him.

She hangs my playthings on the top of the ajar closet door.

"I agree," she tells me, "that those skimpy string monokinis would make ideal cat toys, but I need them for my undercover work."

Perhaps she meant *uncovered* work.

I decide right then that despite my misgivings about Miss Midnight Louise I had better keep an eye on Miss Temple and her midnight ramblings.

So much for taking on a partner. Now I am stuck with a partner missing in action and the previous case of the stripper killer heating up and no one at hand to lend a mitt in either instance.

Perhaps I shall have to hone my delegating skills further, first thing tomorrow.

Meanwhile, Miss Temple has totally thrown off her undercover persona to slip under the covers with yours truly. It is while we are rubbing noses and murmuring sweet little nothings that I resolve to defy logic and physical science and pursue two cases at once.

# Chapter 33

# *Did You Ever See a Dream Walking?*

Temple often thanked her checkered employment history for a brief detour into the thespian arts.

That explained how she was able to call Molina the next morning, as innocent and bright as sunshine.

"I've been thinking about what you said about Max," she began.

"Good."

"Maybe not."

"For you or for me?"

"Well, the thing is"—Temple hated people who used "the thing is," and hoped Molina did too; would bet that Molina did too—"the thing is, I need to know the *exact time* that Cher Smith was killed."

"Why?"

"Well, it could be that I know where Max was, and was *not*, at that time."

"That night? You remember the timetable of that night?"

"He told me about it the next day."

"The killing?" Molina sounded ready to leap through the phone.

"Noooo. Just about meeting Cher. But if I knew the *exact time* that Cher Smith was accosted and killed the next night, I might be able to . . . make more sense of what I do know. You know?"

The silence on the phone line said that Molina definitely did not know.

Good. Temple wanted the homicide lieutenant's frustration level high enough to override her better instincts.

"Are you there?" Temple said. "Look, I'm not even sure I should be calling you." Whined.

"Me too," Molina finally answered. "That's privileged information. Time of death. Besides, it's not an exact science."

"I know. I heard that on C.S.I. Isn't that a cool show?"

"No. Their depiction of forensic work is wildly improbable. Forensics people don't play amateur detective and interview witnesses and suspects. We do that."

Temple relished being the object of that short, biting tone. The madder Molina got, the more disgusted, the more she'd play right into Temple's hands. Or ears, in this case.

"Well, I'm not asking for court evidence here. Just a time. An hour. You know. When? Elevenish? Twelvish? One-ish?"

"How about two-*ish*," Molina gritted through her teeth.

Temple smiled like the Cheshire Cat. "Two-ish, it is. We would need a hyphen in that, though."

"Hyphen?"

"Between two and ish. To look right."

"I don't care how it looks, that's the time Cher was attacked. So. Are you going to give Kinsella an alibi? Was he caressing your lily white body at the time?"

"Lieutenant! That is soooo personal a question to ask. And pure speculation. You have no idea what shade my body is. There are always self-tanning lotions. Two A.M. I'll have to check my diary to be sure."

"Is that just an expression, or do you really keep one?"

"That's for me to know and you to find out," Temple said. "With a warrant," she added in a throaty growl. "G'bye!" Snippy *Weakest Link* tone of voice.

Whew! What a workout for an amateur actress.

She stared at the notebook she always kept by her phone and compulsively doodled on while talking. The number 2 and the capital P.M. were prominent on the pages, outlined by the tilted, houselike shape of the constellation Ophiuchus.

But the two things were not connected: the stripper killing and the Synth. Were they?

Whatever the case, Temple knew more than she had, and more than Molina meant for her to know. That was one thing Temple had learned from Lindy last night: the exact time when Cher was accosted was very important. Now all Temple had to find out was who might have been crossing that parking lot at the same exact time, besides Max Kinsella, who she did soooo not want to be guilty. If Molina was out to see that Rafi Nadir would walk, Temple was determined to see him walking across the right "wrong" parking lot at 2:00 A.M.

Even if the shoe, or glove, fits, you must not call it quits.

# Chapter 34

# *Ritz Cracker*

"I can see," says my dear Miss Temple, "why strippers are so eager to get out of these blasted outfits."

I can see a lot more of my dear Miss Temple than I am accustomed to, but I shut my eyes and try not to think of that noxious Egyptian hairless breed of my kind known as a sphinx. I suppose the Sphinx itself is hairless, probably due to endless sandblasting.

I am sorry to say that even my Miss Temple, left alone with a ring of fifty strip-tease artists' tools of the trade cannot resist slipping into a little nothing in front of her bedroom mirror.

I suppose the most admirable and sensible female harbors a bit of unwholesome curiosity about how well she would pass as a femme fatale. I blame the media.

Still, it is no pleasant task to recline upon our communal couch and watch her preen and pose with such ridiculous articles of nonclothing. Worst of all, she is wearing *my* shoes as an accessory to the crime!

She turns the radio up to a deafening level. It is a rock oldies station playing something with a chorus of "She works hard for the money."

Miss Temple works hard to look like a stripper.

I flatten my ears against the sight and the sound.

At last she turns off the radio and sighs, which is more than I can manage.

"Not even the Midnight Louie shoes can add any class to this outfit," she admits. "I guess I am stuck being Miss Modesto of 1958."

With that she goes through what looks like a straitjacket escape act as she unwinds the assorted elastics before donning her usual underthings, which I find skimpy enough to begin with. What a relief. It is a good thing that I do not talk to humans on principle, as I could certainly shock Miss Temple Barr's friends, co-workers, neighbors, lovers, and enemies with a breathless fashion report on her brief entry into exiting her clothes.

Soon she has donned the long, yellow wig as one would a hat, were one human and had ears oddly placed in the center of one's skull instead of proudly rampant at the top, like the lordly lions on a coat of arms.

Outside our windows the sun is dyeing the day the luscious rosy-orange of a perfectly ripe peach, not that I would ever eat a fruit, but I can appreciate perfection in many forms. Perhaps it takes one to know one.

"Well," says Miss Temple, bending to kiss my ruffled brow, "at least I know that one of us will be safe at home tonight."

Uh-oh. This is a blatant confession that she will be out and up to no good.

I can tail her, of course, but I am counting on an assistant a bit more reliable than Miss Midnight Louise to do the job.

I will wait until apprised of Miss Temple's destination before I hit the trail. So I allow myself to doze off on the zebra comforter that she has thoughtfully left crumpled into a wad in the middle of the bed so I am like Mohammed on top of his mountain, or perhaps the princess who finally got enough mattresses to forever kiss the pea good-bye.

Whilst I nap, gently nodding, suddenly there comes a prodding, prodding at my dreamland's door. Open here I fling my lashes, when with a sound like cymbal clashes, I hear a footstep on the floor. A creak and pause, and nothing more.

Well, Midnight Louie is up and at 'em faster than a mongoose with snake pâté in store.

I leap to the floor and then to the door. I peer through the crack as I plan my attack.

Now I do not know whether to move in the model of "The Raven" or "The Night Before Christmas," because what to my wandering eyes should appear . . .

But a figure all in black.

It could be a raven, a very large raven.

It could be Santa, fresh from a shoot down the soot of a chimney.

However, this is Miss Temple Barr's home, sweet home, so if a large black object appears unannounced, it is likely Mr. Max Kinsella.

This time he is not bearing gifts, like pizza, but is truly checking the place out, like a, ahem, cat burglar.

Before I can pounce, he rushes the bedroom door and pushes it open.

I can barely sidestep the inevitable black eye, which is never a noticeable condition in my case.

"You!" he says, acknowledging my presence. "She must have gone already. Where?"

At that he marches right in and begins searching the premises as if I was not there and to be reckoned with. He does not even pause to give me time to answer, although I admit that I would not.

From the tumble of comforter he lifts the solitary monokini that Miss Temple had tried on in an inexplicable moment of craven feminine weakness. I cringe to have her minor moment of experimentation exposed to other eyes than my own.

He finds the crushed K-Wigs bag on the closet floor.

He stares at me as if he would like to wring an answer from my helpless esophagus (not knowing that he probably could), then turns and ransacks the rest of the apartment.

I follow at a discreet distance.

I fear no man, but I do recognize one at the limits of his patience. And I have seen the strength in Mr. Max Kinsella's clever fingers. I would prefer for them not to be playing Beethoven's *Moonlight* Sonata on my epiglottis.

So I tippy-toe after the human cyclone that Mr. Max has become.

He has searched the kitchen and living room and is now in the second bedroom, aka the office.

I hear a woman's voice.

Has Miss Temple returned for something she forgot, like me?

No such luck. As I near the open door, I notice that the voice has a distant recorded quality. It is as husky as a bull walrus, but it is still a woman.

"Temple, honey," she is saying again, on rewind. "Lindy. Sorry to miss you. I was wrong about that guy you were asking about. He's not going to be where I said he was. He'll be at Secrets tonight. I hope this call isn't too late. Give me a buzz when you have my message so I know you're all right."

"Thanks, lady! All wrong, but at least she's safe," Mr. Max snarls at the answering machine as he bangs the button to stop the machine. "Temple, Temple, Temple . . ." He sighs before leaving.

He does not even notice my presence in the room, although I have assumed a position under the desk that would be extremely difficult to notice.

Still, he *is* the Mystifying Max, and one would hope he would be a little better than this.

I cogitate a bit after he leaves. I am sure that this call came through while Miss Temple was making like Gypsy Rose LeVine to that awful hubbub on the radio. I distinctly heard her murmur "Baby Doll's presents. . . ." Mr. Max is heading in the wrong direction, yet I am sure the action at Secrets will be particularly vibrant tonight when he goes there to find out who Miss Temple had a hankering to follow. I am now a totally free agent, as now I know my roommate has gone off somewhere completely safe.

I hop up on the desk. I have never gotten much into cyber-crime, but I am not ignorant of the possibilities. Besides, what I have in mind is more techno-crime. Thoughtfully, I rewind the message that Mr. Max so heedlessly left unreeled.

My big mitts suffer somewhat from what retired boxers call cauliflower ear. They have been bruised and battered by many months of hitting the pavement when I was a homeless dude. Still, these answering machine buttons are not beyond my manipulations. After some preliminary misdials and abrupt hangups, I manage to find and hit the autodial button that directs my call to Lieutenant C. R. Molina's office at the LVMPD.

When her voice answers—and I do not know if it is real or recorded—I hit replay and let the message Mr. Max heard transfer to the lieutenant's end of the line.

It will certainly be interesting to see who shows up at Secrets tonight. And when. And what they all do about it.

Of course I am heading that way myself.

Every catastrophe in the making deserves an impartial witness.

I am so glad my Miss Temple was headed in a different, utterly safe direction before that—shall I say, fateful?—message came through.

# Chapter 35

# *Diamonds or Dust*

In the dusk Matt walked to the Strip, then took a bus.

He got off downtown and wandered the enclosed area, drifting into the open entries to raucous casinos, veering back onto the canopied concourse to gawk up at the sky-size Las Vegas version of a CineMax screen with the tourists. Images danced like the aurora borealis on crystal meth over them all. No one noticed him.

He caught a cab near the Four Queens and took it to Bally's. He ambled through the hotel to the monorail and took it to the MGM Grand.

He walked through the miles of lobby and gaming areas there, then ducked out a side exit.

Then he hiked to the Goliath.

This was the night.

Act or be acted upon forever.

Do or die.

He killed a half hour in the Goliath lobby before he even approached the front desk.

He had seen no one who knew him.

No one who looked like Kitty in disguise with diamonds, though he'd seen a lot of diamonds in the shopping area.

Diamonds were made under immense pressure, built up for eons in the hidden center of the earth.

He understood that feeling. He knew that pressure.

Tonight it would be diamonds or dust.

# Chapter 36

# Cover Story

Here it had begun.

Molina's dead eyes took in the ersatz elegance of Secrets.

It was an upscale strip club, although that term was a contradiction in terms. Scratch a strip club, no matter how high-class, and you sniffed corruption and exploitation.

She had been laboring late on paperwork when the forwarded call had come through.

"Temple, honey."

No need to guess on whose answering machine that rye-whiskey voice—almost mannish, almost female impersonator—had left the news that Secrets was the place to be tonight.

The first question was who had sent that message to Temple Barr, and why.

The second was, what was Barr doing club-crawling when single white females were the Target of the Month at places like this?

Trying to save the scruffy, shopworn soul of Max Kinsella, no doubt.

Molina's head ached from the wig that clung to it like a moth-balled barnacle, and the incessant smoke and noise.

The glamour of undercover work was way overrated.

This could be a trap or a diversion. Barr could have gotten the message and come here, or not. She could have notified Molina in this cryptic way, or not. Molina assumed not. Barr had a history of independent action, ill-considered or not. So, she herself could have been alerted by . . . Matt Devine, Good Neighbor Matt. Or not. Or by Max Kinsella. Bad Scene Max. Or not.

The whole evening, the entire charade was possibly key to the case. Or not.

She had to assume that Barr at least had the smarts to disguise her appearance.

So now Molina was on the lookout not only for a possible killer, but for a civilian trespassing on police turf.

Still, she wondered what Barr had blundered into. Her informant had the kind of smoky, boozy voice of someone who knew the strip club world inside out from the time of Moses to Madonna.

Who did Barr think she was tracking? A he, of course. If the killer was a woman, it would be a shocker. From the message, it was some-one who was a repeat offender at strip clubs, a regular. That included a lot of customers.

Molina eyed the men standing, sitting, drinking, ogling.

The usual batch of losers and loners. Men whose shoulders slumped, whose jaws dropped, whose eyes were dead with unspoken hopes. And the muscle crowd. Not loners. Guys in gangs, loud, pro-fane, obscene. Pack runners not likely to go beyond the pale in public parking lots, but don't let them run into you alone on a lonely road.

Molina had seen them all, the types. So who didn't you see? Who was conveniently invisible?

"See anybody who ought to be in pictures?" the bartender asked.

This model was female, but she had the same easy-going attitude of her male counterparts, as if Sister Wendy doing the shimmy on the bar wouldn't turn a hair.

"Not yet. I'm really looking for places, not people."

What a lie! Molina was pleased with her latest cover story: loca-tion scout for *C.S.I.* It was the perfect justification for surveillance work: both jobs required lots of sitting and watching and soaking up the atmosphere.

Molina tried some oversalted bar nibblies despite her better judgment. Had to look semioccupied while waiting for Godot, or whoever.

Like most stakeout work, this could turn out to be another dull, wasted evening.

# Chapter 37

# Terra Incognito

Matt eyed himself in the mirror. In the mirrors.

He turned away, displeased as always with his looks.

The place was plastered with mirrors, and it certainly wasn't to visually enlarge the area. The rooms were already king-size.

He went to the window, which gave him a hawk's-eye view of the elaborately tiled areas surrounding the many pools. The mosaic of gold, terra cotta, and white tiles, with rectangles and circles of chlorinated water thrown down among them like area rugs, was like overlooking some Roman ruin, though nothing down there or up here was ruined, except possibly his immortal soul.

The sinking sun sizzled on seminude figures ambling among the bronzed bodies arrayed on lounge chairs. Dozens more people stood in the pools, looking from up here like toothpicks impaled in blue icing. Very few people in the pools actually swam.

The entire scene reminded him of an orgy sequence from a Cecil B. DeMille film epic, *The Last Days of Pompeii*, say, just before the wrath of Mount Etna rained on the pagan parade and turned everybody into ashes, ashes, all fall down.

My, he was getting apocalyptic, wasn't he? If the Devil was in the details, God, unfortunately, was not often in the Big Picture. Las Vegas had been committing a lot of mortal and cardinal sins for decades without a peep from Anybody Upstairs, except possibly the real overseeing deity of the city, the Eye in the Sky cameras posted over all the casino tables.

Paranoid, he turned and examined the room's ceiling for surveillance equipment, despite knowing that any devices would be too sophisticated for him to detect.

What a racket, though. The thousands of men who had done what he was about to do were ripe for blackmail. He supposed that the major hotels had a stake in keeping petty crime off their premises. Better to get their cut on the gambling concessions far below the thousand-dollar suites and million-dollar penthouses than some cheesy blackmail.

Matt eyed the room again. It was half the size of his whole unit at the Circle Ritz, maybe six hundred square feet. A mirrored wall doubled the apparent size of the bedroom. The bed seemed even larger than king-size, and was a mound of piled pillows and bedlinens covered in large, regal designs.

The carpeting was plush, deep, and the color of stale blood.

Beyond the mirrored wall was a hall lined with a long, mirror-doored closet. A door opposite them led into the marble-floored bathroom, as big as his living room at home. A huge matching marble tub reminded Matt of a Roman sarcophagus. It took about fifteen steps to get from the tub to the freestanding marble sink. The toilet and bidet were on the other side of the sink. Of course every wall of the bathroom was mirrored, so you could see yourself coming and going. Literally.

Matt would mostly like to see himself going. Out the door into the wide, well-lit hallway that overlooked a glittering open atrium to the casino attractions far below, down in the stainless-steel-lined elevator car, through the raucous casinos, past the gaudy restaurants, walking a half mile to the exit doors to breath the overheated Las Vegas air and inhale the slightest, distant tang of desert creosote. Wilderness enow.

Omar Khayyám was considered quite the romantic poet, but even he couldn't find a plain loaf of bread in this place to go with the expected and dreaded "thou."

"Thou" was right! It had already cost Matt eight hundred dollars to get this far, and the second stage of the evening was going to run at least another thousand.

Corruption cost, and in Las Vegas, corruption cost big-time.

Matt allowed himself a glance in the closet door mirrors.

He'd better up his estimate of costs incurred for this unconventional outing of his. His clothes were new too, bought in the brightly lit shops lining every hotel's obligatory shopping arcade.

Big winners were expected to blow large wads in these places and they were crammed with designer labels and luxury goods Matt had never heard of.

He suspected some of the high-priced items might not be in the best of taste, but nowadays it was hard to tell highway robbery from high-class prices, especially in Las Vegas.

So he wore a two-hundred-dollar pair of slacks in his favorite khaki color, although the clerk had described it as "lukewarm café au lait." His shirt was a cotton-and-silk blend in stone color. His blazer was a wool-silk blend a bit darker than camel, which the clerk had called "escargot." Had Matt not known this was the French word for the humble and edible snail, or slug, he would have thought it was a synonym for calf-shit brown.

Still, even he, who hated mere appearances, had to admit these clothes had an easy feel and drape that evoked the hushed sound of eurodollars falling to new lows on the Aubusson carpets of the international exchange.

The least a man who was expecting a thousand-dollar whore could do was dress up to the lady's level.

He immediately censored the word "whore." That was the old puritan streak putting unpleasant labels on everything, and everybody.

She was a professional woman of the highest order. Like a well-paid motivational speaker, say. He could identify with that. He got an obscene amount of money for speaking engagements now, being a celibate ex-priest working as a semifamous radio shrink. What was the difference between selling a mind and a body?

Matt paced back to the window, suddenly worried if the "thou" in his unwelcome equation was going to show up. The hundred-dollar bill he'd passed as discreetly as he could to the bellman might be taken as a generous tip, instead of an order for some "classy entertainment." Matt winced at the phrase. He'd been coached, of course, by an expert. Well, Carmen Molina never would or could walk in his shoes, but she ought to know the routine.

So what happened if he was just being ripped off by the bellman? The six-hundred-dollar room, his seven-hundred dollar "casual" outfit, the crisp bulk of fresh hundreds in his new eelskin wallet (she would see that, of course, as well as his new underwear), his desperate gamble that one sleazy act paid for through the nose would liberate him from his demon stalker, what if nothing happened? And he was waiting. For nothing?

Then he'd be relieved. As much as he needed to do what he had set in motion, he most devoutly hoped that something would go wrong and it would never happen.

## Chapter 38

# Baby Doll's
# Brand-new Bag

I am only halfway across the Circle Ritz parking lot when I am
accosted, if one can be accosted by an albino tumbleweed.

"*Oh-oh-oh-oh*," my attacker says, hyperventilating.

"It is about time," I say. "I cannot be about my business until I
know what you have to say."

"*Uh-uh-uh-uh.*"

"Um, words would be nice."

"*Huh-huh-huh-huh-huh.*"

I sit down and prepare to wait, sweeping my posterior member
back and forth like a cranky metronome.

"*I-I-I-I-I . . .*

"*Ran . . .*

"*All . . .*

"*The . . .*

"*Way.*"

"Admirable devotion to duty. But you should have saved a couple breaths for your report."

Frankly, I am impressed. But it never does to let underlings know when they have done well. Management by creative tension has always been the watchword of my breed. Keep 'em guessing, keep 'em on their toes, and keep 'em worrying about what I really think.

"So where did she go?" I finally ask.

"*Ba-ba-ba-ba*—"

"Bally's?"

"*Ba-ba-ba-ba*—"

"The Ali Baba Room at the Alhambra?" Not exactly a strip club, unless you consider it a Las Vegas Strip club, but they do have belly dancers.

"Eee—"

*E*. Now what in Las Vegas begins with *E*, except *E*lvis?

"Duh-duh-duh."

Duh is right!

"Catch your breath and show it who is boss. There, that is the ticket. Give the old brain case a good shake to free all the fleas in your ears. Now, from the top."

"Bah-bee."

"Bobby?"

"Duh-alls."

"Bobby . . . Dulls." Light strikes. "Baby Doll's!"

My informant's head nods like one of those idiotic toys with a spring for a neck and sawdust for brains.

What else can you expect from a mere dog but extreme panting and stupid facial tricks?

"Baby Doll's," I repeat, to make sure I heard the little bowhead correctly. Those cranial barrettes will cramp your cerebellum. "It is a strip club. That makes sense. And you ran all the way to and fro?" This is quite a hike for a three-pound floor-duster like a Maltese.

Nose E. nods his fuzzy little face from which the tongue has protruded like the tag on a zipper the whole time. "I could not . . . keep up."

Some dogs love to chase cars, but this one's legs are so short he should chase Hot Wheels. To be fair, tailing little dolls is not his bailiwick. The Nose Pose is his game and it has made him tops in his field of drug- and bomb-sniffing.

"Did my clever marking technique work?" I ask.

"Oh, yes, Mr. Midnight. The scent you, er, drizzled on the right rear tire was impossible to lose. Unbelievably rank. I have to say you cats have it all over dogs when it comes to the odiferous art. Although I soon lost sight of it—your Miss Temple drives like an Indy Five Hundred speed demon, I might say—I was able to track the Miata all the way to Baby Doll's parking lot. That is not a very nice place, you know."

"I know."

"That was not a very nice thing to do to a human's new car, either."

"I know, but it was for her own good and, beside, humans have the nasal sensitivity of a stainless steel beak. So you left the Miata, and Miss Temple, at Baby Doll's?"

"Yeth."

Funny. I had never noticed that Nose E. lisped before. Why am I not surprised?

"Good work, half ounce. I will take it from here."

He trails me, everything jiggling like a chorus girl's . . . uh, pom-poms: hair, head bow, tiny white whiskers that would look about right on a lab rat.

"Oh, Mr. Midnight. I hate to leave a job half-done. Let me go with you! I like to be in on the search and seizure."

"Trouble is, the action is not going down at Baby Doll's. I just wanted to make sure that my Miss Temple was safely out of harm's way. So trot back to the Old Groove, or whatever it is called, used record store your human, Mr. Earl. E. Byrd, operates. You can rest easy in a job well done. Now it is time for your big-gers to take over."

"Oh! You are just like the Federales!"

"Huh? The only thing Mexican about me is any jumping beans I choose to carry."

"The FBI and the NSA and all those Big-time Initial Guys. They always want me and Earl E. to bow out after I have identified the perp."

"No doubt it is for your own safety. You are civilians, after all."

"And you are not?"

"I am an . . . exception. Your reward will be hearing how well everything went now that I am on the case. See you later, Tater Tot."

I take off at a lope I know the exhausted Nose E. cannot imitate. I have heard Miss Temple bemoan her short-legged stride often enough to realize where his true weakness lies. Industrial strength sniffer, but wimpy ankles.

I try not to gloat as I streak through the dark Las Vegas night, sure and powerful as my own stride.

For once I have both Miss Temple Barr and Miss Midnight Louise safely diverted to the side while the real action is going down elsewhere. Not only am I a knight errant protecting the weaker females of the species, but I am establishing my supreme territory as Crime-Solver Extraordinaire.

My small deposit on the tire of Miss Temple's new car is only a drop in the bucket of my forthcoming triumph in the art of territory marking.

Now I am up against the big boys: Mr. Max Kinsella and, uh, Ms. C. R. Molina.

I am in my proper element: on the prowl alone and pulling everyone else's strings.

How sweet it is!

Chapter 39

# Secret Showdown

He came through the door like an Old West gunfighter.

In fast and hard, so even the heavy metal door swung open and came to a dead stop for a few seconds.

He paused to survey the scene.

In a Western movie, every eye in the place would have been on him.

At Secrets, he went unnoticed.

The door's weight reversed the opening momentum and swung slowly shut. By then he had melted into the mob scene.

Or not quite melted.

One eye in the house had noticed his entrance and still followed his black-clad form through the smoky haze.

Molina couldn't believe her luck.

Kinsella here. Undisguised. Wearing his signature black, looking almost naked in a sleazy turtleneck (which probably meant it was silk) and tailored slacks, looking a lot like a ninja as he circled the crowd and the stage, looking for someone.

Who?

Likely Temple Barr, but Molina would have spotted her even if she had been got up like a Munchkin from *The Wizard of Oz*. The notion was so pleasing that she smiled into her sob-sister margarita . . . it was criminal how weak they mixed these drinks in the strip clubs . . . not her jurisdiction, thank God.

But Max Kinsella was. *Baa baa, black sheep, have you any bull? Yes, sir, yes, sir, three bags full.*

# Chapter 40

# Midnight Choirboy

I cruise by the Secrets parking lot, but not much seems to be happening.

Much as I would like to settle down at the edge of the parking lot and watch two ace trackers from different hunting parties stake out the same watering hole, I find that when I have a chance to sit still, I get antsy instead.

It has been just too long since I last heard head or tail of Miss Midnight Louise.

I know for a fact that my Miss Temple is safely deployed at the one place the dude in question is not likely to show, Baby Doll's.

I do not know anything about the disposition of Miss Midnight Louise other than that she is not at the Crystal Phoenix, or the Circle Ritz, or here or anywhere she should be breaking a nail to get to with a report, at least.

While I sit there chewing my nails I find my noggin cogitating. I am not sanguine about finding Miss Louise in that cavernous place, and I do not like contemplating the many unseen, if not unsniffed, signs of major muscle of a feline nature about the place.

It is quiet here, except for intermittent slices of unholy midnight howls that emanate from Secrets every time the single wide front door opens and shuts to let merrymakers in or out.

I am a bit perturbed that all is normal here. I am even more disturbed to see a stripper leave the premises for the night escorted by a dude with major workout issues. Apparently Secrets has installed a killer security system: see the ladies to and from their cars. With everyone but me carrying cell phones these days, it makes sense.

I had better swing by Baby Doll's on the way to Los Muertos, just in case. It is only a mile or two out of my way.

Oh, my aching pads! When they slapped the tag "gumshoe" on PIs, they must have meant we pound so much pavement pursuing leads that our shuffling feet get so weary they end up sticking to the street.

I am not sorry to leave the dimly heard hell-raising chorus within behind as I plod through the black-and-neon checkerboard of a Las Vegas night, wishing I had at least one of my two little dolls in my sights.

# Chapter 41

# *No Dice*

Max circled the room like a wolf marking his territory. Secrets was doing business as usual, crowded with pleasure-seekers lost in their own vice of choice: booze, babes, or maybe just mind-shattering sound.

The crowd was large and self-absorbed. Even the strippers seemed oddly isolated as they writhed onstage to the music they had chosen. Stripping had always struck Max as a solitary vice on both sides of the spotlights.

He hadn't bothered to disguise himself, not even with attitude. Still, his striking appearance barely registered on Secrets's many employees and clients. Everything was expected, including boredom. Damn it, if Temple had tracked a killer here, he wanted the bastard to be aware of him, his presence. His threat.

Even Temple didn't seem to be here.

Max sighed. He'd have to check the stripper dressing rooms to make sure she wasn't backstage. That would draw out whatever testosterone troops guarded this place. At Secrets they would be fairly discreet.

Rafi Nadir's stint here must have been an aberration. This place's pretensions to business class over coach wouldn't support obvious muscle like him.

Besides, Nadir had never worked here after the night Max had taken Cher away from him in the parking lot. Max had checked. He could have decamped out of shame at being outsmarted and outmuscled by someone as apparently easy as Max.

Max wasn't about to bet on shame being a big part of Rafi Nadir's psychological makeup. Aggression, yes.

Max scanned the entire scene like a panoramic camera, identifying the cast of dozens: the familiar bare figures of girls onstage or lap dancing at the tables, the lapdog circle of guys transfixed like risen mummies before the footlights. Instead of craving revivifying tanna leaves these zombies were shedding leaves of green bills into the teeny-weeny bikini bottoms of various strippers. Down the snatch.

There was even the hard-boiled dame at the bar . . . a retired stripper, or maybe a club photographer. No camera, so she was some other hanger-on in the whole elegantly sleazy scene.

The illusion he required: the instant perception by one and all that he belonged here, that he could go where he wanted with no one objecting.

Max scanned the room again, 360 degrees, and found his course of action.

He walked through the tables, past the obscenely boogy-ing couples, behind the dazed wannabe studs playing hang-dog at the stage lip.

Ducked into the glass-enclosed sound booth at the side of the stage.

"Hey, DJ!" he addressed the slack-jawed youth at the console. "Bitchin' job, man." He flashed a hundred-dollar bill, dropped it onto the feedback dial. "I could use a sharp sound-meister like you at my new club down the Strip, X-treme Dreams. Meanwhile, play 'Misty' for me, huh? Double speed." Max winked. "I gotta see a babe about a takeover bid."

Max was out of the noise-free zone and back on pulse-pounding time. He strode toward the door leading backstage as if he owned the place. His presence in the sound booth would have registered on the edge of everyone's eyes. Once he visibly left a zone normally not intruded on, he could climb every mountain, plow through any door.

Through the door. He held it shut with his body, listened, felt the pounding bass vibrate the wood, his metabolism.

After an unchallenged minute, he moved down the dark hall and through a heavy velvet curtain that shivered to the heavy metal music.

Another door.

Here he knocked.

And waited. Like a gentleman.

This was where the women's world began. Brass knuckles might get you through the hard-knock barriers of sheer muscle. Golden rings would get you through the silken curtains of sheer willpower.

"Yeah?" A distracted feminine voice. Well, mostly feminine.

"Sorry. I need to speak to someone. Can anyone step out?"

He had unconsciously lapsed into an English expression. It called to the women inside like a vodka martini to James Bond.

"Yeah?"

The woman opened the dressing room door a crack only as wide as the seam on a nylon stocking from a '40s film noir. She was tall, rangy, tough. A trans?

"Name's Maximilian. I'm opening a new high-end place, X-treme Dreams, in a couple of months. Looking for talent."

"You've got nerve, coming here." She eyed him up and down.

He nodded. "X-treme Dreams will be a nervy club. I'm looking for ladies who don't hold back."

Hoots and whistles erupted behind the gatekeeper.

"Because then I don't have to hold back on the perks."

More whistles.

"You got a little redhead in there? Visitor?"

"You looking for ET, Maximilian?"

"Only if it stands for 'Extreme Tensions'. I am looking for that little redhead, though, even if she's passing as a blond. I have an emergency message from her mother, Molina."

He had to hope that if Temple was inside, she would hear and get his message.

"We don't have any little women in here," door-babe said. "If your needs are that specialized—"

"X-treme Dreams will encompass every fantasy, every female. But I want the full range. So if a little redhead happens to show, tell her to see Maximilian out front."

Max passed another hundred through the crack in the door that was neither too large or too small, but just right for the bill to be snapped up by a long pair of fingernails.

He ambled out through the hallway, pausing in the door from the dressing room, in no hurry to join the crowd nodding and swaying to the music and the bumps and grinds.

The lone woman at the bar looked about ready to slide off her barstool. She was obviously straight. Straight women found strip clubs boring. So did mature men, not that there were any on the premises.

Max expertly resized up the crowd. No Temple out here, in any guise. No Rafi Nadir.

So think outside the box, as they used to say in the thriving dot-com industry. Maybe the guy Temple was trailing was not Rafi Nadir.

Epiphany.

Maybe Rafi Nadir was *not* the killer.

But the killer had to be here. Temple had been advised to be here by a source she apparently knew. Why wasn't she?

Max checked his watch, which he wore face-out on the inside of his wrist so he could consult it surreptitiously.

Almost half past one.

Something was wrong.

A flash went off in the darkened club.

For a moment Max took it for gunfire, not a camera.

But the only sound was the rat-a-tat of the bass strafing the club through the sound system. Music that made the place sound like a war zone.

Maybe it was: ground zero in the eternal war between the sexes.

The darkness, the sound, the thronging customers, the late hour, it all reminded him of the thick, cloying fellowship of an Irish pub the moment before a terrorist bomb went off.

Max felt the room reel. No, he was reeling.

His fear for Temple, his unease that she wasn't here, concluded that she had already left home before that warning phone call had come, that she might be on a collision course with his cousin Sean, who was only a ghost at this point and could hardly collide with any-one solid. In this weird retro-moment he realized that everything—his life, his love, his future—was out of his control . . .

He crashed through the sound and the milling vacuous faces, heading for the door. The whole place was going to blow. Somewhere. He had to be there. If not here, where? Lindy. The name rang a dis-tant bell. Temple had used it, long ago. Weeks? No. Months? Yes. What he would do outside, he didn't know.

Hear himself think, maybe.

See a path leading to Temple.

Realize who the killer was. Temple thought she knew, surely he could reason it out as well as she. Or could he? Did he care too much, as usual? He had to get out, away. Had to find Temple.

If she wasn't at Secrets, and the killer wasn't, they were both some-where too awful to imagine.

Somewhere he didn't know about, where Sean stood at the bar, waiting with a mixed drink of regret and excitement to hear about Max's assignation with pretty Kathleen, the Irish revolutionary colleen.

No matter who won the girl or the game or the day, the loser would shrug and grin and say "Next time." That's how it was some-times with boys, with men, with brothers.

Only, with Sean, there was no next time.

Max threw his shoulder into the heavy external door as if breaking into somewhere instead of out of his own head.

The night should have felt cool, crisp. Like in Londonderry, like in Minneapolis, like in Wisconsin . . . like where he grew up and could never go home to again.

This air was still, warm, heavy.

Still Las Vegas.

Max lunged for where he thought he might have left his car, almost drunk on panic and guilt and memories.

"Wait," the voice ordered. "Hold it right there."

It spoke with bullets for quotation marks.

## Chapter 42

# *Final Jeopardy*

Matt had given up and thrown himself on the heavily brocaded comforter to watch CNN when someone knocked at the door. Lightly.

He jumped up, trying to punch the mute or power button and
instead sending the huge television screen into paroxysms of alien
images, ending with an apparent pay service for triple-X-rated
movies.

*Oh my God.* This was not what he wanted to see.

He managed to fumble the buttons until the hotel service screen,
innocuous, came up, and went to the door.

Maybe the bellman hoping for another sucker tip.

He unlocked the chain and the dead bolt and opened the door.

He'd been expecting the leather-strapped female who'd domi-
nated the screen for a few frantic moments.

She was . . . well, she was not that.

"You rang?" she said.

"Actually, you knocked."

"But you rang first." Her smile was slow and perfect. "I'm Vassar." She eased over the threshold and Matt was closing (closing!) the door behind her like a good host before he knew it.

"Better lock it again," she said over her shoulder. Her mostly bare shoulder. "This *is* Las Vegas. Besides, we don't want to be interrupted by anything but room service."

She walked to the window like a big cat prowling its territory.

He took in her clothing: gauzy designer something, both expensive and vaguely provocative, though he couldn't say why he knew it was either.

She was tall. Not quite tall enough to be a model. Instinctively, Matt realized that women as short as Temple (five foot aught) did not end up as high-class call girls. No doubt something she would bewail as another inequity of la vida squata.

And this woman was blond, a creamy, caramel blond that must have come from the fairy-godmother fingers at a very expensive salon because it was too shiny and silky and unnaturally natural a color with its fine highlights to be anything but solid gold in the bleaching department.

He applauded his foresight in dressing well for the job.

"Sunset on the Strip," she murmured.

He came over, surprised. The sun was indeed sweltering in the west like melted butter. Everybody below threw long shadows and there were a lot fewer of them now.

"Where'd they all go?" He answered his own question. "Moving indoors to gamble with dice and cards instead of ultraviolet rays."

"Speaking of which"—she cast him a sidelong glance—"do you want to troll the casinos? Eat dinner?"

"Uh, no. I mean, we can eat dinner, but . . . here."

"Oh." She eyed him disconcertingly.

He couldn't imagine what she was thinking. All he had in mind was avoiding public places. That would eliminate the slim chance that Kitty O'Connor had somehow followed him here and would spot him, even though he'd spent three hours getting here to ensure no one followed him.

"I ordered champagne, if that's all right." He gestured to the footed wine cooler, designed like a temple brazier.

"Oh." She ankled over to the bottle.

This was the first woman Matt had ever seen "ankle." She moved as fluidly as a fashion model, all the action in her hips, shoulders and ankles. It was a strut, a stuck-up strut, but as much a strut as any stripper's more obvious locomotion.

*Vassar*, huh?

The waiter had opened the champagne, thank God, although on second thought Matt decided to keep God out of this.

The flutes were etched in frosted designs, like lace embedded in ice. Matt poured carefully, anxious not to agitate the expensive wine, anxious not to regard his guest too closely.

Her fingernails were long, longer than Temple's, and flashed a subtle metallic sheen.

"Some men," she said after an appreciative sip that indicated his hotel bill would rise by two or three hundred dollars, "think a woman brings them luck at the gaming tables. You'd be amazed how much of my time I spend on my feet, bringing luck."

Of course he looked at those bare, long-toed feet, and at the thin-soled, impossibly high-heeled thin-strapped shoes that decorated them. Temple would have wanted a thorough description the way Molina wanted a postmortem. *Think about the shoes, not Molina and postmortems.* They were pale, iridescent snakeskin constructed like a futuristic airport. He'd better leave Temple out of this as well as God. Both of them would be equally wroth with him on this one.

"Tough job," Matt said.

She smiled at him. Gorgeous. Just gorgeous.

"You want dinner?" she asked.

"Yeah." Another delaying tactic. It would be better to get to know her first. Wouldn't it?

She ambled over to the burlwood desk to skim the heavily padded room service menu, like she knew just where it was. She knew just where it was. She'd been at the Goliath many times, maybe in this very room many times.

He was beginning to feel yucky about this as well as guilty, but remembered that Molina had assured him that she would be "clean."

"What do you feel like having?"

"I don't know. You pick. Surprise me."

She raised a pale eyebrow. "A gambler, after all," then lifted the phone receiver and ordered very specific dinners without glancing at the menu again.

What a pro. She'd been here, done that many times before. And that was exactly what he needed. Wasn't it?

After Vassar hung up the phone, she swaggered over to the seating area near the window and arranged herself in one of the upholstered chairs. Her legs crossed higher on the thigh than he would have thought anatomically possible, revealing that her dress's fluttering skirt was split up the side as far as the mind of man could go.

A shame to waste such a show on a fraud. For the first time, he wondered if he *could* do what he had to do. He didn't see her as a person, a woman, but as an exotic variety of show horse, all artificial arched neck and instep, all exaggerated gait and overdressed mane and tail, all unreal.

She leaned back, lifted her elbows and supported her neck with her interlaced fingers.

Matt was able to observe from this new posture that her armpits were preternaturally bare of hair. No doubt permanently removed.

None of this was a turn-on, and he knew he had such a button, because it had been triggered a time or two.

"You're very unusual," she said.

"The feeling is mutual."

She laughed, the first genuine reaction he'd seen. "I'm not unusual. . . . What name do you go by?"

He hesitated long enough for her to continue, "John would do, but it's a bit predictable."

"Thomas," he said quickly, voicing his doubt.

"Thomas. That's better. It may not be your real name, but it's obviously significant to you."

"How do you know that?"

"People are never good at making up totally unrelated things about themselves. There's always a clue. A psychological tic. Thomas. *Thomas Crowne Affair*, maybe. Thomassss . . . Wolfe? Thomasss . . . Mann. Thomasss—what?"

"Merton," he said without thinking.

"Ummm. I knew it would be an author. I didn't know it would be such a good author."

"You know about Thomas Merton?"

"Know? I've read him. Along with Proust and Genet and a lot of very depressed Frenchmen and women."

"Your name—women in your field often take geographic names."

"So. You have experience with women in my field."

"No! No, I don't. I've just observed."

"I went to Vassar, yes. Graduated. Observed." She slid onto her tailbone, revealing an impossibility: yet more leg.

My God, the woman was a stork! He sipped more champagne. Obviously, he needed to be tipsy. He noticed her glass was empty and got up to refill it.

Outside the sky was the color of a Maxfield Parrish print, that heavenly, morning-glory blue that is fading fast to green and will soon flash a fringe of yellow before dousing itself in the utter dark of night.

"I'm glad to see you enjoying something," she said, heavy emphasis on the *something*.

"Nature's hard to beat."

"And you don't think I'm very natural."

"I never said—"

" 'Natural' is not an advantage in my line of work. Or in this town. I love both of them. What's the matter with being unreal? Is reality that great a trip?"

"Reality, usually no. People, though. Authenticity is—"

"Gawd, if I hear that pretentious word again! Au-then-ti-ci-ty. Only phonies flaunt au-then-ti-ci-ty."

"Call it honesty, then."

"Fine. How about you give me some."

"What kind do you want?"

"There are varieties, like . . . dry honesty? Sec, or triple sec? What's your pleasure? Or maybe it's wet honesty, like a wet dream."

Someone knocked at the door. Fortuitously.

Matt jumped up to answer it. A waitress wheeled in a large cart draped in white linen (*a young cowboy draped in white linen*) on which floated silver Merimacs and Monitors of covered dishes. A huge exotic flower blossomed from a vase like a tropical fungus. There were tiny sterling salt and pepper shakers, glittering glasses, another bottle of wine.

"By the window," Matt said, unwilling to let the sunset go and leave him alone with the electric lights. He reached into the slick eel-skin wallet to peel off another hundred.

"Thank you, sir!"

Something in the tone was ironic, forcing Matt to overcome his shame of witnesses to really look at her. She was a clone of Barbara

Eden as the sit-com genie, all bare midriff and glittery lavender veils and long blonde ponytail. She was petite enough to remind him of Temple, although much curvier, an observation that felt disloyal, as if this whole situation wasn't a betrayal enough.

She rolled the hundred tight into cigarette-size and deposited it in the valley of her push-up bodice. Above the veil that covered her lower face, her eyes glittered like the dappled water in the darkened pools below, blue-green.

She winked and left, a real "working woman" who'd hit the jackpot of a big tip in a high-dollar suite. And all she had to do was flash a little flesh, push a cart, and do her job.

Now *her*, she was interesting. A mystery. Who did she really work for? What kid was going to get a special outing out of that hundred? What significant other would she wave it at as proof of a job well done? What small luxury would sit on her crowded bathroom shelf in what ordinary house or apartment . . .

"Hey, Big Spender," said the woman lounging in the chair.

Matt remembered the rest of that line: spend a little time on me.

Matt edged the food cart between them. Vassar was forced to sit up to examine her dinner.

"Oh, this side's yours. Mine's the sea bass."

"Shall we spin the table or change seats?" he asked.

"Spin the table. Do we get a kiss when it's done?"

"Dinner first. It looks superb."

"The dinner he compliments," she said to the window with a shrug. She was slightly tipsy, and he was all too sober.

"You're . . . superb, too."

"Too." She washed away her moue with a sip of champagne and a pointed look at the distant wine cooler.

He rose and filled her glass again.

Outside the night had turned midnight blue.

Was he guilty of rejecting a hooker? Another pretext for anguished self-examination.

"No, really." He sat opposite her, examined her beautiful face, all bones and makeup. Her eyes . . . what color were her eyes? He couldn't tell.

He lifted his champagne glass. "You are beautiful, intelligent, sophisticated. The race of men must bless your existence."

"They reward it, that's for sure." But she seemed mollified.

Matt decided that the condemned man deserved a hearty last meal. He concentrated on the cutting of his tender pepper steak in brandy-whatever sauce. It melted in his mouth like Lady Godiva chocolates.

Everything was superb. The best garlic mashed potatoes he had ever eaten. Even the vegetables were tasty, crisp, worth gobbling down to the last sprig or floret. The champagne bottle was empty, so he had to open the wine and switch to the squatter glasses.

He drank, she drank. The food disappeared and so did the any visible trace of the world outside.

"Most men," she said over dessert, a tiramisù, "would envy you."

"From what I know of most women, and that's not a lot, they'd be wild with jealousy to see how much you can eat and still look like you do."

"That's one of the reasons I decided on this profession. It occurred to me I had certain advantages for it. Some are metabolic. Wealthy men usually like to eat well. I can keep up with them in that respect as well. Men are bored by women who peck at food like chickadees, whining all the while."

"You don't whine."

"Apparently I don't impress you either."

"You do! I can't say how much you impress me."

"But."

"But . . . I'm a special case."

"I'd figured that out. Most men—in other words, my usual clients—fall into two or three, categories."

Matt drank a bit more of the red wine. It was amazing. He glanced at the label, resolved to memorize it so he could find it again, although he might not be able to afford it again, not after tonight.

His watch said a quarter to ten. He didn't have to go to work. It was Monday. The most beautiful woman in the Goliath Hotel was sitting across from him, and if he could get it together, by tomorrow morning when he checked out he'd be a Real Man. A sinner. A human being. A ruined priest. Ex-priest, rather. And no longer Kitty-bait.

All he had to do was what came unnaturally.

"Your usual clients?" he prompted politely, as if he were counseling someone on the radio help line.

"They're powerful men. Rich men. They have insecurities along with many securities of the financial sort. They crave the best of everything to prove their worth, in both senses of the word. I'm one of the bests they can afford. Then there are the other men. They have issues. They can't afford me, but they will. Now I have to add the dot-com geeks who've never felt desired in their lives. I'm something they can't afford *not* to have. I'll make them feel like the billion dollars they made overnight."

"So sometimes you're a reward, sometimes you're an extravagance. And sometimes you're a therapist."

"Oh, you are a quick study, Thomas. Doubting Thomas."

He ought to have gone on red alert at that, but the meal and the wine had made him mellow.

"The problem is," she continued, "you don't fit into my client profile."

"Why not?"

"You're a combination of all three. You have some money, but not enough to keep this sort of thing up. You have issues, but you hide them like a pro, like me. You're not a geek, but you need to be babied along like one. You don't want a trophy, loathe trophies; you're not desperate to lead the high life, la vida loca dinero; and you don't want a therapist. So what do you want? Or should I say, need?"

"Hmm. Cards on the table."

"This *is* Las Vegas."

She leaned forward, elbows on the immaculate linen, like a saloon girl in a cheap Western.

"You're pretty accurate," he said. "I wouldn't be here if I weren't forced to be. You're not my trophy, or my reward, or my Cracker Jack prize for accidentally being somebody. You're my . . . savior."

Her eyes narrowed. He still couldn't see their color, but it didn't matter anymore.

"Savior? I've never been called that before."

"You've never had a client like me. I'm an ex-priest."

"I'm not Catholic."

"But you must know that priests make promises of chastity, to live as celibates."

"Catholic priests."

"You sound like you were raised Episcopal."

"As a matter of fact . . . but that's history."

"Childhood religion is never history."

"You *are* a priest!"

"Ex-priest."

"But not ex-celibate."

"Right."

"So some friendly neighborhood Catholic spinster wouldn't be ecstatic to help you out?"

"Maybe. Maybe not. There's an . . . impediment."

"Oh. You're impotent."

"How the heck would I know?"

"Don't be testy, we're getting somewhere here."

"If I am impotent it's situational. I'm trapped."

"How? You're an ex. You can do whatever you want."

"Leaving the priesthood isn't like leaving a religion. You don't throw over all the traces. You're still obligated to be a moral person."

" 'A moral person.' Listen to yourself. Get real."

"So I'm a geek. Apparently there are a lot of them out there nowadays, cyber and otherwise."

"Okay. So you need someone to break you in to normal life. I've been hired for that before. You're not my first virgin."

"Maybe not, but I'm your first reluctant virgin."

"Why? I'll give you a night to remember. I am very good at what I do."

"I don't doubt it."

"Thomas."

"And I do believe you're a product of Vassar. And I do understand you're an attractive lady."

"But. You'd prefer another lady."

"Maybe I would, but I can't."

"Because you're impotent."

"Because I don't know, and I don't much care. I've got a psycho in my life, my work. A woman who likes to corrupt priests."

"Even ex-priests?"

"Even ex-priests. There aren't too many innocent men out there anymore."

"Tell me about it. Women, either."

"So . . . she'll hurt any woman I have anything to do with. Anything, anyone! My landlady who's sixty-something. A pre-teen daughter of a friend."

"Unless—"

He nodded.

"So you need to sleep with me first."

Silence.

"But you don't want to."

"I don't want to be coerced into sleeping with anyone."

"I get you. I was there once. Yeah, I was a virgin. Everybody was. Almost everybody gets over it, one way or another." She poured some more wine in her glass, her face softening under the makeup. "There was a guy I dated, my freshman year in college. Big, gorgeous guy, football player. Said I was a prick tease one night. Maybe I was, maybe I was just a virgin. I wasn't after that night."

Her eyes of no color were black holes.

"Date rape?"

"Didn't have the phrase all over the newspapers then. I believed that I'd got what I deserved. It's true. I wanted a boyfriend, but I didn't want to sleep with him. Not yet. I didn't know what it was about. I wasn't ready." She smiled over her glass rim. "That's why I'm so good at my job. I can tell the guys who aren't ready from the ones who've always been ready.

"I'm sorry, Thomas, but you're not ready."

"I've got to be. This woman is dangerous. I've got to disarm her. I've got to take away the thing in me that she covets."

"You can sleep with me but you won't lose your innocence."

"You think so? She doesn't really care about innocence, just the fact of it. Did I mention she was insane? Someone told me to try this. There's no way she could suspect that you were in my life, no way she could hurt you. You're the only safe woman in Las Vegas for me."

"Now you've gone and made me feel my work is a duty. I've gotta save you from a date rape. I don't know, Thomas. I work better when the goals are more crass. Orgasm, power, money. Sure, I can handle the insecure. But you're not insecure, just . . . inexperienced. And you don't want to do it. That's kind of insulting. It doesn't exactly turn me on, and I work better when I'm turned on."

"You actually . . . enjoy your work?"

"Yes."

"Because you're in control?"

"How can I be in control? I'm bought and paid for."

"Oh, come on. You're leading the willing sheep by the fleece."

"We call it short hairs in the business."

Matt shook his head. Apparently sexual transactions allowed for no dignity. "You've got to admit I'm an interesting client."

"Unique."

"So, now that you know my problem, can you do anything about it?"

"It takes two. You've got to be willing and able to hold up your end of the bargain. I'm a very sexy lady, but if you really don't want to get into it, I can't make you. How have you managed to remain celibate anyway?"

"I've been looking for the right woman."

"How right does she have to be?"

"Not involved with anyone else."

"And you found one who was."

He shrugged. He didn't have to tell her about Temple.

"So there is one woman somewhere you'd have no trouble sleeping with."

He nodded. "If we were married."

"Married?"

"Married. But . . . I realize that's a high qualification. I believe that I could slip off the straight and narrow if I weren't careful."

"Okay. You have a libido."

He nodded, cautiously.

"Then I can help you."

"I don't seem to be cooperating tonight."

"I haven't done anything yet."

"No, and it's because you sensed that my heart isn't in this. You're not used to dealing with reluctant clients. I don't blame you for feeling insulted. I would be in your shoes."

"If you were in my shoes, honey, you wouldn't be here."

She'd expertly slipped into a vaudeville drag-queen twang that he couldn't help smiling at, even as she waggled a foot in the outlandish high heels.

"I'm really sorry," he said, "to be such an atypical client. I was looking at you as a means, instead of a person."

"That's the way I'm generally looked at."

"How do you stand it?"

"I'm a very desirable, high-paid means. Look at what you've spent on me already."

"True."

"Let me show you I'm worth it."

"What if it doesn't work?"

"I still get my money, right?"

"Right . . ."

At that instant Matt realized that he had invested too much, in every respect, in this evening to chicken out. Or maybe the wine he had drunk realized it.

Vassar had become a person for him in the last few minutes. She was funny, she had a history, she was willing to take him on. And she was a paid professional. At least one of them would know what she was doing.

# Chapter 43

# Max: Gloves Off

"Police shootings of unarmed men these days," Max said as he raised his empty hands, "even white guys, get more bad press these days than they're worth. Suspension. Internal investigation."

"Like you're not armed." Molina's tone was scoffing.

"I'm not. Ever. Once in a blue moon maybe, but when have you last seen a blue moon over Las Vegas?"

"What about police woundings?"

He was silent.

"I'm saying you're wanted for questioning and by God this time you're going to come downtown and sit in an interrogation room and call a lawyer or sweat bullets or whatever you want to do, but you are coming in."

Max finally turned, very slowly, to face her, just as a car's departing headlights pinned him in a moving spotlight glare like a man caught fleeing across a prison yard. "It really messes up an investigation to have a police lieutenant playing undercover agent."

"You're a pro?"

"Maybe."

"Wouldn't doubt it. It messes up *your* plans, you mean."

"Are you pursuing a case, or protecting your ass?"

"My integrity is none of your business."

"And mine is yours?"

"You don't have any."

"What if . . . what if, Lieutenant, in this case I had more integrity than you?"

She laughed. "Is that how you snooker Temple Barr? Pretending to some mysterious higher moral ground? I am not Little Miss Mischief. This is a nine-millimeter Glock, buddy. It, and I, mean business. And if I have to punch a hole in your kneecap to keep you here, I will. Try doing your usual vanishing act with a knee brace, Mr. Moto."

"Mr. Moto wasn't a magician," Max said, as if they were having an idle conversation that required minor corrections.

He had already examined the parking lot for unexpected quick exits and found himself caught disgustingly out in the open. Could it be that Molina had planned her approach that well?

Meanwhile, the sense that Temple was in danger was ticking like a maddened metronome in the back of his head, where migraine headaches start.

Of course, the more he worried, the less he dared show it, feel it. If he lost this game of cat-and-mouse here, he wouldn't be free to rush to Temple's rescue anywhere.

"This isn't the end of the world, Kinsella." Molina neared, the weapon still raised. "All I want to do is talk."

"You want *me* to talk."

"Well, talking usually is a two-way street."

She was using the cajoling tone of interrogation-room cops the world over, a condescending parental teasing: *you want to be a good boy, don't you?*

*No.*

He lowered his arms, a little.

"I think Temple's in danger. I'm not going to hang around discussing whether you're going to destroy your career by shooting me or not, in the knee or not. I'll give you a rain check. Let me go to Temple, and I'll come in to see you in twenty-four hours."

"I do not make appointments with scum. I do not bargain with human vanishing cream. Now."

"No."

He moved closer to a row of parked cars.

Her feet scraped asphalt as she skittered faster than a whipsnake to block his movement.

The gun was leveled at his chest.

Was it going to be a game of shoot-me, shoot-me-not?

Yes, because Max was not going to be stopped. Even now Temple might be . . . Sean.

He moved again.

And stopped at an unexpected sound.

Molina had slammed the Glock down on the hood of the parked Ford-150 behind her.

Max couldn't help wincing for the paint job.

"You can say no. I can say no." She stepped toward him, in front of him, blocking his way, protecting her piece, daring him to go for it.

He lifted his arms from his sides. "You finally believe me about something, that I'm not armed."

"Oh, you're armed, and dangerous. I know that. I'm just saying you'll have to go through me to get out of here."

Max glanced to the pant-legs that covered her ankles. "And your side piece."

She nodded. "I'm not going to drop my guard to bend down to take that off. Maybe you can grab it when I kick your head off."

"That's the most interesting proposition I've had all night, and that's saying something after one too many hours in a strip club or two or three."

"So you admit to patronizing the clubs."

"I admit to doing what you're doing here: investigating the clubs."

"Who made you junior G-man?"

"You'd be surprised."

"I would love to be surprised about you, Kinsella. Unfortunately, that's not possible. Now. Into my car and down to headquarters. Or not?"

She came closer, sideways stance.

It was to be, as the British say, fisticuffs.

That put him off balance. He had to play this out here, in its own time, or he could never get away to go to Temple.

For a nightmarish moment Molina morphed into Kathleen O'Connor, and he was back to the night when a stupid adolescent dalliance became his salvation and his cousin's Sean's death warrant.

But Molina was not the porcelain, poisonous Kitty. Her deadliness was direct: she wanted to wage war, not love, or at least not love as a variety of war.

There was no option. Max would have to fight her. And win.

Given Molina's size, profession, training, and fierce personal stake, he couldn't consider winning as the usual given.

Max, the semiretired, had once been expert in half a dozen martial arts, but he was two years rusty by now. Molina, he would bet, hadn't worked out much recently either.

Still, she had the confidence, and the anger, to challenge him. It went against all the rules of police work. It was deeply personal.

Interesting. The only woman he'd had for a mortal enemy up to now would never confront him physically.

Max began calculating, not how to pass Molina to reach the gun but how to draw her into a weaker position. He didn't feel an ounce of chivalry about the coming struggle. Her slamming the Glock down had released him from all that. If she wouldn't hide behind the gun she certainly wouldn't hide behind her gender. She wouldn't hold back either.

Neither would he.

It was tentative at first, like a knife fight. They danced around, determining each other's reach, reflexes, speed, strategy.

Eerily, the first inward rush to engagement was simultaneous.

The moves came fast and frantic then.

They grappled silently, all their limbs twisting to find a hold that would last, but each move resulted in an effective countermove.

Breaths became pants and then grunts, but neither resorted to martial arts cries, though both had done the drill. At nearly six feet, Molina was solid and surprisingly strong. Max was a steel eel, tensile and limber. Their fighting styles were as violently different as their personalities and made them serious opponents. Molina's determination to subdue a suspect she had hunted for months, come hell or high water, met the skilled desperation of Max's need to end this contest and rush to Temple's aid.

It ended in Max's pinning Molina against the van wall, enforcing a temporary truce as they caught their breath, boxers clenched in each other's arms like dizzy waltzers before breaking away to pound each other to oatmeal.

"We're well matched, Lieutenant," Max admitted between discreet pants.

Not good news. He couldn't count on getting this over quickly and moving on to Temple.

"It's not over," she gritted between her teeth.

"No."

He wasn't really holding her. His hands had flattened against the metal beside her shoulders, one knee was braced between her legs. Technically, she was pinned, but he could see her mind reviewing a half dozen things she might try for the one right move, when he surprised her by speaking again.

"Don't spoil the moment. This has been incredibly erotic."

She broke their eye contact by whipping her head to the side, cheek to the smooth metal. "You'll try anything," she said, contemptuous.

"Yes." He knew he sounded amused, but he meant to startle and irritate her at one and the same time.

She whipped her head to the opposite side. "Get out of my face."

"That's not what you really want."

That brought her eyes forward, blazing. "Right. Next you'll say that what I really need is a good screw."

"It's more complicated than that."

"Complicated! No. This is simple. Me cop, you crook."

They both knew the truce was temporary, that either one could lash back into attack, and that both would be ready for it.

"Sure it's simple. A simple matter of control, Lieutenant. Or over-control. It goes with your job. You're on the job, all the time. You're in charge, all the time. After a while, there's no way *not* to be in control, in charge, on the job. Except this."

"I can be out of this any second I want to."

"But do you really want to?"

# Chapter 44

# The Third Man

Temple nursed her decidedly flat club soda and the sample-perfume-vial-size drop of scotch that went with it.

Your midlevel strip club barware was so tacky: narrow glasses clogged with ice like a backed-up sink. No lowball glasses, no delicate-footed cocktail glasses. Just thick cheap giveaway glass, cloudy ice, squinky drink.

Not that she wanted anything alcoholic. The noise, i.e., music to strip by, had already given her a headache.

So she sat on her barstool, her feet hooked around the top rung, the gaudy selection of monokinis covering her lap, and kept an eye out for her most likely suspect.

It wasn't a brilliant piece of deduction, but talking to Lindy had spurred some ideas.

For one thing, both Cher Smith and the girl whose attack had been interrupted, Gayla, were both new to the Las Vegas strip scene. It could be a coincidence, but Temple thought the killer might be one of those asocial guys who are only bold when they're over-the-top aggressive: no nerve, or all nerve. Someone who explodes. She'd seen so many wimpy guys here, mooning at the strippers like besotted computer nerds in front of a porno-site screen. . . . What if the worm turned? Maybe he picked new girls because they were fresh enough to still be stupid. Maybe they hesitated and talked to him, just to be nice to someone who seemed to need it. Maybe *they* needed to feel glamorous and desired. Two people meeting with so much to overcome, their separate expectations igniting instant disappointment of the other's fantasy, and then . . . violence.

Temple sucked her ice cubes again. There was so little drink in the glass it stayed puddled on the bottom.

That was her theory that saved the neck of everybody she knew. And wrote a satisfying "The End" to the episode that had begun with Cher Smith's dead body being found in this very club's parking lot.

Or, if she wanted to depress herself, there was the Terrible Troika to consider: Max, Rafi Nadir, and Lieutenant C. R. Molina converging seconds apart over the fallen form of Gayla in another strip club parking lot more recently.

Had one of the two men attacked Gayla? The victim couldn't say who had barreled into her in the dark. Temple thought she could eliminate Molina as the perpetrator. That left Max and Rafi. She knew she could eliminate Max, so that left Rafi.

Unless . . . a third man had been there just before these two natural enemies.

So who was the third man?

Temple had an idea, and she was looking for him tonight.

The migraine music stopped.

Temple glanced at the stage.

Temporarily vacant.

In the glassed-in sound booth, she saw a man standing and talking to the kid who ran the sound board. Not the man she was looking for.

Who do you overlook at a strip club?

The man who is looking at you, but from behind a mask.

She was looking for the man in the mask.

The music started up again, so suddenly it nearly snapped her head back. The strips of tissue she had stuffed into her ears barely muted it.

She figured if the guy was a regular, and he probably was, he'd come back to Baby Doll's. To allay suspicion if nothing else. Or just to relive his big moment.

Temple had read the true crime books, some of them anyway. She knew the profiles, yucky as they were.

She knew something else as she scanned the constantly moving crowd of customers: that head of dark, slightly wavy thick hair.

Darn! Rafi Nadir was here too. *Of all the gin joints . . .*

She spun back to the face the bar, hunkered down. When she'd told him this was her next thong gig, he was a suspect worth watching. Who'da thought that Lindy would later tip her off that a new hot suspect would be here tonight?

Unlike Nadir, this was somone too nondescript to describe, although she'd glimpsed him once, more than once when she reviewed all her forays into the clubs.

He was like a mailman, someone made invisible by his function.

Tonight she wanted to spot him, and then really see him.

And she didn't need Raf Nadir playing Big Man to her Little Girl to get in the way.

An off-duty stripper (were they ever off duty?) who was cruising the house paused to twine her arms around his neck.

He must like that, being greeted like a Big Spender. The male ego could be a slippery slope to being taken, and then expected to take it back in spades.

Oh, the music! It was worse than forty alley cats caterwauling. Temple liked high-octane rock, the best stuff, but this was jacked up so that the bass became a punishment.

She glanced in annoyance at the gangly kid in the glass booth, his head bobbing on his scrawny neck (which she'd like to wring), staring sightlessly at the stage where a girl slithered out of her second skin (courtesy of Tess the Thong Girl, as they'd started calling her already). Temple was struck by how fast and easy it was to establish yourself in a subculture like this. Well, easy for her as long as she wasn't masquerading as Suzy Stripper.

It would be that easy for the killer too.

And then she spotted him. Suspect Numero Uno.

That nervous little middle-aged man in the yellow polyester shirt and the polyester-linen sport coat. Hair receding about as much as his belly advanced. A bit officious as he lined the offstage girls up, telling them what to do and clearly liking it.

And that mask he carried everywhere, his ticket to entry into this scene, the reason nobody ever really saw him clearly, because every time they looked right at him, really looked at him, they were thinking of themselves and never saw him, couldn't see him, not through the monocle of glass that made them small in his eyes and him eternally nonexistent in theirs.

Temple nodded to the bartender.

"Another S and S?" he asked.

If she had either scotch or soda in her glass, she couldn't testify to it in court. "Yeah. And . . . that guy."

"Lady, there are sixty guys in here."

"Him. The photographer. Do you know who he is? I mean, who is he shooting the photos for?"

"His bedroom wall." The guy left to run some tapwater and sheltie pee over the ice cubes in Temple's glass.

He plunked the glass beside the ten-dollar bill she'd glued to the water spots on the bar.

"Guys can just come in here and do that?"

"They make copies, give 'em to all the girls. What a racket."

"Well . . ." Temple said, jiggling her thong ring.

"Yeah, but you're selling a product. You don't get off on it unless you're a dyke. These losers, they just gotta be around the girls but they don't want to pay for it. They gotta think they're special."

*And a guy who thought he was special might ask for special treatment, and if he was refused . . .*

"How long has he been doing this?"

"Since I been here?"

"And—?"

"Longer than you've been coming around. Why you want to know?"

"I'm new. Just curious."

"Just curious don't pay in this game. Forget it. He's nobody."

Nobody just might get tired of that condition.

Temple checked out Nadir through a concealing strand of blond Dynel wig.

The same stripper was still with him. His arm circled her waist. They were talking, smiling, flirting.

Revolting! She'd be glad to wash this scene right out of her hair, her fake hair. She glanced at the officious photographer again.

Well, it was an intriguing idea, but there wasn't much she could do

with it except pass it along to Molina, who would sneer at her amateur theories.

Still, she had come up with an alternative to Max, at least, and
they could check on this guy's movements, his history. Who knows
what would show up?

She kissed the ice cubes a less-than-fond farewell and slid off the
stool. Her rear was numb.

"Sold out?" the bartender asked.

She nodded, feeling guilty about the two-hundred-something of
stripper-earned money in the tiny wallet-purse she'd learned to carry
in the clubs on a shoulder strap she wore across her chest like a ban-
dolier.

They worked hard for the money. Temple hated to take any of it
under false pretenses, for vulgar accessories to a lifestyle that still
made her cringe.

She could hardly wait to walk out of here—if only Rafi Nadir
wouldn't notice her! No, he and that stripper were still hanging on
each other.

She had to push with all her might to open the big front door.

The night air wasn't really cooler, but it felt cleaner, rinsed of all
that smoke that made her ears and nose and throat clog up like ice in
a pipestem glass.

She walked across the lot to where she had hidden the Miata
between two huge custom vans. That was the problem with a new
high-profile car. It was a liability for sleazy undercover work.

She missed the snappy click of her high heels on the asphalt, a per-
cussion that had always lifted her spirits since she'd been allowed her
first pair at fourteen, and that made her feel taller. But sneakers were
smarter to wear and her ears still rang from the relentless music
inside, like an infection she couldn't shake.

The parking lot had a wooden fence stretched between brick posts
to present a more seemly view to the street. Facade was all in Las
Vegas.

Temple realized she had mixed emotions: she hoped she'd found a
suspect who would take the heat off Max. She was so sick of the strip
club scene.

She glanced at the fence, lit by the security light.

A cat sat on it. A silhouette in the night. Big cat.

Its mouth opened wide to showcase white shark's teeth in a mouth raw and red against its backlit form.

Maybe it was a black cat.

Temple spotted the Miata's sassy and sleek rear end, looking black, not red, in the vans' shadow, and moved toward it, her door key between her first and second knuckle.

And then she realized what was wrong.

The cat had howled.

And she hadn't heard it.

She was temporarily deaf from the music inside and . . . she hadn't taken out the wads of tissue in her ears.

She was temporarily deaf.

A body slammed into her from behind.

Slammed her up against the van.

"You don't want to leave." The voice was right at her deaf ear, penetrated the soundlessness like a scraping file.

"I'm not a stripper," she said. *Not me. I don't fit the profile.*

If only she could reach up and rip out the tissues, but his body had crushed her against the lukewarm metal, arms pinned at her sides, the ring of costumes cutting into her ribs and hip.

"You're pretty," it said. A hand snagged in the rough fibers of her wig. She could feel the bobby pins that held it on slipping. "Come home with me."

He was pushing her along the van. She felt the side door give behind her, slide open, even heard the sharp crack as it began to move.

His van. She had become a crime of opportunity.

Once inside . . .

Temple squirmed, resisted, tried to scrabble along the moving door so something solid remained behind her, so she wasn't pushed, sucked into that bottomless imprisoning dark within.

The struggle must have knocked some tissue out of her ears. She heard like one cured: an unholy yowling, a whining like the horrible shrieking sound played behind the shower murder scene in *Psycho*.

Oh, Lord, she was *in* the shower murder scene in *Psycho*!

The guy's elbows and hands and knees were jamming into her, hurting her, but she kept scrambling. She didn't know anything about him: how tall, how old, how heavy. He was just an impinging part of the dark.

If she went down, she would never know. . . .

She felt herself slipping, sinking into the off-key shrieking sound, her wrist desperately twisting to turn the big metal ring on her wrist.

He had gotten tangled in the jungle of elastic straps, an arm, Temple thought.

In that instant, her fingers found the small cannister danging from a keychain amid the garish fabrics. Max's so unromantic gift.

She twisted it, twisted her hand half off its joint, and pushed on plastic.

A mist hissed up between them like an invisible serpent's head, as searing and blinding as a sandstorm in her eyes, her nose, her throat.

Force fell away, but Temple tumbled writhing and gagging to the asphalt. After the hard struggle along the metal van side, it felt as cushioning as a warm gingerbread cookie.

Tears blinded her. Her ears, though, were finally clear of tissue. The horrible shrieking, screaming, howling sound never stopped.

# Chapter 45

# Molina: Face-off

Before Molina could answer, he swung her away from the wall.

She was surprised by his strength, quite amazing, almost equal to an angel-dust addict's. The move lifted her off her feet for a second.

She had never experienced in adult life that pit-of-the-stomach carnival-ride thrill she felt now, not in martial arts class and not even in sex, not since she had grown into a tall woman and made herself strong and independent, and ultimately celibate. He only had thirty pounds on her, but he was all muscle and bone, as flexible as a rattlesnake tail.

Now he was pressing her so tightly between the van and himself that she could hardly breathe. She had never allowed herself to speculate about any man's sexuality, not for years, not since she'd become a career woman in a man's world. He was right about one thing: she was all business, all working mother, all bureaucrat and civic servant. And hunter.

He released her, drawing his left hand down her arm to her hand.

His right hand tilted her face to the side. Then his mouth touched her neck over the carotid artery. Every move was music, slow and controlled and perfectly pitched. Not a kiss, a slow-burning brand.

She was back in a crowded high school hallway, a gangly, thick teenager watching the petite bow-head girls as they ransacked their lockers between classes. Giggling and brushing back the careful curls from their necks to show off small lurid bruises. Hickeys. The tattoos of a quarter century ago. Badges of sexual initiation. She knew now that these marks demonstrated the boys' passion and possession more than the girls'. Good Hispanic girls were too repressed to feel passion, but they were good at pretending to it. And they welcomed visible signs of possession, of their own dangerous desirability. Hickeys were the one pimple an adolescent girl could be proud of.

She had never had one.

A departing headlight raked across their figures like a spotlight. She used the distraction to push him away. "Vampire," she accused.

"Vlad the Impaler," he answered.

How could he find sex so amusing, she wondered, especially this explosive kind that defied all previous behavior, all roles, all reason? Maybe he found her amusing.

"You just want to screw me." The accusation, the situation demanded an ugly word for it.

"Right. I just want to screw you." He said the words emphatically, separately, with an undertone of surprise.

Somehow the surprise made the vulgarism sexy, not dirty, as he looked at her mouth, then her eyes. "But I won't. Not until you just want to screw me as much." He had perfectly imitated her tone but his words were an invitation, and hers hadn't been.

She caught her breath. Words were just another weapon to her, but they didn't work for her like this, not in emotional clinches. Only on the street, where they were ugly and effective.

"Don't try your bedroom games on me," she said contemptuously again, softly. She meant the contempt for the games, not the bedroom, but she had to wonder if one hadn't rubbed off on the other for her long ago.

"Bedroom games," he agreed. "We're well matched, Lieutenant," he repeated. "Shall we call it a draw for now?"

The "shall" reminded her of his Continental adventures. Her law enforcement instincts had always told her he could have been, could be, involved in something serious. Something big-time. International. Now she knew it.

She scuttled away along the metal wall, more repelled by herself than by him. He would try anything; she didn't have to.

"You're a criminal."

"Sometimes. To some."

She shook her head, didn't look at him. "Get out of here." Said as shortly as she would dismiss a snitch.

He left, as she said, as he had always wanted to.

And in that momentary turning away, she leaped, kicked a foot out from under him, followed up with a hard knee to the small of the back as he went down, had his right thumb in a painful lock as she forced his arm into an ugly angle behind his back, used her free left hand to slam his head into the asphalt and stun him long enough to grab the handcuffs out of her Excaliber fanny pack, snap the left wrist in, jerk it hard over to . . . finally . . . meet the pinned right wrist and . . . presto.

One magician, hogtied on the rocks.

Molina sat back, both winded and revved. Practice makes perfect, and God knew she had done her share of takedowns in L.A., but that had been years ago.

This one felt better than all of them put together.

For a moment she gloried in being a successful street cop: quarry run down, pinned down, about to go downtown.

She caught her breath and rose, bending to grab his elbow and force him to his feet. She kept his arm in custody while she retrieved the Glock from the truck hood.

"Not leaving your license number?" he asked.

She didn't answer, just hustled him along to her car, trying not to grin in triumph.

Moments later she realized that not once during the whole confrontation—not once—did she ever consider going for her ankle gun.

*Not bedroom games*, she said to herself, breathless but satisfied. *Just old-fashioned, street-smart police work.*

# Chapter 46

# *Hallelujah Chorus*

As I gaze upon my Miss Temple sprawled on the asphalt, coughing and spitting like a half-drowned red tabby, I feel a strong surge of pardonable pride.

Thank Bastet that I decided to pause at Baby Doll's en route to my rescue mission for Midnight Louise!

It looked dicey for a minute or two, when I feared Miss Temple would not heed my clarion call for some reason. Luckily, I had arranged for backup.

Although I have not worked with this gang long enough to unleash them on a perpetrator in an orderly disorderly fashion, they certainly were in fine voice and alerted Miss Temple just in time to upset her attacker.

Our continued caterwauling attracted more help of a human nature, but rather than stick around to answer for such a scruffy band of companions, I decide to press on to the next crisis.

"So that is your live-in," a hoarse voice growls in my ear. "Not much for size or looks. And I think she's deaf. Have you had her tested by the vet? I presume a privileged fellow like you has a vet."

"You are not seeing my Miss Temple at her best angle, Ma. Upright. And she has heard me perfectly well on previous occasions. Must be that awful howling music pouring out of Baby Doll's. We better split before someone mistakes us for street musicians and starts hurling projectiles at us."

At that I jump down from the fence and back into the mean streets, all in the hopes of ending the discussion. My dear mama, I discover, has enough wind to trot alongside me and still belabor my plans, my significant other, and sundry other details about my person and life.

I begin to wonder if this raid on Los Muertos will be worth it.

## Chapter 47

# *I Once Was Deaf but Now I See*

Temple pushed down on the heels of her hands.

She couldn't see, but at least she didn't hear that horrible shrieking anymore. She had a queasy suspicion that she had contributed to it at the end there.

No one was touching her either.

She pulled herself up against the van and tried to open her eyes.

Blinking, burning. She forced her eyes ajar an eyelash-width again, catching her breath.

Then two hands grabbed her arms above the elbows.

She inhaled to screech, solo, when someone shook her slightly.

"Hey. Tess. It's okay."

The voice sounded familiar.

She forced her eyes wider despite the searing saltwater they drowned in.

Rafi Nadir. She was wrong! *He was here and he had always been the one.*

She pulled away, screamed, kicked, punched, spun her ring, grasping for the pepper spray canister again.

"Hey! Simmer down, Tess. It's okay! I decked him pretty good. He's out until someone wants him talkative."

Him?

Temple gasped, stopped flapping like a fish out of water. (She would never eat fish again.)

She tried to focus on the dark asphalt at her feet, between the two vans.

A long figure lay stretched out facedown.

While she stared, Rafi Nadir whipped out a cell phone and dialed 911. "Mugging suspect down at Baby Doll's strip club parking lot, Paradise and Flamingo. We need a squad car fast."

He kept the phone to his ear and frowned at Temple's gaping expression. "If it hadn't of been for those nutsy alley cats serenading the strip club from the fence, I never would have noticed you fighting this creep in the shadows here. Don't you know better than to park your car between two behemoths like this? Put yourself in the dark, a perfect target for a mugger, or worse."

"I—I think it's 'worse'. I think that's the stripper killer."

Temple did not explain that she'd parked in the dark on purpose to hide her car. An undercover operative does not give away trade stupidities . . . er, secrets. Especially not at Secrets. Was she still a little punchy?

"Good thing you had that pepper spray." Nadir paused to answer a question on the open line. "North side of the lot. Yeah." He shook his head at Temple. "I don't know what to do with you, Tess. If this guy *is* the stripper killer, and I kinda think it might not be that bad, you just walked right into his hands. Haven't you got anybody to look out for you?"

"Alley cats?" Temple suggested, shrugging. The tears were stopping and so were the shakes. "Who is it?"

"We'll let the police handle that, little lady."

"No. I really, really want to know. Now."

Rafi Nadir stared at her. She knew she looked worse than a drowned, red-eyed rat. She knew he thought she was stupid and reckless, which she had been, but only because she was smart and tough, in secret. And she knew he thought women needed to be bossed around for their own good. But. She really needed to see who this guy was.

And he saw that she had earned that right.

So he bent down to roll the guy over. Tall, lanky, all in black. Not as tall as Max, but close enough to stop a heart, hers, for a minute. Black Levis, black work shirt. Not Max. Not the photographer.

"Oh, my God!" She pointed as if Nadir couldn't see for himself. "It's that sound machine kid. The club DJ. He gets around from place to place too, like a stripper, doesn't he? Don't the DJs do that?"

"Yeah—" Nadir was looking down at his victim with more respect. "But he's just a kid."

"A kid in a candy store. I bet these guys get the idea they own these women they work around."

Nadir started to say something, looked at Temple, then shut his mouth.

"Listen," he said. "I'd better not hang around." Sirens were wailing like alley cats in the distance. He looked over his shoulder. People who had been peering out the club's open door now were starting to trickle onto the asphalt. "They'll help you keep him down if he gets antsy. Just use your spray. And try not to let it blow back in your face."

Temple regarded the shadowy figure on the ground. Her fingers found the spray can among the spandex.

"Smart idea." Nadir's hand rested on her shoulder for a sexless, bracing second. "You take full credit for this one, kid. You didn't see me."

And then he left.

Temple slumped against the van.

Wow.

She aimed her pepper spray at the ground near the young man's head.

She was wrong. Her hand still shook.

She was thinking about what would happen to Max if she had been left dead like Cher Smith in a strip club parking lot.

# Siren Song

"You're wrong," he said.

"You'll have all the time in the world to prove it."

Her voice was level, strong, intense. But Molina was worried.

He had been the hardest takedown in her career, and she was half-afraid that he had let her win in the end, not because he was a gentleman but because it suited him.

So now she had Max Kinsella, handcuffed, to put in her personal car, which was equipped with nothing but a police radio.

She sure didn't want him behind her, so the passenger seat was the only option and it wasn't a good one.

"Get in," she said, as if she just loved the idea of putting him there.

She shoved him into the seat, pushing down on his head to force him inside.

His height was still too much for the Toyota's roof line, and he banged his skull.

Good, maybe it'd daze him a little. It was a twenty-minute ride to headquarters and she didn't want to distract herself calling in or doing anything but keeping him in custody until he was safely locked up somewhere even an magician couldn't abracadabra his sleazy way out of.

Kinsella sat hunched forward in the seat, partly because of his height, partly because with his hands manacled behind his back he couldn't lean back. Tough.

"Temple's life could be on your head," he said. Sounded strangled, like he really cared. And getting . . . cozy with her if it would help get him free. What a creep!

"Can it."

She snapped on her seatbelt, started the car, put it into gear, checked that he was still bound and pulled out of the Secrets parking lot.

"You don't know that Temple *isn't* in danger," he said, "and you really don't have anything solid on me."

"I'm sure I can work up a probable cause that would curl a judge's hair. You have been caught on too many dirty scenes too many times."

"Not caught. Not until now."

"Why do I think that you think you're not really caught?"

He shrugged, stared ahead, intently watching the street as if he were behind the wheel, not she.

Just fifteen more minutes and she'd be rid of him.

The radio squawked. She wanted to turn up the squelch dial, but couldn't risk leaning down into the well of the car. Perfect opportunity to sandbag her.

After a buzz of competing calls, she heard the words, "Baby Doll's."

Kinsella thrashed a little against his bonds. Solid-steel suspicion, that's what she had on him. It would have to be enough.

She had to lean forward to pick up the mike. Had to. Kept her eyes on him as if she was a staple gun and he was wallpaper.

More voices chimed in, sputtering through the static. Action.

She waited for a break and got on. "Molina. What's going on at Baby Doll's?"

"Perp down. Victim's okay. She's saying it's the stripper killer."

Molina hit the brakes so hard her passenger's forehead tapped the windshield.

She made sure he wasn't using the distraction to attack her, but he was listening as hard as she was.

"Victim is okay?"

"Yeah. She pepper-sprayed the guy"—Kinsella jerked, and she glared him to stillness—"to kingdom come. He's out cold yet."

"Who's the guy?"

"Some DJ kid for the clubs. Tyler something."

Molina gave up and pulled the car over to the curb, putting on the emergency blinkers. Tyler. Who'da thunk it? She had a horrifying suspicion who might have.

"And the intended victim? You got a name yet?"

"Tess, from what some people around here said."

*Tess?*

"But it turns out it's really Temple."

Of course. The awful inevitability of it was almost blinding.

"Yeah," the radio squawked. "That's a first name. Temple Barr. Tiny little thing, but she put this guy down flat."

The radio went silent.

"I think I'll be going now," Kinsella said quietly.

She looked over. The handcuffs dangled from one wrist, then the empty one was snapped on her right wrist, the left one jumped from his wrist to snap shut on the steering wheel.

It all happened faster than the blink of an eye, especially an eye controlled by a mind that was busy absorbing vast new vistas on a series of old problems.

"You bastard." Her tonelessness made the word even uglier. "I ultimately would have had to let you go anyway. This time."

He opened the door, jumped out, leaned his head back in a sliver of open door.

"I know you would have had to." Kinsella rubbed his forehead, grinned. "But ultimately it's more fun this way. You do still have the key somewhere on you, don't you, Lieutenant?"

He slammed the door shut and vanished . . . only because she couldn't move much to see where he had gone.

While she struggled to dig the key one-handed out of her rear paddle holster, fighting the damned seatbelt all the way, the radio buzzed with the happy crosstalk of high adventure and the taunting muted shriek of sirens speeding to the crime scene.

Kinsella had been honest about one thing: a woman in danger.

At least Temple Barr was just dandy, and neither she nor Kinsella would have her damage or death on their conscience.

That would be something in common with Max Kinsella that Carmen Molina absolutely could not bear.

# Chapter 49

# *Serial Chills*

"I did not raise you," my mother says, "to leave a lady lying in the street, even if she is human."

"Look, Ma, you did not raise me, period. It was six weeks and 'You are on your own, kit.' Besides, I know my Miss Temple and she is fine, especially after we sang to high heaven to attract attention to her plight. I do not know that Miss Midnight Louise is fine."

"Usually something 'stinks' to high heaven," Ma says.

"Well, we were not the Mormon Tabernacle Choir, but it got the job done."

We are trotting along at the head of a feline brigade, if a brigade can be as motley a crew as this is.

Only my mother's stern matriarchal influence on the cat colony has permitted this rare outing en masse, so I am best off if I do not irritate the old dear too much.

"So this Midnight Louise is your kit, Grasshopper," she says.

"We have not had a DNA test," I grumble, "so I am not about to claim relationship. She was known as Caviar until some humans got the funny idea she looked like me and renamed her Midnight Louise. You know how it is, humans think all us black cats look alike."

"Hmph. Caviar is a pretty fancy name for a nobody. I do not have any grandkits, that I know of."

"Thank your lucky whiskers! Young kits today have no respect."

"They did not in your day either," says she with a sidelong glance. "This will be good for the colony," she adds. "To leave the safety of their turf, to venture into the Dead Place. They were getting too complacent with the Fixers leaving them food."

I can see that my mama is a leader of cats.

"The days of free-range cats are ending," I say. "It is too dangerous out here and there are plenty of humans to be educated into giving us posh retirement homes off the street."

"And you would be content to sit inside twenty-four/seven and watch the world through a window?"

"Sure." Again I get the green sideways stare. "If I were retired. But I am a professional. There are not many PIs of my persuasion—although sometimes I think there is one too many trying to muscle into my territory—but for the average cat, which is everybody else but me, the domestic life is the best bet. Even dear old Dad has left the seafaring life for a sweet berth with some old guys who run a restaurant on Lake Mead. Heck, they even named it after him. What more could you want?"

"So Three O'Clock is nothing but a house cat. I am glad he left me for that calico floozy from the pawn shop."

I am not about to touch parental history, particularly when it is mine, so I keep trotting and keep it shut.

The pale stucco walls of Los Muertos gleam in the moonlit distance like the white cliffs of Dover. I expect bluebirds any moment, though I have never seen such a mythical beast.

I could use a few helpful Disneyesque birds. They could scout the upper stories and peek in windows and then coming peeping back about what is going on to me.

When we get to the gate I turn to address the mob.

"Okay. Listen up. There are Rottweilers in there and they have a hair-trigger temper . . . mostly triggered by our kind of hair. We want to get in, and then up on whatever we can climb.

"Also, you will find that a couple of major players also occupy the grounds. They are our kind of folks, but they are not used to seeing us types close up and personal. They might mistake us for an appetizer in the heat of the moment. I know these dudes, but they do not know you. So keep your distance if you want to retain your whiskers and any other vital bodily parts."

"These are the Big Cats?" asks poor Gimpy, who has managed to keep up with our march despite his desperately disabled leg. "We will see Big Cats?"

"Yes, but do not let them see you first. I need to explain our mission to them. I am hoping that they will keep the Rottweilers . . . entertained while we approach the house."

"We will see Rottweilers?" Gimpy asks like a kit who thinks dragons are cool.

"The important thing is that they do not see us, kit," I tell him. I cast a significant glance at Snow Off-white, who ankles to my side with a minor hiss.

None of this gang is eager to bow to my leadership, but since I know the way, and the Big Cats, they have to.

"Keep an eye on Gimpy when we get in," I growl sotto voce to her.

"I am not a kit-sitter! *You* keep an eye on him."

"You ferals need to look out for each other. Cooperate, or kiss your whiskers good-bye. When we get Midnight Louise out of that house of horrors, I will have the Big Cats tell you a little story about what intraspecies cooperation can do."

"They are not so big."

"You have not seen them yet." I cuff her lightly to get her on the right track and turn back to Ma Barker.

"You want to take on the Rottweilers, Ma?"

"You bet."

"Remember. Lead them to the arrangement of rocks and fountains in the middle of the grounds."

"They should have park privileges? I would like to lead them off a cliff."

"There is not much here in the way of cliffs, but if you get them to that place, they will wish they had a cliff to jump off of."

"And the colony?"

"I would like to deploy them at high points around the house and grounds."

"And you?"

"I will go in, solo. I am counting on backup when Louise and I escape that place."

"You expect pursuit."

"Yup."

"Worse than Rottweilers?"

"Worse than dogs."

"Hmmm. You are sure that you do not want me to lead the Rottweilers out into major traffic?"

"I do not want them hurt. They are only ignorant indentured servants of a corrupt administration. I just want them out of the way."

"Mercy to dogs? You have been off the streets too long, Grasshopper."

But I think that the old dame will do as I say, instead of as she wishes.


In ten minutes I am past the snoozing snakes, up Sleeping Beauty's hedge of thorns, and doing the Twist to make Chubby Checker plaid with envy as I slither my way down the aluminum vent pipe.

I hit bottom . . . and a unexpected impediment.

The way is blocked!

I do not like the feel of this. It is something solid like . . . wood.

Yuck! It is the head of the dead dummy guy.

Well, I am not Woody Woodpecker so I am momentarily stymied.

Then I tumble. (I am after all, on the ghostly site of a once-proud dryer.)

Aluminum is no different from what they make some food containers out of, and I was busting into garbage cans and aluminum foil and food containers since I was a punk kit.

I manage to get my business end—my powerful hind legs—into position and began rabbiting away at the edges of aluminum surrounding the wooden noggin in my path.

I cannot say that it does not require time, energy, and rhythmic persistence, but in a bit I have managed to kick out a flange of aluminum, a most malleable metal, all around the blockhead.

Then it is merely a matter of drop-kicking the old oaken noggin to Kingdome come. Let us play a little ghostly touch football, Elvis! The head pops out of my way like a ripe melon meeting a sledgehammer.

I am back in the closet.

But not for long.

The fact that the entry hole has been plugged leads me to believe that Miss Midnight Louise has been forced to admit her route of entry.

This gives me a chill. I do not like to think what it would take to force Miss Midnight Louise to do anything.

On the other hand, her presence here, if discovered, could have led to a search party.

I sniff the closet perimeter, detecting again the odd, musky, decidedly alien feline odor I sensed elsewhere in the house.

Just what does Miss Hyacinth use for henchmen these days?

The thought gives me another chill.

There is a lot about this place that gives me serial chills.

Then again, it could be the air conditioning.

Well, there is nothing like brisk activity to get the blood moving. I try the door.

It is now locked, of course.

They are beginning to get me mad.

I sniff the perimeter again, hoping this joint is old enough to have an established mouse and rat population. Great chewers, they are.

However, I turn out to be depressingly alone in my incarceration. And I do so like it when the rodent population has done the preliminary excavating for a job.

I do discover, behind some musty satin and velvet capes, a heating register.

This is as good as a twenty-four-karat golden gate.

In no time flat, I have managed to dislodge two loose screws and have the grate askew in its frame. One last loose screw and it is hanging by one corner.

I gyrate through and find myself once again in the upper hallway, deserted by all except the ghosts from *Omen* movies.

This time I do not waste any (time, that is) exploring the ambiance.

I move, fleet and sure, through the cavernous rooms, past the guardian suits of armor, unabashedly sniffing like the lowest dog.

This time I do not turn and head toward the upper regions when I reach the crossroads to the kitchen but continue on the trail of roast beef, the occasional enterprising rodent, the strange feline scents, and a vague whiff of canna lily that can only betoken my darling . . . cohort.

As I suspected before, the kitchen is a large, old-fashioned affair with a door leading to a . . . butler's pantry. And a door leading to . . . the outside garden. And a door leading to . . . a dining room the size and solemnity of a private medieval chapel. And a door leading to the . . . cellar.

Oh, joy.

Last time I went up and found magicians, Big Cats, and Hyacinth.

I will now descend and hopefully find . . . Midnight Louise.

Of course I must first open the door.

Breaking into a mansion has its drawbacks. Give me a one-room apartment any day.

There is a mitt-wide space under the door.

I stick my mitt into the dark.

When it is not cut off, I use it to nudge and wiggle the door. Sometimes these old doors are as loose as change.

In a couple minutes I hear a welcome click. A loose metal tongue has just given up the ghost.

Or, in this place, a ghost may have just given me entry.

You never know.

I edge through, pull the door shut behind me, thrilled to hear no click of true closure, and descend a flight of stone stairs in the pitch dark.

I am not sure why dark is considered pitch. It does not sing. It does not normally tilt, like stair risers. Anyway, pitch dark is considered blacker than my best formal coat, and so this pathway is.

I move down for so long that I feel the cool dank air rising to meet me.

So does the scent of the alien weasels I scented in the closet, and the faintest sniff of calla lily.

I recall that the lily is the chosen human symbol of death.

Poor Louise. Snatched in her prime, preprime, really, and interred here in this forgotten cellar, with only weasels for pallbearers. *If* they bothered to bury her.

I am smitten by remorse. Or is that smited? Smoted?

Anyway, I realize with a pang that had I not been distracted by human concerns and my Miss Temple's safety, I would have been here sooner and perhaps could have prevented this tragedy.

While the feral folk wait without, I tunnel deeper within, afraid that our quest will have only one certain and sad ending. Ma Barker will not meet her only maybe grandkit. I will be partnerless again. *Hmmm.* The Crystal Phoenix will once again need a new house detective. Chef Song will lose a toadie!

I am nearly choking with loss (and dust) when I touch the cold stone of bottom.

I tiptoe around the rough-hewn stones. The scents have boiled down into an unappetizing stew.

Death leers from unseen corners.

I stumble over a sudden depression in the floor, wrestle with a metal tray until it is dislodged, fall a rib-bruising distance, and find the stingers of a dozen scorpions puncturing my poor hide.

I am done for! Dropped like Indiana Jones into a pit of vipers and vermin, with no way out.

"Get off me, you big oxymoron!"

Only one person—pardon me, individual—would berate me so subtly.

"Louise! You are alive!"

"Not by much, after you landed on me. How did you manage to remove the grating?"

"What grating?"

"As I thought. Dumb luck. Quick, I can climb to the top on you and then . . . well, I do not know if I can pull you out, so I will go to deal with the muscle upstairs and come back for you later."

"Wait a minute. I can climb out on *you*, and then pull you out."

"You would crush me, Popsicle. It is better I crush you."

"Maybe we can both make it out," I suggest, hurling upward until my front shivs catch on a stone rim.

Oooh! That stings.

So do Midnight Louise's shivs as she ratchets up my spine to the cellar floor in a twinkle, just like old St. Nick up the chimney. *Nick* is right! Ow.

"You are not going to leave your old man just hanging here by his nails?"

Something comes hurtling down.

"There is a board. I will scout the stair to make sure your lumbering down here did not awaken all the dogs of war in the house."

Dogs? I thought they were outside.

I manage to scramble up the board, failing to avoid every rusty nail in the dark. If I do not die of tetanus it will be a miracle.

I run and limp my way back up the stairs, running into a furry wall at the top.

"You were a prisoner?" I whisper.

"It suited me to let them think so."

Un-huh. Likely story. "Who are 'they'?"

"Your lady friend Hyacinth and her cronies."

"She is not . . . a lady. Or a friend. Besides, our main goal is to leave here safely."

"My main goal is to eat Siamese tonight."

"Louise, there is more going on than your petty attempts at revenge. I have a whole cat colony waiting outside to back us up, not to mention the Big Cats."

Louise is unmoved. I can feel that by the punishing twitch of her unconvinced tail.

"And your grandmother is waiting to meet you."

"My granddam?"

The family tree will get them every time.

"That is right. I, uh, ran across her again tonight during my investigation."

"You mean you ran and she found you. So where did you dig up the ferals?"

"Your grandmama is their head honcho."

"No kitting!"

"I swear."

"Well, I guess I could wait to make mincemeat of Hyacinth until another day. Revenge is a dish best eaten cold, and there is nothing colder than dead."

"I will hear about your adventures later. Meanwhile, I have

restored our old route into the place, which someone had carefully closed."

"Then let us blow this Bastille."

Bastille? For a moment I think Midnight Louise is referring to the dread Bastet, but the moment passes. One does not wish to invoke Bastet, even inadvertently, unless one wishes to deal with the goddess of cats since the days of ancient Egypt. My tip is: one does not want to deal with Bastet. Ever.

Once I have convinced Midnight Louise that family ties are more important than suicide missions, we rocket up the stairs.

As we pass through the broken-into door, though, my super-sleuth senses go into red-alert. I crush my curled shivs into Louise's shoulder.

She would squeal protest, but I slap a spare mitt over her face. "Shhh! We are not alone."

The kitchen is less dark than the cellar, but not by much.

It takes a few moments for our cellar-dampened senses to reassert themselves, but I can tell by the way Midnight Louise stiffens next to me that she too is taking the measure of the several unseen foes surrounding us.

Among the alien scents, I detect the ineffable perfume of the lady known as Hyacinth.

Midnight Louise turns her head to me, though her eyes remained focused on the smothering dark.

"If we close our eyes for an instant, and run, they will lose track of us," she breathes into my ear.

It is a good stratagem. I nod so she can feel my vibrissae give assent, then shut my eyes and call the fury of Bastet down upon all our enemies.

Then I run.

I hear the soft pound of pads beside me . . . and behind me . . . and ahead of me on an angle.

The thump of meeting bodies erupts into an Etna of scalding hot fury and tufts of soft underfur floating like ash against my nose and pads.

Then I am galloping through the house, following a path of sheer memory and the glint of night lights on the suits of armor.

Something pounds along beside me up the hall stairs.

I head-butt the wall in the dark, eager to find the heat register exit.

Finally my muzzle pushes out and finds air instead of plaster and wallpaper.

I wiggle through, Louise on my tail.

Behind us the dislodged grating scrapes, and scrapes again and again, as a torrent of pursuers pours through the aperture.

I hear claws scrabbling on aluminum pipe.

Either Louise has surged ahead of me, or the rats are deserting the house to avoid the panting, slavering tide of unknown creatures that is on our trail.

It is too dark and confusing to worry about whether Louise is ahead or behind. I must boost myself into the confining vent pipe, then wriggle through it as if my life depended on it. Which it does.

Popping out into the night air gives me no rest. I hurtle down the thorny hedge to the grounds below, my own ingrown thorns out and snagging wherever they can to break what is more of a free-fall than a downward climb. Uh . . . never mind.

Something plunges earthward beside me. In the artificial night light of Las Vegas, I am happy to see that Miss Louise has managed to keep up with me. Or down, depending on how you look at it.

Once we hit terra firma, we leap up. A long sweep of lawn stretches between us and our hidden allies.

The whimpering and growling coming from the rock-park midway between the house and the gate tells me that the Rottweilers (whimpering) have been cowed by the Big Cats (growling).

However, even the best-laid plans of the trained operative can go awry, and my current awry comes plummeting down behind us: a ninja brigade of Havana browns as fresh from Cuba as a fine cigar.

Anyone who has not tangled with the breed known as Havana brown is unaware of the Bruce Lees of catdom. They are all muscle and silent, stalking pads. They wear their hair in a battle-ready buzz-cut and do not waste time on hollow boasts or warning howls.

So they are on us like tobacco-spit shadows, dark and almost liquid of motion.

I box one away, and then another. Beside me, Midnight Louise is similarly occupied.

We manage to work our way a few feet toward where our compadres await, but the Havana browns keep on coming, and those we knock down roll over and leap up again.

I do not know about Louise, but I am trying to head for a sheltered garden construction with vine-twined pillars and a latticed roof dripping hibiscus.

We will have more of an advantage against these numbers there than on open ground.

It is slow progress when you have to pause to repel another onrushing Havana brown every time you take one down for the count.

I am panting like a bellows as we near the edge of our island of safety.

"I have these three, Pop," Louise hisses between pants. "You hide on the porch while you catch your breath."

"It is not a porch! It is a pergola. And my breath has not run anywhere I cannot chase it down and get it back."

After this speech, I do indeed seem to be out of steam.

Louise does some fancy footwork to come alongside of me. There are still about eight Havana browns circling tighter and tighter, their vibrissae lifted in mutual snarls, their canine fangs in doglike evidence.

I would say that it looks black for us, except that they are brown.

And before I could say that, we are suddenly attacked from above.

I see a huge tarantula spider—ten times the size of the big road-runners you glimpse in the desert—all fuzzy brown legs in a noxious cluster as it swings down from the roof above on an invisible rope of spider-silk.

Even Midnight Louise cannot keep a ladylike "Eeek!" from escaping her lips as the creature swings past us and to the ground.

I have been doing a rapid count and realize that I have only toted up five legs on the monster. It is handicapped! Spiders are supposed to sport eight legs.

Still, I shudder at its beady red eyes glimmering from the center of its bloated, pale body, at the dark furry legs churning as it rights itself and reveals. . . .

"Why, Miss Hyacinth, I believe." I am happy to see that while paralyzed with fright I managed to get my breath back.

Now I get it. When the evil Hyacinth leaped down her dark, dangling legs and tail looked like icky unshaven spider gams. Such is the coloring of the Siamese breed, dark at the extremities, light at the core. I wonder if there is any hope that this pattern might pertain to Hyacinth herself. I am immediately disabused of any such notion.

"Back off," she hisses at the gathered Havana browns. "I will handle these intruders myself."

She draws herself up until her back is an arch and prances at us sideways, her narrow face a mask of hatred and death.

Something slaps me in the solar plexus—Miss Midnight Louise's right rear foot in a karate kick.

I rock over, gasping for my recovered breath, which is again AWOL.

"Outa my way, dude," Miss Louise spits. "If this is the hussy that locked me up in the Marquis de Sade's basement apartment, I need to have words with her."

"Louise." I can barely speak yet, and watch with horror as the two circle like prizefighters within an outer ring of Havana browns.

"Louise."

Well, no one is listening but me, of course.

Hyacinth goes up on her toes, up on her razor-honed shivs that glint gangrene-green.

"Her nails," I pant.

"I plan to nail her."

"No. C-curare."

It is too late, they abruptly stop circling and dash toward each other with ear-splitting battle cries. Black and cream and lavender-brown are a blur in the moonlight. Fur floats like feathers to the ground.

Then they are separate again, heads lowered beneath their sharp shoulder blades, glaring, circling, stalking.

"Louise." I do not expect her to take her gaze off her opponent to so much as glance over her shoulder. But she must listen. "Her nails are painted with curare. You cannot let one pierce you."

"Now you tell me," Louise snarls unjustly. I have been trying to tell her all along. "No problem. This chick will not have nails to paint when I am through with her."

Brave words, but how can one engage in a duel to the death without suffering a single scratch?

Although my kind, and even humankind, have always recognized that the death duel of two individuals must be left up to them, for the first time in my life I consider interfering with this untouchable ritual.

Louise did not know her opponent had a secret weapon. Although no one would thank me for it, especially Midnight Louise, I could jump Hyacinth from behind and pin her down. Unfortunately, I doubt Louise would take advantage of my self-sacrifice and run. So I would end up paralyzed spider meat for nothing.

While I am figuring out how to save Midnight Louise without her or me losing face, I notice, speaking of faces, that the Havana browns have turned a beiger shade of brown. Say . . . milk chocolate.

They are retreating, their ring growing wider and sparser.

I decide that my dilemma must have put a fearsome expression on my face, then decide to look over my shoulder.

It is a sight to uncurl the hair on a curly-coated Rex. Even I momentarily consider a craven retreat.

They come stalking up on us like Old West gunfighters: Osiris and Mr. Lucky and at their head Ma Barker.

The Big Cats place one deliberate foot in front of the other. Each pace covers two feet of ground.

"That is our cub," Mr. Lucky growls with a sound like they use in movies to represent demons talking.

Even the evil Hyacinth pauses, her spiked hair wilting a bit.

Midnight Louise has not paid a moment's heed to any of the action around her. The minute Hyacinth backs off, she is on her like a black tornado, feet whirring, fur flying from her shivs.

Hyacinth screams with fury and pain, twists like a pretzel, and rockets across the lawn to the house, driving the craven wave of Havana browns ahead of her.

Midnight Louise sits licking fiercely at her chest ruff, surrounded by tufts of cream fur.

I rush over. "Did she nick you? If we get you to a vet fast

enough, and if I can figure out a way to tell Miss Temple you are a victim of curare poisoning—which I will, somehow—we can get you an antidote. If they have antidotes to curare in Las Vegas."

"Relax," says Miss Louise. "She did not lay a lavender-point glove on me. Besides, you are old enough to know that you cannot believe everything that a feline fatale says."

She looks up from her grooming at the Big Cats. "Thanks, boys, but I had her on the run even before she saw you."

Not one mention of my contemplated desperate dash to sacrifice myself! Talk about ingratitude.

Ma Barker stalks forward. "Very impressive, young lady, but you could interrupt your bath to give your elders a nod of thanks."

"Are you claiming to be an elder?" she asks.

"Only if you are claiming to be a descendant of my son."

Here they both glance at me.

"I do not know about that," Miss Midnight Louise says with a hard look at me, "but I do have a partner who had the smarts to break me out of prison so I had a chance to whip the vibrissae off that witch, so I will say thank you very much to all concerned. Now I really must wash that purported curare out of my hair. Although, according to my connoisseur's tongue from a life of attending Dumpster sales, it is no more toxic than Revlon's Mean Green Glitter nail enamel that is available at Wal-Mart."

While my jaw drops, everybody does not quite laugh, but would have, had they been human enough to indulge in such bizarre expressions of amazement.

# Chapter 50

# The Morning After

Max awoke, still dressed at three A.M., in Temple's bed, with Midnight Louie.

He felt stiff all over, in all the wrong places.

The night lights plugged into outlets on all four walls for Master Midnight's nocturnal convenience cast a moonlit glow on the room.

Midnight Louie blinked reflective amber irises at him—proceed with caution—then the black cat assumed one of those show-offy, impossibly limber cat positions—hindquarters stretching in one direction, extended forelegs reaching in the other, torso torqued in between like a twisted rope.

The black cat yawned, wide and long, flashing white fangs and crimson mouth. He almost seemed to be sticking out a tongue at his crippled human littermate.

Max refused to rise to the bait.

He had earned his strains and bruises, and Temple had tended his scraped face last night with wincing care while they exchanged war stories.

"So my pepper spray was ready for the rescue?" Max asked, glad he had been there to defend her in absentia, somehow. "And Nadir finished that guy off? I would have been there to do it if not for that damn Molina."

"Rafi was a real little gentleman about the whole thing . . . other than decking the Tyler kid. What would make a teenager into a crazed killer?"

"*Rafi?*"

"Whatever."

"I'm sure that the newspapers will dig up the usual background predictors, as the sociologists say. Abusive family situation. Antisocial history. Assumption that women are there to be used and knocked around. *Rafi!*"

"He actually was kind of okay to me . . . or Tess the Thong Girl, even before the parking lot incident."

Max just shook his head. Which hurt. So he stopped. "Crime and punishment make for strange bedfellows."

"Speaking of which, I can't believe you and Molina duked it out. I mean, she's a cop, but she's a woman."

"Barely. She is a pretty good sparring partner, though."

"It must have killed you to let her handcuff you."

"Being handcuffed is second nature to me. Letting her do it . . . yeah, that stung. But I couldn't have put her away without getting pretty rough, and I knew you were in trouble and it'd be easier to get out of the handcuffs and custody than a felonious assault charge on a cop, so. . . ."

"Poor Max! Sacrificing your pride for nothing, when you heard over the radio that 'Pepper Tess' had bagged the baddie. I'd give anything to see Molina's face when she heard that the stripper killer had been stopped by yours truly."

"The incoming news bulletin certainly made my rapid exit from the handcuffs and the car easy."

"That must have fried her fajitas! I not only get the killer, but you get away. She was left with nothing. *Nada!*"

"It's not becoming to gloat, Temple."

"Since when?"

"You're right. It's most becoming. I'm glad one of the three of us is in a position to gloat, and that it's you, and that you're all right. And when I'm feeling better—ow! That stings!"

"It's hydrogen peroxide. It's supposed to sting. Things that heal you are supposed to sting."

Max didn't say anything more about what he'd do when he felt better, lecture her or love her. He just took her hand and kissed it.

"Truer words were never spoken."

Lieutenant C. R. Molina tossed and turned in her old double bed at home. Three o'clock in the morning and she couldn't sleep.

She had worked late enough to know that the gathering reports on Tyler Dain did not give her the sense of closure she had hoped for in finding the Stripper Killer. A kid had done it? He was old enough to try as an adult, but that never quieted the unease a young perpetrator brought to the surface in society, all the way through the police and courts structure, like an ugly undertow in the ocean showing its hidden power. He had confessed to the strip club attacks, including the Cher Smith murder. He was cocky, proud of it.

That still left Gloria Fuentes's parking-lot killing unsolved, and a lot of other questions unanswered, most of them pertaining to magic. Fuentes had been a magician's assistant years ago. Magic also clung to the apparent ritual murder of Jefferson Mangel, the university professor killed among his collection of great magician posters. Missing from the collection? Any trace of the Mystifying Max's admittedly spectacular career. Max Kinsella was the missing link, all right, behind a lot of unsolved crimes in Las Vegas over the past year, and who knew where else, when?

Magic was a boyhood hobby that offered the illusion of power and secret knowledge. Some boys never grew up. Kinsella was one, always hinting that his mysterious past had some clandestine purpose.

Boys could be so dangerous when they reached that cusp between adolescence and adulthood cherishing a secret sense of power. Like Tyler Dain in his sound-proof Peeping Tom booth, who played the music the strippers danced to and came to consider them puppets who should dance to the needs of his immature lust. Girls that age also were walking time bombs, but usually because they often harbored a secret sense of helplessness.

She pictured Mariah, asleep with the tiger-striped cats in her bedroom and surrounded by Technicolor stuffed animals, visions of boy bands dancing in her head. Almost twelve and already hormones were erupting like invisible pimples. A sudden yen for pierced ears. Belly button next? Sass and backtalk becoming common household static. Sending her to Catholic school retarded the inevitable, but didn't stop it.

What would it do to Mariah if she discovered the father her mother had always said was dead was alive and was a loser like Rafi Nadir? What would it do to Mariah's *mother*, she thought wryly, if she had to 'fess up herself for a change? To admit to lying to her daughter. No. Why couldn't Rafi have crashed and burned completely? Died or stayed in L.A.? She had never pegged him as a killer, just as a controller. She would never have tried to keep him out of the stripper cases otherwise. So she wasn't surprised that Tyler Dain and not Rafi Nadir had killed Cher Smith. No, Rafi was only a danger to her. And Mariah. And he didn't have to raise a fist or lift a little finger to be a threat. Just existing did the job nicely.

Molina pictured having to face him again after all these years. The thought made her insides writhe, her hands into fists. Just thinking about him brought back a younger, dumber, weaker version of herself. She didn't fear facing Rafi so much as reverting to a state of vulnerability she'd struggled to escape for many years.

And if they ever met face-to-face, she would indeed be weak: a police officer who'd cut all the corners off procedure to bury a link to a personal issue. Rafi Nadir could ruin her, as he'd tried to do thirteen years ago, and failed. Now, after what she'd done to ensure he stayed out of her and Mariah's lives, he could ruin her utterly.

She spent a few minutes savoring the bitter fact that she'd have been better off confronting the problem directly.

She turned over in bed again, her mind moving with her body into yet another uncomfortable position.

Her encounter with Max Kinsella had been a complete failure too, a humiliating downer.

Everything the man said and did was calculated, like that attempt to eroticize their conflict. What an amoral human chameleon! He had to be guilty of something, and she would find out what and then she would nail him for good.

Meanwhile, she had a souvenir of the evening: the memory of how he'd ducked those handcuffs and left her chained to her own steering wheel. Of course she'd whomped him good first, but she had an ugly feeling he'd let her because it would be easier to escape her in a moving car than in a parking lot. He'd been right in insisting that Temple Barr needed help, but he wasn't the one who should have been giving it.

She mused for an another really ugly moment on where they'd both be now if Temple Barr had not fought free of Tyler Dain to use her pepper spray but had been found dead the next morning.

Hell. In hell. And hating each other even more, if that was possible. It reminded her of the infernal, eternal triangle in Jean-Paul Sartre's hell-set play, *No Exit*.

Things, Molina decided, could not possibly get any worse.

At least that was one ray of hope in a dirty world getting grimier every day.

She hoped to hell that Kinsella had as hard a time getting some shut-eye tonight as she did.


Max left Temple at 3:20 A.M., sleeping like the dead, which she almost had been.

Magicians can do that, slip away and not be noticed. He intended only to be gone for a couple of Temple's deepest sleep-drenched hours.

Midnight Louie apparently never slept. The black cat watched Max go through slitted green eyes. He wasn't about to squeal on a fellow creature of the night, but he just might judge him.

The early-morning air kissed Max a cool fifty-five degree hello as opened the French door to the patio and then worked his way down the Circle Ritz's conveniently stepped exterior. Art Deco had a lot to recommend it. To a second-story man, its step pyramid tendencies were the most pleasing.

The Maxima purred like a panther as he started it. He idled silently past Temple's new red Miata and the silver blob of Electra's Elvis-edition VW bug, glided beyond the white Probe Matt Devine used now. They were all in transition, he realized, changing emotional models and personal identities like cars.

The Hesketh Vampire, chained in the shed like a lone wolf, called to him with a howl higher than human sound as he exited the parking lot.

In mere minutes he was parked outside the bone-white walls of Los Muertos.

The presumed dead remained still beneath their ersatz tombstones. This was Disneyland Macabre, this phony cemetery designed to hide the residence of a magician whose career was built on mocking other magicians. Max would defend the Cloaked Conjuror's life to the death, but he didn't have to like the way he made his living, on the harvest of an honorable land of dead magicians and their once-spectacular illusions.

Magicians were like spiders: you had to keep spinning or the web would fracture and fall. And you with it.

He climbed and leaped down from the wall, thankful for a cushion of expensive sod. He noted the absence of the guardian Rottweilers he'd been prepared to deal with.

Odd, but now he could cross the grounds like a shadow, on foot.

Soon the plink of water on carefully arranged stones told him he was where he wanted to be.

With the big cats.

Mr. Lucky came forward first, rubbing and purring like a housecat, his muscular black-panther side hard enough to knock over an unprepared man. Max was never unprepared among the big cats.

Osiris the leopard kept a wary distance at first, then he too swaggered closer, making a soundless snarl that Max understood was not a threat but a greeting.

Max crouched like the big cats and they rubbed closer, leaving their scents on his shoulders and face. The dogs, if they were loose, would stay away from him now.

The big cats were show-biz veterans and magicians' familiars, used to the spotlights and the long, deep well of darkness before and after. They understood Max as he understood them. Domesticated and wild. Social and asocial. Caged and free. Life was a compromise. So was death.

They permitted him to stroke their furred sides as they paced back and forth, wrapping him in acceptance as if he were a domestic cat, welcoming him to the litter, the cage, the spotlight.

He stood, caressing their wide-cheeked faces, lulled by their high-volume purring, more a rumble. He had come only to see that they were well housed, happy, living as they wanted to live after their various captivities, both benign and malign. That they were themselves, that he had been right to choose the Cloaked Conjuror as their best hope for long, content lives.

Their rhythmic greeting dance paused.

They lifted throats and eyes to the edge of the rock garden that was their home.

A small cat stood there, under the glare of a security light.

Max stared, expecting it to be Midnight Louie, though how he would have gotten here . . .

But this cat's coat was pale, as were the eyes that shone sky-blue in the spill of sodium iodide rays from above.

The darkness beyond the shower of light, behind the cat, turned into a figure as Max's vision adjusted. The form was curlicued like a silhouette portrait cut with manicure scissors from stiff black construction paper. This thing was more solid, more like paper-thin wrought-iron, a creature of razor-sharp extremities . . . gown, nails, the curled ends of hip-length tresses as dark as night would be without security lights.

Shangri-La.

Max templed his fingers, drew himself into one long line of watching black, an impassive vertical of stasis and potential.

Behind him, leopard and panther pushed against his legs, their massive throats growling gently.

He was taken aback that his presence had the capacity to surprise her, but she clearly was shocked. Perhaps she overestimated the estate's security measures.

"You violate this place," she said at last. Her husky soprano trembled slightly with some strong but undecipherable emotion.

Shangri-La was nothing if not feminine, but like many Asians, had a throaty intonation. It reminded him of Temple's voice, so charmingly rough for such a small, smooth package.

"This place is inviolate," he answered. "At least to the cats, and I am their guest."

She stood unmoved, her fluttering pennants of garb frozen as still as the carved draperies on a black jade statue of Quan Yin, the Buddhist goddess of compassion and mercy.

Shangri-La, he was sure, neither possessed nor desired either virtue.

"Guest?" she repeated, outraged by the term.

He offered the truth as a pretext. "I procured them for the

Cloaked Conjuror. I wanted to see how they were doing." He'd also wanted silent but amenable company after the night's extreme stresses: almost losing Temple, almost losing to Molina.

"The cats will not always come when you call," she warned him.

But they would. That was his gift.

The small Siamese in the spotlight hissed at him and retreated to her side, to the dark side. Its blue eyes flashed stoplight-red from the night.

Max studied Shangri-La. She reminded him of something. Something lethal.

Medusa.

That's what her spiky, trailing tendrils of hair and gown recalled. Medusa, the snaked-haired Gorgon whose very glance was fatal poison.

Perseus had needed a mirror to defeat Medusa; he had needed to slay the image to destroy the monster. To see her face was to glimpse your own death, even as she in turn saw your future.

They stared at each other through the dark. Max wondered why this alien magician had allied herself with the Cloaked Conjuror and against him . . . against Temple, for Shangri-La had stolen the ring he gave to Temple and she must have allowed the ring to find its way, for some reason, to Lieutenant Molina.

Was she a professional rival of his in her own mind? Perhaps the intervention was even personal. Perhaps Shangri-La had left Temple's ring . . . his ring . . . on the scene of Gloria Fuentes' murder. But how could this woman know who had given Temple the ring, know of their connection?

What else might she have left, where, for others?

The ritual dagger on Professor Mangel's killing ground?

And why?

Was she an agent of the Synth? One thing was certain. Like him, she was a magician, and she would keep her secrets to the death.

While he had been thinking about her, she had been thinking about him.

"Come here again," she said, "and it will not be worth your life."

She put a period to her threat by choosing to disappear in a fountain of fireworks. And her little cat too.

Max and the big cats were not impressed. They had made such exits many times themselves.

He massaged the sharp shoulder bones behind their heads.

The night held one immutable boon. Cher Smith's killer was finally identified and captured. She had been a child, and her murderer was a child. It was an answer, but not a solution.

Max sighed as the cats pressed closer, as if cold.

At least he could put one lost soul to rest, even if only in the cemetery of his mind. At least he could reduce by one the number of lives on his conscience.

No one could take that away from him, not even Molina.


Matt woke up.

Slowly.

Very slowly.

Woke up early for a man who worked a night shift. Only 9:00 A.M. *It must have been a dream*, he thought.

Then he thought, *This must be how people who get drunk feel the next morning. The classic Morning After.*

And he thought, finally and with the dawning shame of honest recollection, with horror, *No, it's not a dream. It's history. My history now. And forever.*

# Chapter 51

# Life's Little Addenda

The lieutenant slapped the flat of her hand down on the desk, hard.

Between her gritted teeth came a murmured mantra like the *shshshshsh* of waves stroking the beach, only fast and furious.

She rose and stalked out of her office, still *shshsh*ing under her breath like a demented librarian.

"*Sheesh.*" Detective Merry Su's nervous sideways glance met Detective Morris Alch's. "This is bad, Morrie. Triple bad."

"That wasn't some, ah, Chinese curse? Well, I couldn't quite make it out."

"It wasn't Latin, and unless you tell me it was Yiddish—"

"Yeah, I was hoping it was some kind of prayer, too."

"Homicide lieutenants don't pray."

"At least not in public."

"Especially not in public."

They were quiet for a long moment. Morrie Alch was still stunned, like the first time he visited his mother in the assisted care facility and she'd screamed a string of obscenities at him. Alzheimer's will do that to you, to you and your mother.

There could be no doubt. Molina's unprecedented mantra had been *ohshitohshitohshitohshitohshit.*

This would be nothing new in the rough-edged world of cops, except that Molina's management style had been to avoid the obvious, including cuss words.

Hearing her violate her own inviolate rule was surprisingly shocking, like catching your parents having, um, sex.

"She takes these particular murders hard," Su said.

"So hard that I heard from a pal in Vice and Narcotics that she looked into the last case personally, on her own time."

Another meeting pair of sideways glances. Molina was the ultimate delegator. She gave her detectives the widest latitude, expecting them to put it to good use and answer for it any time she asked.

"I suppose," Su said, "after having just solved that stubborn stripper murder case, this new one makes it seem like that never happened."

"This case is nothing like a stripper murder. No, really, it's not. No connection, believe me. A high-end call girl named Vassar, of all things, killed at the Goliath? It's a different class of victim, different venue, different murder weapon. Everything is different. I don't get why the lieutenant should flip at the mere mention of the case."

"She's really put all of our, and her, efforts into nabbing this stripper killer. Having another dead woman turn up the very same night the stripper guy is nailed is discouraging."

"The lieutenant doesn't get discouraged."

"She doesn't swear either."

"It wasn't swearing, really, kinda more like a—"

"Like a whole string of swear words. I've never heard one from her."

Another long silence.

Morrie shuffled his feet and creaked in his chair. Sitting here was like waiting for the principal to come back, only the principal had just gone off cawing like a crow.

"Years ago," he said in a nostalgic vein, "I had the very first woman to make lieutenant for a boss."

"Poor Morrie. You can't get away from us."

"Not that I haven't tried. Anyway, she was from Texas. Stringy woman. Face you'd put a mud fence around to improve the view."

"So what were her other advantages in the job?"

"Other than being as tough as barbed wire, she did one thing that told the guys she meant business."

"Yeah?"

"It was f-word this and f-word that, and freaking f-word in every which way."

"I'm free, yellow, and twenty-one, Morrie. You don't have to sugar-coat it."

He looked away. "I got a daughter your age."

"I suppose that could be Molina's reason for never talking the talk. Her daughter's pretty young yet."

"Kids you take seriously. You don't want the toilet-mouth of the block. Monkey hear, monkey do. You let go at work, you can't hang it up at home."

Su crossed her arms. "A lot of cop talk is pretty sexist."

"It's something a guy's gotta do to make sure the other guys know he's a guy."

"I can take it. Dish it out too."

Morrie shrugged. "Some women overcompensate. You don't. Molina neither. I didn't realize how much she didn't until just now."

"So it's bad."

"She's been working overtime, real overtime."

"You think she's cracking?"

"Naw, but she ain't happy about this last killing. Responsibility will get to you if you let it. We're not here to save anyone, just to find the guilty."

"I can't believe I heard Molina say that."

"Nothing shocks you, remember?"

"That's why I hate it when something does."

Morrie nodded. "I know what you mean. My daughter?"

"Yeah."

"After all that, she grew up to be a real toilet-mouth." He shrugged. "What are you gonna do?"

Su shook her head sympathetically. "Shit."

# Midnight Louie Sings the Blues

Give a dude a dame, and you might as well carve "Finis" on a block of marble bearing his name somewhere, hopefully not at Los Muertos.

I have seen enough of that place to last an entire one of my nine lives.

Here I spend half the case worrying about the welfare of my so-called "partner," and she gets to show up at the curtain call and kick ass.

I get to watch.

This is not the sort of claws-on action I am used to providing.

I can only conclude that this revolting denouement is due to a surfeit of females in my life. There is the errant Miss Temple, who is always getting herself into as much hot water as another infamous redhead, Lucy Ricardo. There is my newly discovered mater, the unfortunately named Ma Barker. There is the vicious

Hyacinth herself. There is the unforgettable and lethal Kitty the Cutter. There is the relentless Lieutenant C. R. Molina.

And there is my partner in crime writing, Miss Carole Nelson Douglas, who appears to revel in showing us guys in a less than flattering light.

Is there a hidden message here? Is this some feminist, humanist tract that I have innocently become entoiled in?

I get to do the dirty work! Do you hear me? Little dolls are supposed to stand on the sidelines and cheer me on. Or swoon at my approach when I deign to make it.

From now on, it is sheaths off.

I am the alpha element here, not to mention the titular hero.

(I like that word "titular." It means the whole enchilada is named after me. Not literally. Aw, now it is getting complicated. Dames must be at work again.)

Of course, when I think about it, that only means that someone else did the naming, and what can be bestowed, can be taken away.

Still, it cannot hurt to reestablish my territory.

I am feline, hear me roar!

Hark? Is that an echo?

Oops. It is Osiris, joining in from across town.

I guess we Big Guys did our part, and we have to give the little ladies a solo bow now and then.

It does not really mean anything.

Unless the little ladies take offense.

Very best fishes,

Midnight Louie, Esq.

For information about getting Midnight Louie's newsletter and/or T-shirt, contact him at *Midnight Louie's Scratching Post-Intelligencer*, PO Box 331555, Fort Worth, TX 76163, by e-mail at **cdouglas@catwriter.com.** or visit the Web page **http://www.catwriter.com.**

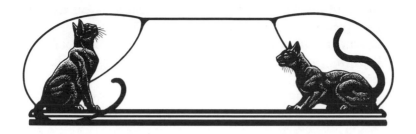

# Carole Nelson Douglas
# Joins the Choir

I totally agree with you this time, Louie.

Don't look so surprised. We *are* in this together.

Frankly, you underestimate your achievements. You're the one who finally tracked down the connection between the murder of Professor Jeff Mangel and the symbol of the Synth. You're the one who found the hidden nest at Los Muertos and Hyacinth and who-knows-what other connections to ongoing villainy.

You managed to call help to Temple's aid, even if it was pretty unappetizing help, and you sprang Midnight Louise from durance vile. She was pretty helpless until you came back on the scene, you know. Just because she and Hyacinth got into a little cat fight at the end doesn't steal your thunder, Louie.

Besides, I thought you macho guys got a kick from watching girls go at it in the ring.

Honestly. Dudes. You can't live with them and you can't live without them.

*BUT WHO WOULD WANT TO? LIVE WITHOUT THEM, I MEAN.*
*I THINK.*